DEAD MAN'S CHEST

DAVID SHERMAN

DEAD MAN'S CHEST

WordCaster Novels
novelier.com
Fort Lauderdale, FL

Fifteen men on a dead man's chest

Yo ho ho and a bottle of rum.

Drink and the devil had done for the rest

Yo ho ho and a bottle of rum.

From *Treasure Island,* by Robert Louis Stevenson

CHAPTER ONE

"Another Saturday night, and I ain't got nobody..."

Try to imagine Sam Cook as sung by Leonard Cohen. I'd never thought of that peculiar combination of words and voice until a hot Saturday night when another Saturday night when "I ain't got nobody" sent me to the Side Car Club, where a young unknown was singing Sam Cook in a junior-Leonard-Cohen voice.

Don't knock it; Sam sang some good songs, and this kid did a respectable Cohen. Somehow, the words and voice worked.

I was at my usual place at the small side bar taking an occasional swig from a bottle of Dock Street Ale-living in Philadelphia, which has its own local brew, I feel it's somehow unpatriotic to drink Boston's Sam Adams Lager. It was getting on toward closing time, and I'd swigged down quite a few of Philly's best brew. Not to the point of feeling no pain, but enough to be on the edge of morose. My judgment was certainly impaired. Which is important to note. Had my judgment not been impaired, the things that happened later that night-had I let them get that far to begin with-would have convinced me to walk away. But my judgment was alcohol dazed; let that be a warning to you-that and Carrie Nation.

Jimmy, the bartender, could tell the mood I was in and, between serving other customers, hung out by me and made comments on the singer and the songs he sang. Jimmy's young enough that his knowledge of Sam Cook, dead before I was born, and Leonard Cohen, who's never become widely famous, surprised me. Still... Jimmy's a nice kid and all, but he's not my type. My taste runs more toward the redhead sitting with two other lovelies at a table about twenty feet away.

That was why I was in the mood I was in; I'd had too many consecutive "ain't got nobody" nights.

A hot Saturday night in July, a music night at the Side Car. A date night. A meet-someone-new-and-wonderful night. Or meet someone just for the night, someone to chase away the lonlyheart blues. So the Side Car Club was more than three-quarters full of couples and seeking-singles-more couples than singles. The crowd was largely collegiate, mostly grad students from one of the nearby universities, probably still in town working on research projects or teaching low-level classes in one or another of the adult education programs. A minority were post-college locals like me, some were from other parts of the city and nearby suburbs. The single women were there in defensive packs, three or more together. The single men were mostly in ones and twos, trying to come up with ways of cutting a single heifer from the herd. Here and there, now and then, one was successful. Especially during the break after young Cook-Cohen's first set, when the dance floor quickly got crowded. The dancing didn't stop when Cohen-Cook came back, instead it got more frenzied.

While Jimmy was off tending to three barflies who were just beginning to get loud, I fixed my gaze on the redhead and tried to gauge my chances if I sent her a drink. I couldn't tell her height because she was sitting, but she didn't look tall-certainly not taller than me. That's an issue with a lot of women, and I've been shot down too many times to count because I'm an inch or two below average height. She was closer to pleasingly plump than model thin, so my Brian Dennehy build might not turn her off. Then I started calculating how many drinks I might have to buy before one of the lovelies would let me keep her company for a while should the redhead turn me down-and wondering if I had enough money on me to buy that many drinks.

I stopped calculating when I remembered a more than slightly tipsy night when a woman I bought a drink for poured it on me. I must have been a bit more than slightly tipsy that night. Or maybe she had a thing against men whose entire wardrobe cost less than the spangled clubbing clothes she was wearing.

Ah well. The young women who come to the Side Car Club are just fantasies anyway. A more realistic fantasy than the young women here on dancing-girl nights, but fantasies nonetheless. And fantasies are best enjoyed in the privacy of one's own home.

Jimmy was back after jollying the three barflies when young Cook-Cohen launched into his rendition of "Closing Time." That's my favorite Leonard Cohen song-and one that can turn me maudlin in a hurry when I've had enough to drink. And Jimmy knew it. So he changed the subject to the Phillies and their current three-game winning streak, which got me to remembering 1993, when the Phillies tore up the league and had Phillies Phans delirious with joy-until our expectations were crushed by the way they fell 4-2 to the Toronto Blue Jays in the World Series.

But before I could get maudlin about the wreck of the '93 World Series, a wreck the Phillies still haven't fully recovered from, Jimmy looked past me in a way that made me stop talking and turn my head to see what had caught his attention.

She made me think of Sister Mary Conception, my ninth grade civics teacher at Archbishop O'Rielly High School, who had the girls sit in the front of the classroom and cross their legs. The first time each year that she did that, she shocked the class by announcing, "Now that the gates of hell are closed, we can begin learning." I strongly suspected that Sister Mary Conception had such gates herself, but had absolutely no desire to know anything about them. Hers, I mean. I was exceedingly curious about those-and other attributes-of my female classmates.

Wending her way through the crowd toward the side bar was a woman who looked about as good as they come; shoulder length blonde hair, nice height, closing on thirty, classic point-seven-to-one waist to hips ratio, enough cleavage to strongly hint that the fullness in her blouse wasn't augmented with silicone.

And she was looking straight at me.

A thought tickled the back of my mind: Her gates of hell are wide open, with "hell" being the operative word.

I should have paid attention to that thought.

I really should have. But I'd had enough to drink that I shrugged the thought off the instant she sat on the stool next to me and stared into my eyes from no more than a foot away.

I swallowed, and would have loosened my collar if I'd been wearing a tie.

But this being a hot July night, I was in an open-necked, short sleeve shirt. "Would you like a drink?" I asked, grasping at the first thing that came to mind, forgetting about the night a drink got poured on me.

She cocked her head in a way that gave a jerk to something inside my chest, then nodded and turned her face to Jimmy. "Scotch, soda."

"Scotch and soda, you got it," Jimmy said, and stepped away to fix her drink.

The blonde turned back to me. "You're Ham Eliot," she husked in a voice rusty from too many years of cigarettes and liquor and other hard use. I felt that voice all the way down to my toenails.

I swallowed again and reached to loosen the tie I hadn't worn in months. "I am," I managed.

"The man at the door pointed you out."

I looked toward the entrance and saw Clyde acting as his own doorman. As manager of the Side Car Club, Clyde Krippendorf doesn't normally hold the door, so I figured one of the hulks he hires as bouncers must be taking a break-Clyde hadn't been on the door when I came in. Clyde was looking my way, but it was too dark for me to make out his expression.

"I need to compliment Clyde on the women he sends to me," I said, looking back at the blonde. I'm pretty sure my face was wearing an Alfred E. Neumann grin.

Cohen-Cook twiddled the dials on his amp, driving the decibels up to a level Leonard never meant "Death of a Ladies' Man" to be played at, making conversation just about impossible.

The blonde leaned closer, almost cheek to cheek, and said near my ear, "I need you." At least that's what I thought I heard-it was certainly what I *wanted* to hear. Either way, I took advantage of her nearness to look down her blouse. Yep, looked real.

I don't ruin my voice by trying to make myself heard in places where music is played way too loud, so I'm not she heard my stammered, "Me too." Even if she could have heard, she was momentarily distracted by Jimmy, who showed up just then with her drink. She gave the glass a suspicious look, then picked it up and drained it in a gulp that made Jimmy and me exchange a wide-eyed look of surprise.

Empty glass back on the bar, she grabbed my hand and shouted, "Let's go someplace where we can talk."

"Talk." The lady said, "Talk." What could I do? I slid off my stool and managed to hold her back long enough to toss some money on the bar, then allowed her to drag me through the crowd toward the entrance.

Up close, I could see Clyde's face clearly. He gave me a "What's this?" look, and the blonde an appraising one. He knuckled me on the shoulder as I went past. He'd been my squad leader in one of the Southwest Asia wars, and had hit my shoulder a lot harder when I made corporal; still, his knuckle stung. He mouthed, "Go for it, buddy." I grinned back.

On the street a few feet from the Side Car Club's entrance, the relative quiet slammed into my ears like a Niagara roar. It's always like that when you go from high decibels to low, but you never get used to it. I shook my head and worked my jaw to bring my eardrums back into equilibrium, then cleared my throat.

"Your place or mine?" It sounded pretty inane to me, but I didn't know what else to say just then.

I blinked when she answered, "We don't need to go to your place, and mine isn't close enough."

Does she have the key to a vacationing girlfriend's apartment that we don't have to go to either of our places? Remember, my judgment was impaired and I'd been fantasizing about picking someone up.

"This should be about right," she said.

Huh? In the street? Then I saw where she was pointing; a nightowl place that catered to the bar and club closing-time crowd. Well, she had said, "Talk." A little conversation before we head for her vacationing girlfriend's apartment is probably a good idea. That's what I told myself as she dragged me into the nighthawk place where she secured us a corner table away from windows. A waitress was on us as soon as we sat down and we both ordered coffee.

"Ham-you don't mind if I call you Ham, do you?"

I blinked. What kind of question was that? I'd hardly expect a woman who'd just picked me up in a bar to call me "Mr. Eliot." "Yeah, sure," I said.

Then, "And what do I call you?" Damn me for a dummy, I'd let her drag me out of the Side Car Club, and I didn't even know her name.

"I'm Sindi DiWagne. That's with an initial 'S' and a ultimate 'i.'" Okay, she knows big words. I said the Side Car Club caters to a collegiate crowd. On any given night there were probably half again as many degrees present as there were people.

"Hi, Sindi," I said, extending my hand across the table. "Pleased to meet you."

She was a shade slow in taking my hand, but before I could wonder about the very businesslike shake she gave it, the waitress showed up with our coffees and cream. The coffees were in sturdy mugs, the type not likely to shatter if someone uncoordinated from drink accidentally knocks one off the table. The cream was in those little peel-off containers in a cereal bowl with ice. A sugar shaker was already on the table, along with a holder with different colored envelopes of fake sugar.

Sindi took a sip of her coffee black and grimaced at it. I laded mine full of cream and sugar before braving it. I normally drink coffee black, but never in the nighthawk places during the hour or two before bar-closing. The coffee then tends to sit too long and gets burnt. After the bars close, the coffee is frequently brewed fresh.

"So what's your sign?" I asked. Dumb question, I know. What I wanted to ask was, "Why did Clyde point me out?" but gift horses, you know?

Sindi waved a hand in front of her face as though batting the question away before it could reach her ears, then said, "I'm told you locate lost things for people."

I sagged back in my chair, lost my grin, and stifled a sigh. So much for fantasies about not ending another Saturday night singing "I ain't got nobody."

Locating lost things is a sideline of mine. I'm a magazine features writer by trade, but freelance magazine features don't provide a reliable living, so I have to do something on the side to bring in extra money. I tried working a regular job after I got out of the Marines, but being tied down to someone else's clock and workplace, doing someone else's work, dragged heavily on me. To lighten things up I tried some writing on the side. It got me a few quick sales to *The Inquirer Magazine*, *Soldier of Fortune*, a little piece in *Philadelphia Magazine*, and a few lesser-paying markets, so I took a look at my bank accounts, decided I had enough to carry me for a few months, and quit my job. I gained a lot of interesting bits of knowledge, and met some interesting people in doing research for my articles, but in less than two years discovered I wasn't making enough to cover all of my bills on a regular basis. So I found a part-time job to take up the slack. The job was two days a week, but I found those two days disrupted my concentration enough that they cost me three and a half days a week of research and writing. I even tried the old standby of freelance writers; find a business client. The steady check was nice, but the work was too much like a part-time job. I decided I needed to find something else to do that would bring in some real money for a few days of concentrated work. Reacquiring lost items, often items that had been purloined, frequently by relatives, friends, or acquaintances, turned out to be it. My fee was twenty-five percent of the market value of the item. Of course, I always made sure that the person wanting my services had legal title to whatever was lost, I didn't break and enter or use strongarm tactics, and I strove mightily to never do anything that could get me fined or sent to jail.

It's not something that I always admit to doing when someone approaches me. "Yeah, sometimes I do," I said. *New Republic*, *Hustler*, *The Atlantic*, *Computing Today*, and *Wired* had all turned down the proposals I sent them. I had a check coming from *Good Housekeeping*, but the rent was due in a week and a half, and I didn't want to take the chance on the check getting delayed in the mail. Or worse yet, my bank might make me wait two weeks before I could draw on the out of state check. Last month was the same, and the month before wasn't much better. As much as I'd wanted my fantasy to come true, I needed a quick influx of money even more.

"So what did you lose?" I asked resignedly.

Sindi looked away and murmured, "A book."

A book? An appointment book? An incunabula-a book published before 1500? A numbers book? "What kind of book?"

"A first edition of a short story collection."

I stared at her as levelly as I could in my state. Most short story collections never have a second edition. Hell, she could buy a replacement on Amazon at thirty or forty percent off! So what's the big deal? Unless there was something really extraordinary about this copy, a book simply wasn't worth hiring someone to locate and return it-and the pay for it wouldn't worth my time and effort.

I blew out a deep breath. Ms Sindi DiWagne was turning out to be a disappointment all the way around. I told her what I thought of the value of a book.

"This book means a great deal to me," she said hastily. "It's very important that I get it back."

I gave her a disbelieving look. I know that some people pay outrageous sums for the first edition of the latest Harry Potter book, but get real-that book had the largest first printing of any book in history, it's not really worth more than its cover price.

"All right, I'll bite. What's the book?"

"A first edition Bret Harte, *The Luck of Roaring Camp*."

"Oh come on, buy another copy!" I blurted. Bret Harte was a major American writer of the Mark Twain era; if there had been bestseller lists at the time, nearly every one of his books would have been at or near the top of them. His first editions aren't as common as Mark Twain's, but they're far easier to find than Herman Melville's. Unless this was Harte's own copy, with margin notes in his hand for a revised second edition that was never published, or something equally esoteric, a first edition of the book would only cost about as much as the latest thriller from Michael Crichton. I know; I wrote an article on collecting Nineteenth Century American literature for *American Heritage* magazine a couple of years ago.

"Look," I said, "I can name four or five bookstores in the city where you can probably just walk in and get another copy for what you'd pay for a, a-," I had to stop to think of what authors were currently popular with women, "-for the latest Catherine Asaro novel." Even in my half-inebriated state, her blank expression told me she didn't know who Catherine Asaro was. Well, shake my head.

"I know how much a copy costs," she snapped. "After all, I bought one. But I'm willing to pay more than it's worth to have that copy returned."

"All right, what's so special about it? Is it a very early presentation copy?"

The enticing way her hair bounced when she shook her head made me forget about books for a moment and return to thinking about more personal matters.

"No, it's nothing like that." She drew a deep breath that drew my attention back to her decolletage, and I swallowed another sigh. Damn, but she looked good. Good enough that I didn't want the evening to end yet, even though it probably wasn't going to go anywhere.

"Tell me about it," I said. I made an attempt to sound interested.

"My apartment was robbed," she began. I didn't bother to tell her that *people* are robbed, homes are *burgled*. Most people make that mistake. "They knew exactly what they wanted," she continued, "the book was the only thing missing."

That raised questions I couldn't ignore. "What did the police say?" was the first of them.

She made her hair bounce again and my eyes nearly crossed watching the golden sway. "I didn't call the police."

It took a few beats for that to sink in, then I sunk farther back into my chair. "Why not?" When a crime victim doesn't call the police, you have to wonder why not.

She looked at me with pleading, Please-help-me-Mister, little girl eyes. "Because the police wouldn't have taken it seriously, they would have thought I was wasting their time. They might even have thought I was trying to make them look foolish by making a fraudulent crime report."

I rolled my head side to side in a slow shake, and asked the second question, "How do you know the book was the only thing taken?"

"I'm in the middle of moving. That book and a few personal effects were all that was in the apartment; none of the personal effects were taken."

"Somebody broke down the door to an apartment that was being vacated, and all they got for their trouble was a book worth less than thirty bucks?"

She made her hair bounce even more than before. "They didn't break the door down. Either they had a key, or they picked the lock."

"How do you know they unlocked the door? Are you sure you left the door locked when you went out? Maybe they came in through a window."

"I always make sure the windows and door are closed and locked before I go to the laundry. They still were when I got back. Whoever it was had to have come in through the door, and there was no sign of it being forced."

"Are you sure it couldn't have been forced? Do you know what a forced door looks like?"

"The door has a vertical deadbolt lock. If it had been forced, the jam would have been broken when I got back from the laundry, wouldn't it?" Her face looked tired, but otherwise she was the image of innocence.

I sighed. She was right about the door being picked, or unlocked with a key. Unless she was leaving out some other minor detail-like a large hole knocked through the ceiling, or an entire section of a wall missing. But why would somebody who could pick a lock waste time on a book that wasn't an incunabula or something almost as valuable? "Was there anything special about that copy of the book?" There better be or it would be impossible to identify.

She hesitated before answering. "You can identify it by a map that was tipped into it, but that's not important. I know who took the book."

I blinked again and tried to think bland thoughts. All I managed was buzzy confusion. "If you know who took it," I finally asked, "why don't you simply go and ask this person to give it back?"

She looked away again. Wringing her hands made her look more embarrassed than before. "Well, I don't know *exactly* who took it. I mean there are two of them, and I don't know which one took it. The reason I need help is," she looked very earnestly into my eyes, "I'm not even sure how to locate them."

"You found me and you didn't even know who I am. Why can't you find two guys who you do know? Right, how *did* you know to ask for me at the Side Car Club?"

"Well, I don't really know them. I mean, I met each of them once and spoke to each of them on the phone one time. Besides, they scare me and I need someone else to find them for me."

I cleared my throat and hauled myself upright. "All right, let's try this again. Who are they?"

It was like hearing a dam burst the way her words suddenly came bubbling out.

"I collect American first editions. Not that I'm some kind of fanatic or anything, I just try to get one representative book by every significant writer this country has produced. I'm a little chauvinistic about it is all. My undergraduate degree is in Am Lit and I'm working part time on a master's at

Penn. Last week I went to the auction at Freeman's." Freeman's is the biggest auction house in town-not big and prestigious like Christie's or Southeby's, but the biggest and best in Philadelphia. "There was this carton of mixed Nineteenth Century novels-mostly reprints of minor stuff. I rooted through it and found this Bret Harte the auctioneer must have overlooked. I was almost the only person bidding on the box and got it for fifteen dollars. Everybody else must have seen the junk on top and decided the lot wasn't worth even what I paid for it. I paid my money and they gave me the box. I took the Harte out of it and started to leave-they could try to resell the rest of those books or throw them out, I didn't care. A very excited man stopped me in the anteroom and offered to buy the book from me for a hundred dollars." She shrugged. "Naturally, I turned him down..."

The way she told it, I could visualize the scene and hear the voices.

CHAPTER TWO

"Excuse me, what did you say?"

"That book you just bought in there, miss? I'd like to buy it from you?" Most of the stranger's sentences rose on the last syllable, like questions.

Sindi studied the man. He was average height and, not quite plump but somehow soft and muscleless-looking. As he talked he bounced nervously up and down on the balls of his feet. His blue serge suit was shiny from many wearings, but didn't look particularly old. He looked like a Disney Tweedle. Dee or Dum doesn't matter. The crowd leaving the auction swirled around them; a few careless people jostled the pudgy man.

"I beg your pardon, but I bought this book for my collection. I'm not selling it before I even get it home." She turned on her heel and took a step away.

"Please, miss?" The Tweedle grabbed Sindi above the elbow. His hand was moist and clammy on her arm. "It's very important that I get that book."

"Then buy another copy." She pulled her arm from his grasp and started off again. "This one is mine."

He grabbed her arm again.

"Let go of me or I'll call a cop."

He jerked back and held both of his hands up. "Oh, p-please don't do that, m-miss," he stammered. "It's just that the copy you have of the book was placed in the wrong lot? It was supposed to have been sold in a different lot, a lot that I bought? But somebody moved that book before the auction started? My employer is very anxious to have that copy. Listen, you paid fifteen dollars for the lot? Here," he pulled a chubby wallet from an inside pocket, "I'll give you two hundred dollars for the book?" He held out a thin sheaf of twenties.

"Come on, mister, I don't know what your game is, but this copy isn't worth that much money, see?" She held the book in front of his eyes and riffled through the front flyleaf and first several pages. "No inscription or anything, no author's notes. Nothing. This is just another copy. You can get one in any well-stocked old book store in the city."

"But, miss?" a note of whining entered his voice. "You don't understand? My employer-this copy was bought by his grandfather when it was new-it has a certain sentimental value to him? He sent me to this auction with strict instructions not to be out-bid for it. He's going to be very upset if I return without it?"

"I understand completely. It's you who don't understand. There's nothing to distinguish this copy from any other except that now it's mine. What you do is, you go out and buy another undistinguished copy and take it to your employer and tell him it's the one you bought here."

The man chewed on his lip; his eyes darted about nervously. "I'll tell you what," he stammered. "Take the two hundred dollars? I'll go out and buy another copy? You give me your book and I'll give you the other copy? Let me have your address and I'll mail it to you?" His eyes pleaded.

"So that's what this is all about," she sniffed. "What you're really after is my address. What are you going to do with it, sneak in when I'm not at home and play with my dirty underwear? Get away from me you pervert." Nose up, she spun away and left the pudgy man standing alone.

*

Sindi was quiet for a long moment, looking down and away, as though remembering. I gave myself a little shake, surprised at how vividly I'd visualized the scene she described. She resumed.

"Then something else strange happened," she continued. "Another man stopped me right outside the door on Chestnut Street and he tried to buy the book for a man whose agent he said he was. This man claimed the book had belonged to his client's father and his client's father read it to him when he was a small child. He also wanted it for its sentimental value."

"What was the price this time?" I asked.

"That's what the real surprise was. He offered the same fifteen dollars I paid for the lot. I said no, that would make my day at Freeman's a total waste and he raised his offer to twenty-five. I laughed and told him about the other man offering two hundred and a replacement copy. He got very angry then and demanded to know who the other man was. There was something about his eyes, he scared me, which the first man hadn't..." And she looked into my eyes again.

*

The man was tall, lean, and hard-faced. His thick eyebrows and dark complexion gave his expression the appearance of a storm cloud. He leaned forward slightly at the hips, and the large hands that hung straight down at his sides looked clenched even though they were open. "Who is he, this other guy?" he asked without moving his jaw.

"How do I know who he is?" Sindi asked. "He's just some chubby jerk who wanted this book and my address. He offered me two hundred dollars and a replacement copy. What are you going to do, just take it from me?" She took a tentative half step backward.

The second stranger leaned closer. The crowd on the sidewalk was thinner than in the anteroom, but that wasn't enough explain the way passers-by avoided bumping into the hard-faced man.

"Maybe I will," he said. Maybe you should have taken his money and replacement copy. Then maybe I'd be mad at him instead of at you." His eyebrows pulled together until they formed a heavy, pointed vee. "I want the book."

"You can't have it, it's mine." She clutched the book to her breast and looked frantically around. "I'm calling a cop," she said.

The hard-eyed man took a quick look up the street and saw a policeman mounted on a tall bay horse coming their way. "You don't gotta call a cop," he said to Sindi. "I'll go now. But I'll be back." He started away from her, but kept watching over his shoulder, to see if she was going to signal the mounted policeman.

Sindi hadn't seen the mounted cop yet, she took another step back, still watching the stranger. She started to turn away when out of the corner of her eye she saw the soft, nervous man leave Freeman's. She turned her head in his direction and the hard man's eyes followed her gaze.

"Is that him?" the hard man mouthed, pointing.

Sindi nodded.

"Hey you," hard-eyes shouted at nervous-pudgy.

The soft man started at the words. He looked at Sindi and the lean stranger, jittered for a moment, then scurried away as fast as he could without running.

The lean man gave the approaching cop another glance and took off after the other man.

Only now did Sindi see the horse and the cop, who was looking at the two men hurry away.

*

"...Then I ran away and went home," she finished, dropping her gaze to her hands.

My body made an involuntary shake. I'd seen Sindi's encounter with the hard man as vividly as the one with the Tweedle. I decided that Sindi DiWagne was a mesmerizing story teller.

I shook my head to clear it and asked, "Who were they, what are their names?" Earlier, she said she knew who they were, just not how to find them. Maybe now she'd tell me. That's why cops and other interrogators keep asking the same questions over and over again; sometimes they get different answers.

"I don't know, I never saw them before."

"Let me make sure I've got this right. Two men, neither of whom you had ever seen before, stopped you and wanted to buy from you a book you had just bought. A week later the book is stolen from the apartment you are moving out of and you think it was one of those two men who took it. Is that right?"

She nodded.

I shook my head. Even in my semi-inebriated state I knew; "That's not much to go on. How could anybody find those two men, assuming one of them is your burglar. And why do you think one of them took it?"

"Three days ago one of the men, the soft one, called me at my job and upped his offer..." She peered into my eyes again.

*

"Who is this?"

"You remember me," the nervous voice on the other end of the line said, "I offered to by a book from you for two hundred dollars? I'm still very interested in buying it and I'd like to discuss price?"

Sindi breathed in sharply when she realized who she was talking to. "You've got some nerve," she said with as much calmness as she could muster, but she was shaken. How did he find out where she worked? Who was this man? Was he some kind of pervert who was going to give her a lot of grief? "What do you think you're doing calling me at work?" She went on the offensive; someone once told her that was one of the best things to do with unwanted callers. "What do you think you're doing calling me at all?"

"Please, miss, don't get upset?" the nervous voice pleaded. "My employer is extremely anxious to possess that book. I am now prepared to increase my offer to five hundred dollars and a replacement copy?"

"Listen, I don't know who you are or what your game is, but I'm tired of it. I don't want to see you again, and I don't want you to call me at work." She hesitated and decided to go all the way with her don'ts. "Or at home or anywhere else."

"We don't have to meet," the voice pleaded, "I can give you an address to mail the book to? I'll even mail you a cashier's check for five hundred dollars and another copy of the book without waiting to see if you mail the book to me?"

"Look, you creep," she shouted, then lowered her voice when several coworkers looked at her, "I'm not giving you my address and I don't want anything from you except for you to leave me completely alone. Do you understand that?"

"Oh, you don't have to give me your address, I've got it. Listen-," Sindi gasped, but he hurried on before she could react to his claiming to have her address, "-you don't even have to give me the entire book? I'll tell you what, I'll give you two-fifty for just the map? The map's the important thing."

"No, mister. You aren't getting the book or the map or anything else from me for any amount of money. And if you do have my address, you better forget it along with my work phone number and my home phone number and anything else you know about me. Goodbye." She was shaking so hard she almost missed the cradle when she slammed the receiver down. The man finding where she worked and calling her there badly shook her. His claim that he had her home address scared her even more and made her glad she was moving soon.

*

"...Even if I was willing to let him have the map I couldn't have without cutting it out because it's bound in." She looked into the coffee cup she was gripping tightly between her hands.

I took a deep, shuddering breath and looked away from her. *Damn!*I could almost swear I'd heard that story from inside Sindi's skin. I twisted my shoulders through a shake to get a grip on myself so I could think, and realized there it was, the map she glossed over a minute ago as being unimportant. "What's so important about the map that he'd offer that much money for it?" It was obviously worth more to somebody than she was letting on.

"I have no idea what's so important about the silly map, but the threatening man wanted it, too. He called me at home two nights ago and said to forget about him buying the book..."

*

"Listen, bitch, if that fucking book's so goddam important to you, you can keep it. Gimme the map," he said. Sindi clutched at her throat. She could see the set of his jaw in his voice. "Well?" he asked when she didn't answer.

"You can't have it," she spoke in a whisper because she felt that if she used a louder voice she would scream. "It's mine." To calm her nerves, she lit a cigarette, forgetting she already had one burning in the ashtray at her side.

The silence on the other end was ominous. Then the voice said, "If you don't give me the map I'll come and take it. How does that sound, Miss Prissy

Pants?"

"You wouldn't!" she gasped.

"I'll take more than the map if you're there when I come to get it." She could hear a leer in his voice. "And, Miss Prissy Pants, if your friend with the jitters gets the map before I do, I'll come and get you when I'm through with him. Do you catch my meaning?"

A tear rolled out of the corner of one of Sindi's wide, staring eyes. Her whole body trembled as she lowered the phone without answering. After she hung up she put her hands over her face and screamed into them.

*

Sindi let my eyes go, and I barely heard her say, "Him calling me at home really upset me. You see, he called my new apartment. The phone wasn't turned on there until that afternoon and it was a new number."

After a moment that felt more like a half hour, or maybe a month or two, her words registered on me and I said the first thing that popped into my mind. "He called your old number and got a recorded voice giving him the change."

"Both the old and new numbers are unlisted. Even if he had gotten the old number somewhere, he would only have gotten a message saying it was disconnected."

We were silent for a moment, Sindi staring into nowhere remembering the phone call, me marveling at her story telling. She twisted her napkin so tightly she shredded it. I put one hand on top of hers and squeezed. The satin smoothness of her skin made me close my eyes and dream a fantasy about this woman. When I opened them, she quickly looked away from me, and the ghost of a smile flickered across her face.

When I felt more in control I asked, "Then what happened?"

"I bought all new furniture for my new apartment." Again, she started slowly. Again, it wasn't long before the words came in a torrent. "But the bed wasn't delivered until yesterday, so I had been sleeping in the old place. The clothes that I needed for work were there and so was my bathroom stuff. You know, cosmetics, toothbrush, like that. Nearly everything else was in the new apartment. My new bed arrived yesterday and I went to the old apartment to pack up and move out the rest of my things. I decided to do the laundry there so that only clean clothes would come into my new place..." She looked back at me.

*

Mary had been in the apartment building's basement laundry, wearing the apron that was her trademark, and Sindi chatted with her while her clothes washed and dried. Mary was in the laundry when Sindi got there and she was still there when Sindi left. Sindi hadn't noticed any machines running except the ones she was using. But Mary always seemed to be in the basement laundry and never seemed to be doing laundry. She was early middle-age and divorced with no children. Rumor had it she had once been raped in an apartment building's laundry room, so she now spent her time in them to prevent the same thing from happening to anyone else. The same rumor said she carried a gun in her apron pocket. It could have been true; Sindi had seen the can of pepper spray Mary had. Anyway, Mary was pleasant

19

company for the time it took to do the wash and Sindi was glad to see her. There probably wasn't anyone like her where she was moving to. She'd miss Mary. Sindi rode the elevator to her apartment alone.

Her clothes were clean and folded, only needing to be packed into the suitcase laying open on the bed. An overnight bag that sat on the toilet seat was already packed with most of the remaining contents of the bathroom. There remained only a couple of stuffed dolls and a few books to go into a shopping bag and she would be able to leave with everything she was taking. The next day someone would come and take away all the old furniture and then Sindi DiWagne could start a new life.

If only those two creeps would leave her alone!

She got off the elevator on the right floor and walked down the dimly lit hallway that wasn't quite wide enough for two people to comfortably walk abreast to the door of the apartment. The key slid into the lock, the tumblers turned easily and the door swung open on well-oiled hinges. That was one thing that could be said about the manager of this old place-he kept the doors and locks in good condition.

Within minutes her clean laundry was packed in the suitcase and it was closed, the remaining toiletries from the medicine cabinet and cosmetics from the vanity were in the overnight bag. Time to make one last sweep through the apartment. Bathroom; an old washcloth and hand towel could go into the trash, the little toilet paper remaining on the roller could stay for the convenience of the next tenant. Living/bedroom; the linen was already disposed of; a Raggedy Ann doll and a stuffed Garfield went into the shopping bag. Three paperbacks went with the dolls. A threadbare dish towel in the kitchenette went into the trash. Hustle the trash bag to the chute and drop it in. Now nothing was left except the furniture. Except for a feeling that something was missing. What was it?

And then she knew.

Quickly, she checked through the apartment again, only this time she looked in every drawer, under the seat cushions, under the bed, on the closet shelves. Nowhere. A shiver went down her spine. One more go around showed the windows were still locked and the door didn't appear to have been tampered with. Frightened, Sindi grabbed the suitcase in one hand and the overnight bag and shopping bag with the other and rushed out to find a cab. She almost forgot to lock the door behind her in her haste.

The next day she made inquiries and finally found Ham Eliot drinking beer from a bottle at the side bar of the Side Car Club.

*

She didn't give me time to recover before saying, "I don't even care that you thought I was picking you up for another reason. Just so long as I got your attention."

I was still too far out of it to look embarrassed.

CHAPTER THREE

I had to think about this one for awhile. On the face of it, there wasn't anything of value to recover-of course, I didn't know what she wasn't telling me about that map. It also seemed there was a degree of danger involved-though she may have been grossly exaggerating there. How much risk was I willing to take for how little reward?

I really do make my living writing feature articles. Some months I bring in five figures on them. This wasn't one of those months, though. *Cosmo* only paid me a kill fee for my piece they decided not to use on how to deal with macho-man mashers in nightclubs. *New Republic, Hustler, Soldier of Fortune, Computing Today*, and *Lear's* all turned down the proposals I sent them. I was due a check from *Good Housekeeping*, but the rent was due next week and I didn't want to take the chance on the check getting delayed in the mail. Or worse yet, my bank might make me wait two weeks before I could draw on the out-of-state check. Last month was the same, and the month before wasn't much better.

I keep telling myself to come up with a couple of business clients, get enough steady work at standard freelance rates to pay my rent. Keep telling myself, but then I remember that I didn't like it when I tried it before.

So I thought about it. Sindi DiWagne was in trouble. Two different people wanted something that one of them evidently now had. The other one was going to be very unhappy with her when he discovered she no longer had it for him to get. Since it was taken from her old apartment and we knew the lean man with the heavy eyebrows had the phone number at her new place, and the pudgy guy said he had her old number and address, the first assumption to make was the pudgy guy had it. On the other hand, the one who made all the threats might have searched her new apartment, not found it there and there's nothing to say he didn't also have her old address. If he had the book there was no way to guess what old jiggles would do. If jiggles had it, the threat from the other guy was obvious. If I was going to do this, I had to find out who those two guys were and, maybe even more important, who they worked for.

So the bottom line was, how much was she willing to pay for the retrieval of a not-very-valuable book? And was that enough for me to take the time to find it, not to mention the risk?

I looked at the clock. It was too late to go back to the Side Car and hope to find the redhead still there.

"You picked me up," I said after thinking it over, "we go to your place."

The bottom-bottom line was, Sindi DiWagne was a good-looking woman who was getting better-looking as the night wore on. Some fantasies just don't want to go away. Especially when you've got a buzz.

"What," she said startled, "why should we go to my place? What do you intend to do there?"

"I'll tell you on the way. Come on, let's go." I was already on my feet and took her arm to get her moving. She snubbed out her third cigarette in the half hour we had been talking and came with me.

Two AM. The bars and nightclubs were closing and the cabs were jockeying for position to get the first fares out. If they got them quickly enough they might have time for a second or even a third fare before everything quieted down for the night. Also, the first folks to leave the clubs and bars at closing were likely to be the least drunk and most likely to give decent tips. I hailed a cab that was losing its race to be the first in line at the Side Car Club and had to tell Sindi to give the driver her address after we climbed in. She scrunched into a corner of the backseat and wrapped her arms around her chest. The way her legs were intertwined, I could tell she really meant to prevent me from ravaging her in the cab. No problem. Even in buzzed fantasy, I wasn't going to ravish her in the cab.

"All right, why are we going to my place," she demanded when the cabbie put shifted into gear and pulled away from the curb.

"Because I don't take pickups home with me," I said. "What do you think?"

Sindi drew into herself more and her face gained an uneasy pout. She believed that macho piece of nonsense.

"Either Fatso or Nasty has your book," I said. "The one who doesn't have it is probably going to come looking for it. If I'm there when he shows up I can ask him who he is and maybe he can tell me who the other one is. Satisfied?" I hoped that sounded plausible.

She nodded and relaxed somewhat, but kept her arms and legs protecting her female attributes.

"We can also talk terms while we wait."

"Terms?" she said in a small voice.

I sighed. "Terms. Money. Payment. Surely whoever told you where to find me also told you I expect to get paid."

The cabbie was paying more attention than I realized. He started looking at me in the rear view mirror in an appraising manner. If he wasn't paying enough attention to my words, he was probably wondering what kind of super stud I was that I expected to get paid for servicing the lady. If I hadn't been buzzed and lonely I would have thought he was thinking something else.

"Oh," she said in a stronger voice and straightened out a bit, "that's right. I wasn't thinking." She sat smoking silently for the rest of the ride.

I sighed again. Is it really true that blondes are dumb? Well, she's had a few tough days. Pudgy and Nasty probably had her shaken up enough she couldn't think straight. We quit talking and I watched the cabbie do his thing. Chestnut Street is a major one way thoroughfare. At this hour of the night it's sometimes as busy as rush hour. This was one of those nights. Most of the other drivers had been drinking and weren't making the lights. Some of them were weaving a bit. Our cabbie wove in and out of the traffic like an Indy car driver and managed to catch each light before it turned red. He knew I wasn't drunk. I guess he thought I would give him a better tip if he made good time.

We were just going across the river, so it wasn't long before he turned onto one of the numbered streets and pulled up in front of a high-rise apartment building that probably went up during the Twenties. We got out and

Sindi went to open the door while I paid the cabbie. He got a couple of dollars extra for his good speed.

Most in-town high-rises have doormen who are supposed to prevent unwelcome people from coming in. Many also have lobby attendants. At night, many of them only have the inside people, who may or may not be able to see the street from their stations. The lobby attendant here couldn't see the street, and this place had an extra fillip; after midnight the front door was locked and tenants had to punch a code into a combination lock to get into the lobby. I turned from paying the cab and what I saw knocked the buzz right out of me; three bozos had Sindi hemmed against the door. She looked terrified.

"Can I help you guys with something?" I said in what was once a parade ground voice. Once upon a time I took some shrapnel in my right knee. After the wound healed enough so I didn't limp too badly, the Marines assigned me to the School of Infantry at Camp Pendleton, California where I taught brand new Marines fresh out of Boot Camp how to use M60 machine guns and 60 millimeter mortars. I lectured to classes of two hundred or more men out in the open. The voice I developed to get all of them to hear every word I said was the one I used on the bozos.

It worked enough to attract the attention of all three of them. Even the cabbie stopped driving away.

"This isn't any of your business," one of the trio said back. "So just go on your way and don't worry about it."

"But I happen to be with the lady, so I'm afraid that makes it my business." In retrospect I can see where I might have been better off if I had just gone on my merry way and let the three bozos do what they wanted to our Miss DiWagne. But, hey, I'm a windmill tilter from way back.

"Then we goan do you, too," the biggest of the three said. He was a crewcut blond with beady eyes and muscles in places where most people don't have places. I could bet he spent most of his free evenings in leather bars with the guys who wear spikes on their wrist bands. Later I learned he was called Moose and the first one to speak was named Kallir. Moose rambled toward me. The ramble made his bulk look even more threatening.

"Want me to call a cop?" It was the cabbie. Made me glad I spent the extra two on the tip.

"No thanks," Kallir answered him, "We can handle this ourselves." Sharp kid, Kallir. If the cabbie didn't know who's who here he might leave without calling for help. But Kallir wasn't sharp enough to not get distracted by the cabbie's question.

Sindi took advantage of Kallir's distraction to break away from the third guy, Hondo, and run over to me. The cabbie popped the back door open and I shoved her in then tried to scramble in after her. Moose was too close, though. He grabbed me and pulled me back out before I was all the way in.

"Get her out of here," I shouted and the cab shot away from the curb.

Moose let go of me and the three of them chased the cab half way down the block. I didn't wait to see if those dogs caught their car, I took off in the other direction and didn't see them when they reversed direction and came after me. I turned at the corner, came down wrong on my right foot and almost fell. Damn, that knee hurt. I saw traffic stopped at a light a couple of blocks away and headed toward it, maybe there was a cab in that traffic that I could get, maybe there was a cop car, maybe if the bozos were following me the traffic would make them peel off. Lots a luck, fella. I never was a fast runner and the bad knee was slowing me down. Hondo jumped on my back before I covered half a block. That slowed me down enough for Moose to catch up and give me a shove and I went down.

Of course I landed on the bad knee, and the pain almost blacked me out. Moose yanked me off the pavement, threw me over his shoulder fireman's carry fashion and followed Kallir at a brisk pace. Hondo tagged along where he could whap me upside the head if I struggled. I know that's where he was because I struggled and he whapped me upside the head for it. I stopped struggling.

Kallir led the way into a dark storefront and into a back room. Once the door closed behind us he flipped a switch and had Moose drop me into a straight back chair and Hondo slapped a pair of handcuffs on me. Then Moose yanked me back to my feet and frisked me. He took the wallet from my hip pocket and gave it to Kallir. He shoved me back down when he was through and tied my hands together.

Kallir flipped through the wallet and puzzled over the driver's license for a few seconds. Then he snickered and dropped the wallet on the floor.

Then the questioning started.

"Okay, buster, where is it?" Kallir wanted to know.

"Where's what?" I asked with as much innocence as I could muster.

"The book," Kallir slowly drew out the words.

"Book? Which one?" I had never seen the book, so why not play dumb? They might fall for it.

Anyway, that's the way it went for most of the next half hour. Kallir patiently asked me the same few questions in as many variations as he could come up with. Hondo sat on a carton looking bored, while Moose leered at me and occasionally licked his lips. Me? I answered each question in the most cooperatively dumb manner I could. Eventually I got as bored with the proceedings as Hondo looked. Then I decided to tell a little truth.

"Okay, okay. She told me something about a book. She said somebody stole it from her. I don't know any more than that."

"Now you know there's a book."

Maybe admitting it wasn't such a hot idea after all.

"Where is it?"

"I don't know. I've never seen it."

"But you're looking for it. You're a private cop or something."

"No, Kallir, it's like I've been telling you. I don't know anything. You're wasting your time on me. I don't have anything to tell you. I'm not a private detective, I'm not a bodyguard, I'm not a cop. None of that. I'm a magazine writer by trade. The lady and I had a few drinks and I was seeing her home, that's all."

Kallir smacked me. "If you don't know anything about the book, what were you doing with her?"

I had to flex my jaw to take out the sting from the slap. "I told you. We met in a bar and had a few drinks. I took her home."

He snickered. I've never heard anyone snicker as much as Kallir. "And what were you going to do when you got her in her apartment?"

I smiled at him, tried to make us two men of the world who know what the score is. "I picked her up in a bar. What do you think?"

"You want to find out if she's a real blonde."

"You got it." The buzz was gone, but the fantasy lived on.

Kallir looked at me, slightly amused, and slowly shook his head. It scared me. I decided it was time to get out of there. Maybe I could bluff my way out.

"Well, guys, it's been fun but I'm leaving now," I said. "I'm going to go home, sit down at my computer, and find an interesting subject to write about. Besides, I'm too old for this kind of shit." I held out my bound hands to be released and gingerly stood up.

Kallir wasn't ready for me to go. "You're not going anywhere," he said. He nodded to Moose. Moose put the flat of his hand on my chest and straightened his wrist.

"Uumph," I said, plopping back onto the chair. They don't call him Moose for nothing. He's big enough that if he could have passed basket-weaving 101 half of the major football factories in the country would have been panting to offer him a scholarship to play offensive guard.

"You're not going anywhere until you tell us everything you know," Kallir said.

"Why didn't you say so, Kallir?" I answered with a brightness I knew was probably too sarcastic. "What do you want to know? I'm not the Encyclopedia Brittanica, so whatever it is you want to know I should be able to tell you in, oh, say, two minutes or so. Five at the outside. Then you'll know everything I do." I looked my dumbest eager to please, but I knew that even the two morons wouldn't accept it, much less Kallir. Take away Kallir's well studied street stupidity and what you had left was an intelligent, perceptive human being with one hell of a mean streak.

"You're a wise ass," Hondo said. He got off his packing crate and swung a fist at my head. Kallir managed to deflect Hondo's hand so it merely glanced off my temple and only left me stunned for a few seconds. Hondo wasn't big like Moose, but the breadth of his shoulders testified to many hours spent pumping iron.

I shook my head to chase out the stars I was seeing and said, "Really guys. Kallir, Moose, Hondo," I wanted to make sure each of them knew he was included in what I said, "I simply want to go home. Nobody ever has to know we met here tonight."

"You're right there, sailor," Hondo said, "nobody has to know we met here tonight." The way he said that sent a chill up my spine.

Kallir pushed the chair he sat backward in against my knees so I couldn't stand up again without moving him.

"Ouch!" I leaned forward and rubbed my bad knee. I had this feeling I might not be able to walk tomorrow-if I was able to do anything at all.

"Did I bang you? Did I make a boo-boo on your knee?" Kallir sneered.

Moose and Hondo chuckled some very unhealthy sounding chuckles.

"No, just an old war wound, don't let it bother you," I tried to laugh along with them, but the knee was no laughing matter. Several doctors have told me to avoid impacting exercises-like running. The shrapnel they weren't able to dig out twenty years ago is still inside the joint, slowly wearing down the cartilage and lacerating the bone surfaces. One of these years I'm going to need a joint prosthetic.

"Let's try it again," Kallir said. "Where's the book?"

"She told me someone took it from her apartment. That's all I know." I kept massaging the knee.

Kallir's face was a patient mask of impassiveness. "Moose, hurt him." His eyes stayed locked on mine. I tried not to swallow, but couldn't prevent an automatic blink.

"That's right," I said bravely, "have Moose get his hands dirty. If you did anything, that blow-dried hairdo of yours might get mussed." I gave him my best sneer, trying to get him off balance. If I was going to manage an escape Kallir was the one I had to have distracted.

Kallir wasn't biting. What the hell, it wasn't much of a sneer. He put up his hand to stop Moose. "That's the advantage of a good blow dry hairdo," he said to me. "If it gets mussed up you just shake your head and it's back in place." He demonstrated by bouncing his fist off my jaw. When my head cleared I saw a lock of hair had fallen across his forehead. He tossed his head and the lock was back in place.

"See, old man? I'm not worried about getting mussed." He still looked patient. "Now where's the book?"

"Someone broke into the DiWagne woman's apartment last night and stole it. I told you that already." Talking wasn't easy with what felt like half the teeth in my mouth ready to fall out.

Kallir sighed. "You keep saying that. Moose."

A pair of heavy hands thudded onto my shoulders with the thumbs lying forward, alongside my neck.

"Where's the book?"

"I don't know. I've never seen it. I already told you someone stole it. I never heard anything about this damn book until an hour ago. And that's the absolute truth."

Kallir looked above my head and nodded. Moose shifted his hands so the palms faced each other, then he twisted one way and back to the other. I screamed, my neck felt like it was breaking.

"Where's the book?"

"I don't know."

Kallir gripped my wrists in his, raised his eyes above my head and said, "Put him under for awhile. Moose shifted his hands so the fingers and palms were on my shoulders. He pressed his thumbs against the sides of my throat. I knew this trick; pressure on the carotid arteries and nerves. It can knock a man out pretty quickly. Keep the pressure on for not a lot longer than that and it'll kill. I struggled, but Moose was too strong and Kallir's chair against my knees restricted my mobility. Hondo spoke just before I blacked out.

"Kallir, we got company."

I didn't hear the rest of it.

CHAPTER FOUR

When I regained consciousness a few minutes later I was lying on my back on the floor and the first thing I saw was Sindi DiWagne's face hovering over mine. On one side of her face I saw Clyde Krippendorf, on the other side was Jimmy's. I could hear other people moving around the room.

"Are you all right, Ham?" Sindi asked. Her worried expression looked like it really mattered to her if I was all right.

"If I'm alive I'm all right," I said. "If I'm dead it doesn't matter one way or the other."

"You're alive, dummy," Clyde snorted.

"Then I'm all right. Help me to my feet." Sindi pulled back and Clyde and Jimmy each took a hand and hauled me up. I rubbed the sides of my neck where Moose had applied the pressure and then rubbed my knee, which wasn't hurting so badly anymore. Aside from Clyde and Jimmy, I saw a couple of other men. Hulks as big as they were, they were probably bouncers at the Side Car.

"Who were those guys?" Jimmy asked.

I shook my head and looked at Sindi. She shook her head and said she'd never seen them before.

"Then why'd they mug you?" Clyde asked.

"They didn't mug me," I said. My knee started hurting again and I looked around for something to sit on.

"Then why did they beat you up?" Clyde asked.

I sighed. "They were looking for something that was stolen from Sindi."

"So where is it?"

"How the hell do I know?" I exclaimed. The buzz was back and I was getting exasperated. People had been repeatedly asking me that same question for far too long and I was tired of hearing it. "Like I said, it was stolen from her and she doesn't know who has it." I looked at the chair I'd been kept in and decided it held too many negative memories. I settled for the shipping crate Hondo had sat on. Then I looked around the room again. "Where's John Wayne?" I asked.

"What?" one of the hulks asked.

"The Seventh Cavalry showed up in the nick of time. John Wayne always led the Seventh Cavalry on its rescue missions. So where is he?"

"I think he's asking how did we get here," Jimmy said. Smart kid. Clyde better fire him pretty soon or he's liable to take over the business and old Clyde'll be out on the street.

"When those men stopped chasing us and started going after you," Sindi said, "I had the cab circle around until we found you again. I saw them carry you into this place and decided to get help. The cab driver wanted to call the police, but I thought they'd need a warrant to come in here. So I made the driver take me back to the Side Car Club."

"I was closed," Clyde picked up the story. "The door was locked and was only being unlocked to let people out. The way she came barging in and yelling I thought the place must be on fire. Jimmy was escorting the last drunk out when she barged in to get us to help. Mack," Clyde jerked a thumb at one of the hulks, "already had his car out front. We piled in and here we are."

"You should have heard Clyde when we got here," Jimmy said. "When he called out, 'open up, it's the police,' he sounded just like Jack Webb." I wondered how he knew what Jack Webb sounded like, he's too young to remember Dragnet.

"That was awful sweet of them to come and help," Sindi said. "Don't you think so, Ham?"

"Sweet" wasn't the word I'd use. "Righteous," I agreed. "Anybody see where they went?"

There were generalized negative murmurings in reply.

"We can find out who owns this building," Clyde said. "That should lead the cops to whoever did this."

One of the hulks came in from the front room and said, "Come here, I want to show you something. "I thought the door opened too easily," he said when we got there. "Look here." He pointed to the door frame. It was splintered around the keeper. "Forget about finding them from who owns this place, they broke in."

He was right. It looked like someone, I'd guess Moose, used a tire-iron to open the door. I thought it was too bad there wasn't a burglar alarm, the cops would have been here long ago. But maybe the owner didn't think there was any point in wiring an empty store front.

Clyde looked around. "Anybody see a phone?" he asked. Nobody did. "Let's go out and find a pay phone so I can call the cops."

Sindi gasped. "Don't do that," she blurted.

Clyde looked at her curiously. So did I.

"Yeah, they didn't hurt me," I said. "This place looks like it's been empty for a while, no need to bother the cops." This was the second time tonight Sindi didn't want the police. I wondered why.

"No hair off my ass," Clyde said. He'd need an explanation later. I'd give him one as soon as I had one to give.

There didn't seem to be much more to do here, except get out before a patrolling cop stopped and we had to explain why we were in an empty store at this hour of the night, so we went out onto the street. Clyde thanked his hulks for helping with the rescue and said he was going to help me escort Sindi home. The hulks said sure thing no problem. Jimmy insisted on tagging along. In less than ten minutes more, Clyde and Jimmy were in the apartment building on the numbered street riding up its elevator with Sindi and me. Sindi wanted to give everyone a drink. She ignored the No Smoking sign on the elevator and lit one which she dropped on the floor and stepped on when we got off.

We exited the elevator on the sixth floor and turned left. This hallway, unlike the old one she'd described to me, was wide enough for us to walk two abreast without crowding, the carpeting was plush enough to deaden the sound of our passage and the light level was almost high enough to read a newspaper by. Sindi stopped in front of 608 and stuck the key in the slot. She stepped inside the door and froze.

I had seen a line of light at the foot of the door, so I was standing slightly to the side and wasn't in line of sight of whoever was inside that stopped her. Clyde and Jimmy were behind me. I motioned to them to be still and waited to hear what came next.

What came next was a slightly gravely voice that said, "Don't just stand there, Miss Prissy Pants, get your sweet little ass in here where we can talk." He followed that with a nasty little snicker. Then he said, "Or whatever I do to that sweet little ass of yours."

I looked over my shoulder at Clyde and Jimmy in a way that meant if they wanted in, fine, if they didn't want to go in with me, that was okay too. I took a deep breath, and stepped through the door and moved quickly off to the side. Clyde and Jimmy were right behind me.

A sofa faced the doorway. A hard-looking, rangy man lounged on it. He had his feet propped on the glass top coffee table in front of the sofa. There was a businesslike scar on his cheek and his heavy eyebrows met in the middle. He was smiling through his teeth. I guessed he was the tough guy Sindi told me wanted her book. There was something bad about him, a feel of evil.

"Gee, Prissy Pants, if I knew you were bringing company I would of popped some corn," he said through those smiling teeth.

"What are you doing here?" Sindi said. Her voice trembled with the effort. "I don't have the book, you do." She confirmed who I thought he was.

"This is Miss DiWagne's apartment," I said to him. "She asked you a question. Now you answer it."

Clyde and Jimmy stood ready. I could only see them out of the corner of my eye so I couldn't see their expressions, but I knew Clyde well enough to know that he looked the same way he did when he was giving the bum's rush to some obnoxious drunk who wouldn't leave the Side Car. It must have been the same look he used to give to defensive linemen when he was winning All American honors at Nebraska. Jimmy was smart enough he was probably looking the same way. The tough guy didn't even look at them.

"But I was here first," he said. "I think she should answer before I do." He chuckled.

"You were here first because you're trespassing," I said.

He shrugged. "Minor point," He removed his feet from the coffee table and sat straighter. "But I'm here for the map. Where is it?" The toothy smile was still on his face.

"You have it," Sindi said. "It was in the book and you stole it."

He shook his head slowly. "True, I have the book, but I don't have the map. Where is it?"

That damn question again. I was tired of it. Sindi also seemed to be getting tired of it.

"If you have the book but don't have the goddam map I don't know where it is," she snapped.

"You telling me Llowlolski has it?" he asked.

"Who's that?" I asked.

"Ask her, he's a buddy of hers." He aimed his smiling teeth at Sindi.

I glanced at her. She looked at me and shrugged an I don't know who he's talking about.

"I told you what I'd do if your jittery friend got the map before I did," he said between his smiling teeth. I was beginning to wonder if that smile was surgically implanted. His eyes weren't smiling along with his teeth.

"The jittery man at Freeman's?" Sindi asked.

He nodded and clapped his hands together twice in sarcastic applause. "See, you do know Llowlolski."

"Listen, pal," I butted in, "I've been hearing about this stupid map for the past couple of hours and nobody's bothered to tell me what it's all about. What say you tell me before I lose my patience?" A not quite seen motion out of the corner of my eye told me Clyde and Jimmy were tensing for action.

"You mean Miss Prissy Pants didn't tell you?" He laughed. "I've met some dumb dicks in my time. Most of them aren't bright enough for the cops to hire as flatfoots, but you take the cake. You took on a client without even knowing what the assignment was. Dumb." He shook his head and slapped his knee to show how hard he was laughing. I didn't bother telling him I'm not a private detective, though I did wonder why he thought I was private fuzz instead of just a friend. He leaned back like he planned on being there for a while and started talking again, "It's a pirate treasure map."

"Sure it is," I said. "Where'd it come from, a box of Cap'n Crunch?"

He laughed again. "Ever hear of a pirate named Teach?" he asked.

A pirate named Teach. The wheels of memory started spinning in my head. Then I had it. I once did an article on pirates of the Caribbean for *Boys Life magazine.* "Teach" isn't the name this pirate is generally known by. "Edward Teach, late Seventeenth, early Eighteenth Century pirate," I said. "Better known by his *nom de guerre*, Blackbeard. Used to tie lit cannon fuses in his beard when his crew boarded a merchantman. Survivors said he looked like the devil incarnate. Really tore up the Spanish Main. Supposed to have left a lot of buried booty which has never been found."

"Smart boy," he said. "That's the one I'm talking about. The map I want is one of Blackbeard's maps."

"That's what was in Miss DiWagne's book?"

"That's what was in it."

I turned and looked full at Sindi. Most likely the map was a fake, but if two different people wanted it, it was hardly as unimportant as she made it out to be. "We're going to have to talk about this some more," I said to her, then turned back to the tough guy. "It's late, you weren't invited in, everybody's tired, there's three of us and only one of you. So what say you take a hike."

He leered. "There's three of you and only one of her, oh my. If seconds is sloppy, what is thirds?"

That was it. When I get tired enough I get cranky. I was tired enough. In three steps I was around the coffee table with my knee planted in his groin and my left hand around his throat. Listen, pal," I growled, "I'm tired of you and I'm tired of your stupid question. You're leaving."

He didn't try to lean away from me, not that he had anywhere to go. He looked up at my eyes. "I get your point," he said. His voice was cool. I didn't feel any tremble or flutter in his throat.

"I'm going to back off, and you're going to get up and go bye-bye."

"Sure thing." Very cool. He was doing a masterful job of convincing me he wasn't afraid. Still, he said, "When you're right, you're right. It's late, I'm going."

He rose to his feet. I know his throat had to hurt at least a little bit, but he didn't touch it or in any other way show pain. When he got half way to the door he looked at Sindi and said, "I'll be back, Miss Prissy Pants. When I do I want that map. You give me the map, I'll give you your book back. I don't get the map, I get you." On his way through the door he added to me, "And don't you be here when I come back. You don't scare me."

Something in his voice made me believe him.

During that whole time, it never occurred to me to ask his name.

CHAPTER FIVE

Clyde and Jimmy let out deep sighs. They both thought they'd have to fight and were relieved they didn't have to. They took over the vacated couch. Sindi collapsed into an overstuffed chair.

My knee started hurting again, I needed a pain reliever. "You offered us a drink," I said. "Where's the bar?"

"In the cabinet." Sindi waved a hand toward the side of the room.

I limped one cautious step in the direction she pointed and Jimmy jumped to his feet. "Sit down, Ham," he said, "I'm the bartender here. Got any ice?" he asked Sindi.

"In the freezer. You'll find mixers in the refrigerator." She was slumped deep into the chair and only stirred enough to gesture toward a hallway. The way she looked the only reason she wasn't curled into a fetal ball was she didn't have the strength to pull her legs up. The tough guy was the one who had been threatening her. Put him on top of Llowlolski, who had to have been upsetting when he called her at her office, and she had the right to be upset. If they both were leaning on me, I'd be concerned too.

Jimmy made himself busy with bottles, glasses, and ice and inside two minutes handed us each a drink. Sindi's was scotch, soda. Mine was bourbon on the rocks. I don't know what he fixed for himself and Clyde. I knocked mine off in two swallows. Clyde was already handing his glass back to Jimmy for a refill by the time I finished mine. Sindi was still holding hers untasted in a limp hand.

"Drink it, Sindi," I said, "it'll make you feel better." She raised it to her lips and sipped. "Knock it back," I told her, and suddenly felt like a pusher for alcoholism. "It makes me feel better," that's one of the standard excuses used by alcoholics. She knocked part of it back and coughed and sputtered, almost spilling the rest of her drink. But then she composed herself and looked more relaxed than limp. "Give me a cigarette, please," she asked. Jimmy found a pack on a table and lit one for her.

Clyde downed his second drink a little slower than the first one. Jimmy managed to get down half of his first by the time Clyde finished his second. I was sipping my second. Clyde stood and looked me in the eye.

"Ham, the next time some broad asks for you in my place I'm going to tell her I never heard of you," he said. "Let's go, Jimmy. If we don't spot a cab right away we can walk back across the bridge. It'll be safer to go together."

"Right," Jimmy said. He followed Clyde out the still open apartment door and finished his drink on the way. Before closing the door behind him he tossed the empty glass to me. I juggled the catch but managed to hang on.

I needed some answers and I needed them badly, but Sindi was almost out in the chair. They'd have to wait until morning-or whenever it was when we woke up. It was after 3:30 AM now.

"Get me a pillow and a sheet," I said, "I'm sleeping on the couch. Then you go to bed and get some sleep yourself." The past hour and a half had knocked the fantasy out of me.

She didn't say anything to acknowledge she heard my words. But she did drag herself out of the chair and through a door I assumed led to her bedroom and a light went on in that room. In a moment she returned with a sheet and pillow. "The bathroom's over there," she said and pointed at another door. Then she turned back to the other room and closed the door behind herself. After a couple of minutes the edge of light at its bottom went out and I heard a quiet sobbing. I ignored it and used the sheet and pillow to turn the couch into a bed and made a quick trip to the bathroom before stripping to my undershorts and lying down to sleep.

It took me a while to start drifting off because my mind was too full of what had happened over the past few hours. The two drinks I had after the tough guy left brought back the buzz. Another thing the buzz does, for me at least, is set my mind to spinning about whatever problem is on it. So my mind spun.

I needed to know more about this map that was supposedly an authentic Blackbeard buried treasure map. Who was the tough guy working for? He claimed to be representing someone else. He admitted having the book, so it must have been him who stole it from Sindi's old apartment. But if the map wasn't in it when he took it, who had it? Llowlolski was the obvious answer. But if Llowlolski had it, who were Kallir, Moose and Hondo working for? They weren't bright enough or sophisticated enough to be looking for it themselves. They obviously weren't with this guy because he had the book and they were looking for it. Who was Llowlolski and who was he working for? Were any of them really working for anyone else? Were any of them aligned with each other or was I up against three different groups?

Then my mind spun in a slightly different direction.

How much was I going to charge Sindi for this job and could she afford it? She wasn't completely unpacked yet, I'd noticed a few cartons sitting about and a Raggedy Ann doll lolling out of the top of a shopping bag. The move had to have cost her something. This apartment was bigger than the one she described moving out of, but still wasn't big. Even though this building was in what real estate agents generously call the Rittenhouse Square area, it wasn't in a luxury high rise and was far enough away from the Square that maybe the rent was relatively moderate. She's putting herself through graduate school part time. I've got to remember to ask what she does for a living. Her coworkers overheard her phone conversation with Llowlolski, that didn't sound like she had an office of her own.

All these things tied themselves together and told me she was probably doing secretarial work or something similar. Not a job or a life in which she had a lot of discretionary money. So the question came again: How much could she afford to pay, and how much was I willing to do for how little? I kept pushing down the fantasy that kept popping up, the one about finding out if she was a real blonde.

The sobbing in the other room stopped and there was only the sound of my own breathing and the noise of predawn traffic on the streets to keep me company. There didn't seem to be anything I could do right away except get the truth about the map from Sindi, and I couldn't do anything about that until she woke up.

The questions spinning in my mind grew fewer and spun in tighter circles and I was drifting into the nirvana of sleep when a small voice from the other room said, "Ham, come here please. I need to be held."

I tried to pretend I was asleep but the voice came again in a moment, "I know you're awake, I can hear the way you're breathing. Please come to me."

I breathed deeply and sat up. If we turned on a lamp maybe I'd find out if she was a real blonde after all. I padded on bare feet to the door, eased it open, and slipped through without closing it behind me. The room was suddenly lit with a soft glow from a table lamp. I blinked against its light and looked through slitted eyelids. I saw Sindi move to the far side of the bed and pull the sheet back so I could get in. She was wearing a short, diaphanous nightgown. I saw no sign of panties, but couldn't tell if she was a real blonde. She held her arms out to me and I crossed the room and got into that bed and into those arms. She snuggled close until my arms folded around her so closely it almost felt like I was hugging myself. Her soft, open lips brushed against mine and her tongue probed lightly at mine. But, even though her thigh was over mine and she gave a little pelvic push, she didn't grind against me.

Sindi DiWagne didn't want sex just then, she needed to be held and was offering me her body in exchange for holding her. When you're forty years old and it's four o'clock in the morning and you've been up longer than you should have and you've been chased through the night streets and been roughed up and threatened and had the adrenaline going up and back down again as often as I have in the past few hours and the lovely woman in your arms just wants to be held, it's possible to simply be tired enough to be content with just holding her-no matter what your fantasies were earlier in the evening. So I held her and rubbed her back until she went all soft in my arms and her breath came slow and shallow and then I went to sleep myself.

*

The clock on the nightstand read a quarter to eleven when I opened my eyes and rolled over to where I could see it. Kitchen noises told me where Sindi was. I rolled out of bed and went into the bathroom where I emptied my bladder and gargled with whatever brand of mouthwash it was she had in the medicine cabinet and went back into the bedroom before I remembered my clothes were in the living room.

"Good morning."

I turned around to see Sindi standing in the doorway. She was smiling at me and holding a small tray with two coffee cups on it. A short terry robe covered whatever else she was wearing, and a cigarette burned in her hand.

"I remember you take yours black when it's fresh," she said. Her eyes flickered to my undershorts and back to my eyes.

Then I remembered how I was dressed and sat on the bed and pulled a corner of the sheet over my lap.

"Thank you for holding me last night," she said and walked to the nightstand and leaned over to put the tray on it and snubbed out her cigarette in the ashtray on the table. Was it my imagination, or was there really a sway in her hips that hadn't been there last night? "I needed to be held, needed it very badly." It wasn't my imagination that when she bent over the front of her robe opened far enough for me to see that under it she was wearing the same nightie as the night before.

"Don't bother thanking me, I always like to hold a woman while I sleep." For some reason, I felt embarrassed. How are you supposed to feel when you're sitting on a strange bed wearing only your undershorts and the woman you just slept with the night before without having sex with is standing over you wearing not much of a nightgown under a shortie robe?

Sindi sat at my left side. Our hips didn't touch, but when I looked I couldn't see any space between us. She sat straight up with her knees primly together and her hands chastely folded in her lap. Her head was turned in my direction but not far enough to look at me directly. She seemed acutely, and uncomfortably, aware of the intimacy of the situation.

"No, really, Ham. I don't know what would have happened if I stayed home last night instead of going out looking for you and that man had come in. It scares me to think about it. Or if you and your friends had left me to come home alone." Her shudder shook her enough that our hips and thighs momentarily pressed together. She darted a quick glance to see if I responded. I did, but not so she could see it. "When it was all over I just wanted to be held, to feel protected. You did that without taking advantage of me. Not even when I offered myself to you." A soft smile curled her lips. "You were such a gentleman. Thank you."

"Gentleman" wasn't quite the way I remembered it, but when people want to think something nice about me, I let them. Still, some sort of reply seemed to be required here. A feeble, "You're welcome," was all I could come up with.

She smiled again and brushed her fingers over my cheek. Then, "Oh." Her shoulders jerked. "This is getting cold." She reached over to the nightstand and handed me a cup of coffee. Our fingers brushed and I couldn't quite hold back a noise that came out half sigh, half groan.

"You were very brave, the way you handled him when he said that nasty thing about sloppy seconds."

I think I turned red. It *had* been a crude remark. "I had a couple of good men backing me up," I mumbled. "It was no big deal."

"I don't care what kind of backup you had. He said that nasty thing and you came to my defense."

I didn't notice her shift her position, but suddenly our hips and thighs were pressed together and our shoulders touched. I licked my lips. My throat went dry and I felt a sheen of perspiration on my brow. I took a sip of coffee so I could swallow, and looked at her. Last night she had looked good and got better-looking as the evening wore on. This morning she looked beautiful. I wondered how on earth I managed to resist last night when I held her in my arms.

She saw how I was reacting to our contact and made a little Mona Lisa smile. She said, "Last night, in the bar, you thought I was picking you up. And you never even tried to cop a cheap feel."

I flushed at that, too.

She put her hand on the sheet where it covered my knee and asked, "How's the old war wound today?"

"It's the other knee," I said. "So far it hasn't bothered me." That wasn't totally true; the knee was throbbing dully, even though there was no active pain.

She reached to caress the right knee and her breast felt full and heavy against my arm.

I drank a little more coffee.

"You were so gallant." She let go of my knee and sipped from her own cup.

I drank a bit more coffee, then reached past her to put my cup down. It wasn't totally an accident on my part that my arm brushed across her breast. I don't think it was fully an accident on her part when her breast pressed into my arm as I brought it back, either. And I know it wasn't an accident when I put my arm around her and she leaned her face into mine. Somehow, she managed to put her cup on the nightstand without spilling any coffee.

Then it got serious and I forgot about last night. I forgot about the book and the map and all the questions from the night before. I forgot about Kallir and company. I forgot about the tough guy with whom I'd traded threats. I almost forgot the meaning of the thing she handed me from the drawer of the nightstand, then remembered what it was and put it on. Safe sex is a byword of the Nineties. I forgot about everything but right now and the most beautiful woman in the entire world being in my arms and what we were doing with each other. She was a real blonde, too.

Maybe I should have remembered that the night before all of her body language made it more than clear that she didn't want any part of me physically.

*

"Oh, god, that was good," she said when we finally untangled and she lay with her head on my shoulder. "It's been so long."

I was panting too hard to answer with words, so I patted her back.

"It's been so long," she repeated. "I needed that so bad. You were the greatest, Ham." She wiggled her entire body against me. "Oh, god, I needed that." Then she settled down quietly for a while.

For me it had been a mindless spasm, a brief, eternal moment when my body remembered all those things I almost thought it had forgotten. It was something that I needed, badly, and it was great for me. But after I had mine, it became a wild ride while I held on as she ran through crest after orgasmic crest. Gave me the impression she enjoyed it more than I did.

When she spoke again, I was still so drained I didn't hear her words the first time she said them and she had to repeat herself.

"It's been way too long since the last time a man wanted me."

I wondered why it had been so long for her. I must have wondered out loud, because she said:

"Why don't men like women over thirty, Ham?"

What? Where did that come from? I didn't think over thirty had anything to do with it-not with her, anyway. She was too beautiful for any man to turn down because she's over thirty.

She asked it again so I gave it a moment's thought. How the hell do I know why some men don't want women over thirty? Is that even true, or is it a myth perpetrated by women who say no to anyone who isn't perfect to explain why they don't get dates? Sure, younger women are normally better-looking than older women. That's in the order of an act of nature.

"It's their job," is the way Clyde explains it. "Young women, that is to say, women of prime breeding age, are supposed to be good-looking. Men are visual critters who tend to be ruled by their testes. The sight of a lithe lass turns men's brains off and their gonads on. This is a biological rule, has to do with propagation of the species. That's why men flock to places like mine on dancing-girl nights, and why there's far fewer such places that cater to women; women aren't visual in the same way men are. It doesn't have anything to do with culture. It has everything to do with biology." And if he's in that kind of mood, Clyde might add, "It's in the nature of the breast, er, beast."

I think there's a lot of truth in what Clyde has to say about that. I know I'd rather see a 23 year-old girlie dancing around nearly naked than a woman twice her age. But when it comes to more than just looking, I want a woman who's been around the block a couple of times. You don't find too many like that who are under thirty.

But Sindi needed to have something said to her, so I improvised. "It's because they can think women under thirty are still kids," I said. "As long as men're with kids they can pretend they're still young themselves and not have to face the fact that they're getting older without necessarily getting better."

She didn't say anything to that right away. When she did it was, "You don't feel like that, do you, Ham?"

I didn't answer immediately either. When I did I said, "Nope. I know I'm getting older and uglier. I want a woman over thirty, someone who I can look good standing next to."

It took a second or two for that to sink in, then she pounded me once on the chest. "Oh, you..."

After we both laughed she squeezed her arms and thighs around me, with a little extra pelvic pressure thrown in to make sure I got the point. "We have to do this again, Ham. Real soon."

My sentiments exactly.

A few minutes later, she plastered a big sloppy kiss all over my mouth, then rolled out of bed and went to the bathroom, saying back at me, "To make you look good, huh?" Then, with what sounded like an edge of harshness in her voice, "You're going to get it one of these days, Ham."

Actually, I thought I *had* just gotten it. Well, maybe the "it" she was thinking of something other than what I was thinking of. Then again, I wasn't thinking very clearly at the time. Or I might have wondered if it was so long, how come she had a rubber ready at hand like that.

When I heard the shower running I thought of something else and got out of bed.

"Hi," I said when I poked my head around the shower curtain. "Want your back scrubbed?"

She gave a surprised but delighted shriek, smiled impishly, and said, "Come on in, big boy, the water's fine."

We proceeded to have a wonderful time washing each other down. At some point in there, she was on her knees in front of me, never mind why, and exclaimed, "You really do have an old war wound!" Her fingers traced the horseshoe shaped surgical scar on my knee. She lingered over the wider part where the scalpel bisected the largest of the entry wounds.

"Did it hurt much?" she asked with apparent concern.

"Hell, yes," I said.

She kissed the old scar, then something else attracted her attention and we forgot all about old war wounds.

It was later when she said, "Hey, I bet I enjoyed that more than you did."

I said I thought so too.

Eventually we got dried off. She shrugged into the shortie robe without bothering with the nightie. "I don't know about you, but I'm starved." I admitted as how I could use some food too. "I'll fix us something to eat while you get dressed," she said, and left me alone.

I got my clothes from the living room and put them on. Damn, I hated putting on the same underwear and socks. But I was feeling good enough my knee didn't hurt at all.

When I got into the kitchen Sindi gave me a smiling peck on the lips and a quick grope before I sat down. I tweeked a tit and she squealed and shimmied girlishly.

Lunch was a bean sprout salad and tuna sandwiches made with thin sliced whole wheat bread. At least I think it was tuna, though it could have been flavored tofu.

"Got any horseradish sauce?" I asked, as good a *non sequitur* as any. I don't go for any health food fad and my opinion of tofu is, well, let's leave that for another time. And there was the incongruity that Sindi has a voice half destroyed by too many years of too many cigarettes and too much booze and here she is into health food. But I'm not about to feel superior about the contradiction, despite having quit smoking myself. After all, I've been known to do dumb things like tangling with Kallir and company and standing up to the tough guy last night on purpose-and last night wasn't as bad as some of the dumb things I've done. That kind of thing is even more inconsistent than her bean sprouts, whole wheat bread, booze, and cigarettes.

We didn't talk much over the meal, but when it was done the first thing I wanted to talk about was money. Once she had made the commitment to pay for my services she'd have to tell me everything she knew about the map. That was what I told myself anyway.

CHAPTER SIX

Money. Even for people who aren't obsessed with it, money's always a very important consideration. You have to pay the landlord or the mortgage company, the electric company, the gas company, the phone company, auto insurance, other insurance, loans, and credit cards bills. You have to buy groceries on a regular basis, buy new clothes once in awhile, and go out from time to time. Everybody needs money. Most people get their money via a regular paycheck from an employer. Some people get it as profit from their manufacturing, retail, or service business. A lucky few inherit it.

Some loonies among us imagine ourselves to be talented. We make something from within ourselves and try to find someone to buy it for, we hope, enough to supply the money for all the things we need. We're the artists; the painters, sculptors, printmakers, craftsmen, writers. Poets aren't dumb enough to think they can make a living doing their art, so they go out and get actual jobs with real paychecks.

Me? Like I told Sindi last night, I'm a magazine feature writer. You probably don't recognize my name because I haven't had any books published. But I sell on an irregular basis to magazines like *Saturday Evening Post, Saturday Review, The Atlantic Monthly, New Guard*, and *New Republic*. I've even made a few sales to the bigs; *Harper's, Playboy, McCall's*, and *Penthouse*. Don't ask what I write about because I can't narrow it down. I'll write about anything somebody will pay me to write about. I've done an article on urban pigeon breeding for *New York Magazine*, one on the hazards of inshore boating near Little Egg Harbor, New Jersey for *Yachting, Racing & Cruising* and a history of the uses of incendiary devices by police departments for *Philadelphia Magazine*. Hell, *Montana Magazine* paid me to write on the modern uses of buffalo chips.

I keep bugging *Rolling Stone* to let me do an article on my kind of music; Commander Cody and the Lost Planet Airmen, NRBQ, Jerry Jeff Walker, Warren Zevon. You know, the ones who approached greatness but were never let in. Maybe they didn't have the right agent or manager or publicist, maybe they're too idiosyncratic, maybe they don't want to do the pandering they think they need to do to make it all that big. Maybe they're just good, but not quite good enough. You know, the singers and bands who never play the major concert halls or the big arenas because they can't fill them. These are the groups and the singles who go on tour and play the same clubs as do the young up and comers who-haven't-made-it-yet-but-are-only-a-year-or-two-away. They play the small clubs like the Side Car Club-except they don't play at the Side Car, except for those who are about to become up and comers. But that's another story.

I go to those clubs, and to the Side Car on music nights when there isn't someone I want to see playing somewhere else. It's a specialized taste that can't be satisfied in the big venues. At least a couple of times a month I can be found in one of those clubs, sometimes as often as twice in a week. I love this music, even when the acoustics are bad and the volume is way too high. Unlike at the major concert halls and big arenas, you can get close to the performers, you can see the wrinkles and get wet from the sweat, you can feel the pain of being so close yet so far away.

Rolling Stone keeps telling me it's been done.

Anyway, I write about anything for anyone and haven't yet made a big splash, so even though you've likely seen my by-line you don't recognize it. I more or less make a living at magazine writing, but the income from it never quite stretches far enough to do everything I want to do, and sometimes it can't handle some of the absolute necessities. What most writers in my position do is find themselves a few business clients to do writing for on the side. I tried that once and didn't like it. What I do instead is take on the occasional private client. Someone who's lost something of value, or had it stolen. I locate it and get it back. My fee is based on the value of the lost item, and I usually try to keep expenses to a minimum. The IRS stays off my back about it because I submit a written report to the client at the end of it, and claim everything leading up to the report as research. On occasion, some of the things I learn in this research works its way into one or another of my magazine articles.

What I do with my private clients isn't any steadier an income producer than writing for magazines. But, hey, it helps pay the bills.

Now I've got a would-be client who dropped in on me out of nowhere and I've got a problem with her. Sindi DiWagne lost a book with a map and she wants it back. She says she wants the book back, but it's not valuable enough to hire someone to get it-it'd be cheaper to go out and buy another copy. I think what she really wants back is the map. That's a toughie. How do you go about putting a dollar value on a pirate's treasure map? There's a lot of them around and nearly every one of them is a fake. The only way to come up with a fair price is to examine the map itself, follow it to its purported pot of gold and see how much is in it. I can't work on that basis. If I did I'd probably wind up having to go out and get a regular job. Repulsive thought.

Sindi DiWagne is a good enough looking woman and all, but expenses and a roll in the hay don't pay the landlord. I was afraid I was going to offend her.

Sometimes I hate having to be pragmatic.

*

She was cuddly and affectionate while we were putting away the lunch dishes, but pulled away when I tried to make something of it. When the tidying up was done I got down to business.

"My normal fee is twenty-five percent of the object's value plus expenses," I said. "What's the value of the map?"

"But it's the book I want," Sindi objected. "I don't know anything about the map." She acted appropriately offended.

"Bullshit," I shook my head to hide the way I felt about talking harshly to the woman I'd just had such a wonderful time with. "The book's only worth fifty or seventy-five dollars. If that was all you were concerned about you would have reported the theft to the police and when they didn't return it to you, you'd go and buy another copy of it. It's not worth hiring someone to get that copy back for you. Now, tell me about the map or I'm outta here." That was a hard thing to say. It had been too long, and she was too beautiful and too good in bed. No way I wanted to be "outta here."

It offended her, as I expected it to. Now we'll see if she really did enjoy it enough to take steps to keep me around.

She pouted and lit a cigarette. "You shouldn't talk to me that way, Ham," she said, which was about how I expected her to start her part of the negotiations. After all, she had given her body to me in copulation and I was supposed to accept anything she said as gospel. It's a female ploy that often works. Resisting wasn't easy for me, but it wasn't going to work this time. She had seemed to enjoy it more than I did, and claimed to need it more. We'll see. This is push coming to shove.

"You shouldn't lie to me, Sindi," I said in what I hoped was a disappointed-but-willing-to-be-conciliatory voice. "You want the map. If I'm going to return it to you I have to know everything there is to know about it. And there's no way I can set a fair price for finding it unless I know all there is to know. So tell me about the map."

She twisted the cigarette between her fingers and puffed on it a couple of times before violently stubbing it out. Then she took a deep breath and glared at me. "All right, here's the map's provenance," she said. "Bastard."

Round one to me. But it didn't feel good-that "bastard" made me flinch.

"In 1693 Edward Teach, better known as Blackbeard, captured the *Oro de Leon*, a heavily laden bullion ship headed for Port o' Prince from Vera Cruz. He took the entire cargo of gold which, if the manifests can be believed, has a current market value of somewhere between twenty and thirty million dollars. Blackbeard and his crew killed everybody on board except for the captain's wife and fourteen year old daughter and an eleven year old cabin boy. The wife and daughter were taken on board Blackbeard's ship, presumably for the sexual use of his officers and maybe his crew. This was after he raped both of them with the captain watching, right before he disemboweled the captain, which he did in front of the wife and daughter. In any event, the wife and daughter were never heard of again. The cabin boy escaped certain death by hiding in a secret compartment in the forecastle, from where he was able to watch everything that happened. His testimony was corroborated by independent sources, which is how we know it was Blackbeard who took the *Oro de Leon*.

"After giving his officers and crew their shares of the booty, Blackbeard sailed up to an isolated area of the Georgia coast where he went ashore with his share and five members of the crew. He came back with only one of the five men. That one had been left with the boat while Blackbeard and the other four went inland to bury the treasure. We can assume he killed the other four crewmen.

"Two years later Blackbeard's first mate, a blackguard known to history only as Grande..."

"El Grande?" I asked.

"No," she shook her head, "just Grande. Grande decided to go into the pirating business for himself and jumped ship. One of the things he took with him when he jumped was Blackbeard's map of the Georgia burial site. He intended to dig up the treasure to use as a stake to set himself up. Unfortunately for him he wasn't close enough to Georgia when he jumped ship to get there in one easy trip; he jumped ship in Trinidad, which is just off the coast of Venezuela. First he had to go into port to round up a crew willing to steal a coastal schooner and kill whatever members of its crew were on board at the time.

"Grande turned out not to be a very good pirate leader. He wasn't able to properly control his crew. They were more interested in landward rape than in pillage on the high seas. It was only a few months before two armed frigates of the Spanish navy cornered Grande on the Atlantic coast of Florida and sank his ship. Half of his crew was killed or escaped in the battle. Grande was sent back to Spain to stand trial while the captured members of his crew went, one by one, to various ports to be hanged as examples to others who might be considering a life of piracy.

"While in prison waiting to be hanged after being found guilty, Grande gave the Blackbeard map to his jailer in exchange for his aid in escaping. The jailer didn't trust Grande to let him keep the map after escaping, so he didn't live up to his end of the bargain and Grande was hanged. But the jailer never managed to find a way to get to Georgia to dig up the treasure, so he eventually sold the map to a Portuguese sea captain for enough money to take care of him in his old age.

"The Portuguese sea captain was a shrewd man. He didn't know how long it would be before he could get to Georgia and, with the state of sailing ships in those days, there was a chance he'd be lost at sea before he could get the treasure. So he made a copy of the map which he carried to sea, and he left the original at home in a strong box with a letter explaining what it was and where it had come from. Eventually he was lost at sea, so far as anyone knows without ever finding the treasure. His son, who inherited the strong box, never opened it to find the map and letter. It seems the captain kept the key on his person and it went down with him.

"Anyway, the grandson of the captain inherited the strong box next and had a metalsmith break its lock. He thought the map and letter were an elaborate ruse and had them framed. They hung in the family's palace until the middle of the Nineteenth Century when the family fell on hard times and had to auction off their belongings.

"The map and letter were bought by an American, a wealthy New York businessman, who believed the map and tried to find the Georgia location and dig up the treasure. He died in the attempt. His son was on the expedition with him and came home with his father's body and the map. He had the map bound into a book, the Bret Harte, for safe keeping until he could raise the resources himself to go back again. He went bankrupt before he could make good on his return and lost everything, including the book with the map, at a sheriff's sale. I found a record of it in an old auction catalog and managed to track it back to Blackbeard. The book remained in the possession of the family of the Philadelphian who had bought it at the sheriff's sale until a few weeks ago, when the latest heir proved to be someone who had no use for books and put the library up for sale.

"I saw the listing for this family's library going at Freeman's and went to find the book." She paused to light another cigarette and didn't start talking again when it was lit.

"And you happened to find this very valuable book by rummaging through the cartons of minor junk," I said. That didn't sound right. Even if the latest heir was so much a philistine he couldn't appreciate books and had no idea of what he had, the auctioneer would surely at least notice something different about this book and put it in a lot of its own, or at least would know it was a first edition and put it with a few other complementary firsts.

Sindi sat quietly for a moment before saying "No. It was with a few presentation copies. I knew there were other people interested in that lot and I didn't want to be outbid, or noticed buying it so, when nobody was looking, I moved it to the box of junk." She had the grace to look embarrassed.

I sat watching her for a while and lightly drumming my fingers on the table top. "You stole it," I said.

"I didn't steal it, I paid for it!"

"No, you paid for the box of junk, not for the book with the map in it. The book with the map in it belongs to whoever bought the lot with the presentation copies." I looked at her speculatively for a moment, then asked, "Who bought the lot of presentation books? Was it your visitor from last night, or maybe this Llowlolski character?"

She shook her head. "No. They both knew I got the book in the box of junk. I don't think either of them bought the lot it was originally in."

"They saw you make the switch."

She nodded. "They must have."

It was beginning to sound like the map might be real. But after all that time, the map might be worthless. Treasure maps were usually cryptic, meant as aides for the hider to find his way back to the loot without giving enough detail for anyone else to find it.

I said, "You want to use the map to find the treasure."

She nodded.

"What is in it that would tell you where to find what you want? The coastline has probably changed since then and any crooked tree it might refer to is long gone."

"It mentions rock landmarks and things like that, that won't collapse in three thousand years, much less in three hundred," she said in a quiet voice that I had trouble hearing.

"What kind of permanent landmarks?"

"A mountain that was used by navigators to mark their passage."

"That tells you if you've reached the right part of the coast. You need more than that."

"A sheer cliff."

"Yes?" She had to give more detail for me to believe the treasure could be found with this map.

"A gully, a granite outcropping, an oddly shaped mountain saddle," she said slowly and lit another cigarette. "The details are enough to find the treasure." I've located all of these things on modern topographical maps. I think I know almost exactly where it is."

A surprising woman. Most men who have military experience have been exposed to topographical maps, but few retain the knowledge of how to read them. Most men just find the lines that indicate elevation confusing. Far fewer women have been exposed to topo maps and know how to read them. I didn't say anything about that, though. Instead I said, "Twenty to thirty million dollars worth on today's market. You're sure of this."

"Yes. It could be more."

I thought some more. Twenty-five percent of that much money would be five million dollars, minimum. Could be seven and a half. Could be even more. That's enough for me to forget about having to earn money from any source for the rest of my life. Only I didn't think she had that much to pay me when I found the map-but if I returned the map to her and she found Blackbeard's treasure and I got my share of it...

Thus doth avarice make accessories of us all. In the meanwhile I had some pressing bills to pay. Besides, Sindi was beautiful and I'd had a wonderful time playing body games with her.

"My normal fee is twenty-five percent plus expenses," I said. "The percentage payable on return of the missing item, expenses on a regular basis."

Sindi blanched.

"Accepting your evaluation of Blackbeard's treasure, that means if I find and return the map to you, you will then owe me a minimum of five million dollars on receipt of the map." I had to discreetly swallow, then silently rolled those words around in my mouth; *Five Million Dollars.*

She paled. "I'll have to pay you your fee when I recover the treasure. I don't have that kind of money," she said. "If I had that kind of money I wouldn't want the map."

"Not necessarily," I said in an automatic reflex. Having millions doesn't make anybody quit wanting more. I shook my head, took a deep breath, hoped she wouldn't get so offended this would be the end of our relationship, and continued. "I know you don't have that kind of money. So this time I'm willing to make an exception. Twenty-five hundred dollars against expenses gets my services for two weeks. If it takes more than two weeks, we discuss further retainer. The balance of my twenty-five percent is due when you find the treasure and cash in on it."

It not a nice thing to admit about oneself, but anybody is susceptible to greed and I'm no exception. I hardly knew this woman and didn't have much idea of who I was up against. I did know that most people will kill for the kind of money we're talking about. And, in effect, Sindi DiWagne stole the map, so I'd be helping her steal it again. And there was little chance that, even if I did get the map back, she'd actually find that much treasure and be able to cash it in. Throughout history there have been quiet, mostly unsubstantiated, tales of people going into the coastal wilds of Georgia, Florida and the Carolinas and coming back out as rich men. All in areas where pirate treasure was rumored to be buried. There have been more tales, documented ones, of people who went into those same wilds on wild goose chases and never found anything. Some even died in the search. I told her most of that, but not the parts about greed or not knowing her very well.

She seemed a little mollified. "Right now the twenty-five hundred is tough to come up with. But I'm pleased you're willing to wait until I actually cash in on the find to collect your money, Ham." Maybe she wasn't mollified, her tone of voice was sarcastic.

"Uh huh. That's why you tried to convince me it was only the book you were interested in. You hoped to get off with some nominal payment. You didn't expect to have to pay out five million dollars." If she was off balance and tipping in my direction, I wanted to keep her that way.

Mollification didn't work so she glared at me. "I expected to give you more than just a token payment," she spat. "What was that this morning? Do you think going to bed with you was just a token?" Okay, she wasn't tipping in my direction. I didn't like to have sex used against me, so I went back on the offensive.

"What you said afterward was it was better for you than it was for me," I said. "You needed it more and got more out of it. Now we're talking business. Besides, you came to me with something you needed, not something you were offering me. I may have to risk my life getting this map back for you. I need more for my efforts than promise of later payment and a fast fuck." Then I ducked. Telling a woman she's a fast fuck when she's trying to make something that wasn't there out of a roll in the hay and she wants something else because of it is dangerous. In this case it was dangerous because Sindi threw her ashtray at me. It missed and she ran crying to her bedroom and slammed the door behind herself.

Sometimes I find it impossible to understand women. Was this real or was it acting? First she tried to screw me, then she fucked me. Now she's mad at me and all upset because I'm trying to play the business angle straight instead of letting the fucking make up for the attempted screwing. Maybe this way of thinking on my part has something to do with why last night was the umpteenth consecutive Saturday night I didn't have a date.

Her hiding in the bedroom gave me more time to think about this whole screwy business.

CHAPTER SEVEN

I poked around while she was hiding in the bedroom. New, inexpensive furniture was all in place, but there were many cartons of belongings that were yet to be unpacked. The break-front cabinet in the living room was empty except for a few assorted bottles of liquor. It wasn't a fluke that she'd gotten things out of cartons to make lunch, the kitchen cabinets were likewise empty. A copy of the Sunday Inquirer sat unopened on a counter. A little voice somewhere in the back of my mind asked why she wasn't doing more unpacking. The voice said there were enough cartons stacked about, and enough empty spaces in the place, it didn't look like someone had been there for an entire week. I told that voice it was because she'd been busy on her job during the week and spent yesterday looking for me, so go away and stop bothering me. The little voice shut up, but I could tell it didn't go away. There were a couple of half-filled bookcases in Sindi's living room. I browsed.

I don't have much idea of the value of her collection, literary, academic, or commercial, but I recognized most of the authors and several of the titles. Cooper, Longfellow, Twain, Poe, Eggleston, Whitman, Melville. Hell, I'd even read a few of them; *Moby Dick, The Song of Hiawatha*, parts of *Leaves of Grass*, most of Poe's stuff. But unless you're into that kind of collecting, or have the concentration to sit down and read some of it, the pleasure of looking at books on a shelf wanes pretty quickly. My knee was hurting about as badly as I'd expect it to after last night. I looked around for something I could do sitting down.

There was a doctor's office selection of magazines sitting on the coffee table. I sat on the sofa and browsed through them. *Redbook, National Geographic, Sports Illustrated*, last week's *Time*. The little voice asked where *Reader's Digest* was. I ignored it. Browsing in magazines is a major source of ideas for people who write for them and I came up with an idea or two to kick around in the part of my subconscious mind that deals with such things.

I was in danger of getting seriously bored by the time she came out of the bedroom and announced, "You'll have your retainer tomorrow." Then she burst into tears and ran back to her bedroom.

I wondered if she was normally given to wild mood swings. I wondered if she was putting on a show for me. I wondered if I had been that cold and callous in the way I made her tell me about the map and told her I wanted a retainer. Whichever it was, what do I do now?

Some women use tears to control men. If Sindi was like that, it wasn't going to work with me. Tears used to yank me around so hard I'd tie myself around a woman's pinky to get them to stop. Too many tears over the years ended in too much scar tissue on my psyche; I don't do that anymore.

If she wasn't the manipulative type, then her tears were legitimate. When a woman is honestly crying a man can either try to comfort her or he can ignore her. If he comforts her it might make matters worse or she might start to fall in love with him because he obviously cares so much. Or she might get the idea he can be controlled by tears. If he ignores her either she gets over it on her own or she thinks he's a cad. It can be a lose-lose situation for a man. In this case, I had the uncomfortable feeling Sindi's histrionics were a put on.

Whether I was through with the magazines or not, I couldn't concentrate on them anymore. I went into the kitchen and got the paper. I read the funnies and tried to blot out the sound of her crying. I skimmed through the "Review and Opinion" section, then tried to bury my consciousness in the sport section.

The great, bursting sobs coming from the bedroom gradually quieted down to soft burbling and faded away to heavy breathing. The heavy breathing came closer accompanied by the slow sound of soft footsteps. When the sounds got close enough I looked up to make sure she wasn't carrying a chainsaw, or anything else psychopathic in nature. The tissue crumpled in her hand looked pacific enough.

Sindi's eyes were red from crying. Her shoulders were drooped. Her mouth was a little girl's pout. She sat on the arm of my chair, settled back with her right arm on its back, and looked down at my upturned face. She reached her left hand across her body and trailed her fingers along the line of my jaw. "I've been acting like a ninny, Haven't I?"

"A bit," I agreed. If this was another act, she still was.

"I'm sorry." She slid her knees over mine and lowered herself from the chair arm to my lap. Her right arm came down from the chair's back and her hand started making curlicues with my hair. "Can you forgive me?"

Her tears hadn't controlled me, if that's what they had been for. Now she was all cuddly and immature. Some women try to control men by acting like penitent little girls. That's a game I'm willing to play, if she was playing it, but only so far. "I don't have to forgive you for anything," I said.

She bent over and kissed me. I kissed her back. Her right hand played with my hair, caressed my neck and shoulder, nibbled my ear. Her left wandered over my chest, unbuttoned my shirt.

My right arm hung down the side of the chair with the forgotten sport section dangling from limp fingers. My left arm lay between my thigh and the arm of the chair, its hand gently curled around her hip where it rested on my lap.

She kissed my forehead, my eyelids, the tip of my nose. Her tongue probed at my lips until they parted. Her right breast crushed itself against my chest and made circles.

The paper dropped from my right hand and Sindi's left breast took its place. My left hand also found something interesting to do. I told the little voice that was telling me there was something cold and calculating about this whole business that it was probably right, but it's been a long time, so shut up and go away. After awhile it did.

*

Our clothes were strewn about the living room and we were lying spent near the coffee table when the phone rang.

It was the doorman announcing, "A Mr. Llowlolski to see you, Miss DiWagne." I nodded at her to have him sent up.

We got dressed in a hurry and I hid in the bedroom, where I could listen in without scaring off the rabbit.

*

"You have seven minutes, mister," Sindi said as soon as she let Llowlolski in. "When the doorman let you in I told him to call the police if he doesn't hear from me in ten minutes. You used three of those minutes getting up here." I was surprised at how tough she sounded.

"Oh, that won't be necessary, miss? The police, I mean? I'll leave here right away." He sounded nervous right from the beginning.

Sindi must have been looking at her watch; she said, "Six and a half."

Where I was, out of sight to the side of the slightly-ajar bedroom door, I couldn't see into the living room, so I didn't see what this map-seeker looked like. But what I could hear was just as Sindi had described. The man positively jittered for the entire few minutes he was in the apartment. I mean I could hear the occasional soft tap of his heels as he bounced on the balls of his feet, the coins or keys in his pockets jangled, his voice wavered in tiny dopplers as he went up and down and probably side to side.

"I've come for the map, miss?" he said hesitantly. "You can save us both a lot of trouble if you just give it to me. Please?"

"I don't have the damn map," Sindi snapped at him. "I don't even have the book anymore."

"Oh dear, oh dear. Did you sell it to someone? If you can tell me who has it now I can acquire it from that person, miss? Please?"

"No I didn't sell it to anyone! Will someone please tell me what's so important about that map?" She was pouring it on, she really sounded innocent and angry. "You've been trying to buy it from me, somebody else stole it from me. I'm tired of all this crap."

"Oh dear, oh dear. Somebody stole it from you? Oh my." He paused, I guess he was trying to figure out something to tell her about the map. He was. "My employer is most anxious to possess this map? You see, it's a map to, a map to... It's a map of a property that was stolen from my employer's family, miss? He needs the map to prove ownership? So he can get the property back? Yes, that's what it is."

"Well, your employer is just out of luck, isn't he? I don't have the book, I don't have the map. You're just going to have to go back to your employer and tell him that you have to leave me alone from now on because he can't get anything from me."

"Who stole it, miss? Do you know?"

"How am I supposed to know the name of a burglar who broke in while I was out?"

Llowlolski must have looked at the door, because Sindi said, "It's been fixed. Do you think I'd live in a dump where the management doesn't fix broken locks?"

"It must have been Greg Hammond who stole the book?"

I thought I heard Sindi gasp, but couldn't be sure because it was a very low sound, masked by the jingling from Llowlolski's pockets.

"You know Greg Hammond? He was that tough-looking man talking to you outside Freeman's when you bought the book?"

"Is that his name?" Sindi's voice sounded strained. I told myself it was because of the shock she had when we got to her place on Saturday morning and found him here.

"Oh dear. You've been through quite a lot lately, haven't you?"

Sindi snorted.

"And I've been responsible for some of it? I want to apologize for any distress my people may have caused on Friday night?"

"Those goons were yours?"

"Well," I could hear him squirming in the whine in his voice, "they didn't hurt you? They only beat up a little bit on your friend for the evening." The way he said "friend for the evening" made it sound prurient.

"You get out of here, right now." It sounded like she pushed him. I heard the door open.

"I'll be in touch, miss? As soon as I find out if Mr. Hammond has the map?"

"Don't bother. If you're interested in dirty underwear, I hear Frederick's of Hollywood opened a store in the Gallery at Market East. Go there instead." She slammed the door and I came out of the bedroom.

"Oh my god, I can't stand that beastly little man," she said and threw herself into my arms. She was trembling.

I hugged her and caressed her and made gentling noises to calm here down, but my mind was somewhere other than on this woman in my arms.

Now I had some information to go on, to try to trace the principals in this whole business. I'd try to locate Greg Hammond first. There wasn't enough information to make the tracing easy, but having a full name and a description makes it a lot easier than just a last. Finding Hammond might make it easier to track down Llowlolski. It was time for me to get busy and start earning my retainer. And Sindi should be free of other unwanted visitors for the rest of today and tonight. Greg Hammond. Llowlolski, first name unknown. Kallir and company worked for, or were otherwise affiliated with, Llowlolski.

But I couldn't leave yet. First Sindi had to talk out the renewed case of nerves she had because of Llowlolski's visit. Then she wanted to make an early dinner for us, a candlelit dinner, even though it was too light outside to need candles, and she didn't have opaque drapes hanging to make it dark inside.

Dinner was a pleasant surprise after lunch. She broiled a decent cut of beef, baked some potatoes-which she served with adequate amounts of butter-peas, and Italian bread. Then she warmed up some apple pie for dessert.

After dinner we made small talk, lover's talk, over coffee. Then we retired to the living room where she found a radio station that played something romantic with lots of strings and we sipped some cognac from a bottle she got out of one of the cartons. The little voice came back long enough to point out to me that she didn't have to root through them, she knew exactly which box to go to. I ignored the little voice and it went away.

Then this poor, deprived lady wanted to dally intimately again.

I objected, she prevailed. I tried to make it seem harder than it was to convince me to stay. The little voice in the back of my brain tried to remind me of the way her body language objected to me in the cab on Friday night, tried to ask me why she changed her mind. I paid attention to that little voice only for as long as it took Sindi to turn my gonads on. Like I've said, gonads on, brain off. It works that way every time. And this was an exceptionally good-looking woman in my arms, a warm and willing woman with silken skin. And it had been a very long time since I'd had anything other than fantasy to keep me warm.

CHAPTER EIGHT

Monday morning after showering I smiled at finding my clothes neatly folded on the side chair in the bedroom. I thought it was a nice, womanly touch on Sindi's part; I couldn't imagine a man doing something like that for a woman who just spent the night with him. I got dressed and took off before it was time for Sindi to leave for work. It always seems to take women three times as long as it takes a man to get ready to go out in the morning. She was no exception. She hadn't dressed farther than underwear and a slip and was busy with her makeup in the bathroom when I was ready to go. So I quickly copied down the number on her phone, scribbled a note, and leaned it against her phone along with my card. I eased the front door closed behind me so she wouldn't hear me leave.

There was a doorman on duty. He looked at me curiously until I grinned at him and gave him the okay sign. He understood, and the next time he saw me he might recognize me as a guy who was banging one of the lady tenants in the building where he worked.

Eight fifteen in the morning is not the best time of the day, and on a Monday morning might be the worse time of the week. At 8:15 AM civilized people, those civilized people who have to be somewhere, are taking a shower, or brushing their teeth, or doing something else bathroomy-either that or eating breakfast. The rest of us civilized people are either still sleeping or doing something about waking up. For the rest of the world, 8:15 on a weekday morning is a mad scramble to get to work. This is rush hour, baby. It being Monday morning, when people most resent having to go to work, makes it worse than it is any other day of the week.

I hate rush hour. Did you ever look at the traffic at rush hour, I mean actually examine it? Here's what it's like: thousands and thousands and tens of thousands of half ton, three quarter ton, one ton, metal, plastic and rubber conveyances hurtling, bursting, ramming their way along crowded, narrow city streets at speeds far greater than the fastest man alive can run. Their brakes squeal, scream, cry out in anger at every breaking vehicle to their front, at each traffic light turned red before they can run it, at all pedestrians, dogs, cats trying to evade them. These vehicles attempt with greater or lesser degrees of success to pass each other, to gain some semblance of superiority over their compatriots. They present a mortal threat to the lives and well-being of all who enter their paths.

Frightening, isn't it.

Now take another look at them. At least eight, maybe nine out of ten, of these behemoths have a driver and no passengers. These drivers are annoyed, irked, vexed, anxious to begin with because they have to go to work that morning-and it's exaggerated on a Monday morning. They're out there, not necessarily fully awake, more or less in control of this one or two thousand pound mass which is in motion in accordance with all the laws of physics, and they're being delayed, challenged, impeded by other such one or two thousand pound masses in motion in equal obedience to all the laws of physics, and more or less under the control of other people who are also not necessarily fully awake and equally annoyed, irked, vexed, anxious. Tell me now, after looking at that, what do you think is likely to happen?

Gad.

There are some forty or fifty thousand vehicular fatalities in this country every year. Personally, I'm surprised there aren't that many every rush hour morning and more on Mondays. If there were it would convince more people to use public transit and those people would very quickly talk the government into providing more funds for mass transit.

Me? I'm no dummy. I didn't even try to hail a cab. I walked. I stayed on the sidewalk away from the curb and didn't step into the street at crosswalks until after my light turned green and the cross traffic stopped. Even then I watched for cars taking the corner without looking for pedestrians crossing the street with the light. I made it through a shooting war and have lived more than a score of years beyond that in spite of doing a lot of dumb and dangerous things along the way. Be damned if I'm going to get my ticket canceled by some bonehead who's driving crazy because he's pissed off about having to go to work on a Monday morning.

I live in an old residential neighborhood some two miles or so from the Center City apartment building Sindi was in. To get home I walked through the University of Pennsylvania campus. Once I got off the main streets and onto the campus, the walk was very nice. The oldest buildings on the Penn campus are more than a century old. The newest just had its dedication last year. During the academic year it has twenty thousand or more students packing its classrooms and laboratories, prowling its corridors, strolling through its grounds. In the summer it almost shuts down. There are only two or three thousand graduate and adult students taking classes or doing research during the hot season. I almost had College Green to myself when I walked through it. A young couple leaned against each other on the Oldenburg Button in front of Van Pelt library. Three women joggers pounded past me on the blue stone walkway. One of them wasn't wearing a bra and jiggled in an entertaining manner. A distracted-looking professor bustled across my path. Some maintenance people were cleaning the weekend's debris off the grounds. It was too early in the day for the sunbathers to be lying about.

Beyond the campus one enters a series of Edwardian and late Victorian housing developments. The term "housing development" wasn't coined until after World War II, but when an area is developed for housing, it's a housing development no matter when the construction was done. I live on a quiet street shaded by trees that were seeded during the nineteen-ought years. The houses are three storey twins built during the Spanish-American War. About half of the houses in this neighborhood are single family dwellings, the others have been divided into three or more apartments.

I walked up the steps of one of the twins and let myself in. Inside the vestibule I checked the mailbox. Most of the mail I get I categorize as send money, spend money, or pay money. I found two charity solicitations, one catalog from a mail order house I never bought anything from, and a bill: two sends, one spend, and one pay. Key through the inner door, up one flight of stairs, and unlock my way into the second floor. The whole floor is mine.

Inside, the bill went onto the dining table in the middle room-the table doubles as a desk for all non-income producing activities that require a desk-and the spend and sends went into the trash unopened.

I was still wearing the same clothes I put on to go out Saturday night. The first thing I did was go to the back, into the bedroom, and strip them off. Then to the bathroom where I climbed into the claw and ball bathtub, closed the curtain, and take a quick shower. Dried off, I padded naked back to the bedroom, through the kitchen that was so small it wasn't good for anything more than cooking and food storage, and put on clean clothes. I hung the jacket on a bedpost. The dirties lay on the floor where I left them; they could go into the hamper after they had a chance to air out.

I've long since accepted the fact that my Brian Dennehy build doesn't lend itself to fashion plate, so I dress for comfort rather than success. Jeans well enough worn to fit like kid gloves, shirt of a hue to reflect the sun's heat, sneakers. When necessary, I throw on a lightweight sport coat and it works for most occasions.

Then to the front room. This is the biggest room in the apartment. I have a friend who rents a modern efficiency in a rehabbed building. Her place could fit inside my front room and she pays more rent for it than I do. Sure, she has a tiny washer-dryer and central air, but to me the price she pays for her place is greater than the inconvenience of walking two blocks to the laundromat and having to exist with a window unit.

This front room is divided into two parts. The first part is a smallish living room, the window half is my office. My computer sits in front of the windows where I can see the world pass by during those long, isolated hours I spend writing. My printers are on a table to one side and the file cabinets on the other. One filing cabinet is devoted to my private clients. Bookcases with all the books and magazines related to my freelance writing form the divider between the two half of the big room.

I sat at the desk and turned on the computer. I let the screen's green glow occupy my eyes while I thought about what I agreed to get involved in.

The first conclusion I came to was someone was lying.

Sindi DiWagne procured a book with a map in it under less than honest circumstances. Greg Hammond wanted the map but didn't particularly care about the book. He had the book but not the map. Llowlolski, first name unknown, also wanted the map and didn't care who had the book. He had neither, despite the best efforts of Kallir and his buddies. So who had the map? If either Greg Hammond or Llowlolski had it he wouldn't still be looking for it. Now that Sindi wasn't around to turn my gonads on, I was able to keep the brain on. My best guess was she had the map hidden someplace. She could be claiming it was stolen to take the heat off herself. I doubted it would work. Hammond and Llowlolski wouldn't quit looking for the map just because she said she didn't have it, and she was the obvious starting point for any search.

What I needed to do right now was find out who Hammond and Llowlolski were, and who their employers were. Eventually one or the other of them would lead me to the map, probably in Sindi's possession. I moved to the end of my computer table and set up a new file for Sindi DiWagne and her missing map.

The *Philadelphia Inquirer* has gone on line with a database containing everything it has printed in the last fifteen or so years. It's working on adding everything it's published in its two and a half centuries of existence to that database. I returned to the computer, activated my modem, and had it call that database. It only took a few commands to convince the *Inky* to download onto my hard disk everything it had on file about Greg Hammond. Getting information about Llowlolski required more inventiveness on my part. I'd only heard the name said by Hammond, not seen it written. Who'd guess that a Polish sounding name began with a double "l" like a Welsh name? For kicks I asked for data on Kallir. I wasn't surprised to not find any.

According to the *Inquirer*, both Hammond and Llowlolski lived on the fringes of organized crime. If life was like Hercule Poirot, whenever the police rounded up the usual suspects in a strong arm case, Greg Hammond would be one of the usuals. He served hard time twice, once as a juvenile and again ten years ago. No other convictions, though the district attorney was convinced he was involved in two or three unsolved homicides. He was married and had two children. His wife's name was Adrianne.

Paul Llowlolski was an accountant who used to work for a major accounting firm and went down once for embezzlement. The DA thinks he now does numbers juggling for the Mafia, but can't prove it. He never married; the names of a couple of homosexual hangouts were in the files with his name, so that might explain why not.

Okay, it seemed they were both what they claimed to be; messengers. Though I still didn't know for whom.

Next I went to a basic reference book that an amazing number of people don't seem to know how to use; the phone book. A Paul Llowlolski was listed with a far Northeast address and an A. Hammond who could have been Adrianne had an East Falls address.

The far Northeast is a collection of middle class neighborhoods where an accountant who had done well but not gotten too big could feel right at home. Free standing, single family homes, mostly built during the Fifties and Sixties, are mixed in with garden court-type housing. Its residents tend to be middle aged, white collar, middle management family people who started out blue collar and have moved up in the world. They drive two year old cars and work for good sized corporations. They are law abiding and unimaginative. Street crime and other violence seldom enters their lives except on television. They are afraid of areas of the city that are not as stolidly middle class as the far Northeast.

East Falls began its existence as a community of scavengers-a more polite term would be salvagers, a less polite term that was sometimes used for them was pirates-along a part of the Schuylkill River where the rough water frequently caused boats to capsize. Because of the Schuylkill, Wissahickon Creek, and the city's park system, there is limited access into East Falls. Over the years it has become a haven for people who started out blue collar and improved themselves. The houses are brick or stone structures set on small wooded lots, except near the river where older row houses are clustered. This is basically a community of professionals. I wondered what Greg Hammond's neighbors would think of his occupation, if the A. Hammond in the book was his wife. There was an easy way to find out if she was.

I dialed the number in the book and listened to the phone ring four times before a child's voice answered.

"Hello," I said, "is your father home?" In the background I could hear a television playing cartoons.

The child didn't answer. I waited for several seconds before repeating my question. "Mom, he wants you," the child shouted away from the phone. I didn't bother repeating I wanted the kid's father. It wouldn't have done any good; the phone bonked down and I heard the sound of comings and goings.

"Hello." The woman's voice was raspy like she had just been screaming, or crying.

"Is Mr. Hammond there," I asked.

"What do you want with him?"

"I'm from Independent Viewing Services," I said. It always helps to have a plausible excuse when you call someone and don't get who you want. "We are conducting a survey of the television viewing habits of middle class men. Could I please speak to Mr. Hammond?"

"He's not here." She was not being communicative, reminded me a little of Sindi DiWagne.

"That's all right, I can call back later. When would be a convenient time for me to call?" Never ask when the person you want will get back, just when would be a good time to call.

"I don't know. I'd have to ask him."

"I'll call back after dinner?"

"It's your dime." Some expressions die hard. Phone calls have cost a quarter for years now.

"All right, I will. Now if you'll be so good as to answer a couple of questions for me, just to make sure I'm calling the right household, I'll let you go."

"I can hang up any time I want." She wasn't asking, she was telling.

"Yes indeed you can." It's so easy to end a phone conversation. I better be brief.

"Mr. Hammond's first name, please."

"Gregory."

"And yours?"

"Adrianne."

I gave her the address from the phone book for confirmation.

"Yes."

"And Mr. Hammond's occupation."

She hung up.

It was pretty certain this was the Greg Hammond I was looking for. I wondered if there was anything going on between him and his wife; her closed-mouth replies may have meant she didn't know where he was. Llowlolski was next. I got a machine at the number in the book. It had the same voice I'd heard in Sindi's apartment. I didn't leave a message.

Since I couldn't get Llowlolski on the phone, I decided to take a drive up his way and eyeball the situation. Maybe I'd see him. Or did I have something else to do first?

Sindi DiWagne said she worked "in an office," with the clear implication she was a secretary, earning a secretary's wages. Her clothes were nice, but not exactly designer stuff. Her apartment wasn't all that great; not as big as mine, and not finely appointed. The books in her collection probably didn't cost all that much. Still, she lived in a decent high-rise just a couple of blocks from Rittenhouse Square. I didn't know what the rents were like in her building and couldn't check it out all that easily because last week's newspapers had already gone out for recycling and the Sunday sport section I read was in Sindi's paper, still at her place. But even without going through the apartments-for-rent ads it occurred to me that the rent on an apartment just a couple of blocks from the Square might be more than a secretary-certainly more than one who was also putting herself through grad school-could pay.

I logged back on to the Inky's database.

There was a reference to her. Only one, and a couple of years old at that. Her name was deep in a story about an insurance company that got caught mismanaging a pension fund into insolvency during the mid- and late-Eighties. The case was dropped when the company insisted on its innocence, paid ten million dollars in court costs and fines, and promised the Justice Department they wouldn't do it again anyway.

Sindi was named as an officer of the insurance company. She was implicated in the alleged mismanagement, though charges against her were dropped along with those against her employer.

That damn little voice in the back of my head said I told you so. I told it to shut up. It did, but it was smug about it.

CHAPTER NINE

I own a Mustang that dates from the late Seventies, and only use it when I'm going someplace I can't easily get to by walking or by public transit. Operating a car costs too damn much and contributes to air pollution, two things that bother me to my soul. The car doesn't look like much on the outside, it has a few dents and the maroon paint has long since faded to the color of rust, but I keep the engine and breaks in good order. It gets me where I want to go, and a few times has gotten me away from people I didn't want to be around.

The morning was nice and it was past rush hour, but the man on the radio said the temperature would rise to blistering levels in the afternoon. I should be through with this trip by then and decided I would find myself a nice air conditioned place to spend the hot time in. The far Northeast is ten miles in a straight line from University City, where I live. It's a mite farther than that driving.

Popular history has it that Philadelphia was the first city in the world to have its streets laid out in a grid. When you look at William Penn's layout for the original city the grid is obvious. But that city only stretched from river to river and was about a mile wide north to south. A large number of other communities sprang up in what became Philadelphia County. The near communities, such as Southwark, Northern Liberties, and West Philadelphia, laid themselves out on the same grid pattern, and even followed the same street lines and kept the same street names. Outlying communities such as Germantown, Manayunk, Kensington, and Tioga also adopted the grid pattern, but they aligned themselves on things other than Philadelphia. Manayunk used the Schuylkill River, Germantown used the highway to Paoli, Kensington followed the highway to the Delaware River Gap, Tioga was on the Delaware River. Eventually all these communities, and many more, were incorporated into the City of Philadelphia.

Today's Philadelphia isn't a city on a grid, it's a city comprised of multiple grids. Unless you're going north and south through the original city, you can't get from one part of it to another in a straight line. To go northeast from where I lived, I started by driving a mile east-southeast to the Schuylkill Expressway, then followed it more or less northwest maybe a mile and a half to the Vine Street Expressway. Then straight east, a little north of Billy Penn's original city, to I-95. On it I was finally able to go northeast until I turned northwest onto Woodhaven Avenue and drove along it until I had to turn southwest to find the development I was looking for.

This is a part of the city that isn't laid out on a grid. It's full of small developments that were inspired by Levittown. The streets here are curved, often so curved that they form "U's," or even circle back on themselves. If a street runs in a straight line it doesn't go for more than two blocks, more likely only one. In this particular development, the streets are named after desserts.

This was originally conceived as a complete community. It not only has a few garden court apartments scattered among the detached and semi-detached houses, it even has a small shopping center to call its own. 154E Custard turned out to be one of the garden court apartment blocks.

The place was three stories high and laid out like a lower case "m;" a straight main building parallel to the street with a wing at each end and a leg in the middle. Tenant parking was between the wings with most of the spaces marked with apartment numbers. I decided the slots without numbers must be for visitors and pulled into one of them. E wing was the rightmost of the three legs. A directory inside the small foyer-lobby gave me Llowlolski's apartment number. Just as I was about to ring a different doorbell the outside door opened and a voice said, "Well, hello. Want to see my hair fall back into place again?"

I turned around and stifled a groan. It was Kallir. Hondo grinned behind him.

"Not really," I said. Whatever I wanted to do today, spending time with Kallir and his buddies wasn't one of them.

"That's a shame. It's wonderful what can be done with a hair dryer." His smile under the blow dried hairdo made him look like a demented version of a television news talking head.

Hondo snickered and made a face at Kallir's hairdo. His own hair had greasy kid stuff dripping off it. With his leather jacket, pegged jeans, and stiletto-toed shoes he looked like he should be hanging on a street corner someplace, hustling change from frightened old ladies.

I gestured at the bank of doorbells and said, "It looks like the person I came to see isn't at home, so I'll be on my way. Excuse me." I tried to edge my way through the door but stopped when a snub nosed .38 appeared in Kallir's hand.

"I think you must have rung the wrong bell and the man you want *is* at home," he said. "Let's go in."

Hondo unlocked the inner door and held it open for me. I shrugged and walked in.

"The stairway's to the right. We're going to the second floor."

I followed his orders. The way I see it, when a man holds a gun on you, you do what he says to until he isn't holding the gun on you any more. Then you get even. It's only in the movies and on television that the unarmed hero can take on a man with a gun with his bare hands and win every time.

The stairwell was unfinished poured concrete walls and steps with iron railings, dimly lit by low wattage bulbs. I turned left when we reached the second floor hallway. The second floor hall looked just like the first-three and a half feet wide with wall to wall runner. Wall sconces gave enough light to avoid tripping.

"That's as far as we go," Kallir said when I was about halfway down the hall. I hoped he meant we were going through the door I stopped next to. The alternative would leave me thinking I should have tried to take him downstairs. Hondo brushed past me and opened the door after tapping out a code on it.

A soft man who looked like he just hopped off a whoopee cushion jittered to us from the next room. Even though I hadn't seen him before I knew this had to be Llowlolski. He looked at me with a confused expression and his hands fluttered a question.

"It's the guy, Eliot," Kallir told him.

Llowlolski's hands stopped fluttering and his jittering even ceased for a moment. The slack jawed way he stared at me you'd think he thought I pulled the Seventh Cavalry act on my own Friday night when Kallir and company were holding me. "What's he doing here?" he finally asked.

"That's what we want to know," Kallir said.

"Bring him in here," said a firm voice from the room Llowlolski had come from.

"You heard the man," Kallir said and poked me in the kidney with his .38. "Let's go meet Mister Big."

"Mister Big," that's what Kallir said. He sounded like a grade B Thirties gangster movie. We went into the other room to meet Mister Big. I'll call the other room a sitting room because it was too small to be a proper living room. An oversized sofa took up one side wall without leaving enough space for an end table. The outer wall was windows with a plant-covered bench in front of it. A Naugahyde lounger stuck half way into the middle of the room from the window corner opposite the sofa. A chair that looked salvaged from a dining room set sat next to the door and a mate to it was in the remaining corner. A chrome and glass coffee table was in front of the sofa and another one sat between the lounger and the second straight back chair. There was very little unoccupied floorspace.

"Mister Big" lounged in the lounger, looking exactly like you'd expect someone to look if a punk like Kallir called him Mister Big. He looked like a man who spends too much of his time sitting behind a custom-built desk in front of a TV camera, reading the local news, or analyzing investment opportunities. Just about nobody else has hair so well groomed it looks like an ill-fitting wig. His three piece pin-stripe must have set him back a thousand bucks-probably pocket change for him, enough to replace most of my wardrobe. The polished wedding band on his left hand could be bright enough to blind you if the light hit it right, and a ring on his right hand held the biggest diamond I've ever seen on a man. His wristwatch looked like a Rolex.

"Let me see it," Mister Big said. His eyes dipped toward my hips. Kallir reached into my hip pocket and pulled out my wallet. He carried it the few feet to Mister Big and handed it to him with just the right degree of deference.

Mister Big took his time going through my wallet, pausing now and then to count the bills, or read one of the little documents that tend to clutter wallets. He made a cut-off laugh when he read my driver's license. When he was through with his rummaging he handed the wallet back to Kallir and gestured for him to return it to me.

He studied me over steepled fingers. His manicure looked as expensive as his suit. After a long moment he said, "Hambletonian Eliot. What an interesting name. Sit down, Hambletonian, do sit down." Kallir shoved me onto the sofa where he and Hondo bookended me.

"Hambletonian is a very unusual name," Mister Big continued. His eyes didn't leave me when he reached unerringly for a glass on the table by his side. "Where did it come from?"

It's a dumb story, one I'm tired of telling. But people who find out my given name always ask, which is why I never volunteer it.

"My parents were trotting fans. They claim I was conceived while they were at the Hambletonian one year, so they named me after it."

"Did their horse win?"

"They said he did, yes. That's why I was conceived, they were celebrating the win."

He nodded in a sage but distracted manner. His glass went back to the table and a gold cigarette case came from an inside pocket of his coat. He withdrew a thin, brown cigarette from the case and carefully inserted it into an ebony and gold holder. The pungent aroma that wreathed his head after he used his gold lighter told me he wasn't smoking a popular domestic brand.

"What if you had been a girl?" he asked.

I thought the question could have been better phrased, say, "What if they'd had a girl," but didn't think I was in the best of positions to correct his rudeness. "Their horse was Hanover Jubilee. If they'd had a daughter they would have named her Jubilee."

"Droll," he said.

I shrugged. My parents tell me it's a true story, but not everyone believes it-not that I blame them.

"What is your involvement in this matter?" he asked without preamble.

I could play it dumb here, but two of the men in this room had seen me with Sindi and done a number on me two nights earlier, and the third had referred to me in conversation just yesterday. It was a reasonable assumption that they'd told their Mister Big all about me. No point in dumbness. "I've been hired by Miss DiWagne to recover her book." Then a quick change of subject; "But you have an advantage on me. You know my name, I don't know yours."

The way he cocked his eyebrow told me he intended to keep his advantage. "Kallir calls me Mister Big. That will do nicely. You don't need to know any more than that." He paused a half beat, enough time to give me a chance to start to say something if I was the type who would start talking before someone else finished, but not long enough to let me talk even if I wanted to. "You don't have the book. We all know who does." He lowered his face to look sternly at me. "At least I imagine Miss DiWagne told you the same thing she told Paul, so you know as well as I do that a Mr. Greg Hammond has it. Now, why are you here? Why aren't you looking for this Hammond person?"

I tried to shrug but Kallir and Hondo were sitting too close and all I managed was to look silly trying. "A lot of people seem to want that book. I'm trying to find out who they are. Maybe that'll help me get hold of it and return it to Miss DiWagne. That's why I'm here, trying to find out who everyone is."

He shook his head slowly. "That's not quite a truth, Hambletonian," he said in the same tone you'd use chiding a naughty child. "You only get one lie when you talk to me. You are supposed to be locating the book, but you know Paul doesn't have it. Moreover, you know who does. So why are you here instead of looking for the man who has it?"

I tried to shrug again. "It's like I said, I'm just following all leads."

"Not good enough, Hambletonian. You should know I want that book and am willing to pay handsomely for it. I don't think you are here to give it to me. Now, last chance, why are you here?"

I had the distinct feeling that nothing I said or did, short of handing him the map, was going to be good enough foi him. And it didn't pass my attention that he never mentioned the map. Well, I had to say something, so I said, "There's more involved here than simply who has the book. I'm trying to find out what it is."

He sat gazing at me with these eyes that said a trust had been betrayed and what he had to do next would hurt him as much as it hurt me. Fat chance. Later, maybe, but not now.

"You are intruding on me, Hambletonian. I don't like being intruded on." His eyes shifted from me. "Kallir, I want you two to take our friend into the bushes out back and convince him that he shouldn't intrude on me unless he is in possession of something I want and he is here to give it to me." He said that in the same tone of voice one might use to thank a pizza delivery guy; it sent a shiver up my spine. Then he turned in the lounger and stared out the window.

Llowlolski fluttered off to the side. He had stood there jittering through the entire meeting without saying a word. He must have been trying to make himself sound important yesterday when he referred to Kallir and Company as "my boys." He sure didn't seem important here.

"Let's go." Kallir was on his feet and jerking on my arm. Hondo stood almost as fast and yanked on my other arm. They quick marched me out of the apartment to the stairs. Kallir was learing about the prospect of convincing me to not intrude on Mister Big. A drop of saliva stood out on Hondo's lower lip. Their eagerness to do me bodily harm wasn't as frightening as Mister Big's casualness.

"Eliot, when we're through with you your hair is going to be so mussed you're going to go right out and buy yourself a blow dryer to keep it neat," Kallir said once the apartment door was closed behind us. "As soon as you get out of the hospital, that is." His laugh echoed in the hallway.

Walking along the first floor hall I paid attention to how tightly they were holding my arms, how I would have to twist to break both of their grips at the same time. I thought about how I would have the advantage of surprise. My big question was, where was the back door they were going to take me out of, and where was it relatively to the ends of the building. We were nearing the front door; I decided to make my break there and couldn't believe my luck when Kallir said:

"Where's the back door?"

"I don't know," Hondo answered. "I never been here before."

Kallir stopped, indecisive, by the vestibule, then made his decision. "We'll go out the front way."

Hondo eased his hold on my arm to open the inner vestibule door. He almost let go at the outer door which wasn't wide enough for two of us to go through at once. I looked at my car to estimate the number of paces before I made my break when markings on a white car passing on the street caught my eye. I looked at the car and almost shouted with joy. It was a police car slowly cruising by. Kallir saw it a flicker after I did and tightened his hand on my arm to pull me back inside. He was too late. I pulled my right arm out of Hondo's grip and spun to my left and buried my fist in Kallir's belly. Then I shoved him into Hondo and ran toward the cop car.

"Officer, officer," I yelled and waved my arms as I ran. During the summer most cops cruise with their windows closed and the air conditioning on. Personally, I don't think police cars should have air. A cruising cop with his windows closed and the air conditioning on can see what's going on around him, but he can't hear much outside the car. This cop had his windows open. Maybe he understood the value of being able to hear outside. Or maybe it wasn't hot enough yet for him to turn on the air conditioning. Whichever it was, he was able to hear me shouting and nosed into the curb fast. The cop was out of his car, looking past me and had his hand on his holster by the time I reached him.

"Excuse me, Officer," I panted, "but I'm lost. I need directions."

"Right," he said, staring hard past me. Then my words sunk in and he double took. "What?"

"Officer, I'm lost and I need directions," I repeated as blandly as I could.

He looked at me hard and then looked past me again with puzzlement showing in his face. I didn't turn around. All I needed this cop for was help in getting away, I didn't want him getting involved with what was going on.

"Cut the bullshit, Mister. I ain't no dummy, you know. Now what the hell's going on over there?"

I looked back. Kallir was leaning against the doorjam clutching his belly and Hondo held an arm, propping him up. They were glaring at me and whispering between themselves.

"Oh, them," I said innocently. "I stopped to ask them for directions and all they could talk about was how the sight of me made the one's stomach hurt. How do I get to I-95 from here?"

He looked at me hard again and examined how I was dressed. I hadn't bothered with the light jacket and obviously didn't belong in the far Northeast. No puzzlement this time, he knew something was wrong, but not what. He knew most burglars and street criminals retire by their mid-twenties, and I was obviously older than that. More mature burglars work suits and work neighborhoods where there are more valuable things to be stolen than were likely to be found in this garden court. "What are you doing in this neighborhood?" he demanded.

"I'm a writer. I was driving round letting some ideas percolate and wasn't paying any attention to where I was going. When I realized I was lost I stopped to ask for directions. All I know is I'm somewhere in the Northeast." I did my best to look honest and law abiding. Why not? There was an element of truth in what I said.

"What part of town you live in?"

"University City."

"You're a long way from home."

I shrugged. "They were long ideas."

He looked past me again and I turned in time to see Kallir pushing Hondo inside and the door close behind them. I'm sure the cop was making mental notes to himself during the moment he stared at the entrance to that wing of the garden court apartment building. Someday he might run into one of us again and he'd want to be prepared for whatever trouble we'd cause. The directions he gave me to I-95 was the same route I used getting here. I thanked him and said something about how helpful policemen in general were and how too few people appreciated them. But I didn't say it too profusely. He was still standing by the side of his patrol car when I drove away. In my rearview mirror I saw him writing something in his notebook. Probably my license number.

CHAPTER TEN

As I promised myself, I found an air conditioned place to spend the hot part of the day. It was a fancy-hamburger joint close to Penn's campus. With most of the students away for the summer, the late lunch crowd was sparse. I chewed slowly on my burger and salad and thought. When the waitress took the empty plate away and brought me another iced tea I sat doodling on a pad of paper. I doodled lists of names, objects, places and incidents. I drew connecting lines between them. I studied the names, objects, places, incidents and connections. None of it made sense. I needed to talk to someone, but Clyde was the only one I could think of. No good. This was Monday, his day off, and he was most likely out of town. I've never asked where he goes on Mondays, but I figure it's either to a religious retreat or he's got a secret girlfriend stashed away someplace where none of his friends can get to her.

None of my other friends know about my private clients and I wasn't about to tell them now. After what I found out about Sindi DiWagne in the *Inky*, I couldn't talk to her, not and expect any truth. And until I had a better idea of what was going on inside her head, there was no way I was going to tell her anything that had any chance of coming back to haunt me. Besides, the best thing would be to talk to someone who wasn't involved to get his feedback, to give me some impartiality, a different viewpoint. I couldn't think of a soul I could talk to about this.

No matter what way I looked I kept coming back to the same conclusion and it didn't make sense. Why would Sindi DiWagne hide the map and make a production of trying to find the book?

And who was this Mister Big?

The more I thought about it, the more I thought this map business was something I shouldn't bother with. There were too many people involved, too many sides, all in conflict. Nobody, not even the person who hired me, was playing straight. I decided that tonight I'd call Sindi and tell her I'm outta here. Call, not visit. I'm a man alone, with all the weaknesses that implies. Sindi DiWagne was a very attractive woman and had made it quite clear over the weekend that she knew how to use that attractiveness and a man's weakness to her advantage. Then a light bulb clicked on and I said out loud:

"Damn, I bet he made a mental note of my address." Sonufabitch. This Mister Big character read my driver's license. Commented about my name. He had to know where I live. Maybe I couldn't get out of this now even though I wanted to. Damn. There had to be a way I could deal with that.

I signaled the waitress for a refill on my iced tea. When it came I sat back and did some more heavy thinking.

After a while I noticed my waitress, the hostess and some of the other waitresses watching me. Even on a slow summer afternoon with few patrons in sight, people who work in restaurants get edgy if one person occupies a table for too long. They want to free it up on the off chance a Shriners convention or something equally large will suddenly descend on them. I was past the unspoken limit on how long one customer can sit. I took the hint and left a ten dollar bill to cover a seven dollar tab.

Outside the temperature was in the high eighties and the ozone level was unhealthful. The time on my meter had expired but I was lucky enough not to have a ticket. There's a two hour limit on parking on Walnut Street and I had passed that limit as well as the restaurant limit. I could only hope I hadn't passed a limit in this map business.

I was only about a mile from home, but I was in no hurry to get there. The thought of a welcoming committee waiting for me was too uncomfortable. I got off Walnut at the first opportunity and tootled along the quiet residential streets. I managed to use up about ten minutes in the trip.

Sure enough, Kallir was lounging on the front steps of my place. Moose sat next to him.

The nearest parking space was a couple of houses down on the other side of the street. I Ubied into it and turned off the ignition. My knee started hurting again.

The neighborhood is slowly being taken over by yuppies, which normally causes me no end of distress, especially since they come in yupples along with their two point eight yuplings per brood pair. Right now, though, I was glad to have those yuplings yammering about-even the point eights dragging their partial selves around and making their fractional noises.

Odd, how the presence of children can make a man feel secure in a threatening situation. It's supposed to work the other way around.

My yuppie neighbors are unfailingly polite and friendly toward me, but I think they really find me suspect; one of the old guard who moved into this neighborhood when it was still a tossup whether it would turn white collar or slum. The feeling's mutual. I wished they'd go away and let the bohemians and artists come back. I liked the neighborhood better back then. Right now, though, I was grateful for the presence of these watchful yuppettes and their rampaging yuplings.

Maybe half of the neighborhood yuppettes with yuplings have opted for the mommie experience instead of returning to their careers. A few of these yuppettes hovered about, trying to be unobtrusive about keeping over-protective eyes on their get. It may have been just my imagination, but it seemed they took turns keeping an eye on my unwelcome visitors as well.

On the way to my place I tousled the hair of one of the tykes, who snarled something unpleasant in return, and said hello to a couple of the doting mothers.

"Friends of yours?" one mother asked nodding at my visitors.

"I know them," was all I was willing to admit.

She turned a baleful look on the pair, then returned her attention to one yupling who was shattering what should have been a quiet afternoon with one of those damnable plastic tricycles that makes a machine gun racket.

I didn't want Kallir and Moose to feel welcome, or get the idea that anyone was keeping them from leaving, so I stood, not sat, to Kallir's side where they could just get up and walk onto the sidewalk without having to go through me to get there.

"Tell your Mister Big that I'm out of this," I said before they could say hello or gotcha or fuck you or whatever greeting they had in mind. "Every time I try to find out something here, I wind up with more questions and less information than I had to begin with. You can tell your Mister Big that Greg Hammond says he doesn't have any idea who has the map-and you can tell him I don't give a good goddam who does."

Kallir gave me a look that would melt methane. "Oh? There's a map now? What do you think about that, Moose?"

"Well, gee, I dunno." Moose grinned at me and yucked.

"Cut the shit, Kallir," I snapped. It was time to stop being a nice guy, or even a wise ass, and talk tough. "You know there's a map and you probably have a better idea than I do who has it. Now go deliver your message like a good little errand boy."

Kallir turned his smile up a few degrees. I felt in danger of frostbite. "When I get around to it. But first, Mister Big told me to find you and hurt you. Bad. Besides," he rubbed his belly, "I owe you one."

Moose yucked again. "That's why Kallir brought me. I hurt people real good."

"Not a good idea," I said. "See all those mommies watching you? They probably think you want to molest their little darlings. Did you notice that one of them is clutching her cellphone?" That was a wild stab on my part, I hadn't seen a handset on any of them. "She's just itching to call 911. The cops respond fast in this neighborhood. Touch me and the fuzz will have your ass in cuffs before you can shake your blow dry back into place."

Kallir looked beyond me and took in the entire street. "I don't see any cellphones." His voice was cocky, but I saw a hint of uncertainty in his eyes.

"You probably can't see it because of the way she's standing. You don't believe me, go ahead and try something. I'd like to hear you explain to Mister Big how some yuppie mommies got you busted."

Kallir stood. "Then we go inside and do it."

Moose also stood and moved so he was almost blocking any escape I might have in mind.

"You'll have to take me in by force. The cops will be here before we get into my apartment."

Kallir looked around again. He fidgeted a bit.

I took a look, too, and breathed a sigh of relief; three of the mothers were openly watching us.

Kallir decided. "Let's go, Moose." Then back to me. "You're not always going to have mommies to protect you, Eliot. When you don't, I'm going to hurt you."

"Give Mister Big my message. He's probably smart enough to call you off."

"That's okay." Kallir rubbed his belly again. "I owe you one. You'll get it."

"Don't even try it."

Kallir hit Moose in the arm and grunted at him. I watched them walk around the corner. After a moment I heard a car start up and peel away. Then I turned and gave the mommies a smile and a wave.

Thank god for yuppettes who opt for the mommie experience instead of returning to their careers as soon as their whelps are old enough for day care.

*

Upstairs I had to do something to occupy my mind, a distraction to help me relax. I went into the bedroom to put my weekend clothes into the hamper. I hadn't bothered to empty the jacket pockets when I changed this morning, there hadn't been anything in them I was going to need. I swore when I finally did. I wasn't out of this yet. Now I knew why Sindi had laid out my clothes so neatly. I also knew who had the map: I did.

I guess it's fair to say I was stunned. At least I lost track of time while I stood there staring at the map in my hand. I shook myself out of it and carried the map to my office to examine it more closely.

It seemed to be parchment, folded in quarters. The folds weren't cracked, so evidently it hadn't been opened and refolded too many times. One edge wasn't of the same wavery quality of the others, indicating it had been cut, though it didn't look like a recent cut. I suspected that what I had was half a sheet of foolscap. The ink was brown with age, and badly faded in spots; it was probably drawn with an inferior grade of ink. I've seen new parchment. It has a very smooth surface and its color is a warm, friendly ivory. The parchment this map was drawn on wasn't as smooth as the new stuff, and its color was darker and mottled. I know there are ways to artificially age papers, but my heart-and probably my sense of greed as well-told me this was old parchment.

The paper's orientation was horizontal. The shoreline appeared along the bottom. There wasn't an indicator arrow, but north was probably to the right. The left side of the sheet was taken up with writing. Styles of penmanship have changed dramatically in the past three centuries. Between that and the crabbed nature of the writing, I couldn't make out more than an occasional word, certainly not enough to understand it.

The map itself didn't look as cryptic as I had expected. There wasn't any attempt at topological lines, they hadn't been invented yet. Many objects were drawn in profile. But the way rivers and the coast were drawn, I got the impression that everything in the map was in an approximately accurate relation to everything else. The more I looked at it the more I felt it could actually lead someone to X-marks-the-spot. Except there wasn't an "X." I guess that's what the writing on the left side was about, to remind the pirate of where the chest, or whatever, was buried once he found his way back to the right place. Probably had a reference to a crooked tree, or something else that wasn't there anymore.

I once did an article on the coastal islands of Georgia for *Adventure Road* and had bought a USGS state map to make sure I got place names and distances right. I pulled that map out now and did a quick comparison. The river mouth Blackbeard, or whoever, had drawn certainly looked like the Little Satilla. But where on earth was that mountain Sindi said she found? According to my map, you have to go some fifty miles inland before you find anything with an elevation of more than 200 feet.

Maybe that's also explained in the legend I can't read. I wondered what the scale of the old map was. My modern one was one to half a million, too big a scale to show the detail I wanted.

Now that I had the actual map in my hands and examined it I started to truly believe it was really what Sindi and Hammond said it was; an authentic pirate treasure map, and Sindi could make out and verify enough detail to follow it to the buried treasure.

My heart fluttered. My share would be five million dollars. Maybe more.

Suddenly I felt so faint I had to lean forward and put my head between my knees and take several deep, slow breaths.

Five million dollars.

I'm forty years old and still scrimping to pay the bills. It isn't even as though I live lavishly. People who live lavishly don't live in apartments in my neighborhood and drive fifteen year old cars. They go to good tailors so they can be fashion plates even if they are built like Brian Dennehy. They don't go snooping around to find other people's lost or stolen property for a cut of the take.

Five Million Dollars.

If I forgot about wise investments and just stuck the whole damn thing in a passbook savings account, it would gross me about two hundred and seventy-five big ones a year. That's a two, and a seven, and a five, followed by three zeros. With a dollar sign in front. And a decimal point all the way at the other end.

FIVE MILLION DOLLARS.

With that kind of money I could buy a brownstone on Spruce Street, stick a Lamborghini in a garage, park a Rolls at the curb, dine at places that don't put prices on the menu, and be a patron of the arts. I could find a good tailor. I could even buy myself a steady girlfriend.

FIVE MILLION DOLLARS!!!

I was giddy with it all and had to do something to bring myself back to earth. I reminded myself of the IRS.

Declare the five million as income. The IRS gets 39.6 percent. The state takes another two plus change. The city wants five percent. That's 47 percent down the tubes. It still leaves me with nearly three million. Passbook interest from that still works out to more than $150,000 per annum.

Okay, forget the Lamborghini and the Rolls. What am I doing with foreign cars anyway? Stick a Lincoln in the garage. Park a Corvette at the curb. Just buy an occasional painting or sculpture instead of being a patron of the arts. Rent a steady girlfriend. I could still afford the brownstone, the tailor, and unpriced menu dining.

And my cut might be more than five million dollars.

Mister Big, get out of my way.

Kallir and company, don't ever show your faces around me.

Llowlolski, crawl back under whatever rock you call home.

Greg Hammond, just go away.

FIVE MILLION DOLLARS!!!

Sindi, darling Sindi, papa's got the map and is bringing it to you. I'll see to it that you're properly outfitted and safely on your way to Georgia. If you want, I'll even come along and help. Maybe even if you don't want, I'll come along and help.

Hey, my five million dollar share has to be protected, you know.

Oh yes. I hate to be picayune, but I still need that twenty-five hundred retainer. The rent's due any day now.

I started walking into town. My mind was so befuddled that I made it all the way to 43rd Street before a rumbling behind me reminded me that there was a faster way. I stopped and waited for the trolley car that was almost on me. I forgot all about the insurance company Sindi worked for and her position in it.

I got off at the 22nd Street subway-surface station and walked on air for the last few blocks. The doorman smiled, it could have been a smirk, but I was in a great mood and every face looked happy to me. He told me to go straight up, I was expected. I saw him reach for the house phone as the elevator door closed.

CHAPTER ELEVEN

The door to 608 was ajar. I bopped in. "Sindi," I trilled. "Where are you, honey buns. Your little trick this morning convinced me. Let's do this..." My voice trailed off and I stopped bouncing when I saw Greg Hammond leaning against the bedroom doorjam. He was smiling. It wasn't a nice smile.

"Honey buns?" he said. "Your little trick this morning?" he said.

I stood as erect as I could and made myself look as solid as possible and tried to look threatening. "What have you done with her?" I snapped in as tough-guy a voice as I could.

"Your honey buns?" he said with a snicker. "Not a damn thing, she's not here. Neither are any of your friends. It's just you and me this time." He pushed away from the doorjam and made himself about four inches taller than me-since he was over six feet tall and I wasn't, that was easy for him.

He looked like he wanted to fight. I didn't. If we fought, one of us was going to get seriously injured. I didn't want to get hurt myself, and I was in too good a mood to feel like hurting someone else.

He chuckled. It was a dry, rasping kind of laugh that sounded unhealthy-to anyone who heard it.

"You came poking in where you weren't wanted," he said. "I'm going to teach you to keep out of places where you aren't wanted." He crossed the room to me in two fast steps. He didn't bother to cock his fist, so I didn't see it coming until almost too late to twist out of its way. His fist slammed through the air and threw him off balance. I completed my spin by giving him enough of a push to slam him into the wall. I should have pushed harder, he bounced off and came right back at me.

"When I'm through with you, you're going to know to keep your fucking hands off her," he said, and threw a roundhouse at my face.

I got too busy to pay attention to what he was saying. I twisted my head to the side and he missed. I turned a foot in and stomped down on his instep. I didn't get full weight into it because he was stepping back, but it was enough to stagger him. I leaned hard into a two-handed shove to keep him reeling back and turned to get out of there.

Hammond staggered but didn't fall. He came back at me and brought his fist up from around shoestring height. I deeked fast but he swung faster. His fist took a glancing blow off the side of my jaw. It was almost enough to knock me down. I hit back, a straight-knuckle jab that sent him into a small table. He knocked the table over and the lamp on it broke.

Fights last a long time only if they're the play-acting you see in movies or on TV-or if they follow the Marquis of Queensbury rules. If one man in a fight knows how, the fight is over in a hurry. I know how to fight, and Hammond did too. This one took longer than it should have. I was trying to avoid hurting or getting hurt, which is a serious mistake in a fight. Hammond wasn't interested in winning right away either, he wanted to inflict as much pain as he could.

That can also be a mistake.

I wasn't able to keep any kind of track of who hit who how, who grappled who, and who threw who down. Somewhere in there my hand got cut on a shard of the broken lamp. All I know is he was on top beating the crap out of me when an angry voice at the door said:

"I'm calling the police."

Hammond stopped pummeling me and looked up. He jumped to his feet, gave me solid kick in the ribs and said, "Remember what I said." Then he ran out.

I heard excited voices in the hall, but didn't pay any attention to them. I slowly sat up and took stock. Trying to avoid getting hurt hadn't worked very well. Something told me it would be a good idea to be gone before the cops showed up, and I wanted to make sure I was in condition to go.

I was bleeding from the corner of my lip, one eye wanted to close and stay closed, my nose felt so clogged I wondered if it was broken. Half my teeth felt loose. My right hand was bleeding from the cut, and my side where he kicked me hurt with every breath I took-I wondered if any ribs were cracked. Amazingly, my knee didn't hurt.

I worked my way to my feet and wobbled a couple of times before I felt steady enough to walk to the bathroom. My idea was to blot off the worst of the blood and grab a towel and find a rear exit from the place. Then catch a cab and go home to tend my wounds.

A familiar, and at the moment not too welcome, voice stopped me before I got to the bathroom.

"Ham, you're hurt!"

"Don't look at me, Sindi," I said. Then I lied, "I'm okay."

"No you're not," she said firmly as she took my arm and turned me to face her. "Oh my god, you're bleeding."

I attempted a grin, but my jaw and mouth hurt too much. "You should see the other guy," I said.

"I did." Right, the voices I heard in the hall when Hammond ran out. "Come with me, I'm going to fix you."

"The cops are coming, Sindi. I think I should leave before they get here." I tried to pull away but she held on harder.

"The cops aren't coming. That was my across the hall neighbor. He came to investigate the racket you two were making. I talked him out of calling the police. Now you're coming with me and I'm going to take care of you."

She wrapped one of her arms around my body and pulled one of my arms around her shoulders. Silly girl. I'm so much bigger than she is she couldn't have carried me anywhere like that. But she draped my arm around her shoulders in a way that my hand just naturally cupped her breast. I went along to wherever she wanted to take me. Gonads, brains. You know how it works.

Where she wanted to take me was the bathroom. She very expertly stripped off my clothes and sat me in the tub so I wouldn't drip blood all over. After quick go-over of my injuries, she left the room for a moment, then came back and put an ice pack on my eye.

"Hold this," she ordered, then busied herself with a carton under the sink for a moment and came back with cotton balls, tape, gauze, merthiolate, astringent, and I don't know what all and knelt by the side of the tub.

She knew enough to not use tap water to clean the cuts. Her touch was gentle. I lay back and relaxed to enjoy her ministrations. She made some exasperated noises as she worked and I opened my good eye to look at her. She had an intent look on her face and the way she leaned over the side of the tub looked awkward. I closed my eye and enjoyed.

Her position must have been as awkward as it looked, because after another minute she said, "This is no good."

I looked again and saw her stand up and undress. She paused when she got down to her underwear, then twitched the corner of her mouth and stripped them off as well. It was all very matter of fact; no coquettishness even though she knew I was watching. Then she got in the tub and straddled me.

"That's better," she said. "Now I can reach everywhere without straining." Her expression stayed intent.

"Ummm," I said, and enjoyed some more. I didn't move, didn't put a hand on her, but I did have exactly the reaction you'd expect under the circumstances.

Sindi raised herself slightly and gave my reaction a sharp rap. "Not now," she said sternly. "I'm fixing your injuries." She smiled briefly and added, "Maybe later-if you're feeling up to it."

I thought I was feeling up to it now. But that didn't seem the right thing to say just then, so I didn't say anything. My reaction came back. She ignored it this time.

But she didn't completely ignore it. When she straightened up to say, "There, all done. Time will take care of the rest of it," her voice was husky.

She wiggled against my reaction and I felt the wetness of her reaction.

"I'm up for it if you are," I said, in a voice just as husky as hers.

She leaned forward and kissed me. Her lips were soft against mine, her breasts were hard against my chest. I let the ice pack slip off my face and put both hands on her. She lifted herself far enough for our reactions to join in the way of male and female.

I still didn't think about the bit about her and the retirement fund. And it hadn't yet clicked on me what Hammond said about "Keep your fucking hands off her."

*

After we showered together I got a good look at myself in the mirror on the back of the bathroom door. What I saw made me wonder what kind of kinks she might be into that I didn't know about. The flesh around my left eye was red and puffy; I knew that red would turn a deep purple before the color faded. There was a cut across the bridge of my nose. At least I knew it wasn't broken, the earlier congestion was just blood from broken capillaries and had cleared out quickly when I blew it. The back of my right hand was covered with a big bandage. There was a large, livid bruise on my left side. It still hurt to breathe, but not as badly as earlier. I didn't feel any grating in the side, so I guess none of the bones were broken. The surgical scar on my right knee was the only injury below my waist, and it didn't count.

Sindi didn't give me much time to admire myself. She bustled about, helping me dry off. Then she wrapped me in a big terry towel and hustled me into the bedroom. She hadn't taken the time to dry herself and didn't bother with a robe. I sometimes say, scratch my back and I'll follow you anywhere. I felt like changing that to, get naked and I'll go anywhere with you. She gave me unnecessary help getting on the bed and said:

"Lay quiet now, you need to rest. I'll be right back with something for the pain."

She walked into the living room and stood where she was still partly in view from the bed. I lay quietly enjoying the view. A part of me admired her talent for keeping a man distracted. She made noises in the living room; a cardboard box made opening and closing noises, glass clinked, liquid glugged. There was a short pause before she came back carrying an Old Fashioned glass. She made a splendid picture of an angel of mercy.

"If hospitals only hired attractive women as nurses," I said, "and they walked around naked, their male patients would get well faster and stay longer."

She glanced down at herself and shook her head. "Men. It's just a body, everybody has one."

I've heard that from other women. They don't understand how the sight of an attractive woman without clothes on affects men, they think we're being adolescent. Clyde must be right about men and women being visual in different ways.

She sat on the edge of the bed and raised my shoulders. "Medicinal brandy," she said. "Drink it." I did as told.

She leaned over to kiss me chastely on the forehead. Straightening up, she pried my hand loose from her breast.

"I'm going to dry off and get dressed," she said. "Then I'm going to fix us some dinner and you can tell me what that was all about."

"Yes, dear."

I watched until she was out of sight, then closed my eyes. Whatever she put in the brandy was working, I thought. The pain was ebbing and I felt too relaxed to move. Then I tried to open my eyes and repeat the thought, *Whatever she put in the...*

*

When I finally got my eyes open, the quality of the outside light flooding the bedroom was different from what it had been. The traffic noises also sounded different. I turned my head to look at the clock on the nightstand, it was a few minutes after eight. I listened and heard water sounds coming from the direction of the bathroom. I realized I was under the sheet and no longer wrapped in a towel. I looked at the other side of the bed. The bed had slept two. Through a fog, I realized the few minutes after eight was AM, not PM.

I sat on the side of the bed and groaned. My face hurt, my hand hurt, my side hurt, one eye wanted to close. My sinuses felt clogged, but my head didn't hurt. Whatever Sindi put in the brandy didn't leave me with a hangover.

I blinked. What *had* she put in that drink? She didn't tell me she put something in my drink; she just did it and knocked me right out. Without finding out what I was doing fighting with Hammond in her apartment. What the hell was going on here? I sat up and almost fell back.

I waited until the dizziness faded. Then moved as though through gelatin. I found if I moved slowly, standing up and dressing hardly hurt at all. It didn't seem to matter that the map wasn't with my clothes. There was a sealed envelope that I didn't recognize in the jacket pocket, but it didn't seem important at the moment, so I left it there and forgot about it.

Sindi came rushing out of the bathroom at the same time I emerged from the bedroom. She was made up and jewelried and wore a half slip under a bra cut so wide it looked designed to go under something that exposed a lot of upper body flesh.

"Ham, good, you're up," she exclaimed, and brushed right past me into the bedroom. I turned and followed with so many questions trying to come out at once that my groggy state wouldn't let put my lips around any of them. "Zip me." She stepped into a dress and presented her back. I zipped.

"I was afraid I'd have to wake you," she said, making adjustments to her clothes in the vanity mirror.

"You put something in the brandy," I finally managed to say.

"You were in pretty bad shape. You needed to sleep."

"The sleep couldn't wait until you found out what was going on when you walked in?"

"I know what happened, you didn't have to tell me." She took my arm and led me into the living room. "I have to go to work now. You're dressed, you may as well leave now too."

She had me by the arm and was moving me fast enough to cause pain in my various injuries and I swayed. She stopped while I took a couple of slow breaths, then let me set the pace.

We were waiting for the elevator by the time I asked, "Where's the map?"

"It's in a safe place."

Then the elevator came. Other people were on it, so I didn't ask any of the other questions burning in my mind. Why hadn't she told me she put the map in my pocket the night before? Why did she put the map in my pocket to begin with? What was Hammond doing in her apartment? How did he get in? I hadn't really looked, but there were no obvious signs of forced entry. He had said something about her, what was it? Oh well, if it's important, it'll come back. What did she think was happening? Where was the safe place for the map? How soon can you leave for Georgia? Thinking of Georgia; where is that mountain mariners used as a landmark?

On the sidewalk, she brushed her lips across mine and said, "Go home. I'll call you as soon as I get a chance." Then to the doorman, "Get him a cab please."

And she was gone, striding away, toward the insurance company that had engaged in some illegal activities, an insurance company where she was an officer. And she wanted me to believe she was a secretary. I managed to think that despite the dulled state of my mind.

I looked at the doorman. It was obvious it took an effort for him to keep a straight face when he looked at me.

A cab came along the street. He tooted his whistle at it, it pulled up to the curb, he held the door for me, I eased myself in and gave driver a location on Baltimore Avenue.

I bought an *Inquirer* at a corner store and went into a lunch place where I ate often enough to be a regular, to have some breakfast.

"What happened to you, Ham?" the counterman asked when he saw me.

"I was at my girlfriend's and walked into something I didn't know was there."

"Yeah? Must have been a big, mean something."

"It was, Tim, it was."

He realized I wasn't going to talk about it, so he asked if I wanted my usual. I did. Three eggs easy over, home fries, ham, coffee. I went to a booth and sipped at my coffee and read the paper while waiting for the eggs. I was nearly through eating when I saw the item. It wasn't much of an item, less than three column inches, and I almost missed it. The headline was;
SLAYING VICTIM FOUND

There are eight or ten murders a week in Philadelphia, so I don't pay too much attention to minor killing items. Something, though, compelled me to read this one. What I read stopped me cold.

It reported a man's body found in Wissahickon Park and described it as a gangland-style murder. It said his hands and feet were bound together and he was shot one time in the back of the head. That much was no big deal, that kind of homicide happens frequently enough. What stopped me was, the paper gave the victim's name as Greg Hammond.

I left without finishing my breakfast.

There were a couple of messages on my machine. My machine time- and date-stamps incoming messages so I know when they came in.

The first message was recorded at 6:17PM the previous evening. It was from *Mother Jones*, they were interested in the proposal I sent them on the significance of smoke filled-rooms in today's anti-smoking climate. Please write the piece and send it in. Hot damn, that would be a nice paycheck.

The second message was stamped at 8:43 this morning. It left me shivering. "You see the paper yet today, Eliot? You're next." The voice sounded like Kallir's. The mist disappeared from my mind.

CHAPTER TWELVE

I stood there shivering for a moment or two while the threat washed over me. Too much had happened over the last three and a half days. Some of it was good; Sindi in bed-and elsewhere-, the yes from *Mother Jones*. Most of it was bad. The time I spent early Sunday morning with Kallir and Company. The inconclusive faceoff with the mysterious Mister Big yesterday morning, along with the confrontation with Kallir and Hondo. Followed by Kallir and Moose showing up at my front steps. Then the beating Hammond gave me. The inescapable feeling that Sindi was manipulating me, using me, lying through her teeth.

It didn't happen to me, but Hammond's murder was a pretty bad thing as well.

Now a threat against my life. A threat I had to take seriously. I had a way of coping with that threat.

One of the things I like about these Victorian and Edwardian houses in University City is, if you're imaginative enough, they've got more hiding places than any burglar could ever ferret out. I use some of those hiding places. Not to hide money or jewels, I never have much cash on hand and own almost no jewelry. I use some of those hiding places to stash my armory.

I'm not a gun-nut-I don't know anyone who has been a foot soldier in a war who is. Mine isn't a big armory, but it is varied. I've got a couple of long arms; a Remington 12 gauge, and a Springfield M1A. I keep telling myself I'm going hunting one of these seasons, but I've never gone. Maybe hunting men in a far-away country twenty odd years ago took the urge to seek-and-kill out of me.

More to the immediate point, I own two handguns. One is a big, bad Ruger Security Six, a .38/.357 with a six-inch barrel. I've fired it on the range often enough to be confident with my ability to quick draw it and hit a man-sized target at seven yards without taking time to use the sights. Snap shooting, it's called. The problem with it is its size. Men smaller than Mike Hammer have trouble carrying big handguns in shoulder holsters without the weapon being obvious.

My other hand gun is a Seecamp .32. It's a cute little thing that looks more like a gag cigarette lighter than a real pistol. Some people call a lady's purse gun. It's got a clever holster, a flat leather rectangle. I can put the pistol in it and when I stick it in a hip pocket it looks like I'm carrying a wallet. The .32 isn't terribly accurate at any distance, but on the range I'd managed to put three rounds in a four-inch circle at seven yards.

There it is again, that magic distance of seven yards.

Few urban gunmen ever learn how to shoot, they seem to have an almost mystical belief that if they point an automatic weapon in the general direction of what they want to hit they somehow will. That means they have to get very close to their targets in order to hit a man. A good example is an incident from a couple of years back. Just a block from City Hall, five punks had a shootout at fifteen or twenty yards. The cops said they fired a total of thirty-eight rounds. Despite all those bullets flying around, all they managed to do was wing a bystander in the leg. Then two unarmed security guards in their forties ran down and caught three of the punks, all of whom were in their twenties. I love a happy ending.

In another incident a few years earlier, a would-be hit man walked up to a parked car, stuck his pistol into the open window, and emptied it at the Mafioso sitting there. He missed.

Seven yards is all the range you ever need in urban combat. Most of these clowns can't hit anything at that range with anything less than a hundred round burst from a machine gun. At seven yards I can hit a man with one shot from this little .32. And at that range, the Winchester Silvertips it's loaded with can do a lot of damage.

I got the little automatic from its hiding place. No, don't ask where I hide it, I don't tell anybody. If I told, it wouldn't be hidden anymore, would it? I made sure it would slide in and out of its wallet-holster easily, then stuck the holster into my right hip pocket. I practiced pulling it out about three or four times. The only glitch was the wallet-holster always came out with it. No problem, my finger was on the trigger and I could shoot it, though I'd have to pull off the holster and manually operate the slide before I could get off a second shot. I loaded it and put an extra magazine for it in my left front pocket.

Maybe this was still nothing more than Dutch courage, but it did make me feel a little more secure. I sat at my computer and turned it on. Not that I planned on doing any work, it's just that the computer's my work place and I automatically hit the power switch when I sit there. I sat in front of the green-glowing screen, not looking at it, gazing unfocused past it to the street below, and tried to think. You know how sometimes when you try to think about a problem you can't string two coherent thoughts together to lead to a third one? That's what it was like-except sometimes when I try to think, I can't even assemble one coherent thought.

I slipped a game disk into the A drive and let a game distract my conscious mind so my subconscious could work on the problem. It often happens that I do my best thinking when I'm playing games on the computer, while reading half-asleep late at night, while waiting for the dryer to stop tumbling at the laundromat, or as I do odds and ends that don't have to be done right now.

It was a quiet morning. I could hear birds singing in the trees along the street. Somewhere a dog barked "Hello" a couple of times, got no reply, didn't bark again. The traffic noise on the through streets was muted.

Soon enough a thought rose to the surface. It was I should warn Sindi; if I was in danger, she most likely was as well, and probably greater danger. The idea of calling her agitated me for a couple of reasons: One, knowing where she worked without her knowing I knew was the only ace I had in this business. Though I couldn't think what advantage an ace in a hand of low-pip garbage gave me. Still, I was reluctant to give up my only high card. Two; I was convinced she was lying to me, so why should I help her?

If only I knew how to get in touch with this Mister Big and tell him I was out of it. Then I thought again of the five million dollars that was going to be mine and knew I wouldn't quit.

Besides, I rationalized, I didn't know who Mister Big was or who else might be involved with him. There are people who won't let you drop out, no matter how pure your motives for doing so.

I wondered how Kallir and Company planned to come after me. Would they try to steer me to a convenient place? They wouldn't try to come here, I was sure I had them convinced the cops would show up before they could get away if they did. Unless they came in the back way.

The back way! I jumped up and ran to the back of my apartment. The view of the backyards from my window resembled a meadow. The yards were grass with some flower patches. No privacy fences broke the sweep of the greensward. The old, hairpin iron fences that were there didn't intrude on the eye from this angle.

Most adults in this neighborhood are at work during the day and the younger children are in day care or some other supervised place. It's nearly abandoned except for the few yuppettes who have opted for the mommie experience. That meant someone could slip into this ersatz meadow and make his way unseen to the back of my place. There was a shed roof immediately below my bedroom windows. It wouldn't be difficult for Kallir and Hondo to climb onto it, though it would present major problems for Moose unless he was far more agile than his bulk implied. That shed roof would put them right where they could climb in the windows with a good chance of nobody seeing them.

I shuddered. I spent several minutes studying the backyards, watching for movement without seeing any. Then I closed and locked the windows. I use a very simple device to keep my windows locked; drilled holes in the corners of the sashes where the bottom one overlaps the top. I stick a couple eight penny nails in those holes. That's a much more effective lock than the regular thumb latch. Now if they wanted to come in the back way they'd have to break the glass and I'd hear them. If they broke in sometime when I was out and they had it in mind to catch me when I got home, a neighbor would hear the breaking glass and call the cops. I hoped. It could happen. If they didn't use a glass cutter and get in quietly. I shuddered again.

I went back to my desk. The birds weren't singing as much. More dogs barked more frequently. The traffic on the through streets seemed louder. A plastic trike ratcheted along the sidewalk. Yuplings shrilled. A mommie-experience yuppette admonished a yupling to be more watchful. The quiet morning had become the day of the dread.

Most days when it's not too cold or too blistering hot, I sit at my computer with open windows while I do my work and hardly notice racket even greater than that assaulting my ears now. The undercurrent of the fear I felt from the threats magnified the annoyance value of the street noises. Then I remembered how the mommies and their spawn had saved me from Kallir and Moose yesterday afternoon and stopped being annoyed. Pray little children yammer.

Why, I thought, I could go outside and hang out with the mommies. Kallir and Moose wouldn't dare try to take me then. I stood to go out.

A different thought stopped me before I was all the way to my feet and I plunked back down. These are the days of drive-by shootings. The presence of innocent bystanders doesn't stop a drive-by shooting, the innocents just get shot by the drive-by shooters.

I went back to my games in hope of more ideas. The first one to hit me was I was still wearing the same clothes as yesterday. I left the computer to correct that and showered. Once clean, I studied the damage to my face in the mirror.

My eye was livid and swollen, but only partly closed. I winced at the pain when I probed the darkened flesh, but nothing grated, so I decided nothing was broken. I closed my good eye and found I could see with the left one. Not as well as with the right, but well enough. The cut on the bridge of my nose was nicely scabbed. I decided a casual observer might believe I walked into a door or fell down. The bruise on my side was larger, but again nothing grated, there wasn't any sharp pain when I probed, so I decided nothing was broken there either.

I dressed and went back to my computer to play more games in search of more ideas. The phone rang before any more ideas came. I let it ring twice while I considered letting the machine answer, maybe start off with the upper hand on my caller. Then I snorted in disgust with myself and picked it up.

"Ham, have you seen the news? They shot Greg."

"I saw," I said, and puzzled over how Sindi said that. She called him "Greg" in a very familiar way, not the way you'd expect if she only knew him as a man who'd recently entered her life and threatened her. There was fear in her voice, as I had felt fear when I saw the item in the paper, but there was also a sound of loss. Now I remembered what Hammond had said during our fight.

"I'm scared, Ham."

"You should be."

"I'm too upset to stay at work, and I'm afraid to go home. What should I do?"

Beats me. I was more sure than ever that she was manipulating and using me. I was also more sure that she was in greater danger than I was.

"Can you meet me at the Cornish Hen? Do you know where it is?"

"I know the place." The Cornish Hen is a coffee shop in a high-class hotel near Rittenhouse Square. You can get a sandwich there or an after-theater dessert. If you like, you can sit for hours over a bottomless cup of coffee. It was frequented by businessmen, artists, students, bohemians, and daters. Despite its yuppie trimmings, I liked the place. Mention of it made me realize it was an hour past noon and that realization made me hungry. "Twenty minutes," I said.

"Please hurry." She made a kissing noise. I didn't reciprocate.

I sat there for a moment after hanging up. My mind was bound with the conflict between wanting to get out of this mess where nobody was dealing with me straight and had now turned deadly, and my desire for that five million dollars.

The jacket I wore yesterday was rumpled and had a bloodstain on one sleeve. Before tossing it aside for the dry cleaner, I emptied the pockets. The sealed envelope I'd found in it when I looked for the map this morning was still there, I'd forgotten about it. I stuck the envelope in the pocket of the jacket I put on and went out. I tried to keep from constantly looking over my shoulder while I walked up to Spruce Street. I managed an unsatisfactory compromise: I looked back often enough to feel silly, but not often enough to be positive nobody was coming at me from behind.

As I hoped, a cab came along a few minutes after I got to Spruce Street. I told the cabbie where I wanted to go and he repeated it. He looked at me in the rearview mirror after he pulled out from the curb. "Who gave you that shiner?"

I grunted. "I thought I'd give my nephew a few pointers in the art of boxing. I should know better than to duke it out with a teenage kid." Then I looked out the window. The cabbie took the hint and didn't try to continue the conversation.

Before we got into town I pulled the envelope out of my pocket to see what was in it. I tore it open and was greeted by a sheaf of greenbacks. I riffled through them. It was the $2,500 retainer.

CHAPTER THIRTEEN

An upholstered bench runs around the inside walls of the Cornish Hen with tiny cafe tables fronting the bench and one or two cafe chairs at each table. More tiny tables, each with two or three chairs, dot the open areas of the floor. The business part of the coffee shop is along the window-side wall and juts into the middle of the room.

Sindi was already there. She saw me, stood up and waved. It wasn't necessary, I saw her right away. She sat on the bench in the far corner where she could see everyone who came in through the street entrance or the door from the hotel. The way she was arranged, I didn't think anybody passing on the street could look in and see her. I waved back and went to the counter to place my order. She looked hurt that I didn't go directly to her.

I ordered a ham and swiss on marble. No, I didn't want sprouts or broccoli on the sandwich. I wanted iceberg, which they didn't have, settled for romaine, which they did. Please pay at the cash register and have a seat, someone will bring it to you when it's ready. The order-taker was cool, after a quick glance she ignored my bruised and swollen eye. I got my coffee cup and took it to the pot on the side counter to fill. Only then did I go to the tiny table where Sindi sat.

She was partly slumped in her seat, partly hunched over the table. Her hands hovered around a cup. A teapot sat in the middle of the small table. A cigarette burned in the ashtray.

I sat on the bench where I could also see the entrances. She huddled against me. "I'm so afraid, Ham," she said. Her voice was much firmer than it had been on the phone. "That terrible Hammond man was murdered. Do you think that wimpy guy, Llowlolski, did it? I didn't think he had it in him to kill anyone." Despite the way she acted, her voice said she'd gotten control of herself in the quarter hour it had taken me to reach her.

"No, I don't think Llowlolski did it. It might have been those other characters though. The ones who got me Saturday night." Okay, it was Sunday morning. Neither of us had gone to bed from Saturday, so it felt like Saturday night no matter what time it was.

She moved against me; I think it was supposed to be a shiver. The way she said "Greg" on the phone contrasted so much with the way she now said "that terrible Hammond man" that it hardened me against her.

"Do you think they'll come after us?"

I noticed the careful "us" rather than "me," and told her about the message from Kallir.

She gasped. "What can we do?"

I looked at her and saw a beautiful woman leaning toward me, into me, seeking protection and offering herself in exchange for that protection. I also saw a beautiful, conniving woman who was manipulating me for ends I wasn't sure of. I saw a beautiful woman putting on an act. I thought goddam, why can't fantasies ever work out right? I said, "I think a good place to start would be you telling me the truth."

She flinched as though I slapped her.

"What do you mean, Ham?" She put her hand on my chest. "What haven't I told you the truth about?"

I thought for a few seconds, wondering where to begin. Finally I said, "When we were fighting, Hammond told me to keep my hands off you. If he was just this bully boy out to scare you into giving him the map, why would he care where my hands were?"

Her eyes widened and she pulled back from me for a second, then she leaned in again and gently touched my swollen eye and split lip. "He was hurting you," she said. "How could you hear anything he said?"

"Easy. I interview people for the articles I write. I don't use a tape recorder and don't take many notes because I can remember nearly everything they say. It was right after the first time Hammond hit me. He said, 'When I'm through with you, you're going to know to keep your fucking hands off her.' That's a direct quote."

She pulled back a little and studied my face for a long moment. I could see when she made up her mind I was telling the truth.

"All right," she said. "You've got me. I know-knew-Greg." She shook her head. "It's hard for me to think of him as dead. Damn." Her shoulders shook. "He was always so strong. It's hard to believe someone could kill him. We had a thing between us once." She took a nervous drag on her cigarette, snubbed out the butt.

"He was married," I said during her momentary silence. Just a little nudge to let her know there were more things I knew.

"I know. They were separated. No they weren't, not really. I mean, it wasn't a legal separation or anything." She looked at me with an open, earnest expression, letting me know she couldn't lie to me, not anymore. As if I could believe it. "They weren't living together. He wanted a no fault divorce, but he still needed someone. If his wife knew, she'd sue for desertion and infidelity. I wanted someone who could keep our relationship quiet, not try to run me around and show me off like a trophy."

"So much for it's been so long."

She flinched and looked away. When she didn't say anything right away I decided to jab her one more time.

"So much for men not wanting women over thirty."

"That's a dirty shot."

So what? She had hurt my feelings. She'd lied to me. I felt dirtied. She may as well share the feeling.

"What happened, why did you stop having your 'thing'?"

She grimaced, I couldn't tell whether at me or at the memory. "Adrianne, that's his wife, got suspicious. He thought she was having him followed. Neither of us wanted to, but we had to break off. He had a record, he was afraid of what someone might find out about him. Sometimes a man on parole has to go back to jail for doing things that are all right for anyone else. She could make a lot of trouble if she knew about me." She paused to light another cigarette.

"Did you know he was still mixed up with the bad guys?"

"That's a lie," she snapped. "He got out of it. He was working for someone, he never told me who. He had a job as a bodyguard for some businessman, I think he said. A couple of months after we broke up he came to see me. He told me his boss was mixed up in something illegal and he was quitting because when things went down he didn't want to get caught up in it. I told him that was a wise move." She took a deep drag. "Then he told me something else..."

*

"I never wanted to break up with you, Sindi. You know that, don't you?"

It was May and they had arranged a seemingly accidental encounter in the Buddhist temple in the Art Museum. It was quiet enough there and had few enough visitors they were certain they could spot anyone following him and break off before being seen themselves. At the moment, the only other people in evidence were a teenage couple necking in a dark recess.

"I know, Greg." She couldn't help herself, she threw her arms around his neck and kissed him passionately. "It was something we had to do. I love you." Her eyes watered.

He kissed her back, long and hungry. His hand groped for her breast through her spring-weight coat. She twisted into his grasp.

After a long moment he broke the kiss. It took another long moment for his breath to come back to normal. "We can get back together, I know how."

"Tell me, Greg. Tell me how!"

"This guy I work for. I found out he's a crook."

"No!"

"Yes. I've got to quit. He's acting dumb. Something's going to happen to him and I don't want to go down with him. I'm a two-time loser. They'll send me away for a long time if they get their hands on me again."

"Yes, Greg, you've got to quit. Right now. Don't go back. Not now, not ever."

"I have to. Just for a couple of days, though. Then we'll be able to get back together and won't have to break up again."

She was full of questions. "Why? How? Who is this man?"

"Why is to get the information I need for us to have the how. But I'm not telling you who he is. He's an important man, you'd recognize his name if I told you. He's also a dangerous man. You're safer if you don't know who he is."

She looked adoringly into his eyes. If Greg said she shouldn't know who he worked for, then she wouldn't ask again. "What do you have to learn?"

"He's buying an authentic pirate treasure map. I'm going to get it before he does. We can dig up the treasure and then we'll be rich enough to go away. Anywhere we want to. And nobody will be able to find us. We won't have to worry about Adrianne, or this guy I work for, or anybody else. Not ever again."

She looked at him, astonished. "Do you believe this? A pirate treasure map?"

Hammond nodded. "I saw the research he had done on it. I'm positive it's real. He thinks its worth forty million dollars and thinks he can get at least half that for it. I read transcriptions of the list of what's supposed to be in the treasure. I'm pretty sure I can get more than twenty million for it. We'll be rich, Sindi."

"And we can go away. We can make a fresh start, just the two of us. Oh, darling!" She kissed him again.

*

She finished her cigarette while telling me the story and lit another when she finished telling it.

"So the whole story about the auction was a lie," I said, and wondered how much of this story was also a lie. The bit about the book had to be true, though. Both Llowlolski and Mister Big had talked about it. Mister Big must be the man Hammond had worked for.

"No." She shook her head. "The auction was a laundry. He stole the map and put it in a box of books that he had someone else put up for sale. Then I bought the lot. It was supposed to take their attention off Greg when they realized the map was missing. Also, I'd be able to claim clear and legal ownership of the map."

"So you got hold of the map the way you told me before?"

She nodded. "Greg and I even did that bit of play acting out front to make them believe he had nothing to do with the theft."

"Who is Llowlolski?"

She laughed. "He's an accountant. He's the guy who was going to make sure the numbers all turned out looking legal."

"And you don't know the name of this man Hammond worked for."

"No." It was a very small voice, one I wasn't sure I could believe.

"Kallir and Company work for the same guy."

She nodded.

"You have the map."

She nodded again. I wondered when she'd speak again. She kept puffing on her cigarette.

"Why did you bring me into it?"

"Greg thought I needed a bodyguard. And he wanted a red herring to distract them from me."

"So you didn't ask around and find me."

She shook her head. "Greg knew about you. He told me where to find you."

"The reason your door wasn't forced at your old apartment is there wasn't really a burglary."

She nodded.

"Hammond was in your apartment when we got there Saturday night, and he was there when I showed up yesterday afternoon because he had a key."

She nodded again.

"You used me." You dirty, rotten, sneaky... "And you cheated on Greg with me."

"No! I used you, yes. But I didn't cheat on Greg with you. It was special with you." She leaned toward me and put her hand on my arm. And I didn't believe her. "Once I met you and saw the contrast between you and Greg, I knew you were much better. I saw what he really was. Don't you see?"

No I didn't see. I didn't see anything but lying and betrayal.

"Greg was a petty crook, he'd always been nothing but a crook. And he involved me in a scheme to commit another crime. You wouldn't do that." She shook her head, denying any possibility I'd do anything like that. As though she wasn't a crook herself with whatever it was she had done helping her employer commit its crimes.

I thought about my own blindness toward her. I thought about my willingness to go ahead and help her get the treasure at the end of that stolen map. I thought about Hammond's death and the threat against me. I thought everyone has a price. I thought of the five million dollars that was my share of the booty and knew what my price was. In that moment I despised myself.

She leaned closer, snuggled her breast into my arm, and kissed me. "Now that I know the difference, now that we've met, now that we love each other, we can get the treasure together and we can disappear, go someplace where these other people will never find us."

But I didn't want to go away. I certainly didn't want to go away with anyone as treacherous as Sindi DiWagne. I wondered how long it would take her to find someone else to help her get rid of me. Yes, it was too easy for me to picture her bedding me until I was delirious with ecstasy, then vanishing with all the money while my mind was too sodden with the physical pleasures of what her body was doing to mine to notice. I could even see her having me killed. It wouldn't even cost her very much of the treasure. In every city there are men available who are willing to murder a stranger for a few hundred dollars. You may have to pay as much as a couple of thousand, but even at that price they're cheap. And they're easy to find. All you have to do is be willing to associate with people like that-and take your chances that they won't figure there's a lot more to be made if they're willing to commit just a little more mayhem.

My price went up and I stopped despising myself. My dreams of the house on Spruce Street, the Rolls at the curb, the good tailor, the steady girlfriend, and all the rest, went bye-bye. My life was worth more to me than the five million dollars I'd probably never see. My self-esteem was worth more than any profit from associating with the likes of Sindi DiWagne. Somehow, I was going to get my hands on that map, find out who Mister Big was, and return the map to him in exchange for him calling off his dogs.

Somewhere during all that, my sandwich arrived. It sat on its tiny tray, untouched. I wasn't hungry anymore.

"What about your job? How much notice do you have to give?"

She shook her head. "I can just walk away from it. They won't have any problem replacing me. None."

I stood up and grabbed Sindi's hand. "Let's go," I ordered.

"Where to?" She stood and, off balance because I was pulling her, followed.

"Your place. If we're going away, we have to get ready. And you have to get the map from its safe place."

CHAPTER FOURTEEN

Hammond was double crossing his boss, presumably this mysterious Mister Big. He and Sindi were using me as a red herring to throw Mister Big off the scent. Sindi, if I read between the lines right, had been using me to double cross Hammond. Mister Big, presumably, had Hammond killed. I'm on the list. It's a good bet Sindi is too. Sindi's still lying to me about her job, so she's probably double crossing me. She may even have in mind to kill me.

Nice people you're hanging out with these days, Eliot. You should have bought a drink for that redhead Saturday night. Gawd, was this only Tuesday? Has this all really taken less than 72 hours? I've been roughed up, tied up, beaten up, threatened with beatings twice more, my life has been threatened, and I've been lied to out the ying-yang. And the most beautiful woman I've ever laid serious hands on used her body to lead me around by the nose. Or some anatomical part.

Now I had to extricate myself. Preferably with my dignity, life, and limb intact. Life and limb, anyway. If necessary, I could forgo the dignity. The first thing was to get hold of the map without being double crossed again. The way to do that was convince Sindi I was going along with her run-away idea.

"Pack a suitcase," I said as soon as we were in her apartment. "If you've got any LL Bean clothes, pack them first. Don't bother with any frilly stuff, you won't be needing it for the next few days."

"What? Pack a bag, why?"

Nice. I was calling her bluff and she didn't know what to do. I ignored her objections. "Just one bag, Sindi. We don't have much time." I hurried her into the bedroom. "Where do you keep your suitcases?"

"Under the bed. But..."

I got down on my hands and knees and looked. There were three of them under there. I pulled out the bigger of the two soft-sided ones and opened it on the bed. "Start putting whatever you're going to need in it. We don't have much time."

"Where are we going?"

I gave her a little push toward the dresser. "Pack a week's worth of underwear, no more." I opened the closet and started rifling through her things. No LL Bean. Not even Banana Republic.

"Ham, will you please tell me what is going on?" She stood looking at me, arms akimbo. She hadn't started packing.

"Sindi," I said patiently, "you said we could get the treasure and then go away where they'll never find us. You were right. The sooner we do it the better. They killed Hammond last night. Kallir told me I'm next. They probably plan to kill you too. We have to get out of town. The sooner the better. Right now's a good time. And you said you can just walk away from your job. Start packing." I went back to the closet.

The only hanging things that looked at all usable on a treasure hunt were a sturdy skirt and two cotton blouses. The rest of the stuff on the hangers was good only for city wear. There was one pair of sensible shoes on the floor. The few pair of boots were fine for doing the South Street Stroll, but useless for digging up a dead man's chest. I tossed the useful things to her, then rooted through the boxes on the shelf. I found a couple of flannel shirts. They'd do. I tossed them on the bed.

She was making busy at the dresser, but not busy packing. Instead, she was going through her undies. I looked. The drawer was filled with frilly, flimsy, and lacy. I think I saw a couple of open-nipple bras and some crotchless panties. Real sexy stuff, but not what the well-dressed woman should be wearing in the wild.

"Do you have any plain cotton?" I asked. "You know, utilitarian stuff, like you'd wear at a Girl Scout jamboree."

"Ham!" She flushed and slammed the drawer shut.

"Sindi." I took her hands in mine and gave her as sincere a look as my battered face would allow. "Our lives are in jeopardy. Any minute now, Kallir and his buddies could come barging in to kill me, get the map, and kill you. They might rape you before they kill you. Or maybe afterward, I wouldn't put it past them. We have to get out of here. We are going straight to Georgia and dig up that treasure. You are going to pack one suitcase, get the map, and withdraw all your money from the bank. Then we'll go to my place and I'll pack one bag. I'll get all my money from the bank. We'll get into my car and head south. Once we have the treasure, you can buy all new frillies and new everything else. I can buy a new computer. But we have to do this now, before anybody comes for us. Do you understand me?"

She gnawed on her lower lip. Her eyes darted around. I was sure she was trying to figure out a way to get rid of me. She figured it.

"You're right, Ham, we have to go now. Why don't you go home and get your stuff and meet me back here? Won't that be faster?"

I shook my head. "Not a chance. Women take a lot longer to pack than men do. That's because women try to take everything they might possibly want, but men only take what they really need. If I left now, by the time I got back you'd probably have three suitcases packed and not be done yet. I'd have to dump out what you've packed and make you start all over again. It's faster my way."

"That's a sexist thing to say," she snapped.

I half expected that accusation after my little speech. It's the basic fallback position for women whenever a man points out a functional difference between the genders. "No it's not. I can be packed and on my way out the door in less than five minutes after we get to my place. We've been here for longer than that and you aren't even started packing yet."

"I have so started!" She looked indignant. "I have to go through my things to see what I need."

"You don't have to go through your things to decide," I said. I tried to look impatient. It wasn't hard. "You need sturdy, utilitarian clothes. Start with jeans. Two pair. Socks-not pantyhose or stockings-a week's supply. Simple underwear, also enough for a week. Walking shoes. If you don't have any clothing like that, we can stop and buy it along the way."

She glared at me, then twisted away to continue rooting. "I have to make sure I'm not leaving behind anything I need."

It goes back to our hunter-gatherer days, is the way Clyde explains it. Women, he says, were responsible for packing up the camp when the nomads moved. They had to make sure nothing usable was left behind. When the men went out hunting, they took their weapons and fire-starters and little else. Women who did a good job of taking care of the camp were more desirable to the men and had a better chance of getting mates and having offspring than the ones who didn't do such a good job. That's why conscientiousness about packing is a female trait. It's one of those inappropriate evolutionary things that continue to this day. I don't know if Clyde is right about how it developed; I do know I've never known a woman who could pack as fast as the average man. At the moment, Sindi seemed to be slower than most.

"You don't seem to get the idea," I said. "We have to get out of here. Our lives are in danger."

"I'm hurrying, I'm hurrying," she said. She found her jeans and folded them into the suitcase. I stuffed the things from the closet on top of them.

"Dammit, Ham, don't do it like that. Fold them and put them in neatly." She demonstrated. Then she made an exasperated sound and unpacked the skirt and one cotton blouse. "I'll need to wear these."

I stuck them back in. "We don't have time for you to change. You can wear what you've got on. Later, when we've got time, we can stop someplace and you can change then."

She glared at me, but returned to her packing without saying anything more. She wound up packing what I told her to, even though it took far longer than it should have.

Then I followed her into the bathroom to make sure she didn't spend too much time going through the medicine cabinet. I really did want to get out of there. Get my hands on that map before any of the bad guys showed up and it would be too late.

The phone rang. We froze and stared at each other for a moment.

"Answer it," I finally said.

It took long enough for her to get to the phone the machine was already answering when she picked up the receiver and she had to turn it off.

"Hello." She listened and went pale. "Yes," she said. Listened again. "But I can't, I don't..." She looked at me and mouthed, "Llowlolski."

I took the phone from her.

"Paul, this is Eliot." First name him, last name me. There's an arrogance in that that can put some people at a disadvantage. I held the receiver so Sindi could listen in.

"Mister Eliot? So that's where you are? My boys went looking for you, but you weren't home?" Kallir and Company were back to being his boys, though it was obvious from my visit to his apartment he wasn't in charge of anybody. "Kallir wanted to apologize to you. For the message he left on your telephone machine? My employer found out about it and told Kallir he's a legitimate businessman. We aren't in that business, you know?" I looked a question at Sindi. She shook her head, she didn't believe him either.

"You're not? Then how do you explain that item in this morning's paper?"

"Oh, Mister Eliot! That was different? Mister Hammond was an employee. A traitorous employee? He had to be taught a lesson, don't you agree? As for you, all we want is the map. If you have it?" I looked at Sindi again. She shook her head.

"I don't have it," into the phone. "Do you have it," aside to Sindi.

"No," loudly enough for Llowlolski to hear.

"It seems you blew it," I said. "Hammond had the map, and now he's in no position to tell you where it is."

"I'm sorry, Mister Eliot, that won't work. Mister Hammond was asked about it very persuasively? He denied having the map. He insisted Miss DiWagne has it?"

"How do you know he wasn't lying?"

"Mister Moose can be very persuasive. Anyway, we checked his home? It wasn't there."

I let out a quick bark of a laugh. "He didn't live with his wife, you dummy."

"Oh, we know that, Mister Eliot. But we took the precaution of checking his wife's house as well?"

There was a sudden, indistinct noise on the phone and a different voice spoke. "Hambletonian, I told you not to intrude on me. I want that map and I want it now. You will suffer most severe consequences if you don't give it to me *post haste*. Hammond's bimbo will suffer even more dire consequences. I may even let you watch what happens to her before turning you over to the boys."

I didn't look at Sindi, my peripheral vision was enough to let me know she paled and put a hand to her throat. I wondered if she knew this was Mister Big. It wouldn't have surprised me if she knew exactly who he was.

"Do you think you can do that?" I asked. Silly me, but I had to say something.

"You bet your sweet bippy, Hambiltonian You remember that expression, don't you?"

Now I looked at Sindi. It was her turn. She looked away.

"Is she listening, Hambiltonian? Can she hear me?"

"Yes."

"Good. This is for you, Miss DiWagne. Kallir fancies himself a bon vivant. But he expects a woman to do exactly what he says, and exactly when he says it. He can be very persuasive about his demands. Do you get my meaning? Hondo is more basic. He likes to pinch things. Making red spots excites him. Raising welts sends him into ecstasy. Moose is simply a slob. Working girls demand extra pay from him. Paul is of a different bent. He approaches from behind.

"I will merely watch them and make the occasional observation on technique. When they are through I will be left with the untidy job of cleaning up the mess they have made. But you won't have to worry about how I clean it up, Miss DiWagne. Indeed, you will be grateful for anything I do to end it. Do you understand me?"

Silence.

"That is a question. I do expect to hear your voice now."

Sindi was shaking violently. Her voice quaked over the one word she said: "Yes." I put my arm around her to hold her up.

"Good. Now, you may have in mind making a break for it at this time. Please feel free to do so. It could save me some trouble. Your building is being watched. You will be followed and, at an appropriate time and place, you will be stopped and the map will be taken from you. If you do not have it on your person, you will tell me where it is. Have no doubt about that. Of course, you could save yourselves a great deal of unpleasantness by the simple expedient of giving me the map now. Which will it be?"

"Hold on a minute," I told Mister Big. Sindi's shaking was more violent and she was making gagging noises. I half led, half carried her to a chair and sat her down.

"Bend over, breathe deeply," I told her and put a hand on her back to help.

She did as I said and after several breaths her shaking quelled. "Give him the map," she finally said.

"I don't have it."

"I'll get it for you. Tell him."

I left her and returned to the phone. "You scared her enough," I said. "She agreed to give you the map."

"Wonderful, Hambiltonian I'll have someone come up and get it."

"No. Not here. Someplace in the open."

"Ah, Hambiltonian, you are so untrusting." He laughed. "As I would be were our positions reversed. I thought you had a wit or two about you. Very well, then. Do you know the Wissahickon commuter station? It's on the Manayunk line."

"I know where it's at."

"Fine. Paul will meet you there in twenty-five minutes. You give him the map and you can go about your business as if none of this ever happened."

"Twenty-five minutes? He can't get there from his place that fast."

"How fast Paul gets there is none of your concern, Hambiltonian Your only concern is getting yourself there in the allotted time-with the map."

"I'll be there." I didn't ask if he was going to have whoever was outside follow me. Or what that person was going to do if he didn't follow me. Nor did I ask if there were enough watchers to follow me and keep an eye on things here. Even if I wanted to ask any further questions I couldn't have. He hung up as soon as I agreed to meet Llowlolski.

I turned to the chair I'd left Sindi in. She wasn't there. Noise in the bedroom told me where she was. I went to her.

"Here it is," Sindi said, crawling out from under the bed. "I hid it in the springs when you were asleep last night."

While I was knocked out, you mean. I thought it, but didn't say it out loud.

"See?" She opened the map and held it for me to look at, then refolded it and put it in a greeting card envelope and sealed it. She didn't give it to me right away. Instead she went into the kitchen and got a brown, clasp envelope from a cabinet drawer. She had her back to me as he put the greeting card envelope into the bigger one. She had the clasp wings up and was licking the flap when she turned to face me.

"Not that I don't trust you, dear," I said, and took the envelope from her. I looked into it to make sure the right envelope was in it. It was, so I handed it back and she finished sealing it.

"Do you have a car?" I asked. If I had to go home to get mine, I might not be able to make the rendezvous in time. I could take the train, but only if one was running at the right time. That wasn't a chance I was willing to take. And I didn't care to go by cab.

"Yes." She got her purse and led me out.

A block away was an old factory that had been converted into luxury apartments. Part of it had been converted to a parking garage. That's where Sindi kept her car. Along the way she looked at me curiously and asked;

"Hambiltonian?"

I shook my head and simply said, "Bad joke."

She took me to her car and gave me the keys along with the envelope with the map. Her car was a year-old Subaru. It didn't surprise me that she had a foreign car. I also understood why she'd never let on to me before that she had a car. The idea of a secretary living in Center City, putting herself through grad school, and driving an expensive car would have been entirely too much to swallow. Even for the easily manipulated dummy she thought I was.

"Take me home, please," she said when we got in.

Okay. She might only be in the way if she went with me. Or Kallir and company might be there with Llowlolski and decide to show me what their Mister Big described about their sexual habits. Better to keep that temptation away from them. I waited at the curb until I saw the elevator close on Sindi, then headed out.

CHAPTER FIFTEEN

Fairmount Park sprawls up both sides of the Schuylkill River from Eakins Oval, in front of the Art Museum, some three and a half miles to the Falls River Bridge. Three and a half miles in a straight line, but closer to five as Kelly Drive winds its way along the river. From the bridge, a small peninsula of the park continues along the east side of the river for another quarter mile to the mouth of Wissahickon Creek. There, the park continues up the creek valley, and is renamed Wissahickon Park. Kelly Drive bends away from the river just as it reaches the creek and ends where it runs into Ridge Avenue. Left onto Ridge a few hundred yards and on the right is the Wissahickon station of the Manayunk commuter train line.

I drove past the station to where Ridge Avenue turns right over the bridge over the tracks and begins its climb onto the ridge that gives it its name. The station entrance is immediately beyond the bridge. I drove in and parked. Only one other car was there. A metallic blue Mitsubishi. Hondo was behind the wheel.

I might have known. Fifty years ago, Zeros and Bettys made by Mitsubishi were killing Americans in the South Pacific. Hondo and his boss want to kill me today. That means the bad guys are still driving Mitsubishis. It follows, if you believe in that sort of thing.

I set the emergency break and put Sindi's car in neutral, but didn't turn off the ignition. I walked over to the Mitsubishi.

Hondo grinned when he saw my face. He didn't say anything, though. Instead, he pointed toward the station.

Wissahickon station is Victorian in design, as are many of the commuter train stations in and around Philadelphia. It is surrounded by a wrought iron fence, and a similar fence keeps commuters from running across the tracks beyond the ends of the platform. There's a ginger-bready station house that's been closed for years. The station doesn't get much use except during rush hour. The traffic rushing past on Ridge couldn't see much of what was happening in the station. It's a great place for an out-in-the-open ambush. The tunnel under the tracks that gives access between the inbound and outbound sides of the right of way is an even better ambush site.

"Mister Eliot, I'm down here?" Llowlolski's voice came to me from the tunnel.

I looked around and didn't see anyone at the station except Hondo, who didn't look like he wanted to get out of the car.

I went down the steps into the tunnel. In the dim light from the small bulbs that illuminated it I saw Llowlolski. Kallir stood off to the side behind him. I wondered where Moose was.

"Somebody beat you up?" Llowlolski said when he saw me, I couldn't tell if it was actually a question or merely his normal way of talking.

"You should see the other guy," I said.

"I did?"

Kallir snickered.

"Do you have the map?" Everything Llowlolski said was still a question, but I couldn't help noticing he wasn't jittering now.

"Yeah. Here, catch." I frizbied the envelope at him.

It sailed straight. He was clumsy about it, but still caught the envelope.

"Okay," I said, "you've got the map everybody's been so hot for. You can tell your employer I'm out of this now and he can forget about me just like I'm going to forget about him."

As I turned to leave he said, "Not so fast, Mister Eliot? I have to make sure I've got the right goods."

I stopped. I had to, Moose was blocking my end of the tunnel. He grinned at me. I turned back to Llowlolski, but not all the way. I wanted to be able to see what Moose was doing.

"All right, I'll wait while you open the envelope. Then I'm out of here."

"Oh, I'm sure." He tapped the envelope to get its contents to one end, then tore off the other end. He dropped the brown envelope and hefted the greeting card envelope. He worked a thumbnail under the flap of the smaller envelope and ripped it open.

"Oh my. What are you trying to pull, Mister Eliot?"

"What do you mean? I'm not pulling anything. You've got the map. I'm going."

Before I could even go one step he said, "Stop him, Moose."

I stopped and held up a hand to Moose. "Wait a minute, that's not the deal."

"Neither is this."

I looked at Llowlolski. He pulled folded newspaper from the inner envelope.

Somehow, Sindi had managed to pull a switch on me while I was watching her.

"Oh shit," I said.

"Hurt him, Moose." All of a sudden, Llowlolski wasn't talking in questions; his voice sounded almost commanding.

Moose yucked and rambled toward me.

"Hold it right there, Moose," I said at the same time I reached into my hip pocket and pulled out the .32. The wallet-holster came with it.

Moose looked at it curiously. "You wanna give me your money?"

I jerked off the holster so he could see the pistol.

He laughed. "You wanna shoot a Moose with that little thing?"

"I don't want to shoot you, Moose." I was edging back.

"Kallir," Llowlolski said.

But he was too late, I'd gotten close enough to Llowlolski to make my move. I spun around and grabbed him. I jammed the muzzle of the .32 under his jaw. He was so soft my knuckles poked into his flesh. "Call them off, Paul."

Llowlolski arched his back as though moving his body from mine could remove the threat to his head. His eyes went wide and his mouth fixed itself in a rictus.

I poked him with the muzzle. "Tell them."

"D-do what he says?" he said. He was talking in questions again.

"That's a good boy, Paul." To the others I said, "Kallir, stand right where you are. Moose, back out."

Kallir glared at me. Moose took a tentative step forward.

I twisted the pistol and my knuckles deeper into Llowlolski's jaw. "Tell him to back up."

"M-Moose, go back?" His voice squeaked.

Moose hesitated, looked at Kallir.

"Moose, if you don't go up the stairs I'm going to kill Paul. Then I'll shoot you. This may be a little gun, but it will hurt you. I promise."

"Do it?" Llowlolski croaked.

"Back up, Moose," Kallir said.

"But..."

"Do what he says. We can get him later." Kallir was taking charge of the situation.

"But I can take him."

"Mister Big will get very upset if his pet accountant gets killed. You don't want Mister Big to be upset with you, do you?"

Moose bent his head and twisted it side to side. He scuffed his feet on the tunnel floor. "No-o-o-o."

"Then go out of the tunnel. Let Eliot pass. When he lets Paul go, then we get him." Like I observed early on, Kallir is an intelligent, perceptive human being. All I had to do now was watch out for the mean streak.

Moose shambled back and slowly climbed the stairs. I followed with Llowlolski. Kallir stayed put.

I looked toward the Mitsubishi when we got outside. Hondo started at the sight of us and opened the door to get out.

"Stay right there," I ordered. "Don't get out of the car, and don't try anything cute." I poked Llowlolski again. "Tell him."

"Stay there?"

Hondo sat back.

"Put your hands on top of the steering wheel where I can see them."

Hondo put his hands on the wheel.

I hauled Llowlolski to Sindi's Subaru and opened the passenger door. I backed in and pulled Llowlolski in. It was a clumsy maneuver, but I managed to climb over the center console into the driver's seat without letting go. "Buckle up," I ordered.

Llowlolski did.

I released the brake, transferred the pistol to my left hand, put the car in gear, and got out of there.

"Wh-where are you taking me?"

"I told your boss I was going to give you the map. We're going to get it."

That was all of our conversation until I pulled into an illegal parking space near Sindi's building.

*

Do I need to say she wasn't there?

The doorman stopped us. He recognized me and didn't have to ask who I

94

was there to see. I hoped he wouldn't also look down and recognize the lump in my right front pocket; I must have dropped the holster in the tunnel when I grabbed Llowlolski.

"Miss DiWagne has gone out, Sir," he said.

"Where did she go?"

"I'm sorry, she didn't say."

I didn't ask him to call upstairs, I believed him. There was a slim, very slim chance that she didn't have the map with her, so I asked if I could go to her apartment and wait for her.

He said no.

I pleaded and wheedled, stopped just short of outright begging.

"If you have a key to her apartment, I guess it would be all right, sir."

"I don't have it with me." What's a little lie when my life's at stake?

"If you can't get into her apartment, sir, I can't let you into the building."

I knew when I was beaten. It wouldn't have been so bad, though, if the doorman hadn't been supercilious about it.

I thanked the doorman for his trouble and gave Llowlolski a little push in the direction of the car. A uniformed employee of the Philadelphia Parking Authority was standing in back of it writing out a ticket. I stopped Llowlolski and waited until she was finished. Hey, it wasn't my car. Besides, after this stunt, I figured Sindi was due some aggravation of her own. And the lump the pistol made in my pocket seemed huge, I was convinced anyone could see it and call a cop.

When the coast was clear we got into the car. I sat looking nowhere out the windshield, hands on the wheel, engine idling.

"Now what are you going to do?" Llowlolski asked when enough time had gone by. He sounded like he was getting his courage back.

"Now I try to stay out of a world of hurt." I looked at him and patted my pocket over the pistol. "You better root for me. If I'm in a world of hurt, so are you. If they try for me, I'm taking you out first."

Llowlolski looked like he lost his courage again. He didn't realize all he had to do was open the door and walk away. Only a total fool would shoot him there on the street. Even if I was a total fool, all he had to do was run. By the time I got out of the car and got the pistol out of my pocket he would be out of range and far enough away I'd be better off trying to catch him another time.

"Who was watching the building to see if I'd do what your boss said?"

"Hondo?"

"But he was at the station when I got there."

"As soon as he saw you drop the woman off at her apartment he went to the station? He was sure that's where you were going."

I started the car and drove off.

*

I had a prisoner. Okay, he was a hostage. What could I do with him? It wasn't like I could take him home and lock him in a closet. Someone might be watching my place, so I couldn't go there with or without him. I didn't think he'd be much good as a shield. If nothing else, maybe I could get some information from him. I drove in circles until I found a legal parking space near the Cornish Hen and took him in for a cup of coffee.

"Pay the man," I said when we got our cups.

Llowlolski looked resentful. After all, the coffee shop was my idea, not his. But he paid anyway.

There was someone new behind the counter. He looked openly at my face and batted his eyelashes. He smiled. Probably thought I was rough trade. I ignored him.

We sat at the same tiny table I shared with Sindi just a couple of hours ago. I was in the corner so I could see both entrances and sat Llowlolski with his back to them. If there were going to be any surprises, let them surprise him.

"So there was nobody left watching the building to see where she went?"

"No?"

"Do you have any ideas where she might have gone?"

"No?"

"You're a lot of help, aren't you?"

"I only know what my employer wants me to know? He doesn't want me to know very much about this business."

"But he lets you be his messenger and errand boy?"

He shrugged. "Maybe he finds me more trustworthy than some of his other employees?"

I studied him for a moment. "Yeah, I can see that. You're not the type that would come up with a scheme to steal the map from under him, like Hammond did."

He blinked. "I beg your pardon?"

"You know, the map this is all about. Sin... Miss DiWagne told me how Hammond came to her and got her to help him steal the map. If he had been more trustworthy, like you, he wouldn't have done that."

Llowlolski laughed. "Oh dear, the little twat certainly has misled you, hasn't she?"

If it was Clyde calling Sindi a little twat, I would have grinned sheepishly and gone, ah shucks, a-yup. Hearing it from Llowlolski, I wanted to bash his face in. He lucked out, we were in a public place and I didn't want to attract too much attention. Instead of bashing his face in, I grabbed his conservative, accountant's necktie, and yanked him close to me so hard he jarred the table and slopped coffee from our cups.

"Watch your mouth, Paul. There are names people can call you, but I'm restraining myself." I let go and he flopped back heavily into his chair.

The eyelashes at the counter took a tentative step in our direction and I glared him back. He assayed a sweet smile at me and swallowed nervously when I didn't return it. I kept glaring at him until he stopped looking at us.

"What do you mean she misled me?"

"Mister Hammond was most anxious for my employer to acquire the map. You see, he was the one who first learned of it. He knew he wouldn't be able to locate the treasure and sell it himself. My employer was very happy with Mister Hammond for this intelligence and promised him a twenty percent share when it was found."

Why did I feel there was something somehow ominous about him not talking in questions? "So Hammond came up with a way to get fifty percent."

"Mister Hammond was a very tough man, but a man of somewhat limited intellectual capacity. In two or three more years, Mister Kallir would have been his superior. But that would have been all right, because Mister Hammond was intensely loyal. And our mutual employer treated Mister Hammond very well, rewarded him for his loyalty."

"If he was so loyal, what happened?"

"We knew Mister Hammond had a girlfriend. We even suspected she was instrumental in him leaving his wife. The girlfriend, Miss DiWagne, was investigated and found not to be trustworthy. I don't know the details, but I think there was something a couple of years ago about her threatening to turn state's evidence." That could explain why no charges were brought against her. "My employer was about to tell Mister Hammond to stop seeing her when he disappeared. The next thing we knew, he was involved in the theft of the map from its rightful owner."

"And you think it was Sindi's idea."

"Oh yes, we know it was. Mister Hammond said so under circumstances where we couldn't help but believe him."

And was killed in the process. Llowlolski's story was believable, but I wasn't sure I could believe it any more than I believed the stories Sindi told me. There was so much double-dealing and double crossing going on I didn't know who to believe. Dammit, I wished people would stop telling me things that sounded like the truth. It made me feel more of a fool than I already did.

"So who's this employer of yours, the one Kallir calls 'Mister Big'?"

He shook his head. "There are many things I can tell you, Mr. Eliot. However, that is something I am not at liberty to divulge."

"Come on, Paul. At least give me a hint. He's obviously a businessman. What kind of business is he in?"

Llowlolski smirked. "He is in the business of making money." His smirk went away. "However, as so many businessmen did during the past decade, he made a few mistakes. Mistakes that cost him dearly. It became necessary for him to make an alliance with some rather unsavory people." He leaned into the table and lowered his voice so that I had to lean into the table as well to hear him. "He began trafficking in drugs in order to recoup his losses." He looked very earnest when he concluded, "So you see, there are very good reasons why I am not at liberty to divulge his identity. Should you live to go to the police, there could be very serious repercussions."

I believed the "should you live" business. Drugs. Damn. "Uh, who are his unsavory associates?"

He shook his head. "Some sort of South Americans, I don't know exactly who they are. Now he is in debt to them. They want him to succeed in securing the treasure so he can pay them. They will be very displeased with anyone who stands in his way."

Oh no. It's a tossup who's worse, the Colombians or the Jamaicans. How I felt must have shown on my face because Llowlolski laughed.

"Don't worry, Mr Eliot," he said. "They aren't Colombians." There was a nasty edge to his smile. "They won't kill your family."

My reaction to that also must have shown, because he gave a little chuckle and said, "Mr Eliot, I find you a frightening man. I think very few men could have been as cool as you were in that tunnel and gotten away unharmed like you did. It is refreshing to be able to frighten you."

"I don't know about refreshing, but you scared me all right."

He laughed again, but it sounded introspective. "Mr. Eliot, I don't think my employer's unsavory associates care about you one way or the other. All they care about is getting their money from him. If he can't pay, he is the one in trouble with them, not you."

Maybe I showed some relief.

"However, if you keep my employer from the map, you are in serious trouble with him."

"I want to talk to him. Let's go."

*

The price of a call on a pay phone has gone up a hundred and fifty percent in the past decade-far more than can be justified by inflation. It must be the improvements in service that you get, right? Well, what you get is a phone with no phone books, sheltered by a little shell that protects the phone from the weather in all directions but the business end. You don't get a cozy little booth with a door you can shut for privacy, to keep the rain off, and cut down on traffic noises. When I use a pay phone these days it somehow seems that I'm paying a lot more for a lot less.

One other thing you don't get today is, it's a lot harder to see what someone's dialing on a touch tone than with a rotary dial. I watched Llowlolski finger the keypad anyway, and memorized what I thought he dialed.

He identified himself, said he wanted to speak to the boss, and waited patiently. Then he flinched and started talking in questions again. He was with me? he was at a pay phone? he started to say where? and stopped when I jabbed him in the ribs. He said I wanted to talk, and handed me the receiver.

"Hambiltonian," Mister Big said. "I thought you were going to give Paul the map."

"I thought so too. It seems someone pulled a switch on me. She seems to be good at that. She did a switch on you at Freeman's. Now she did it to me with me watching her."

"You don't have the wit I thought you had, Hambiltonian Though that was clever of you, the way you got away from the station."

"Look, Mister," I wasn't about to call him Mister Big to his face, "I don't have your damn map. If I did I'd give it to Paul right now, no questions asked. You're the one who had the building watched, you're the one who let her get away. Listen, I didn't ask for any of this. I never liked it from the beginning. I'm out of it. You don't fuck with me, I don't fuck with you. Okay?"

"No, that's not okay. You have intruded on me and you have obstructed me in obtaining what is mine. You are not out of this."

"Tell you what. Give me your name and a number where I can reach you. If I see the broad, I'll give you a call and let you know where she is. How's that sound?"

"That sounds no good, Hambiltonian You disappoint me. The next time I, or any of my people, see you, you will immediately hand over the map. If you don't, you will be killed on the spot. Now send Paul home, he doesn't do you any good as a hostage." He hung up.

I stood there for a moment before gently cradling the receiver. "Take a hike," I told Llowlolski. "Your master wants you."

Llowlolski looked at me like he suspected some sort of trick. He backed away a few steps, his eyes flickering between my face and the pocket holding my pistol, then he spun and ran, waving and calling for a cab he saw coming his way.

And I was left all alone.

CHAPTER SIXTEEN

Okay, bright-eyes, what do you do next? The streets were filling up with office workers buzzing from the hives they toiled in. Probably most of the ones buzzing past me were buzzing their way to other hives that they lived in. I looked at them and considered the implications of hive-life. Maybe one of these days I'll write an article for *Psychology Today* on the effect on the psyche of both living and working in tall buildings. But not now. At the moment, I didn't feel like dwelling on the implications of hive-dweller. At the moment, what I felt was lonely. I also felt hungry. I'd carelessly left my lunch uneaten in the Cornish Hen when I dragged Sindi out to pack a bag. I'll bet she finished packing that bag after I left. Probably by now she was on a big silver bird, making her way to Georgia to dig up Blackbeard's treasure to keep all to herself. And maybe not.

It wasn't much of a chance, but I gave it the old college try anyway. I turned back to the phone and dropped a quarter in the slot. Directory assistance gave me the number of the insurance company Sindi worked for. Another quarter in the slot and a very professional sounding woman transferred me to another professional sounding woman who said Miss DiWagne is out of the office, no I can't tell you where she is.

I didn't leave a message.

I was a couple of blocks from an unpretentious eatery that I like, so I went there to have an early dinner. I bought a copy of the *Daily News to* see if it had any more information about Hammond's murder. It had even less than that morning's *Inquirer.* I ate in a corner where I could see out the windows and watch the door. Nobody I recognized walked past or came in.

I would have dallied longer over my after dinner coffee, but the serious dinner crowd started coming in about half past six and by seven they needed my table, so I paid my check and left. But now where to? I had to assume my apartment was being watched, so going home didn't sound safe. I checked the time and decided it was late enough Clyde might be at work. Even if the Side Car Club was being watched, at least there I wouldn't be alone. On the street I looked around, didn't see any familiar faces, and caught a cab. I had the cabbie drop me off on the Drexel University campus, which abuts the Penn campus at its northeast corner.

Even if the Side Car was being watched, I thought I could get in without being seen. There's a small parking lot in back, it's used by the staff and musicians. There's no indication from the front that it's there; the lot's entrance is nearly a block away, through an alley off Arch Street. I zigged and zagged a bit on foot, keeping an eye out for followers who didn't seem to be there, then went in that back way. I didn't see any loiterers in the alley either.

I didn't expect the back door to be locked. It usually isn't, because the bouncers, musicians, bartenders, and dancing-girls often take their breaks out back. A young dolly with long, straight hair right out of the Sixties, and wrapped in a pink robe I'd seen often enough on one or another stage inside, was dragging on a cigarette and chatting with a guy I didn't recognize, but who didn't look big enough to be a bouncer. I guessed he was a new bartender.

"Hi, Ham," the dolly said. "This is Charlie. He's a new bartender. Charlie just started today." She didn't express any surprise at seeing me come in the back way instead of the front.

"Hi, Eve. Hi, Charlie," I said, and offered my hand to the new guy.

"Ham's a regular," Eve said. "And he's a friend of Clyde's. So be nice to him."

I gave Eve a warm smile. "Is Clyde in now?"

"Yeah. I think he's in his office."

Charlie looked at my eye but didn't ask about it. Eve ignored it. She's a cute little dolly, but I think she's tough as nails. She probably never pays attention to fight injuries on men.

I went in and Eve returned to chatting up Charlie. He probably thought he was in for a good time later that night. But Eve chats up everybody in the Side Car without ever, so far as I know, even acknowledging their existence once she hits the street at the end of her shift.

The crowd was decent for the hour. A lot of the customers were in suits and ties, still dressed from the office. Most of the stools around the big circular bar across the dance floor from the now-empty main stage were occupied. Several men stood in small clumps of three or four; but they stood because they wanted to, not because there were no seats available. On those Fridays and Saturdays that are dancing-girl nights, that bar can get stacked three and four deep with customers. Two nearly naked girls danced on the small stage in the middle of the bar. Three more shimmied and gyrated their way around its inside perimeter, soliciting tips.

Jimmy was behind the small side bar, waiting for an order from one of the four men at it. Sheela bopped and ground on the stage behind the bar. She saw me and blew a kiss my way. Toni leaned on the bar in deep, giggling conversation with two of the customers.

I waved at Jimmy, he grinned widely and waved back. I headed down the short corridor that led to the men's room and went past it to the door marked "No Admittance Without Authorization." Inside was the dancing-girls' dressing room. A privacy wall just beyond the door prevented anyone outside from spying on the girls as they changed between street clothes and costumes. Also inside that door was Clyde's office. The office door was ajar. I poked my head in and rapped on the door frame. Clyde was hunched over a computer, intent on a spreadsheet. He waved me in without looking to see who was there. No lights were on in the office; a window onto the street provided all the illumination it needed. At dusk, Clyde would draw the blinds. He sometimes jokes that the window's on the wrong wall: it should look into the dressing room because that's where all the action is. I know he's joking when he says that because he's scrupulous about observing the privacy of the dressing room when he goes between his office and the club floor.

He tapped a rapid staccato of keys, gave the screen a final scrutiny, hit the save command, exited, and cut the power. Only when the computer was off did he look up to see who his visitor was.

"Well, Ham," he drawled out the words. If Jimmy had grinned widely at me, Clyde's grin was huge. "I was beginning to wonder when you'd come up for air." He seemed to notice my eye for the first time and his grin vanished. "What happened, did your friends come back that night?"

I shook my head. "No."

"So tell Uncle Clyde about it, lad." He sometimes calls himself that and me lad. Not because he's older than me, I'm few months older than him, but because he's so much bigger than I am. "Does she play that rough? And more important, did you get some?"

"No, she doesn't play rough, not that way. And, yeah, I got some. Both kinds."

He cocked a questioning eyebrow. "Meaning?"

"Meaning I got laid and I got screwed."

"The way you say that, I can tell there's a difference. Spell it out."

I told him everything that happened during the 64 or 65 hours since he and Jimmy left Sindi's apartment. Well, not everything. There are details of bedmanship a man won't tell even his best friend. I also didn't tell him how she used her body to lead me around by the nose-or some anatomical part. Too much basic masculine pride on my part, you know?

While I told my story, Clyde turned to the counter behind himself and poured two cups from a coffee maker. He didn't ask, he just gave me a cup. When I finished telling him about the weekend and since, we were ready for a refill, which he again poured without asking.

"No shit. So, when she grabbed you by the wienie, you concentrated your attention on her titties, and lost all of your good sense."

So much for my masculine pride. "Well, yeah, I guess. Something like that. Sort of." Masculine pride doesn't want to come right out and admit when it's been beaten.

Clyde leaned way back on his chair and heaved his feet onto the desk. The chair is a big, old-fashioned wooden swiveler. Clyde says the big old wooden chairs are the only ones strong enough to support his bulk. The chair didn't seem to agree, it squealed a protest.

"Let us analyze this thing," Clyde said. "First off, I wish I knew who your 'Mister Big' is. But at least we know what kind of businessman he is, that may narrow down the search for his identity."

"Search for his identity?" I repeated. "How can we do that?"

He glanced at me over steepled fingers. "How old did you say this guy is?" He'd get around to answering my question in his own good time.

"Late forties, maybe fifty."

"Okay, that kills my first guess, but all I have to do is shift it a bit and it still works."

I waited, knowing he'd explain himself. He did.

"Something bad happened to business in this country during the Eighties. The means to management became advanced degrees rather than experience. The ends of management became quick, high profits. The bigger and faster the profits, the better. Back in prehistoric times-that's when you and I were schoolboys-we learned in history class about the robber barons of the Nineteenth Century. They raped the land, abused their employees, fought their competition in ways that look like warfare. They lied, they cheated, and they stole. And they amassed fortunes that would have been the envy of any Oriental potentate.

"In other words, they were rapacious and greedy, they were unscrupulous in attaining what they wanted. They weren't nice people.

"But, and this is a very big but, in the process, they built things. They built mining, the steel industry, the petroleum industry, railroads, shipyards, international shipping, banking. They built the infrastructure that allowed Teddy Roosevelt to build the Great White Fleet for the navy and send it on a round-the-world cruise to announce to the known universe that the United States had arrived as a power to be reckoned with. They built the base on which the United States built itself into the richest, most powerful nation on earth."

He shifted into a more comfortable position and continued. "Their descendants a century later forgot how the robber barons made their wealth. They didn't want to build things because building things takes too long. They became impatient to make their own fortunes. The MBA degree became the route to captain of industry. They got advanced degrees in finance and banking. They bought companies in order to sell off the companies' assets rather than to make a better widget. They shuffled paper around on the stock market. When they built something, it wasn't new factories or new mercantile outlets, they built luxury hotels and resorts that were beyond the means of most people to stay at, and too often in locations where the people who could afford them didn't want to go. They built luxury office buildings that turned out to have too much space at too high rentals to get filled up. They thought the luxury places would work and reap vast profits on short order. Turned out they were wrong and many of them went bust."

He paused and gave me a professorial look. "Sounds like education is bad for the country, doesn't it?"

"Keep going," I said. Clyde's no dummy. While playing major league college football, he actually got a degree-in biology. When his college ball days were over, he could have gone pro, but he was a late-round draft choice. In those days, late-round offensive linemen got paid so little many of them had to hold off-season jobs. Instead, Clyde came east and got a second bachelors degree, in anthropology this time, from Penn. He worked his way through that second degree by tending bar. He stuck with bartending afterward and worked his way up. Next, he wants to open his own place, but hasn't yet decided whether he wants a music place or a dancing-girl one.

"When I was at Penn," Clyde went on, "I knew a young man, I forget his name, who was working on a Wharton MBA. I was in school for knowledge, I enjoyed learning. Business seemed to me to be an awfully dull subject to study. One day I asked this fellow why he was going for an MBA. He looked off somewhere and thought about it for a few seconds. Then he said, 'To make money.' Damn, that sounded to me like a really dumb reason to pick a topic to study." He shook his head and dropped his feet off the desk to lean forward on his elbows.

"But that's the result of the materialism of the Fifties. You remember; a

David Sherman

house in the suburbs, a two-car garage, a 21-inch TV, a swimming pool in the backyard, annual vacations in Disneyland or Yellowstone. The whole Ozzie and Harriet business. And everybody expected their kids to do better than they did. The World War II generation sent their kids-that's us-to college. The generation between us and our kids went to grad school.

"But somewhere the message that captains of industry have to make things got lost. Making money not only became the object of the game, it became the entire game.

"Remember the Tee shirt that said, 'He who dies with the most toys wins'? How about the people who say, 'Money is only a way of keeping score.' That's a very Eighties attitude. Nobody before the Nineteen-eighties would have said that.

"These people didn't make things. They moved paper around, they bought and sold production facilities to make a quick buck. If the production facility happened to have to quit producing because its assets got sold off and hundreds or even thousands of working stiffs lost their jobs, tough. If they were in banking, they made loans that promised big returns fast, not long-term loans for primary manufacturing or reasonable housing."

"That's all very interesting, Clyde," I said when he'd run on for longer than I wanted to listen to an economics lecture, "but what does it have to do with finding Mister Big?"

"Well, that's simple." He didn't say the word, but I heard it anyway; *Dummy*. "Llowlolski said your mysterious Mister Big is in the business of making money. I read that he's one of those businessmen who made a lot of money by moving paper around, by buying and selling without producing anything or adding value to what he bought and sold, and got into serious trouble because of it. All we have to do is check out the clowns who meet that description."

"Where do the drugs come in?"

He laughed loudly. "You know how lawyers tell the difference between right and wrong?"

He was obviously waiting for an answer, so I gave him one, "No."

"Whether or not they get paid." He laughed heartily. When he was through laughing he said, "Here's the corollary for business types. When the objective is to make money without making things or adding value to holdings, the difference between right and wrong becomes very fuzzy. There's very little difference, either psychologically or philosophically, between insider trading, corporate raiding, and drug dealing. The end is making a buck, with little or no concern for the means."

That was one I'd have to think over for a while before deciding whether or not I agreed. But I find Clyde right often enough, I imagined I would agree.

"Okay, now, practical matters." Clyde became business-like. "You can't go home, it's probably not safe. Stay here this evening, go home with me when I close up." Then he got back to the beginning of his economics lecture, "Tomorrow we'll find out who your Mister Big is."

I was through waiting for his explanation. "How the hell are we going to do that?"

He leaned forward, conspiratorial. "Who do you think my main customers

104

are, Penn and Drexel students? Huh! Most of them aren't old enough to come in here. Blue collar types? Be real, this location is surrounded by universities. I've got businessmen, executives, stock brokers, doctors, lawyers, professors, people like that-on the stage as well as as customers. I can ask a few people and if they don't know off the top of their heads, they can make a few inquiries. Believe me, by this time tomorrow we'll probably know who this character is. We may even know where your blonde bimbo's hiding."

Sometimes Clyde astonishes me, and I told him so. Since I didn't have a better plan-or any plan at all-I said okay.

"Now, I gotta get out on the floor, make sure everything's all hunky-dory and nobody's doing anything that'll get me closed down. You grab a stool at Jimmy's bar and have a beer. When I get a chance, I'll talk to some people."

He ushered me out of the office. There was chatter going on in the dressing room, but neither of us looked. The dancing-girls who spend their work hours on display deserve their privacy when they're off stage.

It was after nine by now. I could tell because a Dee Jay was on duty playing dance music way too loud; the dancing-girl night Dee Jay doesn't come on 'til nine. Clyde caught Jimmy's eye and made a sign to him. Jimmy signaled back "got-it." All but two of the stools at the side bar were occupied now. One of them was the end stool, the one I wanted. I slid onto it and sat so I could see the entrance and the entire room. Jimmy opened a Heineken and put it down for me. I pulled out a five, Jimmy shook it off. "On the house tonight," he said.

I nodded thanks and left the money on the bar anyway.

Shela and Toni weren't at the side bar anymore. They might have been at the big, main bar, or that could have been their voices I heard in the dressing rooms, but I hadn't looked so I didn't know. Maybe their shifts were over. I've sometimes wondered about the scheduling on dancing-girl nights. Some of the dancing-girls come in late, some leave early, some seem to be there all the time, some only show up for an hour or two. One of these days I'll have to ask Clyde about that.

Two different dancing-girls were working the side bar now. The one on the stage looked vaguely familiar. I couldn't place her, but didn't think I'd seen her here before. The way she looked at me I felt I should know her from somewhere, but couldn't conjure up where. I didn't know the name of the one shimmying for tips, though I'd seen her often enough; she's one of my favorite dancing-girls. Make that my very favorite. But the dancing-girls are pure fantasy and I know there's no chance of me leaving the Side Car with one of them, so I make a point of not remembering the names of my favorites. Fantasies must be recognized as such. Fantasies that get confused with reality, yet remain unfulfilled, can be just too damn painful. Not knowing a favorite dancing-girl's name keeps me from confusing fantasy with reality. Not remembering certain names is how I keep fantasy from hurting me. That's what I tell myself, anyway.

"Hi, Ham." She shimmied her way to me and stood there in all her glorious femaleness for my pseudo-private viewing. Her green eyes sat in an oval Mediterranean face, glossy black hair cascaded halfway down her back, satin skin, about a handful of breast on each side, tucked-in waist, broad swelling of hip, contralto voice. She could be Spanish, Italian, Greek, Semitic, or North African, with an admixture of something else. It's a physical type that turns my knees to jelly and my brains to mush; it raises my testosterone to Tarzan of the Jungle levels and can make me act like Sylvester Stallone. I couldn't tell for sure how old she was, but I thought somewhere over thirty. She wore a few bangles and beads, dancing slippers, tiny bikini panties, and pasties, nothing more. A marvelous fantasy for me to dream on.

But tonight all I could see was blonde, all I could hear was rusty-husky.

I gave her a wan smile. "Hi," I said back, and slipped a dollar-bill tip between her offered breasts.

"Who'd you walk into?" She looked at my injured eye.

"Shouldn't that be 'what'?" I asked.

She laughed. In a different state of mind, I'd love that laugh.

She raised her eyebrows in question, nibbled her lip, jiggled at me a couple of times, but I didn't answer her question or pay awed attention to her display. She said "See you later," and continued her rounds. When she worked her way around to me again she presented her derriere to me and wiggled it. I dutifully tipped her, but my heart wasn't in it. She leaned on the bar and asked, "Problems?"

"Yeah." I nodded.

She cocked her head. "Woman?"

I thought about it. "Partly. Partly something else."

"Do you want to talk about it?"

I shook my head.

"There may be something I could do to help you with it."

I tried to smile and speak carefully. I didn't want to offend her, didn't want to sound like I was putting her down. "Maybe another time, another problem. I don't think there's anything you can do to help me with this one."

The way she studied my face made me uncomfortable-I felt like a specimen under a microscope. I looked at the stage to escape her eyes.

"Ham," she finally said, "there are things I can do that you don't have any idea of." She patted my hand in a friendly way. "Another time, another problem. But only if you promise."

I tried to smile again. "Thanks."

She left me alone after that, and I felt strangely empty because of it. I wondered what I might have missed in what she said. Then I reminded myself the dancing-girls are fantasy and put her out of my mind. She must have said something to the other girls, because they all left me alone for the rest of the night. Except for one little thing.

About ten o'clock these two dancing-girls left the side bar and two others took their place. A few minutes later this favorite of mine appeared at my side, close enough to make a slight contact between our bodies. She wore a short, nearly transparent shift over her bikini bottoms and pasties.

"I don't think this is the right color match," she handed me a tiny, flat, plastic container, "but use it anyway. Put it on your eye, it'll mask the color." Her fingertips lightly touched the puffy flesh around my eye, then she left to do her dancing-girl thing at the main bar.

I looked after her wistfully; another time, another problem. I remembered blonde and rusty-husky. I thought about fantasy and its meaning to the human psyche. I sighed. The little voice inside me said go ahead and cry. I told it to shut up and go away, big boys don't cry.

Eventually, I had to make a pit-stop. In the men's room I ignored the glances of the other customers and the curious observation of the attendant while I applied the makeup to my eye. The dancing-girl was right; it wasn't a good color match, but it did mask the bruising. It would pass in dim light.

Each time I finished a beer, Jimmy put another one down for me and never took any money, even though I put more on the bar each time. I drank slowly, but drank for enough hours to get a buzz. When I was near to being in my cups I thought back to what Clyde said about "on the stage as well as as customers," and wondered what he meant. Was it possible that...? No, it couldn't be. The dancing-girls were fantasy, no more than that. Weren't they?

Last call sounded at a quarter of two. On the stroke of two, the remaining dancing-girls dashed for the sanctuary of the dressing room and Clyde and his bouncers cleared out all the remaining customers but me.

Clyde supervised a cleanup for ten or fifteen minutes, then collected me. We went out back and got into his pride and joy, a black '57 Thunderbird. In less than fifteen minutes more we were in his Olde City condo.

He looked at my glazing eyes and said, "Ham, I'm going to have a nightcap. I don't think you need one."

"Yer right, Clyde. You usually are."

"You know where the guest room is. Find your way there. There's clean sheets on the bed."

I found the guest room on the first try. I stripped down to skin and climbed into bed. During those silent, idle moments between head hitting the pillow and landing in Nod, I thought it was a long time since I last slept in my own bed, a long time since I last had clean underwear and socks to put on when I got up.

CHAPTER SEVENTEEN

The smell of fresh-brewed coffee woke me.

"Rise and shine, sleepy head," Clyde's voice boomed at me.

I groaned at the noise, opened my eyes, blinked at the light, buried my face in the pillow. I felt ill. My head hurt-oddly enough, none of my injuries from the fight with Hammond did. How much did I drink last night?

"Up and at 'em, Ham. Your coffee's getting cold."

I groaned again. I didn't feel like having a cup of coffee. I wanted about ten more hours of sleep. But I didn't remember drinking enough to be hungover.

"Come on, lad. I had Jimmy keep track of what you were costing me last night. You didn't drink all that much."

He was right. I may have had more to drink than I wanted to, but not enough to account for how badly I felt. It must be emotional letdown that made me feel lousy. This had been a roller coaster few days. I groaned a third time as I sat up and held my head. A mug of steaming coffee sat on the night table. I took a sip. It wasn't too hot, so I drank a little more. It didn't make me feel any more human.

I looked at Clyde. He was sitting on a chair looking at me. "What time is it?" I asked.

"Going on eleven."

I reached for my watch; it said ten of. "Geeze, I must be wiped out. More than eight hours. I hardly ever sleep that long. You got any aspirin?"

"I'm not surprised-that you need sleep or that you have a headache. You've been through a lot of turn-arounds the past few days. You probably couldn't hear your own voice, but you sounded pretty depressed last night. Depression can make you sleep longer. It's a basic survival mechanism. When things get too bad, the subconscious thinks the bad things might go away by themselves if you sleep long enough. What you might call a basic ostrich reaction. Depression can also give you a headache." As he talked, he opened the drawer of the nightstand and got a couple of aspirin out of a bottle for me.

I downed the aspirin with some more coffee. After a few minutes I started feeling better; partly because of the aspirin, partly because Clyde tends to talk sense and good sense helps. I finished the coffee and held out the mug. "More."

"Good lad. I'll get you more while you hit the bathroom. I already put your clean clothes in there."

"What clean clothes?"

"I've got a washer and dryer, remember?" I did a load of wash while I had my nightcap and put it in the dryer right before I sacked out. It was ready when I got up this morning." He smiled crookedly. "I don't know about you, but I hate not having clean underwear and socks when I get up. I also laid out a fresh towel and washcloth for you."

"Thanks, Clyde." Good friends are thoughtful that way. In the bathroom, I discovered that Clyde had even put out a new toothbrush. When I got out of the shower I found a second mug of coffee waiting on the sink. The second mug was empty by the time I was through in the bath. I even reapplied the makeup to my eye. Now instead of a dark, swollen shiner, I had puffiness and a slight discoloration. The cut on the bridge of my nose didn't look too bad today.

The kitchen was right where I remembered it. I poured myself another coffee and joined Clyde at the dining table. He looked up from the papers he was doodling on.

"Cereal's in the cupboard above the left counter. Bacon and eggs in the refrigerator. What do you want from me? I'm not going to do everything for you." He mock-glowered. "Anyway, I'll bet I've already done more for you than your blonde bimbo did. Except pounding the sheets, that is."

I laughed, I was definitely feeling better. "You have, old buddy. Sindi didn't do my laundry." Or put out a new toothbrush.

"Now get yourself some breakfast and sit down here, I've got some information for you. By the way, that's a great improvement on your face."

I almost jumped. "What information?"

"Get food. Then I'll tell you."

I shook my head. "It's too early. I have to be up for a while before I get hungry."

"Suit yourself. I've got three names here. It's not an exhaustive list, but there's an excellent chance that one of these is your Mister Big." He picked up the papers he'd been doodling on and referred to them as he talked. "J. Michael Horton did some fancy juggling with junk bonds, among other things. He likes to live high and has been hurting pretty badly since the junk bond market went bust. Recently, he's seemed to be solvent again, but nobody seems to know how. Arnold Lowry may be the nation's only officer of a failed S&L who didn't come out of the experience as a rich man. He also is on a financial rebound without any visible means of support. Edward Bigler," he paused over the name, "invested heavily in shopping malls in Arizona and in a Toronto holding company. All of those investments went belly up. The evidence is he's still broke, but he's been seen recently spending a lot of time being palsy-walsy with some folks neither of us would care to hang out with."

I looked gape-mouthed at him. "Where the hell did you get all that?"

"I told you I was going to ask a few people. Hell's bells, man, I had two of those names before I closed up last night."

"Clyde, I'm amazed. And you don't even look smug."

He shrugged. Just another day's work-and it wasn't even noon yet. "There's more. I'm expecting a call that may give us a line on your blonde bimbo."

"Don't tell me, I know. You asked a few people about her."

"Actually, I only asked one. She said she knew the name, and knows somebody who can probably tell her more."

I just sat there staring at him for a moment, unable to put my mind all the way around what he'd just told me. Finally, "I think I'm ready for breakfast," I said.

"I'm still not cooking for you."

Bacon and eggs weren't the only things in the refrigerator. I got out sandwich fixings and made myself a ham and cheese on rye. I was nearly through with it when a phone on a side table in easy reach from where Clyde sat rang.

"What'cha got for me," Clyde asked when the hellos had been said. He listened, made I-hear-you noises, took some notes, asked a couple of questions, finished with, "Thanks a lot, Martha. I owe you one." Pause to listen. "He's not feeling too well, but he'll get over it." Pause. "Okay. No promises, but I'll give it a shot." Goodbyes were said and he hung up.

"That was Martha, she asked after you."

I drew a blank. "Who's Martha?"

"Sorry, I should have known better. I guess you only know her stage name. She's..."

"Stop."

"Say what? All I'm doing is telling you who that was."

"You said her 'stage name.' She's one of your dancing-girls?"

"Yeah. So?"

"If she's one of the dancing-girls I don't want to know which one. You already told me her real name. I don't want to know more."

"Ham, I wouldn't have thought it of you."

"Thought what?"

He shook his head. "I wouldn't have thought you'd only see my girls as bodies. I thought you saw them as people."

"I do think of them as people." Then I realized I didn't, I see them strictly as fantasies-and there are a few whose names I deliberately don't know because those fantasies are too real. "Oh, gawd," I moaned. That was a harsh revelation.

"Talk to me, Ham."

I'm sure my face was red while I rushed through telling him how I saw the dancing-girls as fantasies, and why there were some whose names I didn't know. If I saw any of them with real names and real lives outside the Side Car, it would destroy them as fantasies for me.

He laughed. "Martha will get a kick out of that when I tell her."

"Oh shit, please don't tell her."

He laughed again. "Okay, I'll let you tell her yourself the next time you see her. She's the one with..."

"Stop. Don't tell me. I can't afford to confuse fantasy and reality. Especially not now."

He looked at me for a moment, thinking. Then he said, "All right, I won't. You're on your own."

I wanted to ask what he meant, but he went on. "What she called about was your blonde bimbo." He shook his head. "You sure know how to pick them, Ham. This Sindi DiWagne character ran quite a scam on you."

I wanted to ask how this Martha dancing-girl knew anything about a woman who was an officer of an insurance company. What I asked instead was, "What do you mean, she pulled a scam? Other than what I already know."

"Well, she's not in grad school for one."

"I suspected that."

"And that isn't her apartment she took us to."

I looked quizzical.

"She rented it, all right, but it's not where she lives. Actually, she sublet it for one month." He looked thoughtful. "Did you get the impression the place wasn't really moved into?"

"Not exactly. But I did notice she wasn't any more unpacked yesterday than when I first saw the place. I chalked that up to her not having any time, between the time she spent with me and her job."

Clyde got the phone book and thumbed through it. "You're sure of that spelling, D-i-W-a-g-n-e, and Sindi with an S?" I nodded and he said, "Unlisted."

"That's what she told me."

"Do you still have the number where she works?" he asked, and reached for the Yellow Pages.

"Better yet. I've got her extension." I fished a piece of paper from my pocket and he reached for it.

A moment later he was talking to Sindi's secretary. He used a voice I'd never heard from him before: It was very Main Line; weighted down with many generations of big money. These many generations of money needed Miss DiWagne's personal attention on a vital matter. If Miss DiWagne isn't available in the office, is there somewhere else she can be contacted? "I appreciate your kind assistance," he said at last, and hung up.

"She's flying the coop," he told me. "She's got a plane to catch. Her secretary doesn't know where she's going or how long she'll be gone, it came up rather suddenly. She's supposed to call in with an itinerary later today when she reaches her first destination."

Her first destination, that would probably be, "Atlanta," I said. "She must have taken off after the treasure while everyone else's attention was focused on me. It's buried in Georgia, so Atlanta's her logical first stop."

"Except you couldn't locate anything higher than two hundred feet within fifty miles of the Georgia coast. So where's the mariner's mountain the map shows?"

I didn't have an answer for that one.

"She lied to you about everything else, lad. You've got no reason to expect she wouldn't lie to you about where the treasure's buried."

"But I found the river mouth on the map."

He shook his head. "You found something on the map that resembled the Seventeenth Century mouth of a river in Georgia. River mouths change over the course of three hundred years, especially on coastal plains. You found a resemblance because you were looking at a map of Georgia and you wanted to find something."

"But..." I couldn't argue the point, I knew too well he was right. The Little Sapilla was just another fantasy. I shook my head. "Shit, I'm just full of fantasies lately."

"The prospect of five million dollars landing in your lap is enough to make anyone fantasize."

"The money's not all it was."

"Yeah, well, that's going to create fantasies as well."

He reached for the phone, I'm sure he meant to distract me. "Let me make a couple more calls, see if I can make anymore headway on this Mister Big."

Then it clicked that he said, "...has a plane to catch."

"What time's her flight? Sindi's flight?"

"I was afraid you'd ask that. One thirty-two."

Less than an hour and a half. I had a chance. "Lend me your car."

"No."

"Yes. Clyde, I'm not going to hurt your car."

"That's not what I'm worried about. I'm thinking about your well-being if you go off on this wild goose chase."

"Are you positive it's a wild goose I'm after?"

"Pretty damn sure, right. We already know this woman can twist you around. What's she going to do if you show up at the airport when she's trying to get on a plane?"

"I'm over that. She won't be able to manipulate me this time."

"How sure are you of that?"

"Very."

We argued a little longer, but there are things a man has to do-things that any reasonable person will think are stupid or worse-if he's not going to doubt himself ever after. Clyde's a reasonable person, but he's also a man and understands the imperatives.

"Okay, I'll lend you my car. You be nice to her. But first, drop me off at the club. I can make my calls from there."

"Thanks, Clyde, you're a real friend."

He grunted. He knew friends have to let each other do dumb things, but he didn't necessarily think they should.

Twenty minutes later, Clyde was at the Side Car Club and I was on the Schuylkill Expressway headed for Philadelphia International Airport. I was so intent on intercepting Sindi before she boarded the plane, I didn't notice the metallic blue Mitsubishi parked on 33rd Street where it could watch anyone pulling up to the Side Car. Neither did I notice it follow me. Nor did I notice its driver talking on a cellular phone. I was aware enough to stick my .32 under the driver's seat before getting out of the T-bird.

*

I've been in a lot of big-city airports over the years, and in most ways, Philadelphia International doesn't take a back seat to any of them. It's closer to the heart of the city than most, which is an advantage. It has short and long term parking, shops, eating and drinking facilities, and passenger lounges. It's serviced by major highways, taxi cab service, hotel and public limousine service, and a commuter train terminus. You can rent a car or a hotel room there.

Philadelphia International consists of one very long concourse with five long terminals jutting out from one side, rather like a very long, very tall centipede. Not counting the international terminal, it's nearly a half mile from end to end. The four domestic terminals that jut out from the main concourse are more than two football fields in length.

In San Francisco, a much smaller airport, there is a moving walkway to carry passengers between the entrance and the gate area. St Louis is a big airport, it also has a moving walkway to transport passengers on their journey to the gates. In Atlanta, if you need to go from one terminal to another, there are moving walkways under the aprons. LAX had a moving walkway back in the mid-sixties. This is where Philadelphia International falls on its face; it is the only large airport I've been in anywhere in the country that doesn't have a moving walkway.

By the time I parked Clyde's T-bird, I only had 45 minutes to find Sindi. Less than that by the time I got onto the ground floor of the main concourse. Nowhere near enough time to go it entire length and all four terminals to look for her at each gate. I tried to save time by going the concourse's length looking at the TV screens that announced departure times.

When I got to the end I thought I must have missed something, because I didn't see any listing for an Atlanta flight with a scheduled 1:32 departure time. I headed for the upper level thinking maybe the screens there would show additional information. Silly idea, I know, but when you're clutching at straws...

Between B and C Terminals is where I ran into Kallir.

"Having trouble finding your flight?" he asked.

The whole masculine pride bit came back uninvited; I couldn't tell him I was there looking for a woman who used me and dropped me. "I'm meeting a friend, Kallir," I snapped. "Beat it."

"I don't think so," he said, and grabbed my arm. "Not unless your friend plans to leave town on the same flight you think you are. I don't think she's going to leave, either."

I wrenched my arm from his grasp. "I don't know what you're talking about and I don't think you do either. Beat it, punk."

"O-o-oh, tough guy," he said. "You're meeting someone, go to the gate. I want to see you go through the metal detector." He smirked.

Not a bad idea. Kallir must have thought I had my little gun on me. He might be carrying himself. If he was he couldn't follow me. Maybe, just maybe, once through the metal detector, I could find a way to evade him. If only he's carrying and can't get through the airport's security system himself. I looked lost, as though I was armed and had nowhere to go.

"I can't go through them either." He smiled that nasty smile of his. "I think you should come with me. Someone else will meet your friend."

"I don't want to go with you, Kallir, so forget it."

"You really should. You see, I've got something you don't. I've got the balls to shoot you here, you don't."

"That doesn't sound like balls to me, that sounds like stupidity."

"Whatever you want to call it. I've got what it takes and you don't."

Lately it takes me a long time to catch on to some things. Like, I didn't realize until he said that, that he might be a sociopath, maybe even a psychopath. Sometimes even a heavy duty nut like that exhibits some survival traits.

"Fuck you, Kallir," I said. "I'm calling a cop." And hoped I could get away while the cop was dealing with him.

He smiled wider. "Like my good buddy Clint Eastwood says, make my day." From nowhere, I felt something hard pressing in my side. I flinched, it was the same place Hammond kicked me Monday afternoon.

"Put it away, Kallir." I tried to put disgust in my voice, and not show the nervousness that I felt. "You'll have cops all over you before you can get away."

He didn't move his head, just let his eyes do the walking. An expression flickered across his face, but it was too rapid for me to be sure it was fear; I thought he saw a cop somewhere behind me. I took a chance.

"I'm going in to meet my flight. You can come if you want to."

"What flight?" he snapped.

"That one." I turned until I saw a screen announcing arrivals. "United flight 843 from Atlanta, due in at 1:32." It took a major effort on my part not to sound surprised at that. Had Clyde gotten the information wrong? Had I misunderstood him? I was looking for a flight leaving Philadelphia for Atlanta at 1:32, and here was one coming in from Atlanta at that very same time. Was Sindi meeting someone on that flight and they were getting another flight together? The screen said gate C-21.

"Are you coming?" I didn't give him time to answer, I turned on my heel and headed for the mouth of Terminal C. I heard the clatter of feet on the concourse behind me. They got close, and Kallir grabbed my left arm. I wrenched it out of his grip and held up my wrist, I wanted it to look like I was just looking at my watch.

"I don't have time to stop now," I said. "The flight's due in just a couple of minutes. C-21 is all the way down at the end. It'll unboarding by the time I reach the gate as it is." I didn't even look at him, just kept striding along. I sensed uncertainty at my side and stepped out more briskly. "Time's wasting, gotta run." I reached Terminal C and headed into it. Ahead was the metal detector and safety. I walked as fast as I could without running. The queue at the portal was moving briskly, hardly any wait at all. Kallir yelled at me as I got a clean bill of health and was allowed entry to the gates. There was sudden commotion behind me, but I didn't turn to look at it.

C-21 was down at the end. It seems every time I catch a flight in or out of Philadelphia International, my plane is at a gate all the way down at the end. For once, I was glad of it. I was just past the first gates when a dark-suited man appeared at my side.

"Excuse me, sir," he said. His tone of voice made me stop and look at him. He was in his thirties and about average in height and build, but there was a hardness about that made him look very strong and capable. His suit bore a plastic badge that identified him as airport security. "Do you know that gentleman back there?"

I looked where he was pointing. Kallir was in the grip of two men. When he saw me look at him, Kallir started struggling and tried to point an arm at me.

"No, I don't know him," I said, acting the offended innocent. "He's a Moonie or something. He accosted me in the concourse and kept opportuning me all the way to the metal detector. I tried to tell him I wasn't interested, but he kept insisting I make a donation, or read a pamphlet, or something." I looked earnestly at the security man. "Aren't you supposed to keep people like that out of the airport? Isn't there some sort of city ordinance against soliciting?"

He almost cracked a smile at that. "Do you have a ticket, sir?"

"No. I'm meeting someone." I made a production of looking at my watch.

"What flight, may I ask?"

"United 843. It's due in at C-21 right about now. I better get there because this is my friend's first trip to Philadelphia and she's afraid of strange airports.

He looked at an arrival screen to verify the flight. This time the smile did appear. Small, but it was there. "Thank you. Sorry to bother you, sir." I had this feeling he didn't quite believe me.

"No problem." As I headed toward the end of Terminal C, I could feel him watching me. I felt he'd be watching for me to come back, and he'd have more questions if I came back alone.

CHAPTER EIGHTEEN

The first of the departing passengers from United 843 bubbled past me before I reached the gate. Most of them were businessmen traveling alone, only a few were with someone who met the plane. The rest of the passengers were still straggling out of the flexible tunnel from the plane, milling about, getting their bearings, joyfully greeting meeters, when I got there. I looked and looked and didn't see Sindi anywhere. The crowd started to clear out. Soon I'd be standing alone in the waiting area, standing out too clearly.

Across the way C-22 was filling up with people waiting for another flight. I went over there and took a seat in the smoking area to plan my next step. No, I wasn't going to take up smoking again. In today's climate, people who smoke are too often ignored or looked upon with approbation. Most people would not look at this small seating area with its rising tendrils of blue-gray smoke, or would look with disgusted superiority if they did look. Those who looked would not see people sitting there, they would see anonymous, antisocial creatures who have no consideration for other people's comfort or health. They'd identify these miscreants as "smokers." It's always seemed to me that smoking is something one does rather than something one is. Smoking, to me, isn't a characteristic, except in so far as it may be an indicator of an addictive or self-destructive personality, it's an action.

I saw sitting in the smoking section as camouflage of a purloined letter sort.

Okay, there was missed communication. Either between Clyde and Sindi's secretary, or between him and me. There didn't seem to be a 1:32 to Atlanta. Then I realized Clyde didn't say the flight was to Atlanta, he just said it was at 1:32. He did object to my guess, reminded me that I couldn't find the mariner's mountain on my map, and said she could have been lying to me about what state the treasure was in. The more I thought about it, the more likely that sounded. I was about to get up and head back to the concourse to see if there was a flight going anywhere that departed at 1:32 when I remembered airport security. Were they waiting for me? The terminals were dead ends, the only way out was the way I came in. How could I get out without being seen?

I looked out the window and saw a plane pulling in at a gate with a lower number. I waited for a few minutes, then headed back up the terminal to where I saw people leaving a gate. What I wanted was to find a nervous looking woman who would let me carry her onboard bag. I suspected trying to find one could land me in trouble in a hurry. I settled for joining a clump of men tall enough to be basketball players. Maybe their height would shield me from the view of any security people who might be watching for me.

Either the shield worked or no one was looking for me.

What didn't work was checking the departure monitors in the concourse. It was now far enough past 1:32 that none of those flights showed anymore. I sagged. Finding Sindi before she left was my last chance at the five million dollars. Now she was gone and I had no idea where. Missing out on that money hurt. I told myself it was only a fantasy anyway. Knowing that Sindi herself and our love-making that had seemed to me so real and honest was only a fantasy, that she'd merely been using her body to blind my eyes so she could use me, that hurt more. That's two strikes. They say three and you're out.

I went outside and got reminded of my third strike. Mister Big had told me to hand over the map or die.

Hondo stepped in front of me and giggled. Moose stood next to him and yucked.

"You going somewhere?" Hondo asked.

"I'm going home. Now get the fuck out of my way." I tried to step around them, but Moose's hand on my chest put an stop to that idea.

I improvised. I ignored Moose and talked to Hondo. "I came to meet Sindi DiWagne. She's going to get the treasure. I was going to see her off. When I got to the gate Kallir was with her. She looked pretty down. He had the map-I saw it in his hand. There wasn't anything I could do, so I left before they saw me."

"Kallir's at B-8?" Hondo asked, excitement growing in his voice. "And he's got the map?"

"What'd I just say?"

"Watch him, Moose." Hondo ran into the airport.

Moose grinned at me. "I'm gonna enjoy this," he said.

"What do you think you are going to enjoy?"

"Doing you and the bitch."

I shook my head sadly. "Moose, I'm going to walk away from you and you aren't going to do anything about it. I'm going to get into my car and go home. Kallir's got the map. It's over. I'm out of it."

He ponderously shook his head. "Uh-uh. You going with us when Kallir and Hondo get back."

"No, Moose. Look over there." I nodded to his left rear. Two Philadelphia Highway Patrolmen were standing about twenty feet away from us. "I'm going. You don't want to try to stop me with two cops standing right there, do you?"

Moose looked confused. "But Hondo said..."

"You've got the map, that's what you came here for. You can let me go. You'll only get into trouble if you try to stop me. You'll be in jail, you'll miss out on your share. You may even screw things up so the treasure is lost for everybody. So long, Moose."

I could hardly believe he let me go so easily.

*

I thought Kallir was being held for questioning. He might even get turned over to the city police and locked up while they decided whether or not to charge him with something. Hondo was sure to waste some time looking for him when he didn't see him at gate B-8. It would likely take Moose several minutes to decide not to stand there waiting any longer. Llowlolski was no kind of threat without backup. I didn't think Mister Big was either. All of which meant I had a few minutes head start, long enough to go home and grab some clean clothes. No matter what I'd told Moose, it wasn't over yet.

On the drive back I returned the .32 to my pocket. I was able to park almost right in front of my place. The street was quiet, not a single trike ratcheted the peace away. Maybe the yuplings were all in for their afternoon naps, their mommies gathered for tea. Maybe they'd all gone to a private swim club. It was too much to hope for that they'd moved away. Go in, check the mail, check the phone machine, throw a few things into an overnight bag, and I'm outta there. It would only take three or four minutes. Unless I had a lot of calls waiting on the machine. If I did, I could always pull that tape and take it with me to play back somewhere safer.

Sure.

The mailbox held one send money, one spend money, two pay moneys. Nothing to take up my time there.

Inside my apartment was another matter. It was very thoroughly ransacked. No subtlety at all. Every drawer in the kitchen and bedroom was dumped. The bed was upended. All the clothes in the closet were off their hangers. The medicine cabinet's contents were strewn about. My overstuffed chair was upside down and its bottom cover torn out. The file cabinets were on their sides and their contents thrown all over the office area. Nothing had been left untouched. My computer was on the floor, one printer was on its side, the other was upside down. The TV and VCR were moved. The stereo system was dismantled and the records were all out of their cabinets. The paintings and prints were off the walls. Even the rugs were pulled up and tossed aside. The bottle of champagne I keep in the pantry for a special occasion was empty.

That particular bottle had been in the pantry for over a year.

Whoever did this had gone through everything. Almost. I checked the hiding places. They hadn't found any of my firearms.

Give thanks for small favors, I guess.

The light was blinking on the answering machine. I played it back. One message, ten words:

"Welcome home, Hambiltonian I want it. You know the consequences." The message scared me.

The call was time-stamped right about when Clyde got the call from Martha about Sindi. That told me my place was probably trashed this morning.

I didn't bother straightening anything out. I half-blindly stuffed a few things into an overnight bag and got out of there. On the way I took a closer look at the doors. On the inner vestibule lock, I thought I saw scratches that might have been made by someone picking it, but I wasn't sure, though I couldn't think of any other way anyone might have gotten in. Surveying the mess had taken extra time-it was five minutes from when I went in until I got back into the T-bird.

It was about a quarter of three when I parked behind the Side Car Club. Nobody was taking a break in the small parking lot. I didn't know if the back door was unlocked, I didn't even know if the place was open for business at this hour.

The answer to both was yes. The side bar was closed. Maybe a dozen men were at the main bar. One dancing-girl was gyrating on its stage to the strains of something pop on the jukebox, another was collecting tips. No one noticed me as I went through the dark recesses to the office.

"You look like hell," Clyde said. "Want a drink?"

I shook my head and tossed him the keys to his car.

"You go first," he said.

I sat heavily and started talking. I told him about my futile attempt to find a 1:32 flight to Atlanta. I told him about running into Kallir and getting away from him because he wasn't able to go through the metal detector. He laughed when I told him about the security man who questioned me. He nodded approval at the way I got out of Terminal C without being seen. He liked my getaway from Hondo and Moose. I laughed along with him in all the right places. But the laughter was hollow, the hurt from the two lost fantasies was too great for real laughter.

I started trembling when I told him about going home and what I found there.

"You're having that drink," he said, and picked up the phone. I hadn't known, but wasn't surprised to learn, that the phone had an intercom function.

A moment later a big guy came in carrying a glass on a small tray. He one of the bouncers I guess. I pay far less attention to the men in the Side Car than I do the women. The big guy put the tray on the desk and left when Clyde told him there wasn't anything else.

"Bourbon. See if it'll calm your nerves any." Clyde picked up the glass and handed it to me.

I obediently took a sip.

"Drink it all."

I took another sip, then knocked it back. The liquor burned all the way down. I felt it hit my stomach and had to make myself sag in the chair. It's funny the way people treat alcohol. They use it to celebrate, but it's actually a depressant. That makes it good for relaxing. I relaxed. Maybe a little too much. I could feel it going to my head, not the best shape to be in right now. I stopped trembling.

"Later I'll get a couple of the guys and we can go to your place and help you straighten up."

I wasn't sure that was such a great idea, but didn't object.

"Now for more bad news," he said and I sagged emotionally. I didn't need any more bad news. "Martha did some more checking and wasn't able to find out anything about where your blonde bimbo took off to. Martha is..." he paused and looked at me, gave me time to interrupt if I still didn't want to know who Martha was.

"Don't tell me. You know what I said about the dancing-girls as fantasies. I've had enough fantasies blow up in my face over the last few days."

He shrugged and started talking again. "The good news is, I'm pretty sure Edward Bigler is your Mister Big."

Now I got excited. "Tell me."

"There are couple of real strong indicators. First," he held up his index finger, "the word on the street is he's gotten involved with designer drugs as a way out of his current financial difficulties."

119

"Wait a minute," I interrupted. "What do South Americans have to do with designer drugs? I thought they were always made locally."

He nodded. "Right. That's a discrepancy between what Llowlolski told you and what I've found out. Let me finish, though." His middle finger joined the index in standing up. "Second, he's come up with a real hush-hush scheme for buying his way out of the drug trade. Third, he's got some strong-arm punks working for him. Fourth, he's got an accountant with a shady past working for him. Fifth," his hand opened all the way and he grinned, "the accountant's name is Paul Llowlolski."

I was excited. This Edward Bigler had to be my man. "Llowlolski was blowing smoke about the South Americans, he just wanted to scare me."

"Seems that way."

"Okay, now what do I do with this?"

"Isn't it obvious? You call the son of a bitch and tell him you don't have the map, so he should go fuck himself. That'll shake him up." He shoved a piece of paper at me. "His phone numbers. Home and office." He looked smug.

My hands trembled again when I picked up the paper with the numbers. One was a Center City exchange, the other might have been Society Hill. I held out a hand for the phone, Clyde pushed it across the desk to me.

"Speaker?" he asked.

"Sure," I said, and punched out the Center City number. Clyde hit a button on the phone as soon as I hit the seventh digit and I put the receiver down.

"Bigler Entrepreneurships." An officious female voice answered on the second ring.

"Yes, let me speak to Mister Bigler, please."

"Is he expecting your call, sir?"

"No, but he'll want to talk to me."

"One moment, please."

There was a soft click on the line, a dead space, another soft click, and a different voice said, "Mister Bigler's office, may I help you?"

"Yes, I'd like to talk to the big man."

"I'm sorry, sir, Mister Bigler is in conference and can't come to the phone. Perhaps I can help you?"

"I'd love it if you could, but this is private business between Mister Bigler and me. This is urgent. He will want to talk to me. So why don't you step into the conference and slip him a note. Say it's the horse race guy."

"I'm sorry, sir." There was no sorrow in her voice, neither was there any amusement. "Mister Bigler left strict instructions he was not to be interrupted by anything less than the building being on fire."

"What about nuclear war?"

"Only if a bomb is headed this way." Her voice held just the slightest hint of amusement.

People who make big enough bucks hire layers of people to keep them isolated from the riff-raff. In normal circumstances it successfully keeps them from being bothered by nuisance calls. It also has the unfortunate side-effect of keeping them from some important calls-such as this one. This secretary's voice told me she wasn't going to put her boss on the phone with me. Not even if I told her the building was on fire.

"All right, dollface, you win. Tell him I'll call him at home tonight. Love ya." I broke the connection.

"She sounded like a good executive secretary," Clyde said. "Sometimes I wish I had someone like that to run interference for me. Keep some people out of my office."

I shot him a sharp glance. Was he saying he wished I never showed up yesterday? He was grinning, just yanking on my chain. I didn't need my chain yanked.

I started trembling again. "What if this is the wrong guy?" I asked.

"Come on, Ham, you know he's the right guy. Shit, man, his accountant's your jittery guy. What more do you want?"

"You're right." How many crooks in pinstripes could Llowlolski be working for?

Clyde looked at his watch. "I've got an idea. Let's go." He stood, showed me another piece of paper, and grinned.

I read what was on the paper and grinned back. I led him out of his office.

We didn't leave immediately. First Clyde stopped and spoke quietly with one of the bouncers. When we reached the back door, I looked back and saw that bouncer on the phone. I wondered what kind of surprise Clyde was cooking.

CHAPTER NINETEEN

Networking is what it's called. I needed to know the identity of a man who was making threats. I told Clyde about him. Clyde asked a few people he knows. One or more of them gave him enough information about one individual to confirm that individual's identity as the man making the threats. Easy.

Many people have speculated that no one is more than three or four people removed from anyone else in the country. All you have to do is ask your barber, who asks another one of his customers, who asks his brother-in-law who is married to a secretary at Chrysler, and you've got Lee Iaccoca's home phone number. Well, that's the theory, anyway.

It does work to some degree. I can testify that I myself have gotten direct access to financiers, engineers, nationally famed lawyers, corporate CEOs, publishers, inventors, and musicians by that route. In a city like this, it's easy. Many Philadelphians claim this isn't a big city, it's a small town where everybody knows everybody else. That's not quite accurate, but it is true that, with relative ease, anybody who is anybody can likely locate anybody else who is anybody. I don't have much excuse for not having thought of this myself in this instance. It's just that I had no clue as to 'Mister Big's' identity, I was upset over the threats made against me, and I was distracted by a beautiful blonde fantasy with a rusty-husky voice.

I'll get over it.

Clyde's contacts not only gave him Bigler's home and office phone numbers, they came up with his home address. That's where we went a bit after three in the afternoon. I was right about the phone exchange. Bigler lived on one of the little streets that make a warren of the older parts of the city. He was on Panama Street, just off 4th, in the heart of Society Hill.

This is a part of the city that was constructed during Federalist times, some if it even dates back to the late Colonial period. A walking tour of certain pockets of Society Hill can be like reading a living history book. In these small pockets it seems as though every house at one time or another was the residence of someone famous from the Revolution or the early United States. And if no one famous lived in the house, some organization or another held a meeting in it. You can tell because of the historical location plaques bolted to the fronts of so many of the houses.

It's also an area of you-can't-get-there-from-here streets. All the streets are one way. You may find yourself less than half a block from your destination and have to go another six blocks of curlicues to park in front of it. And many of the little streets are off-limits to auto traffic.

This block of Panama Street was open to traffic, but it was too narrow to allow parking. Clyde toodled his T-bird around until he found an open space on 4th Street below Pine. He pulled into the curb right behind a metallic blue Mitsubishi. That car made me wish I'd noted the license number of the car

Hondo was in at the Wissahickon Station. On the way back to Panama Street, Clyde waved at three big men in a passing Chevy. They waved back. I didn't ask. He told me anyway.

"Insurance."

If the metallic blue Mitsubishi was Hondo's car, backup sounded good to me.

Bigler's house was about a third of the way up the block and it stood out. It was one of only a few on the block that didn't have a "George Washington Slept Here" marker. It was also the only Federalist house on a block of late Colonials. It was twice as wide as its neighbors and about ten feet higher. We couldn't tell from the street, but it probably extended ten or fifteen feet deeper than the others as well.

"Yeah," Clyde said as soon as he saw which house was the number he had, "they say he's a big spender. This sucker had to set him back more than half a million."

I nodded. "At least," I said. The Edwardian I live in is big, but Bigler's house was bigger, and property values are several orders of magnitude higher in Society Hill than in University City.

"Just walk by like we're passing through on our way somewhere else," Clyde said.

Sounded excellent to me. He was on the curb side. I walked as close to the houses as I could. The windows of Bigler's house were high enough that somebody inside looking out might not see me unless they were right at the window. Clyde had a better angle and casually glanced in as we passed.

"You say Moose is a big, dumb looking guy?" he asked when we neared 5th Street.

I nodded.

"And Hondo looks like he should be hanging on a corner in South Philadelphia?"

"Yep."

"Then the one with the Jimmy Johnson wig must be Kallir."

"Did you see them?"

"All three."

"Anybody else?"

He shook his head. "They looked like they were waiting."

"Now what?" Clyde was doing such a good job I thought I'd continue following his lead.

He pensively shook his head. "I wish they weren't there."

The Chevy that passed us on 4th Street pulled up just as we reached 5th Street. "Wait here." Clyde went to it and leaned in the passenger side window. I couldn't hear any of the conversation, but I did see the three men in the car nod agreement. Clyde came back.

"They're going to watch the place. If anybody leaves, or when Bigler comes home if that happens first, they'll call me. Until then, we don't have a damn thing to do. So let's go back to the club and let me finish my accounts while we wait."

*

There were four messages waiting for Clyde. One was a would-be promoter who wanted to book a teenie-bopper band into the club. Clyde was the very soul of diplomacy when he explained to the guy that the Side Car Club was a bar and the acts had to be old enough to drink. No, he never had all-age nights. The second was from his beer distributor saying his shipment of Moose Head Ale was delayed getting in from the brewery, but he'd have it tomorrow for sure. Clyde swore, but said okay it's not your fault. Then he told me he was going to have to find another distributor because this one kept not paying his bills on time and deliveries got screwed up at least once a month because of it. The third call was another one of Clyde's contacts who confirmed some things about Bigler that we already knew. The call Clyde saved for last was from Martha.

"I don't want to know," I said when it looked like he was going to tell me which of the dancing-girls she was.

He shrugged, "Your loss," and dialed the number. "Miss Puller, please. This is Mister Krippendorf returning her call." He put his hand over the mouthpiece and said to me, "She's at her day job." Then into the receiver, "Hi, Martha. We just got back in." He mostly listened for about a minute and made a few I'm-listening noises. "Very interesting," he said at last. The thot plickens, as someone once said." He listened again, then said, "I don't know, you may be wasting your time. Right now he's kind of snake bit, you know?" Pause. "Okay, well, that's up to you... Um-hum... Yes, dear, I owe you... Okay. Thanks a ton."

He hung up and looked at me. "Ham, you're blushing."

My face was hot, so I guess I was. "You two were talking about me."

"Sure, why not? Martha's a nice lady and she likes you. Why? Damned if I know, you're certainly no great prize."

He let me stew in that one for a moment before saying, "She found out more about your blonde bimbo."

"Stop calling her that, please."

"Why? You told me she's really a blonde, and any woman who uses her body like that has to be a bimbo."

I made a face. "Because it reminds me of how easily she buffaloed me, okay?"

"If that's the way you want it."

"That's the way I want it."

He nodded. "Here's the latest," he continued, as though we hadn't just been talking about things painful to me, "She didn't go to Atlanta, but we already had that pretty well figured out. She went to Wilmington, North Carolina, which makes a lot more sense, because we know there actually were mariner's mountains in North Carolina, while there couldn't have been any in Georgia. Unfortunately, we don't know where she went from there. She rented a car so there's no immediate way of tracking her."

My curiosity finally got to me. "How the hell does she find out these things?"

"I'll tell you, but only if you'll let me tell you which dancer she is."

My curiosity wasn't that great. "It'll remain a mystery to me."

"I don't know why. She's nice. You'd like her in real life. Really."

"If she's so nice, why don't you go after her?"

"Policy. I don't play footsie with the help. Besides, I'm not her type. Or something."

"Does that mean you've tried?"

"No. We had that out when I hired her. She said she was glad to hear that policy. She enforces a similar one on her day job."

I tried not to let any expression show, but I did wonder what kind of day job this dancing-girl had that she enforced policy.

Clyde laughed. "Lad, you should see your face. You look like you tried to swallow an egg without shelling it first. Listen," he leaned forward and lowered his voice. "Don't worry, I'm not going to tell you who she is, not until you're ready. Most of my girls are full-time dancers, it's what they do for living. A few are college girls putting themselves through school. But would it surprise you to know that I've got a lawyer, three doctors-one MD and two PhDs, an associate professor at one of the suburban universities, a Main Line housewife, and three corporate middle managers working for me part-time?"

My expression must have registered surprise, because he laughed again. "Well, I do, lad."

"They told you what they do full-time and you believe them?"

"Hell no. None of them told me up front, most of them don't know that I know. But you don't think I'd hire somebody without checking her out, do you? I don't want any junkies in here. I don't want any ripoff artists. Or trouble makers of any sort. Some places, they'll hire anybody who comes in off the street, looks decent, likes to take off most of her clothes in public, and is willing to let the customers cop a feel for a tip. I'm pickier. I do background checks on my girls. I know who they are and where they're from before I let them get on my stage.

"Martha caught me checking her out and I had to explain myself. When I did she told me she hadn't sure she wanted to work for me-until she saw the care I took in hiring dancers. Especially since I do the same thing with bartenders and bouncers."

"But, aren't women like that opening themselves up for blackmail?"

"No shit, Sherlock. But they know how I look after them. Besides, honestly, how much attention to you pay to their faces?"

It was my turn to laugh. "I see your point. I know their faces, but most men probably don't look at much above their clavicles."

He cocked an eyebrow at me. "Is that so now, lad. I happen to know that you've met a couple of my girls away from here and didn't recognize them."

I felt my face go hot again. Yes, I see the dancing-girls as fantasy figures, I readily admit that. But I do look at their faces. I would recognize them as real people off the job. Wouldn't I? Then I remembered the vaguely familiar dancing-girl from last night, the one I thought I knew from somewhere but couldn't place, and had to admit maybe I wasn't doing as good a job of acknowledging their humanity as I'd thought.

"Uh, is Martha one of them?"

It seemed Clyde was doing a lot of laughing at my expense. "No, as far as I know, you've never seen her away from here."

I felt uncomfortable and it showed.

"Don't let it bother you, Ham. Listen. A lot of women are exhibitionistic.

Most content themselves with wearing tight clothing, short skirts, plunging necklines, T-shirts with no bras. Some of them are in jobs or social positions where they have to be very circumspect about what they do. A very few of those come to work in a place like this where they get to show off their bodies in fairly complete anonymity."

"Anonymity? How the hell is being nearly naked up on that stage anonymous?"

"It's easy, lad. Remember, men here don't really look at their faces. Besides, it's amazing how different a woman can look with a change of make up and a wig."

I gave him a skeptical look.

"Really," he said. "A friend of mine once found himself at a party his ex-wife was also at. She'd changed her hair, from long and straight to permed with highlights, and began wearing cat's-eye glasses. It wasn't until she spoke and he heard her voice that he recognized her. Another friend was meeting a woman he'd known for years. She'd changed her hair from natural to something a runway model might have as a wig. He didn't recognize her until she spoke to him." He shrugged. "That's the way the titty bounces."

"Bouncing titties," I said. "Sure. And nobody recognizes the women they know."

"That's right. You want examples from here? The lawyer told me that one night she thought she was going to get fired and maybe even disbarred. One of the senior partners in her firm came in with a client who also knew her. You know what happened? Between them, they tipped her a hundred bucks before the night was over! And they never recognized her. The professor told me sometimes one or more of her students comes in. They never recognize her. One of the corporate managers has a subordinate who's a regular here. He has no idea his boss is one of the dancers he tips.

"My customers are just like you. They look at the bodies of the dancers. It never occurs to them that the woman they're ogling might be someone respectable. They hardly ever look at the girls' faces. Most of them are even worse than you. Sometimes one of these characters will approach me like he thinks I'm a procurer and ask to rent one of the girls for an hour or so. The yahoos always describe the girl's tits, her ass, her legs. If she's a blonde or a redhead, he'll mention that. But he never describes her face." He shook his head in mock amazement. Or maybe it wasn't mock.

Clyde's story didn't make me feel any better about having met two of the dancing-girls out of context and not recognizing them. I decided it was something I'd have to think about.

"Nothing wrong with it, it's in our genes. Women are bred to be looked at, men are bred to look at them. It's only bad if a man never sees a woman as a person, if he always only sees her as a body.

Clyde looked like he was settling in for one of his long lectures on the mammalian nature of *Homo Sap*, or maybe a dissertation on how our modern attitudes, actions, and political incorrectnesses were formed by our evolution as hunter-gatherers. The phone rang and saved me from that fate.

"Bigler just got home," Clyde told me when he hung up. He pushed the phone across the desk to me.

CHAPTER TWENTY

It wasn't five o'clock yet. I told Clyde that Bigler must have gotten my message and been so shaken up he fled to the safety of his goons. Clyde grinned and said might be. He put the phone on speaker as soon as I finished dialing so he could listen in. I recognized the voice as soon as Bigler said hello. He was Mister Big, all right. He sounded on edge. I decided to keep him that way and press any advantage this unexpected call might give me.

"Eddie," I said condescendingly, "that wasn't nice what you did to my place this morning. What are you going to do to make it up to me? Never mind, I'll figure something out, and then you'll recompense me. I'll be interested to hear how pretty-boy got away from security at the airport this afternoon. You know, if I was you I'd fire the three of them. They keep coming after me and I keep getting away. They just aren't very good at what they're supposed to do, are they? Well, I guess it's hard to find good help these days."

He was trying to talk, but I rambled on, not giving much thought to what I was saying, mostly letting him know that I was in charge of our little conversation.

"Kallir missed the DiWagne woman. I guess she's safely in Wilmington by now. With the map. You know, she's pretty sharp. The way she used me to distract you so she could get away." I laughed, a harsh bark. "The bimbo promised me a cut of the take. I was going to be quite well off, or so I thought. But she really did a number on you, you poor sucker. Now you're stuck with your new friends and they're turning on you. Kind of sounds like you're in deep shit." I finally stopped to let him have his say.

"What do you mean, calling me at home, Hambiltonian?" He sounded angry, I could understand that. "How did you get this number? Who do you think you are? You don't have idea of who you're up against."

"You don't have any idea who you're up against either, Eddie," I snapped. "Puts us on a more even footing, doesn't it? And I'm calling you at home because you wouldn't take my call at the office."

He didn't say anything to that immediately, not that there was much he could say. It must have come as a tremendously bad surprise when I called him at the office, then called him at home. And calling him Eddie was calculated to anger him.

"Hambiltonian, I told you never to intrude on me, not unless you came to hand over the map. You are intruding on me. You will pay the price."

"Eddie, I keep trying not to intrude on you. But you just won't leave me alone. How can I not intrude on you when every time I turn around your bully-boys are annoying me?"

"Hambiltonian," he sounded cool, fully back in control of himself, "I haven't begun to annoy you yet. You aren't going to have any peace until I have that map."

"Eddie, you just aren't listening to me. I've told you repeatedly I don't have the damn map. I tried to give it to you once, but she pulled a switch on me. You keep ignoring me when I say I'm out of this, that I don't want anything more to do with it or with you. Listen to me this time, Eddie. I'm out. I don't have the map. I don't know where the bimbo is going with it. I don't know where the treasure is buried. I don't ever want to see you again. Or Paul, or Kallir, or Hondo, or Moose. Not ever again. Is that clear, Eddie?"

While I was talking I heard another phone ringing in the background and the muted sounds of someone answering it. Then a closer voice said something and Bigler laughed. It was a confident laugh that had a chilling effect on me. "You're such a stupid amateur, Hambiltonian Did you hear the other phone ringing a moment ago? It was a message I've been waiting for. When Kallir failed to intercept the bitch, thanks to your meddling, I arranged for someone to meet her when she got through checkout in Wilmington. She didn't have the map. That must mean you have it, doesn't it? Rest assured, Hambiltonian, I'm going to get it."

"What have you done with her?" I demanded. There was a rasp in my voice; no matter what I might say about her using me, or how I'm through with her, Sindi DiWagne still had a hold on my heart. Or some part of me.

Bigler laughed harshly. "Wouldn't you like to know. Don't worry, she's in good hands. Hands that owe me." He hung up. So much for any advantage I thought I had.

"Shit," I said, and sat way back in my chair.

Clyde took the phone off the speaker. "Everybody's lying here. Bigler said he's got her, but Martha told me she rented a car in Wilmington and took off."

"So who do we believe? Either of them? Neither of them?"

"Believe Martha. Bigler was probably just trying to psych you." Clyde paused in thought, then asked, "Any chance you have the map and don't know it, like before?"

"None. The last time I saw it, she was putting it in an envelope. I haven't seen her or been in her place since. And I don't think there's any way she could have gotten into my apartment after it was trashed to hide it there." Still, I checked all of my pockets. No map.

"So what did she do with it?"

"Damned if I know. Mailed it to herself?"

"You say she put it in a greeting card envelope?"

"And sealed it, right in front of me."

"It would have been no problem to write an address on that envelope, stick a stamp on it, and drop it in a mailbox as soon as you took off."

"Where'd she mail it to herself at?"

Clyde shrugged. "I'd like to say she called ahead, booked herself a room at a HoJo or someplace, and mailed it care of there."

"You'd like to say that, but you won't. Why not?"

"Because Martha already checked. There's no Sindi DiWagne registered in any hotel or motel in Wilmington."

Once again I wondered what this Martha's day job was that she could find out so easily where Sindi DiWagne went, and that she wasn't registered in any hotels there. But I didn't wonder enough to ask. Not with Clyde's condition that he'll tell me only if he also tells me which dancing-girl she was. I felt a desperate need to keep fantasy and reality separate in my mind.

"Maybe she registered under an assumed name," I said. "She's resourceful enough, it probably wouldn't be hard to get a credit card under another name." Then I leaned back and tried to think. I knew better, of course-sharp concentration on anything only blunts my mind. Mine is the kind of thought process that works best when the subconscious is left alone to do its own work, the conscious mind only gets in the way. Thoughts swirled, jumbled, and failed to cohere.

Clyde let me go through this futile exercise for a few moments, then yanked me back. "Right now, I think our best next step is getting some dinner," he said. "It's going on half past five and I haven't eaten since breakfast."

A glance at my watch confirmed the time. My stomach growled at me, I hadn't eaten since breakfast either. "Sounds like a good idea," I said.

"Go to the bar and have a drink. Give me a couple minutes to give instructions and make a phone call. Then we'll go."

"Right." I went out and he stayed to make his phone call. The side bar still wasn't open, so I found an empty spot at the main bar and ordered a soda. One dancing-girl was on the stage, four others were circulating around its inside. The first one reached me and I made a point of looking at her face rather than her body. She was all bright eyes and coy smile and looked barely old enough to be in a bar. And I couldn't think of her name.

"Hi, Ham," she said. "I didn't see you come in."

"I was in the back with Clyde." Her voice didn't tell me who she was either.

"Sneaking a peek in the dressing room, I bet." She giggled.

"You know better than that," I said, mock sternly.

"Do I?" She wiggled her shoulders, brought to mind a cat preening herself, cupped her breasts toward me for a tip.

I looked to see where I was putting the dollar bill. "You know better than that, Shela," I said. I managed to hold off any expression of disgust with myself until she had moved on to the next man. Clyde was right. I don't really look at their faces. But I can sure match the tits with names.

I saw Clyde huddling in a corner with one of his hulks. Giving instructions, I guess. Another hulk came in the front door. I couldn't tell for sure in the dim light, but he looked like one of the three I saw in the Chevy in town. He looked around, saw Clyde, joined him. Something changed hands. Clyde seemed pleased. He gave whatever it was to the hulk he was first talking to and said some final thing. Finished, he took a step toward me, saw me looking, gave a come-here wave. Another dancing-girl reached me as I stood up. I didn't feel like testing myself with any more do-I-know-you games. I looked at her chest. "Hi, Toni," I said and pushed a dollar bill across the bar for her to pick up. On the way across the dance floor I felt like kicking myself, but was content with snorting and cursing myself for being several kinds of male chauvinistic pig asshole.

"Let's walk," Clyde said. "Neither of us gets enough exercise. And walking'll give us a chance to see if anybody's watching the place."

"Fine by me. Where we going?"

"Fortieth Street."

"Sounds good."

"Maybe you saw Mack come in," Clyde said as we cut through the Drexel campus. "He's one of the guys I had watching Bigler's place. Kallir and the other goons left while they were watching. Mack took some Polaroids of them. I left instructions for the men on the door to keep an eye out for them."

"Clyde, you're a genius."

He nodded. "That's something I never call myself. Enough other people do I never have to.

We didn't see a metallic blue Mitsubishi parked nearby, but that didn't mean anything by itself. No cars started up behind us, a casual look to the rear didn't show anyone following in trace-maybe that meant something. Maybe they were looking for me at home. Maybe they were biding their time for some other reason.

*

Everyplace there's a college with more than a few hundred students, there's a nearby commercial development to provide the student body with goods and services not provided by the college-and separate the students from their money in the process. University City with its several colleges and universities is no exception.

"Fortieth Street" is what this commercial area is called, but 40th Street is only its main axis. It sprawls from 38th Street to 41st, from Market to below Spruce. It's got all the fast food joints, video arcades, sandwich shops, apartment blocks, bars, laundromats, movie houses, and sundries stores you'd expect to find in a commercial development designed to attract the college kiddies. It also has restaurants of various ethnic cuisines, nightclubs, pharmacies, clothing, and fine shops. Fortieth Street doesn't only attract students and faculty from Penn and the other colleges and universities that give University City its name, it attracts people from all over University City, and beyond. Some residents of University City do nearly all of their shopping on 40th Street and within a few blocks of it.

"We have to be back by eight," Clyde said when we settled into a Hungarian place. "I've got a couple bands coming in at nine. The dancers get off at eight and I want to be there to pay them at quitting time."

We kept the dinner conversation on safe topics that wouldn't upset our digestion. You know; what movies we'd seen recently, which books we'd read, what were our upcoming vacation plans. We didn't talk religion, politics, work, or my problem. It was the conversation of strangers who are feeling each other out, or the banter of old friends who don't need to probe around the edges. What we talked about was inconsequential, the thing that mattered was we talked. Old friends don't need to talk to be companionable. We are old friends, but we needed to talk. Not talking would have left me brooding over my problem. Old friend Clyde wasn't going to abandon me to brooding.

It was nearly seven we were ready to leave. Plenty of time to get back so Clyde could pay the dancing-girls when they got off work. Neither of us felt like walking that far so soon after eating. We caught a cab.

*

Music nights at the Side Car Club are potluck. You never know what you're going to get. The touring acts, the guys I want to write about for Rolling Stone, don't get booked here, they go to the clubs where every night is music night. It isn't that Clyde hasn't tried. He's told their managers and agents the place has the same capacity as the clubs they play in, which is true, and that it has better acoustics, which is a maybe. He's given these managers and agents the demographics of his music night crowds, which are exactly the demographics they want in an audience. But he never manages to book those acts.

The managers and agents always say their guys don't play go-go bars. They don't care that there are no dancing-girls on music nights.

So Clyde gets the local acts. The starters play the Side Car Club before they become up-and-comers. So do the never-gonna-make-its. Some of these local bands are good. Some go on to cut an album or two. Some find themselves opening for big names. A few wind up doing some headlining themselves. A few, a very few, make it big. Tonight's acts were more along the lines of garage bands that should have stayed in the garage.

The opener practiced and practiced until he had the sound of the young Dylan down pat, but hadn't a clue to what his music was about. I wouldn't have thought it was possible to botch "Lay, Lady, Lay" that badly. He received a round of polite applause when he bowed his way off at the end of his set. Nobody was all that enthusiastic when he came back on for the obligatory encore. Had he played later when the audience had drunk more, maybe they would have been more receptive-and maybe they would have booed him off the stage. There's no predicting what an audience will do once it's had enough to drink.

Faux Dylan was followed by a gangly group of post-teens who must have thought the name was The Rolling Stoneds. They got their drinks from the side bar, and Jimmy swore to me he was only feeding them soda, no alcohol. The cigarettes they were toking on looked store-bought from where I sat, but there are ways to turn a store-bought into something home-grown. I wasn't close enough to get a whiff of what they were blowing, and didn't think I wanted to-I want to be sober tonight. The audience got into the mood, drank a little faster, and Rolled with the Stoneds.

I stayed out of the way at closing time while Clyde supervised the straightening up. The bartenders and bouncers wiped the bars and tables clean, put up the stools and chairs, cased and stacked the empty bottles, refilled the coolers-the floors and food areas would wait until the cleaners showed up in the morning. Clyde and one of his hulks counted the take, which two hulks took out for night deposit. A little after 2:30 we all left.

Over a nightcap I said, "Tomorrow I've got to go home for a little while. Check the mail, check the answering machine, straighten up a bit."

"I'll get a couple of the guys," Clyde said.

I wasn't about to argue the point.

CHAPTER TWENTY-ONE

Two of Clyde's hulks showed up shortly after we finished our late breakfast. A couple of the dancing-girls, in mufti, were with them. So was Jimmy. Clyde had prepared me for the dancing-girls by saying, "Women are better at straightening up and cleaning than men are." I tried to tell him not to bother any kind of cleaning crew for me, but the hulks were okay-just in case. He said it was too late, they were already on their way, and he wasn't going to send them home.

Sometimes I think there must be a secret society or something; big men seem to congregate together. Clyde was six foot one, these strapping young bucks were taller. One of them, who looked like he wastes a significant portion of his life maneuvering Nautilus machines, flexed his biceps and rolled his shoulders at me.

"Take you long to learn how to do that?" I asked.

He barked out a laugh and didn't do it again. He'd tested the old bull and thought it ended in a draw.

Clyde caught that byplay. "You know what that's about," he said to me.

Yeah, I know, Clyde's told me. That behavior is endemic to the Class Mammalia. Come rutting season male mammals fight each other for the privilege of mating. It gets fuzzed up a bit when you get away from the herd animals. Females of the Orders Carnivorae and Primatae don't have their "seasons" according to the calendar; some females are always in estrus, so those males have more occasion to fight among themselves. Most Primates, that includes monkeys, apes, and us, live in social units bigger than what you might call the nuclear family. Those males vie for primacy, to be the Alpha Male. The biggest male almost always wins. In our two point seven million years of human evolution, Clyde claims, the bigger man was better able to get food for his woman and better able to fend off the saber tooth tiger. Therefore, he had his pick of the women. The young big men kept challenging the old big guys until the young guys beat the old guys. The big guys, who had first pick, usually got the best looking babes, according to Clyde.

He'd say that explains a phenomenon I observed when these two hulks and two off-duty dancing-girls showed up. The guys were certainly big, and the girls were certainly good-looking. The girls positioned themselves about equidistant between Clyde and the hulks. They were torn, Clyde would claim, between going for him, the alpha male, and going for the younger guys, who were bigger and someday would supplant him as the alpha. Jimmy wasn't as big as the two hulks, the girls paid him as little attention as they did me.

It makes sense of a sort. But then Clyde has to go and ruin it by saying that's why the rest of us, men like me who aren't the big hulks, go to places like his: it's the only way we can get the good-looking babes to entertain us like that.

Clyde's a good friend, but there are times when I hate him.

Nobody bothered with introductions. They all worked together and knew each other. I was both a regular at the Side Car and a friend of Clyde's, so they assumed I knew all their names. But I don't pay that much attention to the men, and-I hated to admit it to myself, but after my little experiment with Shela last night I had to-I couldn't be sure of who the dancing-girls were in their street clothes.

"I think you all remember what I told you last night, but just in case, I'll refresh your memory," Clyde told them when we were all assembled. "Some tough-guys have been giving Ham a very hard time. Yesterday morning they broke into his place and pretty thoroughly trashed it. Ham wants to straighten up. He doesn't think they took anything, but they might come back. We're going to help pick the place up. We're also going to be there with him in case the tough guys show up. If anybody wants out, say so. No problem."

The dancing-girls twittered. The hulks looked strong and invincible. Jimmy said, "Ham's a good guy." It was settled. We went outside and piled into three cars: Clyde and me in his T-bird; the girls had come together for primordial female protection; Jimmy had brought the hulks. "The problem with big guys," Clyde told me when we were on the way, "is so many of them think they're already on top of the shit heap just because they're big, and they don't have to do anything. So you gotta keep on top of them if you want anything to get done."

At midday on a Thursday there's plenty of parking in my neighborhood and we all were able to park close to my place. Several of the mommie-experience yuppettes were being watchful over their rampaging yuplings. Several looked suspiciously at my companions. Probably wondering what kind of orgy I had planned, what kind of bad influence I was going to be on their hubbies. I waved at them, they waved back. A yupling on a machine-gun trike tried to run me down. I thought of the .32 in my pocket, decided it wasn't a big enough caliber to kill the infernal machine, and dodged out of the way.

There was nothing notable in the mail, just a normal selection of sends and spends. No pays today.

Upstairs the place looked to be exactly as it was yesterday afternoon, though with that kind of chaos it would be impossible to tell if someone had come in and gone through everything again. Nobody said anything for a long moment. I guess it's like the aftermath of a tornado or an earthquake. Nothing prepares you for it, words are inadequate.

"Where do you want to start?" Clyde finally asked.

"I'll do the office myself," I said. "Otherwise, pick a place."

"All right, we'll start in the back and work our way toward you."

"Okay fine." I started to make my way to the front when Clyde stopped me with another question:

"Do you have anything in the bedroom you don't want anyone to see?"

I looked at him. "Like what?"

He shrugged. "How do I know what you don't want anybody to see?"

He could be talking about pornography, weapons, drugs, or any of a huge number of other things. I couldn't think of anything. "If I do have anything like that it's already been seen by someone I don't want to see it. We're all friends here, right?"

Without waiting for an answer I turned my back on them and continued to my office. Behind me I heard low voices and occasional expressions of whatever, but paid them no mind. I've always found moving to be ultimately a lot easier if I do all the packing myself. That way when it comes time to do the unpacking I know where everything is and get myself into shape more quickly. This was like letting someone else pack and unpack me. It would be a while, possibly a long while, before I'd be able to find half of my belongings. But the office was the most important, that's why I was doing it myself.

The first thing I did was turn the computer on and run a disk-checking utility to find out if there was any damage. I didn't bother to put the box on the table first, just left it on the floor. While that program was running, I sat in the middle of the mounds of paper on the floor and sorted through them. No sorting into individual files now, that would be a more long term proposition. The first step was to stack them according to which filing cabinet they went into. Everything for bookkeeping and tax use over here. General data and research material there. Research material, copies of proposals and manuscripts for published-and unpublished-articles in a third pile. Private clients on the left.

The disk utility finished running long before I finished what I was doing. There were a couple of bad sectors I don't think were on the hard drive before, but otherwise everything seemed to be fine. If they were in the middle of a program I wouldn't find out until I tried to run that program. Well, I'd be careful for a while, that's all. I made sure those sectors were isolated so they wouldn't cause any storage problems, then parked the drive, turned the machine off, and put it back on the table where it belonged. Then I went back to the papers on the floor.

When I finished making the first sort I went to see how everybody was doing. One of the dancing-girls was almost through in the bathroom. Jimmy and one of the hulks were putting the books back on the shelves in the middle room. That's something else I'll have to spend time on later; I've got a couple thousand volumes. If they aren't in order, I'll never be able to find anything. The other dancing-girl was putting things away in the kitchen.

"Sorry, Ham," she said when she saw me. "I don't like anybody messing around in my kitchen because they never put anything back where it belongs. I guess that's what I'm doing to you."

I assured her it was okay, I'd be able to find things.

Clyde and the other hulk were in the bedroom. The bed was back together, the closet clothes were hung, the drawers were back in place, and they were putting everything back in the drawers.

"There are too many of us to fit in here at once," Clyde said. "So I split us up. We're almost through in here."

"Everything else seems to be nearly through, too," I said. My voice was flat. I felt numbed by the magnitude of it all. "I don't know how to thank you."

"They're all on payroll," Clyde said. "I'll bill you." He didn't laugh, but I could tell he was making a joke.

"Fine," I said in the same flat voice. "That's only fair." I did think it was fair, Clyde shouldn't have to pay to help me. But I didn't feel like making jokes. I stood there watching dumbly for another moment, then said thanks again and left them to finish. Both dancing-girls were in the kitchen.

"We'll be finished here in a couple of minutes, Ham," one of them said.

"You'll have to rearrange the medicine cabinet, but the bathroom's done," said the other.

I mumbled thanks and continued on my way.

"Damn, you've got a lot of books," said the hulk who was shelving them.

"He's a writer," Jimmy said. "What do you expect?"

The hulk grunted.

Back in my office, I started filing the bookkeeping and tax stuff, that should be the easiest. In a few moments I heard noises in the other half of the big room. I looked; the two dancing-girls were straightening up. They'd brought the hulk from the bedroom to move furniture for them. Not that there was much furniture or that it was heavy. Most women, when a man is available, will use him for lifting and moving, even if the lifting and moving is something she can do herself. Clyde says women bred men to be pack animals.

"Let me in here," Clyde said a minute later.

Half of the bookkeeping stuff was filed. I put the rest of it in a neat stack out of Clyde's way and moved to the other side to work on the private client files while he started shelving the books and magazines in the divider bookcase.

In not more than another half hour it was all done. All except most of my filing. The major sorts were done and some of the paperwork was back where it belonged. The rest of the place was looking good, except most of it probably wasn't where I'd put it. Give me a couple of weeks and I'll have everything back where I can find it. I think.

I held the sparse Sindi DiWagne file in my hand. It seemed to be complete. I wondered why they didn't take it. Maybe they read it and didn't see anything of any apparent value. Maybe they weren't looking at the papers, only looking for parchment. I looked at the file, there wasn't much in it. A name, address, phone number. Less than two pages of scrawled notes, most of which I now knew to be false. If they looked at it, they wouldn't have found it to be good for anything but a few laughs. No wonder they left it intact.

I looked at Clyde and his crew-my crew. They didn't have to help me. Clyde, okay. He and I are old friends, I'd do the same for him if our positions were reversed. Jimmy, all right. He's a good guy and we get along fine. I'd probably give him a hand if he was in trouble. The two hulks and two dancing-girls, there was no need at all for them to help me. The few bucks Clyde was paying them for their time wasn't enough to explain why they'd bother.

And I couldn't even think of any of their names. It made me feel humble and grateful; an ass and an ingrate.

"It's inadequate, but I want to say thanks to all of you for your assistance," I said. "Let me do this, let me take you all out to dinner."

The dancing-girls and the hulks begged off, they had other commitments, I was a good guy and they were glad to help, any friend of Clyde's. Various excuses.

"Some other time, Ham," Jimmy said.

I felt more humbled and grateful. Maybe people in general are better than I give them credit for. Maybe I'm more cynical than I realized.

In another minute they were all gone except for Clyde.

Before they left, one of the dancing-girls gave me a quick kiss and said, "It'll be okay, Ham. In the meantime, if there's anything I can do, anything at all, just say so. I'll be glad to help." The kiss was on the cheek and the look she gave me was the kind of fondness a young woman might display toward a favorite uncle. She was cute and perky, and didn't look mature enough or old enough to be somebody who enforced policy on a day job.

I looked a question at Clyde when they were gone.

He looked amused. "Goddam, Ham," he said. "I'll bet if she was running around with her bare tits hanging out you'd know her name."

I sort of shrugged, too embarrassed to say anything. "Is that...?" was all I could manage to say.

"No, lad, that isn't Martha. I'm not going to do anything to help you figure out who Martha is until you're ready to meet her and deal with her as a real human being instead of just an entertaining pair of tits."

"That's right, rub it in, I deserve it." I felt shame, something I'd thought I left behind me years ago. Even the term by which I thought of and called these women, "dancing-girls," now seemed to me to be demeaning and dehumanizing. I felt like kicking myself, or crawling into a hole and pulling it in on top of me. Damn Sindi DiWagne. In the past week, I'd come face to face with so many things I didn't like about myself, things I hadn't had any idea were there, I was beginning to strongly dislike this guy Ham Eliot.

"Cut the shit, lad," Clyde boomed. "Stop feeling so sorry for yourself. All that's happened is you've demonstrated that you're just as male as the next man when it comes to women. The difference is that most men never realize what you do, and the ones who do mostly don't see anything wrong with it. Now what you do is, you buy a bottle of something nice for each of the guys and some flowers for the girls. They'll appreciate the gesture and know you gave a damn about their help."

He stopped talking and looked around. "Doesn't look like there's anything more to do here. Let's go."

"Where are we going?"

"To a flower shop and a state store. Where else?"

The bell rang as we were going out the door. We looked at each other, wondering who it could be. I brushed past Clyde on the small landing in front of my door and led the way down. If it was danger, it was only right that I should face it first. If it was a neighbor, that neighbor would expect to see me.

It was Jimmy. He looked worried.

"That's your Mustang out there, isn't it?" he asked as soon as I opened the door. "The maroon one?"

"Yeah, why?"

Jimmy went out and walked toward my car, he talked at me over his shoulder as he went. "When I was a kid, my dad had a Mustang just like yours. "I learned how to work on cars on it. I thought it would be fun to look under the hood. You know, for old time sake? There's something you should see."

The hood was up. I saw the two hulks standing on the other side of

Jimmy's car from mine. The dancing-girls were gone.

"What?" I looked under the hood.

"That wire." He pointed at the battery.

"What about it?" I ride in cars and I drive them, but I'm not a mechanic. I can usually find the carburetor, the battery, the air filter, the fan belt, and the radiator. I'm real good at pointing out the engine block first time. Beyond that I don't know, and don't want to know the workings of the internal combustion engine. But even I could recognize that there was something amiss under my hood.

Two heavy duty cables are locked onto the top of the battery. I'd never before seen an extra wire coming out along side one of the cables, but one was now. I looked closer and found another wire under the other cable.

"Shit," I said. "Does this mean what I think it does?"

Jimmy didn't say anything, he just looked at the wires.

Clyde crowded in. "Oh my god," he said softly.

"Shit, shit, shit." I got down on the pavement and looked under the front of the car. I had to crawl halfway under before I could see the wires and where they went. Then I lay there looking at it for what seemed like a very long time before easing myself back out and standing up.

"Anybody here into explosive ordnance disposal?" I asked.

"What do you mean?" Clyde asked.

"I mean there's what looks like a two-pound block of C-4 taped to the firewall. Those wires lead to a fuse in it."

"Jesus H fucking Christ," Clyde said softly. "You turn the key in the ignition and it's no more Ham Eliot."

I nodded.

"Give me your keys," Jimmy said. "I'll go inside and call the cops, tell them there's a bomb."

"Wait," Clyde said at the same time I said:

"Don't." I think I looked pale. I know I felt weak. I didn't look at them, I just said, "Back off to a safe distance," and went to open the trunk of my car. "Do it!" I snapped when they argued. "Do it right now." I didn't look to see where they went.

The trunk of my car is, I guess, just like the trunk of any car that's had only one owner for as long as mine. It's full of all kinds of stuff that got put in it one time or another and forgotten about. It also has a toolbox. I got a pair of wire cutters from the box and rooted around to see if there was anything else that might be useful. There was. Once upon a time I helped a friend build an addition to his house. Just to be cautious, I wore a hardhat. After one day working with the circular saw, I got tired of sawdust on my face, and attached a Plexiglas shield to the back of it. That way, if I wore the hardhat backward, I could both protect my brain-box and keep sawdust out of my eyes. That hardhat was still in the trunk where I tossed it when the job was finished. There was also an old pair of heavy duty work gloves. I put on the hardhat and gloves and went back to the business end of the car.

A long time ago I suffered through a day of instruction on explosives. I remembered what C-4 looked like, and that all by itself it was basically inert- you can take a hammer and pound on it, or burn it in a fire without anything happening. It takes an explosion to set it off. It's the fuse and the wires that can trip you up. And hidden detonators. I remembered clearly the steps in disarming a bomb. I strained to remember the things you could do wrong in disarming one, and couldn't come up with anything. Shit, shit, triple shit. The only thing to do was follow the steps and hope I didn't do any of the things I couldn't remember not to do.

The first step was cut the wires. Then remove the detonator from the bomb. That neutralizes it, makes it harmless. I squatted down in front of the grill so the engine block was between as much of me and the C-4 as possible. Even though the bomb looked very straight-forward, I didn't want to take any chances. This way, if the bomb was booby-trapped, maybe all I had to worry about was concussion and the hood falling on me. I reached in and clipped one wire. Nothing happened, so I pulled the clipped end away from the battery. Then I clipped the other end. Again, nothing happened. I bent that end away and realized I'd been holding my breath. I took a couple of deep slow breaths to calm myself and stood up.

I heard someone ask, "Is it safe?" I didn't look, just held up one hand and signaled them to stay put. Then I went around to the side and leaned under the hood to see if I could locate the explosive from above. It was right there. I had a clear view of the fuse as well. I squirreled a hand in and found I could get a secure grip on the fuse. All I had to do now was pull the fuse straight out and it would all be safe. If the fuse wasn't booby-trapped. If I didn't do anything wrong. If I did anything wrong now, there was nothing to protect me from the explosion. I still couldn't remember any of the things that I could do wrong.

I drew the fuse straight out, didn't twist it or press on it too hard. It came out easily. I carefully laid it on top of the engine and peeled off the duct tape that held the C-4 to the firewall. There wasn't a pressure-release fuse under it. I breathed a deep sigh of relief, then went to the trunk, dropped the C-4 into it, peeled off the gloves, tossed them and the hardhat into the trunk, and closed it. Clyde and Jimmy were already at the front of the car when I got back to it.

"I always suspected you had more balls than brains," Clyde said. "Now I know it." He sounded relieved.

"That's the bomb?" Jimmy asked, looking at the fuse. "It doesn't look like much."

"That's just the fuse. It's the dangerous part, don't touch it."

"You put the C-4 in the trunk?" Clyde asked.

I nodded. "It's safe there. At least for awhile."

Jimmy needed an explanation. "C-4's inert. You can burn it and it'll make a fire, just like Sterno. You can beat it with a hammer and probably all that will happen is you'll make smaller pieces. It needs an explosion to set it off, that's what the fuse is for. It doesn't take much to set it off." While I talked I removed the wires from the fuse. "Watch," I said when the fuse was free of the wires. I threw it high into the air. It arched up and hit in the middle of the street about thirty feet away. The impact set it off with a very satisfying bang.

"See what I mean?"

Jimmy nodded, mouth open and eyes wide. I didn't think he fully understood the danger.

"We should leave before you get scolded," Clyde said. He was looking at one of the houses. A yuppette stood on her porch, arms folded sternly across her chest, glowering at me.

I shrugged at her apologetically and went to pick up the debris from the fuse.

"Mommies disapprove of fireworks," I said when I got back to Clyde.

"I don't blame them," he said.

"Neither do I."

We got into his T-Bird and drove off.

CHAPTER TWENTY-TWO

"They tried to kill me, Clyde. I mean this was for real. If Jimmy hadn't just happened to look under my hood, the next time I started my car would have been it." I shivered.

"Sure seems that way."

"They must have done it yesterday morning when they trashed my place."

"They could have done it this morning, or anytime since the last time you drove your car."

"They planted that bomb before I could give them the map, if I had it."

"What does that tell you?"

"They don't care if I give them the map."

"Yeah. What else does it tell you?"

"It tells me they don't think I have the map."

"Right on. Anything else?"

"Shit. It tells me they plan to kill me no matter what." Now I started trembling.

"Nice people you're hanging out with these days, Ham."

"Shit. Clyde, the next time I'm in your place and some floozy comes over and says you sent her to me, I'm going to throw her out the door. Then I'm coming after you." Neither of us said anything for a block, then I added, "If I live through this."

"You will." But I noticed he didn't say how.

One step at a time. The first step was a stop at the florist at Fortieth Street. Clyde took care of buying the flowers and saying where to deliver them. The only thing I had to do with it was, when he told me how much, I paid for them.

There are only two State Stores in all of University City, one of which is on Market Street right near the Fortieth Street commercial district. We didn't go to it, though. The Pennsylvania Liquor Control Board provisions both of the University City stores more with the wino in mind than the vinophile. Once every few years the PLCB proposes opening another University City store, one which will appeal to the latter. But every time they do members of the community rise up in indignation and protest that liquor stores only serve to attract winos from outside the community. That's always struck me as falling under the heading of self-fulfilling prophesy. If the store was patronized by vinophiles it wouldn't need to cater to the winos. So the way it works out is, nearly all of the white collar types and academics who live in University City go elsewhere to do their liquor shopping. So Clyde drove into town to the State Store on Chestnut Street. Here, as in the florist shop, he did the buying and told me how much to pay the man.

Throughout, Clyde kept up a running patter. His intent in doing the mundane and making small talk was obvious. He wanted to distract me, maybe get my mind running in constructive patterns. It didn't work. My mind kept spiraling around they-tried-to-kill-me.

I'm a grown-up living in a nominally civilized society. Things like this aren't supposed to happen. Nobody goes out and gratuitously tries to kill someone. Warfare is different, that's collective insanity on a national level. Clyde would say it's something else, but that's Clyde's hangup. Yes, I went away to war once and actively tried to kill people who were just as actively trying to kill me. But I had the excuse of only being nineteen and not knowing any better. My country and the other two countries involved were going through a phase of collective insanity at the time, so. But since I came back to this civilized society, nobody has tried to kill me. I mean, it's not done, is it?

Okay, one time I was doing some work for a private client and found myself running afoul of the local Mafia. Even they didn't try to kill me. A couple of nice Italian boys from South Philadelphia came around to teach me to keep-a my nose out of places it didn't belong. They didn't want to kill me, they wanted to put me in the hospital. Fortunately for me, they were doing it for the sport of it, where I didn't understand their intent and fought for survival. That meant I fought dirtier than they did. They were treated and released. Then I was able to explain to an emissary of the capo that it was all a misunderstanding and please accept my apologies, it won't happen again. The capo liked my style and appreciated my skill in sending his nice boys to the hospital. So much so that he offered me a job. He took no offense when I politely refused his offer. We parted company with the understanding that I'd never cross his path again.

The Mafia played tough, but they didn't try to kill me.

Dopeheads sometimes commit murder in the course of committing whatever crimes they are committing to dope their heads. Drug dealers kill each other over territory, or kill someone for stealing their drugs or money. Family members and close friends sometimes kill each other when interpersonal stresses get so high they see no way out of them. Once in awhile a member of organized crime gets killed as a warning or as an object lesson. There are the young punks on the street today who have no concept of life and death other than what they've gleaned from a lifetime of TV and movies, the ones who casually kill robbery victims for not handing over their money fast enough, or kill other punks for looking at them the wrong way. Nearly all other homicides are the result of accident or negligence.

I didn't see how that bomb against my Mustang's firewall fit into any of those categories. Even conceding that Bigler had gotten himself involved with designer drugs, I hadn't stolen drugs or money from him. I wasn't muscling in on his territory. I came into things late, with no understanding of what was happening or knowledge of who was involved. After briefly being infected with greed, I tried to get out. And said so. He knows I don't have the map he wants-I think he knows. Yet he tried to kill me anyway. More accurately, he had someone try for him.

It takes a special mindset to look at someone and kill him. Maybe it doesn't take that same mindset to tell someone else to commit murder. Bigler threatened my life. Kallir and company planted a bomb rather than try to take me out face to face. They'd made threats often enough, but it was always to "hurt," never to kill.

I used to be able to kill people. But that was a long time ago, in a far away place. And they were never people I talked to. They were always people I could find a way of looking at as not quite human, not really people. I could probably get that mindset back, but I knew it would not be easy, and it could only be in extremis. Maybe none of these people had what it took to walk up to someone and kill him.

Well, hell, Bigler made his money by unscrupulously manipulating paper. He lost it the same way. He never made anything in his life. He didn't know what life was about. He wouldn't know how to deal with someone who has always made things, who knows the nitty-gritty. Maybe he'll freak out if his instrument of murder lands on his desk.

"I'm going to give it back to him," I said.

"Give what back?" Clyde asked.

"The C-4. Let's go back to my place so I can wrap it in some gift paper."

"First tell me more."

"You have his office address?"

"Yes."

"Good. I'll get a clipboard and deliver the package myself. Have someone sign for it. Include a note."

"Telling him to fuck off?"

"Approximately."

"You got it."

*

It only took about fifteen minutes to write a note, compose a delivery signature slip on my computer, print out a dozen copies, and make the copies look like they'd been carried around for a while. Clyde wrapped the block of explosive and the note in kraft paper while I took care of the signature-slips. He addressed the package and marked it "personal" while I did the work on the computer. He and I filled out a few of the slips. We used different pens to make signatures on them. We made plans as we headed into town. Clyde dropped me off in front of the right Penn Center building about half past four. I took the elevator to the twelfth floor, got off and looked dumb.

"Can I help you, sir?" The receptionist was about thirty. Her blonde-streaked hair looked like it received weekly attention from a hair dresser. Her dress was conservative while still being stylish. Evidently Bigler Entrepreneurships occupied the entire floor; the reception desk blocked one end of the elevator lobby, a closed door shut off the other end. A nameplate on the desk said she was Ms. Rosario.

"Yeah," I said. "I have a delivery for a Mister," I looked at the brown wrapped package and made a show of comparing it with the paper on my clipboard-I even flipped through a couple of sheets to make sure I had the right one, "Mister Bigler. Where can I find him?"

Her manner was amused superiority. "I'll take it."

"I don't know. It's got to be signed for." I looked uncertainly at the package and the slip.

"That's all right, I sign for everything that comes in."

"You sure a that?" I looked a little suspicious.

"I'm sure." She almost concealed her mockery.

"It says personal on the package, and my instructions are to make sure it's signed for." A touch of wariness.

She held out a hand for the clipboard. I reluctantly gave it to her. She looked at the top page, peeled up a couple of other pages to glance at, reached for the package. When I didn't immediately hand it over she said, "I do this all the time, every day."

As if to prove her point, an elevator opened and courier from a real delivery service stepped out. "Hi, Cathy," he said as he came to the desk.

She greeted him by name, took the offered clipboard and package, signed, returned the clipboard. "See?" she said as he returned to the elevator. "All the time, every day." She flipped open a red-bound diary and logged in the package. Then she looked at me expectantly. "I'm sure your boss wouldn't like to know how you're just standing around not letting me sign for the package. What do you think?"

"Well, you signed for that other one, so I guess it's okay." I handed her the package.

She looked at the address, signed briskly, handed back the clipboard, logged in the delivery. She looked at me still standing there. "Anything else?"

"Um. I go now? That's it?"

"Yes, you go now. I'll make sure Mister Bigler gets the package."

"Oh. Okay," I said uncertainly. "It's my first day on the job. You know?"

"I know. It's a tough world out there. But hang in, you'll do all right."

"Um. Okay. Thank you." I retreated to the elevators, looked at them like I wasn't too sure of what they were supposed to do, or how to get them to do it, and pushed the button for a down box. One came and I went. The receptionist started laughing before the doors were completely closed.

Yes, I overdid it. Deliberately. The receptionist would want to tell somebody about this incredibly dumb delivery guy right away. I was sure she'd see to it that Bigler would get the package before he left for the day. If he was in. I hoped he was in.

I had to wait at the curb for almost two minutes before Clyde pulled up.

"I drove around the block twice and still had time to make a phone call. What took you so long?"

"I wanted to make sure Bigler got the package today."

"Did he?"

"If he's still in he will." I told him what I did with the receptionist. He got quite a laugh out of it.

Clyde put his car in a parking garage and we went back and stood in a bus-stop crowd where we could watch Bigler's Penn Center building without being noticed by anyone coming out of it who might be looking for us. At a quarter after five our quarry came out and flagged a cab. We split up; Clyde to redeem his car, me to get another cab and follow Bigler.

The cabbie draped his arm over the back of the driver's seat and turned to look at me when I told him where to go. "You're kidding me, right?"

"No I'm not kidding. Follow that cab. Now let's go before we lose him." I didn't look at the cabbie, I kept my eyes on the cab Bigler was in.

"Am I on Candid Camera?" The cabbie was still looking at me.

"No, you're not on Candid Camera. Let's go." To demonstrate my sincerity and get him moving, I handed him a ten. "That's over and above fare and tip if we don't lose him."

The cabbie looked at the ten, then faced front and asked, "Any particular cab?"

"The one that's got its left turn signal on."

"Got it," he said, and pulled into traffic. Between there and 18th Street, he cut off a Honda, caused a Toyota to swerve and nearly hit an Olds, and made a Beemer hit its brakes so hard it fishtailed. "Damn foreign cars," he muttered. "If they can't drive in American traffic they should go home." The light changed just before we reached 18th Street and he barely made the turn in front of the southbound traffic.

"If I live through this, that ten's yours," I said. "You get another one if we don't lose him."

The cabbie laughed. "I like a big tipper." He maneuvered to two cars behind Bigler's cab and stayed there.

I thought Bigler would go home, but followed him just in case. By the time Clyde got his car and got to Bigler's neighborhood, I'd already be there if that's where he went. In that case, we'd meet on the corner of 4th and Pine. If I wasn't there, he'd find a pay phone, call the Side Car, and leave the number of that phone. Then, when Bigler got to where he was going, I'd call the Side Car, get the number, and call Clyde at the pay phone so we could plan our next step.

Bigler made it easy for us, he went home. I had my cab go a block farther before I got out. As promised, I gave the cabbie a second ten over and above the fare and tip.

Clyde reached the intersection a few minutes after I did and found a parking space.

"Ready?" I asked.

"In a minute." I followed him up Pine Street. He stopped next to a red Buick parked by a fire hydrant. The three men in it got out. I recognized two of them as the hulks who helped me at my apartment this afternoon. The third was one of Clyde's other bouncers.

"Watch where we go," he told them after we said our hellos "If we don't come out in five minutes, make like the Marines on Iwo Jima."

"Sounds like fun," the third man said grinning. He flexed his muscles.

"If you have to come in," Clyde said, "it won't be fun, it'll be deadly serious."

That didn't seem to subdue muscles very much. Clyde's mouth made a disgusted twitch. "Keep him out of trouble," he told the others. "Let's go."

The hulks followed us as far as Panama Street. Clyde stopped them where they couldn't be seen from Bigler's house and told them to wait there. Once we were around the corner and far enough down the street that we could talk quietly without being overheard by his guys, I stopped.

"Clyde, I don't want to go inside and I don't think we should let Bigler see you. He may not know about you. If not, I'd rather keep it that way."

"What do you propose?"

"You stay out of sight. I'll talk to him in the doorway. If he tries to pull anything, I'll yell and you come running."

He thought about it for a moment, then nodded. "All right. I'll walk past and take a look in the windows. I'll let you know whether or not it looks clear.

Okay?"

Good old Clyde. He's concerned about my safety and doesn't want me going into a lion's den. But all he'd be able to see from the sidewalk was part of the front rooms on the first floor. He wouldn't see anything or anyone deeper in the house or on a higher floor.

"Thanks, Clyde," I said. "I'll wait for your signal."

He walked along the opposite side of the street. I smiled, that hadn't occurred to me. He'll get a better angle of view that way. When he was well past Bigler's house he turned back and gave me the okay sign. I swallowed and started down the block.

These old houses don't have porches. They abut the sidewalk and have stone, usually limestone, steps that jut into the walk. Bigler's house had four steps. The top one was about two feet deep. I stood on it and looked for a doorbell. It was a plain button set into the inner side of the frame, about a foot above the door handle. It looked like it was the original doorbell, installed when the house was first wired. I pushed it and heard a raspy, electrical buzzing somewhere inside. After ten or fifteen seconds with no response I pushed it again, a longer push this time.

A female voice from somewhere deep in the recesses of the house cried out, "I'm coming, I'm coming." A moment later she opened the door.

She was dressed for going out, though I couldn't tell whether it was for the boardroom, a society ladies' charity function, or dinner. Her hair was the kind that so often seems to come with money-chemically created blonde that looks like it was chiseled out of concrete. Her face was long, drawn, and from the horsey set. The product, I thought, of too many generations of Main Line inbreeding. The way she looked at me, she obviously thought I was the product of too many generations of gutter inbreeding.

"Mrs. Bigler?"

"Yes?"

"Would you tell Eddie that Mr. Eliot is here to see him, please." I didn't think she was going to invite me in.

She blinked at the "Eddie." "I'm afraid that Mr. Bigler is busy at the moment and can't come to the door." I was right about her not inviting me in.

"Mrs. Bigler, just tell him I'm here. He'll want to see me." She hesitated, looked a bit uncertain, so I went on. "Tell him if he doesn't want to see me now, the next package he gets from me will be an even bigger surprise." She still hesitated. "If you don't go and get him for me, I'll just go to the nearest pay phone and call him." To prove my point I recited their phone number.

She still seemed uncertain, but said, "Wait here, I'll see if he wants to come to the door." She closed it on me. I heard a rattling that might have been a security chain being attached.

The wait before I heard the security chain rattling again and the door flung open wasn't as long as when I first rang the bell. Bigler glared at me furiously. His breath came in snorts, I could smell alcohol on it. A wisp of hair was out of place.

"Hambletonian, I told you never to intrude on me. What are you doing at my home?" The doorsill was a step higher than where I stood, he tried to use his additional height over me to intimidate.

It didn't work. "Eddie," I spoke in a condescending tone, "you had your goons try to kill me. They weren't any more successful at that than any of the other things you've had them try recently. Only this time they pissed me off."

"I don't know what you're talking about." Fire was in his eyes-and lies on his tongue.

"Cut the shit, Eddie. You got my package."

"Why didn't you go to the police if you think I tried to have you killed? You can't prove I did it, that's why."

"I don't need to prove it to know it. I'm here, Eddie, to tell you to stop fucking with me. I don't have the map and I don't know where it is. I'm out of this. You're going to leave me alone from now on. Do you understand?"

The smile he gave me would have done a Great White shark proud. "Hambletonian, it's you who doesn't understand. You know who I am. You know where I live. You know where my office is. You present a clear and present danger to me. There's only one way you can get out of this."

I didn't like the sound of that, but I wasn't going to let him know it bothered me. "Eddie, don't fuck with me. That's the bottom line. You're a businessman, you understand bottom line. You stay away from me. You leave me alone, I leave you alone. You fuck with me, you're fucked." My words were much calmer and more confident than I felt.

"You poor, dumb, stupid bastard."

"I'm going home now, Eddie. You're going to leave me alone."

He shut the door on me. My knees were weak, but I went down the steps and, looking for all the world like nothing was wrong, walked to the end of the block where Clyde waited for me.

CHAPTER TWENTY-THREE

Clyde wanted me to stay with him until everything blew over. I told him either it was already over, or it was going to get a lot worse. Either way, hiding out wasn't going to make anything any bit better-and me hiding out with him might make his life a whole log harder. He argued, he fought, he pleaded. I insisted I'm forty years old, I don't need a mama hen watching over me. I told him it's nice to have friends who give a enough of a damn to want to help and protect me, but if there was something to be faced here, I had to face it. Anybody else around would be in the way-like an innocent victim is in the way.

Over dinner I finally agreed to check in with him three times a day; 11:00 AM, six PM, and midnight. He swore he'd round up a posse and come after me if I didn't. I told him don't bother. He swore vengeance if anything happened to me. I told him to forget it, nothing was going to happen. I wished I felt as confident as I talked.

It was after eight when I got home. I told myself I had to get busy on the smoke-filled rooms piece for Mother Jones. So I headed straight to my office. The light wasn't blinking on my phone machine, so I settled myself on the floor and started going through the pile of papers destined to be refiled into the research material for proposals and articles cabinet. Somewhere in there I had a few notes and clippings, and a copy of the proposal. First I ordered the manila folders, then looked at each piece of paper in turn and put it into the right folder. No point rooting through the stuff now just to pull out the contents of one slim file, and then sort the rest of it later. Do both at the same time, save time later, I told myself. What I was really doing, of course, was giving my conscious mind something to concentrate on so it wouldn't start running itself in circles and entirely knot up my mental abilities.

After a couple of hours the sorting and refiling got boring enough my mind started doing its curlicues anyway and I turned on the tube to give it another distraction. The distraction turned out to be an annoying distraction, because I didn't know what the program was, who the characters were, or anything about the on-going story line. Back in the Eighties I was a TV addict. I watched four or five hours a night, more on the weekends. In '89 my TV broke. I decided to break the addiction before getting a new idiot box. I suffered through about three days of withdrawal, and believe me it was suffering, then learned to live quite nicely without it. After a few months I decided I liked not having a TV anymore. It did leave me at something of a disadvantage in social situations when the people I was with started discussing current programs, but hey, that was the price I had to pay for being intellectually superior, right?

In the beginning of '92, I decided to get a new TV in time for the Winter Olympics. At first I thought I'd spend about three weeks glued to the tube, watching all the programs I'd heard so much about but never seen.

In two days of conscientious watching, the most intelligent program I saw was a rerun episode of The Untouchables from when I was a kid. I concluded that three years earlier TV had been dumb, and in the intervening time the lowest common denominator had dumbed down. Since then I've watched the Olympics, the Somalia intervention, the Phillies, Flyers, and Eagles-when they are winning-and a few things on PBS. In social situations I still sometimes have to be pseudo-superior intellectually, but at least I no longer have the feeling that maybe I'm missing something.

I don't watch the local news, either. The news directors seem to be constitutionally incapable of presenting national or international news without putting a local slant on it. The field reporters are constantly sticking microphones in the faces of people who have just undergone personal tragedy and asking how they feel, or other inane questions. The anchors are so-o-o sincere and coif their hair into such ill-fitting wigs I can't stand to hear or look at them.

I left the local news on when 11:00 arrived. Sure enough, one of the lead stories was a tragedy that happened someplace else. Sure enough, it was presented with a local angle. Sure enough, a reporter stuck a microphone in the face of a grieving brother and asked how he felt. Believe it or not, that local angle got me off the floor and sitting in front of the TV.

The story was about a commuter plane that went down in North Carolina. According to an eye-witness, who had a microphone stuck in his wide-eyed face, there was an explosion and when he looked up he saw this fireball and a plane fell out of the sky. All fifteen people on board were killed. The plane disintegrated in mid-air. Bodies and burning debris were strewn over nearly a hundred acres of farmland. A local reporter in North Carolina came on camera and speculated about a bomb being aboard the plane. He said the National Transit Safety Board was investigating, but so far had no comment about anything.

The local angle was a Delaware Valley resident was one of the victims. They showed a picture of her and gave her name. Both were Sindi DiWagne.

I sat numbed in front of the flickering pictures and droning voices without making a bit of sense of any of them. There was probably a story about a fire or a broken water main; one about a party at a city recreation center, a church, or a suburban synagogue; one or two murders. They did the weather and sports. I neither saw nor heard any of it.

It took time to sort through my feelings about her being dead. I hadn't known she had a brother. Then again, we never got into that sort of intimate discussion with each other. A brother I didn't know about somehow made her more of a fantasy than she already was. In the past week I had been been madly, passionately, infatuated with her. She had manipulated me, used me, and set me up as a diversion so she could make her getaway with a possible fortune. I had hated her. I had sold myself to her, and redeemed myself. I had been confronted by some very bad people and was lucky to get away with nothing more than a moderate beating. I faced some things I hadn't known and didn't like about myself.

How did I feel about her? I felt manipulated, used, and betrayed. I felt angry. I felt-oh god what a body-I felt lust. I felt what-might-have-been. If she'd been honest with me. If there really was a pot of gold at the end of that map. If I'd gotten my share. If she'd loved me as she once claimed. If we'd gone off together and started our lives anew.

If. The saddest, most rueful, most depressing word in the language. The word most used to place blame and make excuses.

If. There was no if here. It was over. It was done. She lied to me. She cheated me. There was no pot of gold. There was no share for me. There never had been any love.

All there had ever been was a lonely man's hopes and dreams. A poor man's greed. Nothing real. Only fantasy. That's all there ever was. Always and forever, 'til death do us part.

And now Sindi DiWagne was dead. Murdered by Edward Bigler.

There was no explanation other than murder for the explosion that blew her plane out of the sky. It was asking too much of coincidence to think she just happened to be on an airplane that blew up for any other reason. Bigler wanted her dead so badly he was willing to kill fourteen other people in order to make sure Sindi DiWagne died.

It was done, she was dead. I could only assume he had the map. I was out of it. If he didn't have the map there was no way to find it. It might have been a bit of the reported burning debris from the plane. Maybe it got loose in the fall and blew away to never be found again, or be too damaged by the elements to be readable if it ever was found. Maybe she had mailed it to herself and died before it arrived at its destination, now destined to spend eternity in a dead letter office. Possibly it would make its way back to her brother in Warminster. What would he make of it? He'd probably get rid of it with her other effects-in a garage sale or in a grief-cleansing fire. The chances of Bigler getting his hands on it if he didn't already have it were diminishingly small. My chances had diminished into a black hole in some inaccessible galaxy in an unknown part of the universe. I was out of it. Sayanora, Sindi DiWagne. So long, Eddie Bigler.

Then I remembered a few hours ago Bigler as much as said he wanted me dead regardless.

Shit.

But why? He had what he wanted. I never had anything to do with this map business, not really. There was no reason for him to come after me. No matter what I knew, I had no proof. So what if I knew who he was, where he lived, where his office was? I had no way to claim any share of any treasure, nor did I love Sindi DiWagne; so I had no revenge motive to go after him. I had no evidence to give to the FBI or to any police department. I decided to call him tomorrow and declare a truce.

I did my damnest to ignore the fact that either he deliberately had fourteen innocent people murdered in order to kill Sindi DiWagne, or he gave his orders in a way that didn't preclude such a mass murder. I did my best not to think about how ruthless and uncaring this said he was. If I tried hard enough, I could even ignore for the moment the probability that Edward Bigler would allow no truce.

I wanted a drink.

The special-occasion champagne I had in the pantry was the only alcohol

I'd had on hand. If I wanted a drink I had to go out for it. Even if the champagne was still there, this didn't count as a special occasion. I went out to one of the neighborhood bars on Baltimore Avenue.

None of my yuppie neighbors were in it. They never are. They do their tippling in private clubs, faculty clubs, lounges near their offices. Or they buy well known brands of booze and wine at the better State Stores outside of University City and do their drinking in the comfort and privacy of their own homes. They don't drink in the neighborhood bars. These local bars are richly populated by the blue collar and unemployed people whose apartments and houses haven't yet been taken over by the upwardly-mobile middle class infestation that has been the bane of the neighborhood, with a liberal sprinkling of students and folks like me. No one dresses to impress in these bars. People go to them to get comfortable, be friendly, and do some serious or not-so-serious drinking.

The Mud In Your Eye had a cheerful, not quite raucous, crowd that night. Most of them knew most of the others by first name. Most of them knew me by name and shouted out greetings when I came through the door. First they tried to include me in the frivolity, but I wasn't in the mood. Several saw I was feeling down and tried to cheer me up, but I didn't want cheering up. I wanted a few quiet drinks and time to think. Time to mourn? I wasn't sure I wanted to mourn Sindi DiWagne. I wasn't sure she deserved mourning. That thought almost made me cry.

I couldn't think in there, and nobody was going to let me drink quietly, so after one beer I bought a six-pack and headed home. It was a couple minutes of midnight and I considered calling Clyde from the pay phone before I left, but didn't want to make the call in front of all these people who knew my name. Besides, Clyde wouldn't round up a posse and come after me before I could walk the few blocks from the bar to my apartment.

Tomorrow night there'd be a lot of people on the streets, but not as Thursday turns to Friday. Most people have to get up for work in the morning, most of the worker bees are already in bed by midnight. I had the street to myself once I got off Baltimore Avenue. I guess that's why I noticed the footsteps behind me. That and the fact they didn't sound until I was in the middle of the block-and they were already close.

I walked along without apparent concern-and listened. There were two sets of steps behind me, coming faster than I was going. I was in a dark spot between two street lamps when they got close enough for me to hear them coming up one on each side of me. That sounded threatening; regular people out for a late night walk talk to each other, these two were silent except for the sound of their footsteps. I knew that muggers who work in teams often grab their victims from opposite sides. I got ready.

Before I reached the next pool of light a hand grabbed my right arm. I immediately twisted down and to my left, and kept going into a roll that threw my body into the shins and feet belonging to that hand. I curled the six-pack in one arm, like a running back protects the ball when he's being tackled.

My maneuver took him by surprise and threw him off balance. I could feel his upper body swinging through the space I had just occupied. In such rapid succession that I was only afterward able to put it in order, I heard the swish of something cutting through the air, a solid thunk of something hard striking skull, he made a sound like "gaahgh," and fell heavily over me. If I'd had the time to think about it, I wouldn't have liked the sound his head made when it slammed into the sidewalk.

I rolled away before whatever hit him could strike again and left the six-pack where I went down. I came up in a crouch, pulling my .32 out of my pocket.

A vagrant beam of light glanced off my little pistol. The other man said, "Shit," and dashed into the deeper shadows between two houses. He made a muted racket going through the backyards. Did he look vaguely familiar or was it my imagination?

From the time the hand first grabbed me until the second man ran couldn't have been more than five seconds. Other than the gaahgh and the "shit," none of us had said anything. It was all very fast and very quiet.

I fixed my gaze on the downed man for a long moment while I listened. He was limp and motionless. No one gave any cry of alarm. I didn't hear anyone creeping about.

I went over to check my first attacker. I turned his face to look at it in the dim light. It was Hondo. No wonder the one who fled looked familiar; he must have been Kallir. The left side of Hondo's forehead was bashed. I probed at it with a fingertip. It yielded. I turned his head the other way, it felt wet in the back. That area was also soft to the touch. I don't know why in books they always check the neck for a pulse, that one's too easy to miss. I know exactly where the pulse is in the wrist, but didn't see much point in looking for it. With two head injuries like that, Hondo's chances weren't good.

I looked around and didn't see anyone on the street or peering from between parted drapes. I retrieved my six-pack and headed rapidly back to Baltimore Avenue and found a working pay phone. I dialed 911 and said, "Send an ambulance. There's a man with head injuries on the sidewalk," and said where. Then I hung up without answering any questions. I went home by a different route.

CHAPTER TWENTY-FOUR

The phone was ringing when I got home. It was Clyde. He tried to cover his worry by sounding angry.

"Come on, Clyde," I said. "Stop being such a mama hen. I was just out having a beer." For some atavistic reason I didn't want to tell him about Kallir and Hondo jumping me. He'd really want to protect me if he knew.

"You want a beer, you come to my place. How do you know who's in those places by you? Who's going to back you up if you need it?"

"Cut the crap dammit. I've been drinking in those places for years. I know who goes there, they know me. I'm safe drinking in my own neighborhood." Sure I am-it's on the way home I'm not safe.

"You're not near as safe as you think you are. Did you catch the news tonight?"

"What about it?" Clyde didn't have a TV at the Side Car, what could he know?

"Sindi DiWagne's been found. Dead."

"Yeah, I saw that. How'd you get it?"

"Martha saw it on the tube. It upset her. She's on the stage dancing now."

"She's got a day job and she's scheduled to work the last couple of hours on a Thursday?"

"No. She came here to tell me. She hoped you'd be here so she could tell you, too. Lad, the lady's concerned about you. She's dancing now because it's her way of relieving tension. Come on in. She'll feel better knowing you're safe. She can help you forget about that other woman."

"No!" I snapped the word. It was odd. Not ten minutes ago I knew I was about to be attacked by two men, yet I remained calm. I moved instantly and with precision as soon as Hondo touched me and I handled the situation with a minimum of fuss-though Hondo might argue the point about minimal fuss. If he wasn't dead he'd likely be a vegetable for the rest of his life. But the prospect of meeting Martha Puller, of seeing this dancing-girl as a real human being instead of as a fantasy, seeing her as someone with a real day job, someone with concern for me as a person, that made me break out in a cold sweat. "No, Clyde. I've told you before, I don't want to know who she is. I mean it. I'm not coming over tonight." I grabbed for a straw. "I'm not coming over any time I know she's there. I have to get out of this week with at least one fantasy intact. You got it?"

"All right, lad, all right. I'll tell her you're okay and you're tired is all. But it's your loss. And I'm still worried. If he killed your blonde, he might well want to kill you." I noticed that after the first time when he used her name, he referred to Sindi in other ways. But he wasn't calling her a bimbo anymore. Respect for the dead, maybe.

I was almost hyperventilating and had to get my breath under control before I could go on. "Okay, here it is," I said when I felt able to talk without giving away how I was feeling. "Bigler killed Sindi, we can be pretty sure that was his doing. It's possible he'll come after me. I'm going to look for something I can use to keep him off me." And I'm going to put the son of a bitch out of business. Put him where he can't get to me.

"All right. I have something that might help. One of my contacts tells me he bought a building in Northern Liberties six months ago. My guess is that's where the drug lab is."

That sounded likely to me as well. "Thanks, Clyde. I'll follow up on it tomorrow." And then I'm going to get him.

"Remember to call me at eleven. This isn't just some asshole who will try to bankrupt you or defame your character. Bigler's a killer. You have to be careful dealing with him."

"I'll be careful, Clyde. I promise. And if I need help, I'll holler." But this is my fight. It's personal, and I wasn't going to involve any of my friends in it.

"Okay. Call at eleven."

"I will."

"I'm coming for you if you don't."

We hung up.

I had a beer and tried to plan my moves for tomorrow. What I really wanted to do was tie one on, but I didn't have enough beer to do the job. Besides, the first one didn't taste so good. The second one didn't taste any better. I went to bed.

As I lay there drifting off I decided to see Maxie Stein in the morning.

*

A few years ago I did a story on urban pioneering for *Philadelphia Magazine*. Urban pioneering isn't what they were looking for, of course. *Philly Mag* called me wanting an article on gentrification, with a positive slant on the process. They saw gentrification as the taking of blighted areas of the city and turning them into nice places for decent people to live, and increasing the property tax base. Their definition of blighted is low income residents living in low rent, low tax rate housing, and probably all black. To them, decent people are middle-class baby-boomers, probably white. The same kind of people I wish I didn't have for neighbors.

The pioneers I was interested in were generally baby-boomers, but they lacked the middle-class values of their generational cohort. They tended to be artists, craftsmen, intellectuals. They bought into marginal neighborhoods because, frankly, they usually couldn't afford more than a small apartment in middle-class neighborhoods. They sometimes had problems early on with their new neighbors because they were usually whites moving into a black neighborhood. Too many of the middle-aged and older blacks saw them as a threat because property values might rise and they'd be taxed out of their homes. Too many of the young blacks saw all white people as rich, and therefore proper targets for robbery and burglary. But the pioneers generally made good neighbors and didn't drive up property values all that much, so the problems usually lapsed-until the follow-on echelon showed up.

Once there was a great enough density of pioneers in a marginal neighborhood, certain members of the upwardly-mobile middle-class could see a marginal neighborhood in a different light. They could see a clear choice between paying mid- to upper-six figure prices for Society Hill, and spending in the mid- to upper-five figures for a house in a marginal area and another mid-five figures on fixing it up. In the former case, they'd have to live tightly for several years until their income caught up with their housing costs. In the latter they'd have a better house than they could otherwise afford and their life-style wouldn't suffer as much. This follow-on echelon did drive up property taxes, which in turn drove out the older residents-including most of the pioneers who had made their moving in possible to begin with. This time, the problems wouldn't stop until all the old residents were gone, and even then required on-going security measures unnecessary in older middle-class neighborhoods.

That's the way I saw it, that's the way I wrote it. It wasn't the "up" piece *Philly Mag* expected and they didn't want to use it. But they had a hole to fill in that issue and nothing else they had on hand was big enough. So a staff writer took out my slant and put in theirs. *Philly Mag* hasn't bought from me since.

Maxie Stein is a real estate agent who helped me with my research on that article. His office is on 19th Street near Graduate Hospital. His territory is the area from South Street to Washington Avenue in the numbered streets from the upper teens to the low twenties. The way he presents himself, his income is totally dependent on encouraging the pioneers and follow-on echelon I checked him out and learned that's only a sideline with him. He gets most of his income from owning decrepit housing in his target area and renting it out to poor blacks for more than it's worth. Every time he sells a house to a pioneer or a gentrifier he makes enough money to buy two or three more rental properties, so the sales he claims are his primary business are actually a very lucrative sideline for him.

Every time Maxie sees me he tries to sell me a house. I keep telling him I'm too old to be a pioneer and not middle-class enough to be a gentrifier. We go back and forth on that for a while with him insisting that a homeowner in his area doesn't have to be either a pioneer or a gentrifier. Eventually he runs out of steam and the subject is dropped until the next time we meet.

Real estate agents have more than listings of properties for sale or rent. They also have a book, a computer printout really, that lists all the properties in the city. The book gives the address, zoning and construction classification, owner of record, purchase date, purchase price, and tax assessment value of each property. Real estate agents use it to determine comparable values for properties they want to sell-or buy.

I went to see Maxie because I wanted to look at that book. A friendly real estate agent will let you do that. Other real estate agents won't admit that it exists. Maxie wants to sell to me. He also likes the way *Philly Mag* rewrote what I said about him in that piece. He claims he made seven sales as direct result of it. He's a friendly agent.

"Ham, old friend," Maxie almost shouted when he saw me at the security-glassed cashier window. He jumped up and ran to open the door to the inner office. "Come in, Ham, come in." He bustled me through, made sure the door was locked again, and rushed me to the visitor's chair next to his desk. I managed to exchange hellos with Mrs. Anderson, Maxie's assistant-an acne-scarred, middle-aged woman who did the book-keeping and collected the rents from tenants who came to the cashier window. Maxie had another person who worked for him part time, a big man who collected the rent from tenants who didn't come to the office.

"Let me give you a cup of coffee. How about tea? Would you like a hard donut?"

That's a stale joke. Once he gave me a stale bagel and I called it a hard donut. He's called them that ever since.

"Thanks, Maxie, but I just had breakfast."

He poured two cups of coffee and went on. "Are you ready to settle down now? Start building your own nest egg instead of paying rent into somebody else's nest egg?" He ignored my head shake. "I've got a choice property on 21st Street near Christian. Prime rental. Right now it's six apartments, but the owner could move out the tenants on one floor and turn that floor into one apartment. The rent from the remaining apartments would pay the mortgage, taxes, insurance, and maintenance costs. All you got to pay is for the heat. After a year, raise the rents and they'll pay for the heat, too. A year after that, you're showing a profit and building your own nest egg. How 'bout it? Let's go, I'll show it to you now."

I put a hand on his arm to keep him from getting up. "No, Maxie. I know what 21st and Christian is like. And I'm not ready to buy a house."

"You don't like that, how about Kater Street? I got a nice little fixer-upper in the low twenties you can have for a song. Forty, fifty thou in fix-up costs and you've got yourself a real cozy gem."

"Cozy" is real estatese for too-damn-small.

"No, Maxie, I'm not in the market."

"I don't blame you for not wanting Kater. The houses are too small and the neighbors are all into EST or something. I got a nice one family on Carpenter. Big. Four bedroom. Original bath and kitchen. Get some antique furniture and you can turn it into a real showplace."

"Original" is real estatese for needs to be replaced.

"Maxie, I'm not buying."

I may not have been buying, but Maxie was sure trying to sell. He told me about five more properties he was trying to unload before he gave it up as a lost cause and let me tell him why I was there.

"You pain me, my friend," he wailed when I said I wanted to see the book. "You misuse me, you abuse me. You come to Maxie because you want to learn the comps in a different part of town so you know how badly you're getting ripped off on what you want to buy there."

"Shut up, Maxie. I told you I'm not buying. I didn't mean I'm not buying from you. I meant I'm not buying period."

"All right, all right. Tell me what you're interested in and I'll look after your interests, make sure you're not getting ripped off by someone who doesn't know and love you like I do."

I had to laugh at that one, Maxie doesn't like to give up. "No, Maxie. I'm not buying somewhere else. I'm trying to match somebody with a property he bought six months ago."

"Oh, why didn't you say so? Give me the address of the property, I'll tell you who bought it." He reached for the book.

"I can't. I know who bought it and what part of town it's in. I need to get the address."

Maxie stopped talking and leaned back in his chair to study me for a long moment. "Do you realize what you're asking for? I can't get that for you, not without more information."

"Yes, Maxie, I know what it takes. No, I'm not asking you to do it for me. Let me see the book. I'll do it myself." His expression told me he wasn't sure he could believe I wasn't taking advantage of him, so I decided to tell him more. "About six months ago a man by the name of Edward Bigler bought a property in Northern Liberties. I need to find the address of that property so I can find out what he's doing with it."

"This Bigler, you're doing research on him for something you're writing?"

"Yes." True enough.

"Did you try to look him up in the phone book?"

"It's not where he lives. I don't know what he calls the place or what he's doing with it. I could read the whole damn phone book and probably not find it."

We were interrupted by Mrs. Anderson who reminded him he had an appointment to show an apartment.

"Okay, Ham," he said grudgingly. "I have to go out. You look at the book. But if you decide to buy that property, remember who helped you."

"I will, Maxie, I will. Thanks." When he was gone I asked Mrs. Anderson to let me know when it was almost eleven. Then I settled down to do my digging.

Finding a property in the book is easy if you know the address. If you don't it's another matter altogether. The book is laid out the same way as a reverse phone directory; by streets. I wasn't sure of the exact boundaries of Northern Liberties, and I knew a real estate office wasn't the right place to ask. Real estate agents have a habit of extending the limits of desirable areas to make potential buyers and renters think they're getting something they're not. If I had to guess, I'd say Northern Liberties is from Fairmount Avenue on the south to Girard on the north, Front Street on the east out to 8th or 9th Street. But that might be too conservative, so I extended my search to include all the way down to Spring Garden Avenue up to a couple of blocks above Girard and west to 10th. That could still be too conservative, but it approximately doubled my search area.

I started the search by looking through the numbered streets for sales dates in the past year. About halfway through 4th, I realized looking for Bigler's name might not be the best idea. Entirely too many of the properties had corporations listed as owners. Bigler Entrepreneurships probably wasn't the only corporation he owned, and he might have bought the property through one of the others. I went back to the beginning and wrote down the name of every corporation I didn't recognize, along with the addresses it owned.

Along the way the Mrs. Anderson told me the time and I interrupted my reading long enough to call Clyde. I told him where I was, what I was doing, and forget about the next scheduled call, I'd call when I left. Once he was sure I was okay, he didn't keep me on the phone and I went back to work.

Maxie came back before I reached 10th Street. He clucked over me and made a fuss over the three sheets of paper I had filled with corporate names and property holdings. I took it from his attitude, less effusive than normal, he hadn't gotten the tenant and didn't like being stuck with an empty unit. He poured me another cup of coffee. It had sat in the pot long enough to get that burnt flavor. I went back to work and ignored the coffee. I could have done the named streets alphabetically; Brown, Fairmount, Girard, Parrish, et cetera, but didn't want to risk missing any, so I did them geographically, south to north. No Bigler, but page upon page of what the law calls fictitious names.

When I stopped to check a map for the names of all the little streets tucked in between the through streets, many of which ran anywhere from a half block in length to three or four blocks long, Maxie asked if I was ever going to come up for lunch. I looked at my watch, it was just past two. We went a block or so up to South Street and into a pizza shop for hoagies. Maxie talked through the walk up, through waiting for our sandwiches to be made, through eating, and through the walk back. I don't know what he talked about or what I might have said in reply. The kind of concentrated digging I was doing numbs my mind. I lose track of time and the ability to relate to people. If someone with mayhem in mind caught me at a time like this I'd be dead meat-or a reasonable facsimile thereof.

Back in Maxie's office, I peered closely at the large city map hanging on the wall and wrote down all the little-street names I could find. Then I buried myself back in the book. By the time I was through, Mrs. Anderson had gone for the day and Maxie was getting impatient to leave himself; he said his wife was waiting dinner. He also said my friend the saloon-keeper called and I hadn't seemed to notice the phone ringing. I looked at the stack of paper I'd filled out with names and addresses. I had long since run out of my own paper and had used several sheets of Maxie's. Nowhere had I seen the name Bigler.

"Maxie, thanks."

"Now what are you going to do with all of that?"

"Find out who's behind these corporations."

"You think your man is?"

"I do. I know he bought a property in that area about six months ago, but his name isn't listed as an owner. So one of these corporations must be his."

"Is he trouble for you?"

"He is that."

"Are you going to make trouble for him?"

"I certainly am."

"When you're done with this, come back to me. I'll find for you a house that will leave you not having problems with landlords." He escorted me out of his office, turned on the burglar alarm, and locked up the steel security gate over his office front. "Can I give you a ride someplace?"

"No, I need to walk, clear my head. That kind of research wipes me out, fills my skull with cobwebs. Thanks again, Maxie."

We shook hands. He got into his Cadillac and drove off. I walked up 19th Street and found a cab on Lombard Street. I gave the driver the address of the Side Car Club.

CHAPTER TWENTY-FIVE

I paid my way in through the front door and got my two free drink tickets. It was so dark inside I could hardly make out anything more than a few feet beyond the bright lights on the stage inside the main bar. One dancing-girl was on the stage, three others were making the circuit of the bar. I couldn't make out who they were. I headed toward the lights. Clyde collared me before I reached them.

"I thought you were going to call when you were through at that real estate place?" he said gruffly.

I faced him and blinked against the darkness, trying to get my night vision working. The blink didn't help any. Time spent in the dark is the only thing that brings on night vision.

"Sorry." No I wasn't. "What the fuck, I came straight here when I finished there." When my mind is fogged up I get either very amenable or very snappy. I was in no mood to feel amenable.

"You stop anyplace for dinner?"

"No. What time is it?"

"Six thirty."

"I'm not hungry. I had a late lunch." I tried to go to the bar, one drink ticket held ready to trade in.

"No you don't. I know you, Ham. You're not having a drink on an empty stomach. Not in my place. Not anyplace tonight."

I didn't like that and started to say something, but remembered I was probably in immanent danger and changed my mind. "Okay, I'll hit the lunch bar, then get a drink."

"I've got a better idea. Let's go out to dinner."

"Bullshit, Clyde. I just paid my way in. I'm not leaving again right away."

"Dummy. You don't have to pay to get in here."

"You're running a business, you can't afford to go letting everybody in free."

"I'm not talking about everybody, I'm talking about you."

"Clyde, fuck off. I've had my head buried in records all day and I've just come up for air. Give me time to get oxygenated." Digging through records really can put me in a rotten mood. This rotten mood was probably exacerbated by knowing I was in danger.

Clyde clamped a hand on my upper arm. "I'm not fucking off and we're going out to get some dinner. I'm hungry even if you aren't. You don't want to eat, fine. Keep me company."

He dragged me into the shadows where he said something to one of his hulks, then dragged me to the entrance. "Give him his admission back," he told the doorman.

"I'm not taking it, Clyde," I snapped. "And I'm keeping the drink tickets." I didn't like being dragged about by the arm and was feeling feisty, but didn't have the energy to physically resist. At the moment, snapping seemed the only way I could resist.

"I don't know why I put up with you, Ham," he snarled.

I went along limply as he dragged me to the back door.

"It's my car, I'm driving. Any objections?" It sounded like my obstinacy was getting to him.

I knew I was beaten. "No objections." We got into his T-bird. As we drove over the Market Street bridge I said, "Bear with me, Clyde. Really, when I do that kind of research my mind goes on me. It takes an hour or two to get back to normal. Okay?"

He said okay back, but it sounded like he meant "we'll see about that."

He drove around Rittenhouse Square a couple of times, looking in the rearview mirror most of the way. "Doesn't look like anybody's following us," he said at last, and found a parking space.

We went in someplace where nobody outside could look in through the window and see us at a table. Clyde told the hostess to give us a table where we could see anyone coming in and nobody could sit behind us. She shook her head, but smiled and did what he asked when he explained, "It's a guy thing."

The smell of food and the sight of diners got my digestive juices going. I tried to focus on the menu, but my mind wasn't working well enough. When the waitress came to take our orders I pointed almost randomly at something on the menu. "Coffee first," I said. Clyde said me too.

"So tell me what happened today," Clyde said when the waitress was gone.

"Not much to tell," I said. "I buried myself in the book and came up with a lot of nothing."

"That folder you're carrying doesn't look like nothing." He held his hand out for it. I handed it over. He flipped through it and whistled. "What's it mean?"

"It means Bigler bought the property under a fictitious name. Monday I'm going to have to go to the State Office Building and dig through the corporate records to see who owns these names." Not a chore I was looking forward to. But at least there wasn't as much to go through as I'd dealt with today.

"Why the SOB?"

"Because he lives in Pennsylvania and bought property in Philadelphia. Any corporation he used to make the purchase is probably incorporated in this state and not in New Jersey or someplace else."

He grunted.

The coffee arrived and I concentrated on it in the hope it would do some defogging for me.

Clyde also drank quietly, gave me the space I needed to come out of it.

Food came and we made sparse small talk over it. Back in the car we went out Walnut Street. Clyde didn't turn off at 33rd like I expected him to. I asked why not.

"Tonight's a music night, that's why." That didn't make any sense to me and I said so. "I've got this customer, he's pretty much a regular on music nights. He works for the state. If he comes in tonight I'll give him a copy of your list. Maybe he can get the information you're looking for before Monday."

It was my turn to grunt. I didn't want Clyde to do this, but neither did I want to wait until Monday to find out which of these corporations belonged to Bigler.

We went to an all-night photocopy place near Penn. I used a self-serve machine to duplicate my list and gave it to Clyde.

"Think he'll be able to read my chicken-scratching?" I asked when I handed it over.

"Don't see why not. I didn't have any trouble with it."

Friday. Another music night at the Side Car Club. A night just like the night it all began. I sat at my favorite stool at the small side bar and resolved to not talk to any women in the place. As it turned out, I was too distracted to enjoy the music. Enough so that when the volume got turned up too high it became an annoyance. I sought out Clyde and told him I was going home.

"You have your car?"

"No."

"I'll have one of the guys give you a lift. Tomorrow, when you call me at eleven, I'll let you know if my state guy shows tonight."

The hulk who got the taxi job, I think it was Mack, insisted on coming inside to make sure there were no unwelcome visitors waiting for me. I didn't tell him if there were they were probably armed and coming in might only get him shot. I didn't tell myself that if the hulk went in first and got shot, that could give me time to get out unshot.

No one was there. I thanked the hulk for the lift, offered him a cup of coffee, he said no thanks I gotta get back, and then I had to figure out what to do with myself until Monday. I relied on my old fallback and played a couple hours of computer games. When that got too boring, or the concentration the games demanded was more than I could come up with, I played some CDs and had a couple beers. They tasted better than last night, but not enough for me to want to kill the rest of the six-pack.

*

I had missed the newspaper on Friday, but there wasn't any mention of Hondo's death on the TV news that night. Neither was there anything in Saturday's paper. Maybe he wasn't dead. Maybe it was too small-time for the news media to deal with. Maybe Kallir came back after I left and got the body before the police arrived. Whatever. I felt relieved not to hear anything.

Saturday was uneventful. I focused my attention on refilling my file cabinets. At eleven I checked in with Clyde. His state guy had showed up and went away with my list, but hadn't called in with anything yet. By the time I broke for lunch, one and a half of the cabinets were finished. I went back to them after I ate. I almost had three of them done by my six o'clock check in. If not the end, at least the beginning of the end was in sight, so I plodded on, just nibbling on whatever seemed convenient instead of stopping for dinner. I felt a great sense of accomplishment when the last piece of paper went into the last folder and that was put in place in the last drawer of the last filing cabinet. I felt so good about it I started right in on putting the books and magazines in the divider bookcase in order. Halfway through that I realized it was midnight and I better check in with Clyde. Really, there was no need for him to come charging to the rescue. Then I sat back, played a couple of CDs, and drank the last two beers.

Warren Zevon's "Roland the Headless Thompson Gunner" had never held so much meaning for me.

*

Saturday had been my first uneventful day in a week. It felt so good I looked forward to a repeat on Sunday. After a shower I examined myself in the bathroom mirror. My left eye was more than half open and the bruising was turning a stale yellow. The cut on the bridge of my nose was thinly scabbed, almost completely healed. The bruise on my side was still big, but the color was now a dull purple, it was healing as well. It seemed such a long time since I'd examined my injuries. The fight with Hammond seemed so far in the past. It was nine thirty, plenty of time before Clyde was going to charge in if he didn't hear from me. I dressed and went out to get a newspaper and have breakfast.

Traffic was light. Those people who were up and out at this hour must be in church or on the golf course rather than on the way to or from. I had a red light at Baltimore Avenue but there weren't any moving cars on 46th Street and none westbound on Baltimore that might be making a right-turn-on-red, so I crossed. I didn't pay any attention to the eastbound car that was rolling to a stop.

Not until I heard its engine roar and its wheels squeal, that is. My head jerked to the right and I saw that car twisting and accelerating through a left turn onto 46th. It was coming straight at me.

I dashed for the safety of the far sidewalk, still looking at the mad car. 46th Street had never seemed so wide, thirty feet had never seemed so great a distance. A small bit of my brain wondered why the nut behind the wheel was straightening out his turn, why he kept pointing at me. Running wasn't fast enough-I dove out of the way.

The driver suddenly twisted his steering wheel hard to the left and fishtailed. I rolled away. The right side of the car smacked into the back of a car parked at the corner. The mad driver managed to get his car under control, whipped out of his spin, and shot up 46th.

I jumped to my feet and ran back into the street, looking after him. I saw through the cabin, back to front. I couldn't see the driver's face, of course. But the hairdo certainly looked familiar. So did the car, now that I wasn't dodging it-it was a metallic blue Mitsubishi.

It was Kallir. Thursday night must have taught him jumping me on the street wasn't such a great idea. So he tried to run me down.

I was trembling, my knees wanted to buckle. My chest heaved with deep breaths. But I couldn't just stand there. If I stuck around to be the good-neighbor witness and the cops managed to find Kallir, I could find myself answering questions I wanted to avoid about the death of a mugger a couple of nights ago. I looked around quickly. Nobody was running out of any of the houses screaming "My car, my car." My clothes were dirty from landing and rolling on the sidewalk. I decided I could fix my own breakfast and do without the Sunday paper. I went briskly home.

The third attempt on my life in four days left me more shaken than I expected. I tried computer games to distract myself enough to calm me down.

No such luck. Listening to CDs didn't help either. I couldn't read. The Phillies game wouldn't be on the tube until 1:00. I'd lost my appetite. The next thing I knew it was eleven and Clyde was going to jump on his horse if I didn't call him. But I didn't want to talk to him. I was certain my voice would give away that something was amiss. I made an effort and made the call.

"You been trying to get me?" Clyde started. "Sorry you weren't able to get through. I've been on the phone with my state guy." He was, blessedly, so wrapped up with his news he didn't hear the numbness in my voice. "He used his modem at home to get the information on those corporations. Bigler wasn't listed as an owner or officer on any of them. But a whole bunch are owned by other corporations. What do you think of that? I think Bigler built himself a screen of corporations to hide his ownership. Now it's a matter of backtracking until his name crops up. At least the list is a lot shorter now than it was. My guy said he'd be happy to get the rest of the information for me, but he's got a noon date on the golf course. You've got a modem, right? Give me the number and he can have his computer feed your computer the information he's already got. How 'bout it?"

I was doubly glad Clyde ran on so. For one, he didn't notice my voice. For two, he told me enough to distract me from the murder attempt and lift my spirits. I dreaded tomorrow's visit to the SOB. This was going to make it far less difficult. I gave Clyde my modem's number.

"Hang up and stand by, lad. Your computer can expect a call inside two minutes."

"Make it three," I said and hung up.

It took nearly the entire three minutes to crank up my machine, let it run through its autodiagnosis, and get it ready to receive. The call came through almost immediately. I don't know who this guy is, but I love him. He dumped the data and stored it on my hard disk in ASCII. That flat eliminated any possibility of me not being able to read it in case my software was incompatible with his.

I called Clyde right back. "Damn, this took a bunch of work," I said. "What'd you give him to do it?"

Clyde laughed. "I didn't have to give him a damn thing. He's a hacker dweeb, he loves doing this kind of stuff. You see, he doesn't have a password authorizing him to get into those files. This was an exercise for him to get around the security system. He loved it. He said if the rest can wait until tomorrow night, he'll do the rest of it for you." He paused for a moment, then said. "I gave him a pass to the club. He gets in free every night for the next month. The pass includes the two drink tickets on girlie nights."

"Clyde, you're amazing."

"Nothing to it, lad. Nothing to it." But the pride came through in his voice. Then he wanted to know if I was okay, I said I was, he took my word for it, we hung up.

The complete file was more than 20k long. Clyde's state guy, the hacker dweeb, had gotten far more information than I asked for. He not only gave me the principals for each corporation on my list, he included their addresses and phone numbers of record. Each corporate listing was followed by the address or addresses it owned.

I finally got around to fixing my breakfast. While eating, I read through the file. I'm not one of those people who doesn't allow food or beverage near his computer. A couple of times a year I have to disassemble the keyboard and clean the debris out of it.

Most of the officers' names on the list were strangers to me, but I did recognize a substantial portion of them from business or politics, and a few from the arts world. Here and there was the name of someone I had personally encountered in research for one article or another. A couple were acquaintances who I hadn't known were incorporated. I was through the bulk of the file before I discovered just how good a screen Bigler had set up.

By the time I wrote down the name, Pharm Designs, Inc., at Maxie's office on Friday, my mind was too far gone to catch the significance. I probably thought it was the name of a Vietnamese clothing or furniture manufacturer. The French didn't give the Vietnamese the letter F when they gave them the Roman alphabet, so they always use the diphthong "ph" for the "f" sound. I didn't recognize the names of the president or vice president of Pharm Designs, Inc., but I knew the secretary-treasurer. It was Paul Llowlolski.

CHAPTER TWENTY-SIX

The two-story, turn-of-the-century building on Orianna Street occupied a quarter of the block. It looked derelict. Faded lettering that ran the length of the building on a wide molding between the first and second floors proclaimed it to have once been a proud factory, a manufacturer of "fine women's clothing." The ground floor windows were boarded up. A third of those on the second floor were broken, but looked like they were covered on the inside. The main entrance, a recessed double door centered on the street side, was chained and padlocked. There was a smaller door at each of the corners of the building. One of them had a doorknob shiny with recent use. I parked out of sight on Green Street and walked back to take a look at the rear of the building.

In back was a narrow, refuse littered alley that deadended at the far end of the building's rear. Crack vials crunched underfoot as I made my cautious way down it. Outhouse odors made the air fetid. Flies buzzed in greater density than I could remember ever having seen in the city. I batted a swarm away from my face and tried to ignore them. Unless I stepped in something unpleasant, the only danger the alley presented was if I ran into a crazed crackhead. I watched where I put my feet. The crackheads were spending this early Sunday afternoon somewhere else.

The back of the clothing factory came as a surprise. The building's front was many-windowed yellow brick, the back was weathered clapboard with only three small windows on each floor. A small door, almost flush with the pavement, was set into the middle of the back wall. It had been forced sometime in the past, probably more than once. Now it was broken almost in half and was off its top hinge. A steel door inside it rendered it redundant as well as useless. I tried to look in the windows. They were painted black on the inside, and there were no chips in the paint through which I could see. The farthest window had a broken pane, but that didn't do me any good either. A sheet of metal was bolted to the inside of the frame. Probably all three windows were secured like that. It was likely the second floor windows were as well.

It was pretty likely that before Bigler bought this building it was used by druggies to get themselves out of the weather and the sight of prying cops. They must have been furious when he sealed it off from them. I was surprised all the windows weren't knocked out. Maybe the crackheads didn't have the initiative to try that hard. Maybe only a couple of crackheads had used the building and they died back here. That would certainly explain the stench and the flies. Except there didn't seem to be any center to the malodorousness, and the flies didn't seem to be paying more attention to any one part of the alley than any other. I sensed an irony here; drug users being evicted by drug manufacturers. The crackheads were welcome to spend their money on the product, but weren't allowed to enter the sacred premises where they were made.

Idly, I wondered how big a crew Bigler used to clean the inside of the place, and how long the cleaning had taken.

The second floor windows were at least fifteen feet up, and there was no fire escape I could climb to check them out. I looked up at the surrounding buildings to see if there was a way to get to the second floor. One, three stories high, had a ladder leading from the roof down to the third floor and a fire escape from there to the second. The counter-balanced ladder that should have given access from the second floor to the alley was missing. It may have been under the debris in the alley, more likely the ladder was long gone. The dead end of the alley was blank cinder block that went handholdless up to the level of the second story windows, it was no help. The drainpipe on the building adjoining the factory may have been strong enough to scale, but I didn't want to risk it.

I would have stayed there longer to ponder the problem of gaining access to the second floor, but the fetid odor and hordes of flies lighting on me discouraged that idea and I decided to do my thinking elsewhere.

This isn't a residential area and the businesses in it were closed, so there were few people about. Those few paid me little attention as I walked back to my car. I got in and headed for I-95. I drove out as far as Bucks County with the windows open to drive the memory of the alley's smell from my nostrils. Then I turned around and drove back to Orianna Street. I didn't particularly want to go back, but I did feel a need to get inside the building.

I parked on 4th Street this time. I walked north on Orianna on the opposite side from the building. I didn't see anything usable. Then back south on the building's side. I examined the boarding on the windows, it all looked sound. The chain and padlock securing the main entrance looked like they'd last longer than the door they secured. The unused side door hadn't been used in uncounted years. It was sealed with what looked like every paint job the place had had in the past seventy-five years. The door with the shiny knob also had a shiny new lock set in it. My guess was the entire place was very strongly secured on the inside of every door and window.

I wanted to get inside, but it looked like the only way in, front or back, was through this door. Unless I returned after dark and tried the back with a ladder. But then I'd have to deal with the crackheads. Crack does a lot of nasty things to people before it kills them. One of those things is, it can turn them very violent. Another is, it can dope their nervous systems so they don't feel the injuries they're receiving in a fight. That makes even a small, weak crackhead an excessively dangerous person to tangle with. So I was left with this door. It was unlikely that if anyone was in now, he'd let me in just because I came knocking. I needed to find another way in.

Once in a great infrequency, providence smiles. I left the corner door, passing the front of the building again, heading back to my car, when I heard the door opening behind me. I ran the last few steps to the old main entrance and ducked into its recess. Maybe whoever was coming out would say something I could use. Maybe I'd get a look at the person. Maybe it was someone I didn't want to see me.

Voices came from the door, clear enough in the quiet of an otherwise unoccupied area.

"You gonna leave this unlocked, right? I'm gonna be right back, just two minutes." The voice had a whiny, nerdy quality.

"Yeah, right," said a duller, tougher voice. "Just two minutes. Last time you said that it was ten minutes."

"But I just gotta get something from my car. It's parked onna corner. It ain't like I'm going to no store or nothing like last time they made me wait."

A brief pause, then the tough voice said, "I don't see no car onna corner."

"It's there, it's just around the corner you can't see it from here. I dint want nobody seeing it in front of here, dint want nobody thinking maybe someone was home here." He was a native Philadelphian, nobody else says "dint" for "didn't."

Another brief pause, then the tough voice said, "Two minutes. You ain't back in two minutes, I lock this door. Then you explain to the boss how you got your dumb ass locked out when you was suppose to be working."

"Two minutes. That's all, I'll be back in two minutes."

"You better."

I heard the sound of footsteps going away, then the door closed. I looked at my watch and watched the sweep hand mark off twenty seconds before I looked out. No one was in sight. I dashed back to the door and tried it. It was unlocked. I ducked inside and closed it softly behind me. It seemed I was right about interior security; a sheet of steel plate covered the inside of the door. The vestibule was lit only by splash-light from the ajar inner door. That door was also steel. I stood close to the narrow opening and listened. Hollow echoes from somewhere in the recesses of the building were all I heard. I looked through the slit between the hinge side of the door and the door frame. It opened into a short corridor lit only by one low-watt bulb hanging from the ceiling at this end and another at the far end.

I opened the door wider and stepped softly into the corridor. I examined the corridor and the first thing I saw almost made me run right back out. On the wall next to the door was a combination box for an alarm. Then I noticed that only the green light was on, indicating power, not the red light that signaled activation. The alarm must have been turned off so the whiny guy wouldn't set it off when he came back. Halfway down on the right side, toward the back of the building, was a stairway. It was dark and I didn't see any light upstairs. At its end, the corridor turned right. That's where the echoes were coming from, that's where I headed.

I was looking around the corner wondering what was immediately behind the curtain a few feet away when I heard a noise behind me; it must have been whiny coming back. Could it be two minutes already? I dashed back to the steps and up them.

The outer door closed, then the inner. There was a pause. It was long enough to make me wonder what noise I made, or what other clue I left to alert whiny Then I heard his footsteps going down the hall and realized he must have stopped to reset the alarm. That was confirmed when the tough voice welcomed him back, on time for a change, and asked if he'd set the alarm. Yeah, yeah, he had, he had. The voices were closer than I wanted to hear them, they sounded like right on the other side of the curtain. It was enough to make me glad I hadn't had time to go to it and look through. I decided to check out the second floor as long as I was there.

No light came through or around any part of the windows. There was a glow from a place in the floor, though, about fifteen or twenty feet away from where I stood at the top of the stairs. I headed for it, waving my hands through the air in front of me, probing for obstacles I might bump into or knock over. I shuffled my feet, probing for things to trip over, holes to step in, and avoiding footfalls that might be heard downstairs.

Near the glow I found a desk. It was positioned so whoever sat at it could look through a window in the floor and observe the work going on in the laboratory directly below. I watched for a few minutes, intrigued. I'd never before seen an illegal drug lab in operation.

There were three people in sight. One wore a sweatshirt, spandex pants, and jock shoes; he wore the headset of a Walkman. His hair was cut in an orange, spiky Mohawk. The second was in a lab coat that had a fully loaded pocket protector. He looked like what I imagine a dweeb looks like. The third was a bearish clod. His sport jacket stood in sharp contrast to the unshaved stubble on his face.

From where I sat at the desk, I could see two glass-doored, enamel painted cabinets such as you find in doctor's offices along one wall. A utility sink with what looked like an extra-wide drain was against another wall. Two stainless steel tables were in the middle of the floor. One of them held an assemblage of equipment that looked like a still. The other held a balance scale, stacks of small plastic bags, rolls of tape, and other packaging materials. A drying oven sat on cinder blocks in the middle of the third wall. I couldn't see the fourth wall, which was below where I sat.

I suppose it's not quite accurate to say the bear was in charge. The Mohawk and the labcoat moved about doing arcane things with their condensers, reaction flasks, evaporators, beakers, and Bunsons. Even though I recognized the equipment they were using, my knowledge of chemistry was too small for any of it to make sense to me. The bear sat on a high stool near the curtain and watched. He must have been a guard. Guarding the product from being pilfered by the help as well as guarding the building from intruders like me. Maybe he was better at preventing pilferage than he was at keeping me out. I could see their mouths move occasionally and them looking at each other; they were talking, but I couldn't hear their conversation.

After a while they all looked at the oven, a timer must have sounded. Mohawk went to it and opened the door. He carefully drew out a low-sided glass tray filled with what looked like talcum powder and carried it to the table with the packaging materials. Bear watched him closely, then carried his stool closer to that table to keep an eye on labcoat, who used a tiny spoon to measure amounts of the powder into plastic bags, which he weighed.

Labcoat must have been very experienced at the weighing, because he didn't often have to adjust the amounts he put in the bags. Either that or the weights were merely approximates. He used clear plastic tape to seal each bag as he filled it. The bags were very small, no more than half a teaspoon of the powder went into each. Probably destined for a pusher rather than a wholesaler. I wondered what kind of drug this was that got sold as a powder-the only powder I knew was cocaine. But what do I know about drugs? I mean, beyond what's printed on the label of an aspirin bottle.

While the bagging was going on under the watchful eye of the bear, Mohawk carefully filled another glass tray and put it into the kiln. He set a dial on the side of the oven and pressed a red button. Then he went to look over the bear's shoulder at the bagging. Sharp words were exchanged, it looked like the bear didn't want Mohawk behind him, wanted him where he could see him. Mohawk went back to the oven and leaned against the wall, pouting.

I decided I'd seen enough, it was time to leave. I got up and cautiously headed toward the stairs. Then I stopped and thought about it for a moment. There was an alarm on the door. One or both of the doors might have a lock that required a key to open-I remembered the inner door was left ajar while one of the workers went out. I visualized the street outside and where the building was relative to the corners. Even if I didn't need a key to open either door, I didn't think I could get out of sight before the bear came out after me. Then, even if I outran him and managed to get to my car and away without him being able to see it and give a description to Bigler, or anybody else in the organization, Bigler would know his security had been compromised and probably close shop before I could get anything done about it.

Wonderful, I thought. The only thing I could do to make things harder on myself at the moment would be to go downstairs and try to collect a sample of whatever it was they were cooking.

I needed to occupy my conscious mind for awhile so my subconscious could work on the problem. I shuffled carefully to the building's back wall and probed along it until I found a window. My guess in the alley was right, it was covered by a sheet of metal. I felt around its edges to see how it was attached and found the rounded, slotless heads of rivets. The only way to unblock the windows was to batter or pry the plates off.

A more detailed inspection revealed that the second floor of the building was one big room with closets built into three of the corners. All three were padlocked. Most of the floorspace was bare. Other than the desk and chair next to the observation window, there were only a few shipping crates scattered about. A couple of them were open, their lids propped against their sides. The others were solidly nailed shut. The only other thing I could see was a filing cabinet near the desk.

I could see! My night vision was working. The small amount of light spilling from the observation window was enough to allow me to see dimly. As soon as I realized I could see, no matter how faintly, I realized there had to be some sort of access to the roof. I went around again on another inspection tour, this time looking at the ceiling. I found it.

Near the middle of the room there was a hatch set in the ceiling. A roof support beam was next to it and rungs were set into the beam to allow whoever needed to get to the roof to do it without having to pull over a ladder.

I climbed up the rungs and felt around the hatch. There was a simple hook-and-eye holding down the near edge. The other end was hinged. The hook slid easily out of the eye. The hinges didn't squeak very much. I held the hatch open without letting it fall back onto the roof and make noise, then shimmied out into the daylight. I squinched my eyes shut against the brightness, then opened them a slit and blinked rapidly a few times to adjust to the light.

Okay, I was outside. Now how do I get down to the street? One thing I didn't want to do was go walking around up here-someone might see me and do something I'd find unpleasant. The only thing I remembered from my earlier inspection was the drain pipe on the building next door. It hadn't looked very sturdy from ground level, but it seemed to be my only route down.

When I closed the hatch, I held the hook up until there was no longer space for my fingers between it and the roof lip. I pulled my fingers out and lowered the hatch as quickly as I could. As easily as the hook had slid out of the eye, maybe it would swing right back in if my timing was right. It wasn't something I was going to worry about now. Maybe nobody would notice the hook wasn't in the eye until it was too late to prevent what I had in mind. Maybe the hook re-eyed itself.

The roof of the adjacent building was about four feet below the roof I was on. I lowered myself onto it and lay flat to find the drain pipe. I grasped it with both hands and gave it a shake. It barely budged. Being careful to keep my weight off the pipe, I lowered my feet over the edge and clamped them to the pipe. I held onto the roof with both hands until I was hanging at arm's length. Only then did I put a hand on the pipe and slowly ease my weight onto it. It held. I used my feet to guide me and walked my hands down the pipe in something so fast it was almost a guided fall. I made it down safely.

This time the flies and I had company in the alley. A crackhead raised himself from a pile of rubble that concealed him from view from the street.

"My man," he half mumbled, half slurred, "you gi' me a dolla buy some food. I hungry." He leaned forward from the hips and swayed. He didn't put out a hand for the requested handout. His face looked like the nerves that give the features mobility had been severed. Flies crawled on it, one went between his open lips and I could see it dining on the crud on his teeth. A smell worse than the stench of the alley rose from him.

I knew any money he got from me or anyone else would go for drugs, not food. If I gave him a dollar it would only put him a dollar's worth closer to death. If I gave him nothing, he'd die just as soon. I told myself he was just another rotting piece of litter in this alley and went past.

Behind me I heard him mumble, "My man, dolla, hungry, my man, dolla, hungry," like a mantra. I tried not to wonder how long it would be before he noticed he was alone again and lay back down in his garbage. I tried not to wonder if he would imagine I had been a hallucination.

*

I was home in time for my six o'clock check in with Clyde. We spoke briefly. Then I settled down with some graph paper and an office furnishings template and did the most accurate floor plan I could of the drug lab. There was someone I wanted to give it to in the morning.

At the end of my midnight check in, I said, "Well, I'll talk to you on Tuesday, Clyde."

"What do you mean, Tuesday? Tomorrow's Monday."

"That's what I mean. You're out of town on Monday, I can't get hold of you."

"Don't you worry about that, lad. I'll call you. Just be sure you're at home at eleven, six, and midnight."

"You know, Clyde, sometimes you can be a real pain in the ass."

"I'd rather be a pain in the ass than a pall-bearer."

CHAPTER TWENTY-SEVEN

A while back I did a two parter for *The Barrister*, a magazine for lawyers. Like I said, I'll write for anyone who'll pay me. Part one was on how lawyers select juries, mostly what kind of people they try to get and the criteria they use to make challenges-to reject prospective jurors. In doing the research, I wasn't surprised to learn that lawyers want as jurors people they think they can manipulate. Some of the criteria for rejecting people were surprising, though. They generally don't like men who wear bow ties. Men with beards are also out-unless they're blue collar, where beards are more socially acceptable. Lawyers see bow-tied, bearded men as independent thinkers who aren't easily swayed. Part two was on how jurors feel about the manipulative tactics of trial lawyers. I'll admit I slanted that part, put the emphasis on jurors who base their decisions on the facts and merits of a case and resent the courtroom tactics of lawyers.

One of my sources for the first part was Jim O'Donnell, an assistant district attorney. I wouldn't say we became friends, but we have kept in touch. I called him on Monday morning. Partly because I know him, partly because he's now the head of the DA's organized crime unit.

I got right to the point. "Jim, how'd you like to bust a designer drug lab?"

He laughed. "Ham, busting designer drug labs is one of life's little pleasures. You plan on turning informant on one of your sources?"

"You know better than that, Jim. I treat my sources with a confidentiality most lawyers would envy. This is a scumbag who fired a warning shot across my bow when I was doing research on something totally unrelated to drugs." The nautical term seemed natural considering that just last week I was searching for a pirate's treasure map.

"You just happened to come across something and had a warning shot fired your way. Nothing more than a warning shot?"

"I'm not sure it can even be called that much." I wasn't going to admit to what had been going on, I'd done too many things of questionable legality recently. "But I've come into some information I think you'll find very useful."

"Well, give it up."

"Nope, not on the phone. Let's meet someplace." The DA's office gets requests like that all the time and doesn't insist on getting things on the phone-I hoped.

"Well, gee, I don't know. Normal procedure is for a potential source to say enough on the phone to let me know whether or not it's worth an interview. But since I know you and consider you reliable, come on in."

Well, I guess I was wrong. Still, I didn't want to do it that way. "No good. Let's meet away from your office."

He took a few seconds to think about that, then asked, "Ham, are you in some kind of trouble?"

"I haven't done anything, if that's what you're asking." Not with making or dealing drugs, anyway. "Somebody knows who I am and I'd rather not take the risk of being seen going into the DA's office. Okay?"

"Are you sure that's all?"

It was my turn to think about his question for a few seconds. Then I said, "Let me put it this way. Don't ask me any questions that might cause me to plead the Fifth if I was under oath."

"Sounds serious."

"Serious enough."

"Let me take a look at my calendar. "There was a pause while he did that. "I've got a 1:30 at Penn's law school. You still live in University City?"

"Sure do. Let's have lunch in 3400 Walnut. That way we can take as much time as we need and you'll be less than a block from your 1:30."

"Can't. I'm having lunch with. . . No. I can change that. This is for real, right?"

"This is for real."

"Okay, I'm going to reschedule my lunch date. Let's meet at 12:15."

"I'll be inside waiting for you."

That left me three hours to occupy. There was no point in going anywhere, and I knew I wouldn't be able to concentrate on any work. I rearranged the books Jimmy and one of Clyde's hulks had put back on the shelves last week.

True to his word, Clyde called at eleven. I assured him I was okay and didn't say anything about my coming meeting with Jim O'Donnell.

*

3400 Walnut is a University of Pennsylvania office building, the first floor of which is given over to shops. A food court is prominent among them. At ten minutes past noon, I settled into a high-backed booth where I could see the entrance. Jim O'Donnell walked in promptly at a quarter after. I stood and signaled him.

My mind wasn't on food, it was on how to give the DA's office enough information to act without incriminating myself in the process. So I let Jim decide which vendor we were going to get our lunch from. That could have been a mistake, since he made me pay for both of us.

"If you knew who I was supposed to have lunch with," he said, "You'd think buying me lunch was the least you could do to make up for tearing me away from her."

"Ever hear of a guy by the name of Edward Bigler?" I asked once we had our food.

He looked at me oddly. "I've heard the name."

"Then you may know that he went bust trying to get richer fast and that lately he's been getting his fortune back."

"Ye-e-s."

I looked at him oddly, wondering why he drew out his answer like that. So I said, "And I suspect you may know that he's been doing his recouping through the expedient of manufacturing designer drugs."

"That's quite a claim."

"That you know it, or that he's doing it?"

He paused, then, "Both."

"Do you know that?"

"What do you know about it?" A typical lawyer's ploy, answer a question with a question.

"I know it's true. I know where the lab is. I know what its layout is."

Jim pushed his lunch aside and leaned in close so he could talk in a low voice. "What's your involvement in this, Ham. Tell me the truth. "He looked serious and concerned.

"None. Absolute truth. I have zero involvement with drugs or anybody's designer lab. "I also leaned close and spoke low.

"What's your involvement with Bigler?" He did know the name, he didn't ask if that was the right name.

"By total happenstance, while I was working on a project that had nothing to do with him or with drugs, I crossed his path and he fired a warning shot." Well, I hadn't known of his involvement at first.

"And he told you about the drugs."

"No."

"Come clean with me, Ham."

"You know about him and his drugs, don't you, Jim. Are you investigating him?"

"Let's just say I'm aware of it and am interested in learning more. Let's also say I want to know if you're going to go down with him and want to cop a plea."

"I am not involved with him or his drugs. There is nothing to implicate me in any way, because I haven't done or acquiesced, aided or abetted in anything. I'm not going down with him. Good enough?"

He leaned back and smiled broadly. "What do you have for me, Ham?" He pulled his sandwich back and took a big bite.

"How about you tell me how far along your investigation is and I'll fill in what blanks I can."

He shook his head. "I didn't say anything about an investigation."

I got out the graph paper and shoved it across the table to him. He looked at it, then looked a question at me.

"That's the layout of his lab. Or at least as much of it as I know."

"You're not involved in any way, yet he invited you into his lab and showed you around?" I shook my head. "You knocked on the door and they let you in?" I shook my head again. "You broke in?"

"None of the above."

"Then how did you get this?"

"Like I said on the phone, don't ask me any questions that could cause me to take the Fifth."

He looked at the layouts. "How accurate are these?"

"As accurate as I could make them without taking measurements." Then I explained them to him. One sheet showed the alley in back, complete with the incomplete fire escape, the drain pipe, and the roof hatch. The second showed the approximate location of the crates on the second floor, indicating which two were open and empty, the desk and observation window, the three padlocked closets, and the metal-covered windows. The third only showed the vestibule, the two corridors I'd seen, and the layout of the lab room under the window.

"Where is it?"

I gave him the address, then asked, "How does this fit in with what you already know?"

He grinned like a wolf. "We know he's been making drugs for the past two years. We know the principals involved, and his distribution system. We even know where the lab is. What we haven't been able to do is get anyone inside."

My information suddenly didn't seem very important. "Why haven't you moved on him yet?"

"Didn't you hear me? We haven't gotten anyone inside. That means we would waste valuable time if we broke in, time during which they could get rid of evidence. But now," he hefted the three sheets of graph paper, "we know right where to go."

"You're going to get him off the street?"

"We're going to put him-and his people-away for a long, long time."

"When?"

"At 1:30, Judge Donazio and I are addressing a third year class at the law school. I'll show him these layouts, swear to him they're accurate, and he'll give me a warrant. They are accurate, aren't they?" I nodded. "Watch the five o'clock news."

"One more question before you go," I said. "I heard he's involved with South Americans in this. Are they Columbians?"

He looked at me oddly. "Hell no. He's got a Canadian partner, but everybody else in it is homegrown American."

That was a relief to hear.

*

The raid was one of the lead stories on the five o'clock news. They promised film at 5:30. At 5:30 they showed footage of the inside of the lab, and the chemists and bear I saw the day before being taken away. The six o'clock news showed Bigler and what the newscast called "his associates" being taken into the Round House, as Philadelphia's police headquarters is called, for arraignment. I didn't see Kallir or Moose.

Clyde called as soon as that bit was over. "You catch the news?" he asked.

"Yeah. Wonderful, ain't it?"

"Sure is. Could be better, though. I didn't see your three friends. "Good, he didn't know about Hondo.

"The talking head said the cops got everybody, they didn't say that was pictures of all of them."

A couple of minutes later we hung up. I didn't tell him about my part in the bust. I wondered, not for the first time, where Clyde went on his Mondays. It had to be fairly nearby if he was able to see the local news.

The 11:00 news showed more pictures and put names to many of Bigler's "associates. "I didn't see the pictures or hear the names I was looking for.

*

Tuesday morning's *Inquirer* didn't have pictures or names for Kallir and Moose either. Nor did the *Daily News* when it came out. They did, however, say Bigler's bail was set at a million dollars and he was in jail until it was posted.

If Bigler and all of his people were locked up that meant I was safe. Even if Kallir and Moose were free. Even if Bigler had contact with Kallir and Moose on the outside, he was too busy with the drug bust to worry about me. Kallir and Moose were spear-bearers, they wouldn't try anything on their own, they only jump to their master's voice. After dinner I decided to walk over to the Side Car Club. Except for my excursion to Northern Liberties on Sunday afternoon and lunch with Jim O'Donnell on Monday, I'd been cooped up inside my apartment since Friday night. And my movement had been restricted for longer than that. I needed to get out, I needed some exercise.

I didn't make it all the way to the sidewalk out front before I decided walking the couple of miles to the Side Car was a bad idea.

Usually when I go out I just let the outer vestibule door close behind me, but sometimes I make sure it's shut. When I take the first step down I turn a one-eighty and pull on the door handle. I did that and there was this pffftt and a thunk and a hole appeared in the door frame and I dropped and half rolled, half slid, down the rest of the stairs. When I did that, a car parked across the street revved its engine and laid rubber pulling out into the street and speeding away.

It all happened so fast the only make I could get on the car was it was white, probably a Hyundai. I couldn't see the driver. I got back to my feet and climbed the stairs. I had to go inside to get something to dig the bullet out with. It was small, maybe a .380, and went into the wood less than half an inch. It had to have been fired from an automatic, its powder charge reduced so it wouldn't recoil the slide, or it would have gone in deeper. Some sort of silencer had to have been attached to the muzzle of the pistol because I didn't hear a report. I guesstimated where the car had sat waiting for me, what the bullet's trajectory was, and where my head would have been relative to the trajectory if I had simply continued down the stairs instead of turning back to make sure the door was closed.

My best guesstimate put that bullet right into my head. When I dropped and rolled-slid, the shooter must have though he hit me. I thought of how close he came and sat down heavily. Then I though how this was the fourth attempt on my life in six days. According to the TV news, Bigler was still in jail. Either he was in contact with Kallir and Moose and still telling them to kill me, or Kallir and Moose had standing orders to do it regardless. Shit. The situation sucked.

After a while I decided I didn't want to be alone. I went over to Baltimore Avenue and stood in a store front, watching for a cab. Where I stood I could see who was in the passing cars before they could see me. No unwelcome familiar faces came by during the few minutes before an unoccupied cab came by. I ran to the curb and flagged it down. I hunkered down with my back wedged between the seat back and the right side door. With a simple turn of my head, I could look in all directions, see a threat coming from anywhere. The driver gave his paranoid passenger a wary look in the rearview mirror and didn't try to make conversation.

It was a music night, unusual for a Tuesday. The crowd was moderate in size, in drinking, and enthusiasm, which was fine by me. Neither the opener nor the headliner turned the volume up too high. They were neo-bands; both were neophyte, one was neo-Dire Straits, the other neo-Grateful Dead. The crowd wasn't big enough to open the side bar where I usually sit, so I took one of the small tables off the dance floor. Clyde joined me after a while and we made small talk between sets. I was glad he didn't propose that I stop making my check in calls, but I didn't tell him about the three attempts on my life, and he didn't know about or my part in getting Bigler busted.

I drank soda until midnight. Bartenders don't like soda drinkers, they generally don't tip as much as people who drink alcohol. Bar owners like them, though. They charge almost as much for a Pepsi as they do for a mixed drink, and the Pepsi costs less than the shot that goes into the mixed drink, so the profit margin's bigger. I switched over to beer at the witching hour and drank them slowly enough to only consume three by closing time. Clyde gave me a lift home. He thought my remoteness was simple emotional letdown from the previous week or so. I didn't disabuse him of that notion.

CHAPTER TWENTY-EIGHT

There's a saying about best laid plans. They have a tendency to go awry. Everyone of my plans, best- or worst laid, for the past week and a half, beginning with my attempt to get Sindi DiWagne away from Kallir and Company in front of her apartment building that first night, had bombed. I planned to get out and got snookered back in. I planned to give Bigler the map and got suckered by a neat little bit of slight of hand. I told Bigler I didn't have the map and he had his goons put a bomb in my car. I told him I was out and he sent Kallir and Hondo to kill me. Then Kallir a second time. I sicced the DA's office on his drug lab to tie him up so much he'd be too busy to bother with me, and someone came a-shooting.

I could go back to Jim O'Donnell and tell him all, ask for protection, get Bigler brought up on attempted murder charges, maybe get his bail jacked up even higher. But he'd also have to get Kallir and Moose and I didn't know where to find them.

Then there were the questions he'd have that I didn't have good enough answers for. Like, why hadn't I said something before? Why hadn't I reported the alleged burglary of Sindi DiWagne's old apartment to the police? Why didn't I tell the authorities I was engaged to look for an admittedly stolen object, the map? When I met Llowlolski at the Wissahickon Station I was illegally carrying a firearm and I committed a kidnapping. I left the scene of a felony when Kallir and Hondo jumped me and Hondo got killed. Again, when Kallir tried to run me over and smacked into a parked car. Not to mention that I didn't say anything to anybody when someone took a shot at me last evening. Oh yes, I didn't report a car-bomb, either. Instead, I delivered that block of C-4 to Bigler. That could certainly be construed as me making a death threat.

And those were only the highlights. I was a more or less innocent victim in all of this. But at the very least, I was guilty of weapons offenses and obstruction of justice.

I'm an independent cuss and I like me that way. I like making up my own rules as I go along, marching to the beat of my own drum. It's important to me that I take responsibility for my own actions, that what I do is on me. When I fail, I take the blame-which can be tough. But when I succeed, I don't have to share the glory-which is awful nice. But damn, it gets me in trouble sometimes.

So what's my next step? How do I stay alive and not have to pay any penalties?

On Wednesday, Bigler made bail.

I thought it was time he and I came to an accord.

*

Right after my six o'clock check in with Clyde I called Bigler at home. His machine answered, which was just as well. His line was probably tapped, and he might make a mistake and call me Hambletonian There's not many people around with that as a first name, a good investigator might find me relatively easy to track down with just that much information. Then I'd be asked a ton of questions and have so few good answers I'd probably be locked up as an accomplice in the drug ring. Maybe he'd call me Hambletonian and it wouldn't be a slip, maybe he'd want me in jail where I'd be easier to get at.

"Eddie, I saw you on TV," I said into the machine after the beep. "Looks like you're going to be real busy for a while. I'm sure your dogs have better things to do with their time now, so call them off. You don't fuck with me, I don't fuck with you." I hung up and hoped Jim O'Donnell never listened to that message; he might recognize my voice, and then I'd have those questions to deal with.

A couple of days went by during which nothing happened and I started feeling secure. I thought Bigler must have seen the wisdom in the message I left for him. I started the article for *Mother Jones* and wrote and mailed out five or six proposals on as many topics to an equal number of magazines. As long as I didn't let myself think about Sindi DiWagne, the map and the money it represented, Bigler, or Kallir and Company, life was getting back to normal. I unilaterally stopped checking in with Clyde and he didn't make any objection. Everything was hunky-dory as long as I didn't consider the possibility that Bigler was biding his time.

*

Someone I wanted to interview for a proposed article on the near future prospects of the aerospace industry was in town for the weekend. He was staying at the Adam's Mark hotel on City Line. On Friday I drove out there and took him to lunch at the TGI Friday near the hotel. He was an exceptional interview, so eager to get out his point of view that all I had to do was ask an opening question and he was off to the races. By the time we finished one after-lunch cup of coffee I had more than I needed and thanked him profusely. The interview had only taken half the time I'd allotted for it, so I decided to take the scenic route home.

Presidential Avenue comes off City Line, turns left, and becomes Neill Drive. Neill Drive looks like nothing you'd expect to see in a big city. It's a windey, poorly paved road that goes down a steep slope through a wooded area. It's called a drive because it's in Fairmount Park and most of the roadways in the park are called drives. It reaches the bottom of the hill at Falls River Bridge and makes a sharp right turn before it merges into West River Drive. Near the bottom it goes under a railroad tressel. Neill Drive is busy at rush hour, but not heavily traveled at other times of the day.

Halfway down a car closed on me from behind and tapped my rear bumper. I automatically goosed the gas to put a little space between us and got tapped again. I looked in the rearview mirror. It was a white Hyundai. Kallir was behind the wheel. He made contact again and put a little muscle into it this time. Our speed was far too fast for this road. The pressure Kallir was putting on my bumper could make me spin out. Even if we made it all the way down all right, we were going too fast to safely make the turn at the bottom.

I tapped the brakes and the pressure from behind made my rear slew to the side. I accelerated to straighten out and broke contact. The tressel was in sight now, coming up fast. I knew the sharp right was just past it. I also knew we were going too fast to make it. Just then Kallir pulled up along side and leaned into me. He planned to drive me smack into the bridge abutment. I nudged my wheel to the right and back, just enough to break contact with him, and stood on the brakes. Kallir shot past and his brake lights went on as he tried to slow down for the turn. He took it wide, but he made it. I fought the wheel to maintain control of my car and was almost at a safe speed by the time I reached the turn. I saw Kallir still slowing down ahead of me on West River Drive, and I whipped into the turn onto the Falls River bridge. By the time he could make a U-turn and come after me, I'd be lost in the maze of streets on the other side of the river.

I had to find a place to park for awhile and calm down. The ride down Neill Drive was brief, but horrifying. Only quick thinking and quicker reflexes on my part had kept me from becoming part of the bridge abutment. I found a rundown scrap of residential street and pulled over to the curb. It took several minutes for my heart to stop thudding like it wanted to find a new home, and even longer for my ragged breath to become regular.

Way back when I was just a whelp, probably not long after I was out of swaddling clothes, I decided that five was my lucky number. Why? Who knows why younglings decide things like that. If I was correct in assuming that Kallir was involved in planting the bomb in my car, and if it was him who took the shot at me, this was the fifth time he tried to kill me. Five was my lucky number and I'd survived five attempts on my life. I didn't know what six augured and didn't particularly want to find out. Bigler made it obvious he wasn't going to let matters drop. Or maybe it was Kallir on his own, trying to make good on his promise to pay me back for hitting him and getting away when he and Hondo were supposed to take me out back of Llowlolski's apartment building and hurt me. So far as I knew, Moose wasn't coming around to kill me. Maybe that meant Kallir was working on his own, that it wasn't Bigler trying to get me.

Either way, I didn't think the attempts on my life were going to stop until the matter was finally settled. I decided it was time for me to be proactive instead of waiting for the next try. Maybe six was Kallir's lucky number.

I put the car in gear and found a place that no one would ever think of as one of my regular haunts. Later this evening I'd go to the Side Car and talk to Clyde. He proved so good at tracking people down, maybe he could get a line on where I could find Kallir.

I drove for an hour before settling on a restaurant-bar in Kensington. No one would look for me there, I haven't been in that part of town in years. I explained to the waitress that I'd be there for some time, reading the paper and drinking coffee. Then I'd have dinner. She said business was slow until six, so it was no problem. I slipped her a couple bucks and she smiled widely enough to display the gaps where an upper eyetooth and lower molar used to be. She said, "Don't worry about anything, hon, I'll take good care of you."

I was through with the paper by the time the local news came on the TV over the bar and decided to watch it. What I saw ruined my appetite. There had been a riot in Holmsburg Prison. That's not enough to upset my appetite, that sort of thing happens in prisons, especially overcrowded prisons like

Holmsburg. Two prisoners died in the riot. That bare fact didn't upset me, either. There are a lot of very nasty people locked up in Holmsburg and once in a while one of them kills another one of them. If I have any reaction to that at all, it's most likely to be good riddance. As far as I was concerned, though, this riot was different.

The talking head stared all google-eyed and solemn into the camera while telling his viewers that both dead men had been arrested in Monday's dramatic raid on an illegal designer drug lab in Northern Liberties. The DA's office, he said, had hoped these two men would turn state's evidence in the case. The talking head gave their names while two bits of tape ran. One showed the bear and the two chemists being taken out of the lab by Philadelphia police detectives; the chemist with the Mohawk was highlighted. I didn't recognize his name. The other showed Bigler and a couple of other men in suits being taken into the Round House. Paul Llowlolski's name was said, and it was him highlighted in the picture.

I had promised the patient waitress I'd order dinner. She kept her promise to take good care of me. I ordered dinner to go, gave a decent tip, and headed back to University City. Fortunately, most of the rush hour traffic was going the other way and by the time I hit the Vine Street Expressway, most of it had died down altogether.

*

Greg Hammond was dead, on Bigler's orders. Sindi DiWagne was dead, along with fourteen innocent people, also presumably on Bigler's orders. Hondo had died in the one attempt on my life he was involved in. Now Llowlolski and one of the chemists were dead. That was entirely too many bodies piling up.

There had been five attempts on my life in the past week, Kallir made three of them, probably made the other two. The way it looked to me was Bigler was systematically killing off everybody he didn't consider absolutely trustworthy who knew anything about the map or was involved with the drug lab. I was now certain he was behind Kallir's continued attempts to kill me. I had thought of going to Jim O'Donnell and telling him about the attempts but decided against that because there were too many things I didn't want to explain. If Bigler could cause a riot in the prison to kill Llowlolski and one of his chemists, there was absolutely no reason for me to think the authorities could protect me. This was a problem I'd have to deal with on my own.

So far I hadn't been able to convince Bigler he didn't need to worry about me. Driving to the Side Car, I decided I had to convince him I was too dangerous to continue going after. But how could I do that? Bigler probably had his own security system to keep him safe. Beyond that, the police were probably watching him. I didn't see any way I could get to the man himself. I had to get to Kallir-but I had no idea of where to find him.

*

Jimmy was inside the door with one of the bouncers when I got to the Side Car.

"Where's Clyde?" I asked.

Jimmy looked serious. "He's at Graduate Hospital."

"Who's he visiting?" Clyde hadn't said anything to me about a sick relative or friend.

"Himself. He's hurt pretty badly."

"What happened?"

"Someone jumped him from behind when he was leaving home this afternoon to come here. He said to tell you it was Moose." He shook his head. "I don't know who Moose is, but he must be one mean son of a bitch. Raul was with Clyde when it happened, and he's in the hospital too."

"Who's Raul?" I didn't give a damn who Raul was, I was delaying dealing with the fact of Clyde being hurt.

Jimmy gave me a crooked smile. "He's the assistant manager. You know him. He's the real big guy Clyde talks to before he goes out with you. They took him to Hannehman."

"Oh. Yeah, I know who you mean now." Damn me, but I really don't pay much attention to anything but the tits and asses on dancing-girl nights, or the music on music nights. So many of Clyde's people have helped me out in the past few days. Now Clyde and one of his hulks were in the hospital because of me. And the only man I knew by name was Jimmy. Damn me. It was time I took control of the situation.

"The other day Mack took some Polaroids. Clyde gave them to Raul. Do you have any idea where they are now?"

"Right here." Jimmy reached onto the shelf under the doorman's lectern and pulled them out. "We weren't ever told to stop keeping an eye out for these guys."

"Let me have them. I'll bring them right back."

"Sure thing, Ham. Just a sec." Jimmy looked into the darkness of the club and signaled someone. In a moment one of the hulks joined us. "Go with Ham, Mack," Jimmy said. Then to me, "Clyde gave orders that if you showed up you were to have a bodyguard." He smiled crookedly again. "He told me I'm in charge until either he or Raul gets back."

I didn't want the bodyguard, but I didn't want to take the time to argue, either. I shuffled through the photos and gave back all but the best shots of Kallir and Moose. "Thanks, Jimmy." Then to Mack, "Let's go."

We got into my car and went to the all-night copy place on Walnut Street. They had a color copying machine and I made fifty copies of each of the Polaroids. They weren't great copies, but they'd do. Back at the Side Car I huddled with Jimmy, Mack, and as many of the other hulks as I could in the few minutes I was willing to spend. Jimmy could brief the rest of them when he got the chance.

"This is Moose," I told them and handed out copies of the picture. "He's the one who hurt Clyde and Raul. This other one is called Kallir." I passed out his picture. "You all know people who work in other places. Show these pictures around, find out where these two characters live, or at least where they hang out. Then let me know." I looked each of them in the eye, I wanted to make sure they understood the next thing I said. "Don't, I say again, do not, under any circumstances, try to do anything with either of these guys yourselves. Kallir is a killer. We all know what Moose can do. These men are very dangerous. One more time, don't try to do anything about them yourselves. Do you understand me?"

They all said they did. They told me they would find out where I could find Kallir and Moose, and they wouldn't do anything about them themselves. I hoped I could believe them. I didn't want any more nameless men hospitalized on my behalf.

Then I went to visit Clyde.

*

I didn't wonder why the cops put Clyde in one hospital and Raul in a different one, the Philadelphia cops constantly put people injured together in separate hospitals. I didn't even concern myself with why didn't they put him in one closer to his home, off hand I could think of two or three closer to where he was hurt than either the one he was in or the one Raul was in. That again, is normal procedure for the Philadelphia police. I was glad, though, that the one they took him to was relatively close to the Side Car.

I would have left Mack behind, but didn't want to upset Clyde by letting him know I was turning down his offer of a bodyguard. I'd get rid of Mack later.

The guard at the desk told us Clyde was only allowed one visitor at a time. Mack said I should go first. The guard got my name, then picked up his phone and told me to check in at the nurses' station when I got to the floor; he'd let them know I was on my way.

A nurse was standing in front of the elevator waiting when I got there.

"Mr. Eliot?" she asked.

I nodded.

"Mr. Krippendorf is conscious but sedated. I'll show you to his room. You can have ten minutes. Please don't agitate him." She stood in front of the elevator door blocking my way until I agreed not to agitate her patient. On the way to the room, she briefed me on his injuries.

"He's not pretty. Multiple abrasions and lacerations, a broken arm, a broken clavicle, and a concussion. The concussion is why he's sedated. Don't be alarmed if he seems to drift in and out on you, that's perfectly normal for his condition."

I said right, sure. Normal.

Clyde's was the only occupied bed of three in a dimly lit room. He mumbled something I couldn't make out from six feet away when the nurse bent over and said something to him. She gave me a look that said, remember, ten minutes, don't agitate him.

I nodded back I understood the rules, and moved a chair to where I could sit close to Clyde. His head was bandaged. One arm was in a cast that held it to his lower chest and included most of his upper chest. Even in the dim light I could see that half of his face was discolored. A couple of tubes ran into his good arm. A few wires snaked out from under the covers and connected to machines mounted near the bed. Their monitor faces glowed with blips flowing across them, or with bright squiggles spiking up and down.

Right. He looked absolutely normal.

"They're only letting us come up one at a time," I started. I wanted to avoid agitating him, if he thought I'd come without my bodyguard he probably would be. "Mack's downstairs. He can come up when I leave."

Clyde's lips moved, but the words were too soft to hear. He tried again and croaked out, "Good." His hand moved on the sheet and I took it. He squeezed my hand, but there was about as much force in it as a baby's grip.

It was strange, and very sad, that hand that was so big and strong was now so limp and weak. I felt responsible for what happened to him, I should have warned him that something might happen. Then maybe he would have been ready and he wouldn't have been beaten like this.

I had to lean close to make out what he said next.

"That Moose. Tough." Clyde tried to sit up but could barely lift his head an inch above the pillow. "Raul. Out before I knew what. Happening." He was too weak and dopey to speak in complete sentences, I had to fill in the blanks. "Got me. Club. Something. Watch. Out. Wants. You. Kill. You. Came to me. Find out. Where you are." He stopped talking and fell back, panting from the effort his warning had taken.

"Don't worry, Clyde. I'll watch out. Moose won't get me. He's the one in trouble now."

Clyde's eyes closed and his breath came easier. He was asleep. I sat quietly, holding his hand. I tried to visualize the scene, Clyde coming out of his apartment, meeting Raul, heading for his car. Moose coming out of nowhere, clubbing Raul into unconsciousness, knocking Clyde down, asking where I was, breaking Clyde's bones.

I tried, but I couldn't see it happening, it was too bizarre. Clyde was too big and strong, too physically capable. If Raul was the one I was thinking of, he was also too big to go down with just one blow. Moose was big and strong, yes. But. . . But I didn't know how strong. Maybe I was very lucky that he was never able to hurt me when he was told to.

While I sat there, holding Clyde's hand, I forgot about the attempts against me. I forgot about all the people Bigler had killed. All I could think of was Moose hurt my friend. He wasn't going to get away with it. No more than Bigler was.

The nurse came for me when my ten minutes were up. I told her Mack was waiting downstairs. She said not to bother sending him up, Clyde would most likely sleep through the night.

I didn't try to dump Mack. Instead I took him back to the Side Car, and I stayed there until closing when I helped clean up and close up. Don't ask me if it was a dancing-girl night or a music night-I flat don't know.

CHAPTER TWENTY-NINE

It was Friday, not quite two weeks since Sindi DiWagne-the late Sindi DiWagne-sat next to me at the small side bar at the Side Car Club. How many people had died? I didn't want to add them up. Especially not the fourteen innocent people who went down with Sindi in the commuter plane. How much of it was my fault? The beating of Clyde and Raul, that I could place on me. If I hadn't gone to Clyde for help, he and Raul wouldn't be in the hospital now. Of the others, Hammond had betrayed his boss and his days were numbered before I got involved. Sindi had something of value that a greedy, unscrupulous man wanted. She was going to die if she didn't give it to him. She may have died regardless. Hondo? It was just a matter of time before somebody did that punk. Were Llowlolski and the Mohawk chemist my fault? After all, they got killed in prison after I blew the whistle on the illegal drug lab. No, I decided, they weren't on me. When you play with bad people, bad things can happen to you-maybe even put you into a premature coffin. And I firmly believe that when you deliberately do things that hurt other people, and working for a gangster or making illegal drugs certainly qualify as deliberately hurting other people, you deserve whatever happens to you. Their deaths were on them.

But Clyde and Raul were definitely mine. It was up to me to make amends.

Mack showed up at my door about breakfast time. That's my breakfast time, which is closer to most people's lunch time. He was wearing a lightweight sports coat, which made me wonder if he was carrying a handgun. Instead of asking about that, I told him he didn't have to babysit me. He said Clyde wanted me watched after. When a man is as much bigger than you as Mack was bigger than me, it's sometimes best to just go along with what he says. Besides, even though I wouldn't admit it out loud, I felt a lot safer with a bodyguard. I took him down the street and bought him breakfast. Turned out it was his second of the morning.

We visited Clyde that afternoon. They still wouldn't let him have more than one visitor at a time, so Mack waited downstairs while I went up. Clyde was alert this time, they'd taken him off the pain killers. But he still had the same tubes feeding into his arms, the same wires leading from his body, the same green-glowing monitors blipping their blips.

He was alert, but very weak. I had to lean in to hear what he said. "Did you come to see me last night, or was I dreaming?" he asked when I pulled the same chair I'd sat in last evening next to his bed.

"Come on, Clyde, you're too big a boy to have nightmares like that. You know I was here."

He laughed at my little joke, but it wasn't much of a laugh-it wasn't much of a joke, either. "Was I coherent? I know I tried to warn you."

"Coherent enough. You and Raul were on your way to your car. Moose came up behind you, knocked Raul out from behind and knocked you down before you could react." I shook my head in amazement. "I never would have thought he was that fast. Or are you getting old and slow?"

Clyde laughed again and winced from the pain that the movement shot through his head when he shook it. "That big lummox is fast."

"He tried to beat where I was out of you. You were too dumb to tell him and wound up here." My jokes were feeble, but Clyde was weak enough they were all he could handle. His laughs were as weak as the jokes.

"Did I warn you?"

"You told me Moose is dangerous and I should watch out for him." He looked disturbed, as though he failed to let me know enough, so I added, "You said he wants to kill me."

He nodded and looked sad. Somehow I didn't think his sadness was for himself or Raul, I thought it was for me, for the danger I was in. I felt like a shit. My old friend, my best friend, was hurt on my account, and he was feeling badly for me.

"I told you I'd watch out. I have been. I also told you that Moose is the one in trouble now."

He smiled. "Yeah, I thought that's what you said." The smile went away and he looked at me seriously. "Don't do anything rash."

"Don't worry, old buddy. I won't do anything you wouldn't."

"That's what I'm afraid of."

I laughed at his weak joke.

"Mack's with you?"

"Downstairs. These people seem to think you can't handle more than one of us at a time."

"I'm getting sleepy. Send him up before I zonk out, will you?"

I felt awful, but didn't show it. "He'll be here in a couple minutes," I said and stood up. I put a gentle hand on his shoulder. "You get well now, you hear?"

"Positively."

I got out of there before I started blubbering. Downstairs I paced back and forth in the lobby while Mack visited. Mack came back in less than five minutes.

"He fell asleep right after I got there," he said. I couldn't get anything more out of him except, "Let's drop by Hahnemann, I want to say hello to Raul."

I found an illegal parking place close to the entrance to the hospital and pulled into it. "If I'm not here when you get back, don't panic," I said before Mack got out. If a meter maid comes along, I'm going to drive around the block. I'm not going to run off and leave you here. Okay?"

"Okay," Mack said, and went into the hospital.

I don't know how long I sat there, not particularly thinking, mostly just feeling shitty, waiting for Mack to finish his visit. After a while I noticed in the rearview mirror a uniformed employee of the Philadelphia Parking Authority coming my way, checking meters, writing the occasional ticket. We don't really call them meter maids anymore, not since the pay for the job went up enough that more men started working for the PPA. The meter maid coming toward me was a case in point; he wasn't and had never been a maid. His mustache gave him the appearance of a black Cossack. I started flicking my eyes back and forth between the hospital entrance and the rearview mirror, wanting Mack to come back out before the ticket-writer reached me. A lot of people must have overstayed their two hour welcome at the meters, because it took him a long time to reach me. When he was two cars behind, I turned on the ignition and got ready to get in gear and go. Mack came out just as I was ready to leave.

"Thanks for waiting, Ham," he said when he got in. He didn't say anything about how Raul was, and the way he looked I didn't think he wanted to be asked about it, so I didn't. Besides, I knew what kind of shape Clyde was in and didn't want to know how badly someone else got hurt on my account.

I didn't know what my next step was, and didn't think I could figure it out until I got the reports from the Side Car's bouncers and bartenders, so I drove across the river and parked in back of the club.

*

Jimmy was inside, sitting on a tall stool near the entrance. I waved to the dancing-girls making their living within the security of the main bar, got something fizzy and non-alcoholic from the bartender, and joined Jimmy.

"Clyde looks like shit," I said, and pulled over another stool.

"I know. I visited him right before I opened up." He barked a brief laugh. "Ain't it a bitch? I'm the only one here who ever sees him outside the club except when he wants some work done, but I had to wait in the lobby because other people were lined up to see him." He shook his head. "I was a half hour late opening today. Three dancers, one bartender, two bouncers, and seven customers were waiting outside for me when I got here."

"Yeah, ironic," I agreed.

None of the early arrivals had any information on Kallir or Moose, but I hadn't expected to learn anything this early. Even though bar and restaurant people have their own after hours social life separate from the rest of society, I expected it would take several days to get anything. If there was anything to be found out. Though as pretty as Kallir made himself, I'm sure he hung out someplace. Probably someplace with naugahide stools and plastic ferns.

All the employees checked in and out with Jimmy and he kept track of their comings and goings on a clipboard. He asked each new arrival, but none had found out anything yet.

I stayed away from the bar except to get refills of my non-alcoholic fizzies-this was a dancing-girl night, but it wasn't a good idea for me to get too close and risk losing myself in a fantasy world. When I got hungry I ate sandwiches from the food bar.

The Mediterranean beauty came in around nine. At first I was proud of myself; I recognized her face, I didn't need to see her tits to know who she was-even though she was one whose name I deliberately didn't know.

She peered intently at my face for a long moment, then said, "You aren't using the makeup anymore. That's good. You're healing well." She stood so close that the smell of her femaleness totally drowned out the spilled-beer and stale-cigarette odors of the club without being overwhelming itself. When she looked deep into my eyes and asked, "Is there anything else I can do for you?" I had to swallow before croaking out no.

"You're sure?"

Even in her street clothes, she was the richest female fantasy I could imagine. I didn't trust my voice so I just nodded.

She stood there, maybe waiting for me to say something. After a minute or so of vocal silence on my part, even though my eyes were probably saying things I didn't want to say, she shook her head, snorted "Men, I'll never understand them," and went to the dressing room.

I had to control my breath to keep from hyperventilating. I saw the way Jimmy was looking at me and had to turn my head away, glad it was so dark inside so he couldn't see how red my face was.

"Damn, Ham," he said softly enough I wasn't sure he meant for me to hear him, "if I had a woman that looks like that come on to me that way, I'd be on her so fast she'd be the only one who'd see me move." In my peripheral vision I saw him shake his head. "Clyde told me there were ways you were dumb. But I wouldn't have guessed this if I hadn't seen it myself."

That made me even more embarrassed and I turned totally away from him. Not a good move-the turn had me facing the main bar. The dark-haired beauty was already inside it, dancing nearly naked on the stage. He arms were stretched out, sinuously weaving a come-hither through the air. Her arms were pointed at me, she was looking at me. I had to look away before she mesmerized me.

"Jimmy, just shut up," I snapped.

He gave me a "what did I say" look, but didn't say anything else about the dancing-girl or my ways of being dumb. Every now and again through the evening, though, I did catch him looking at me oddly.

By midnight everyone who was scheduled to work had shown up and we still didn't know anything about where Kallir and Moose hung out. I decided to stick around and help close up. That way one or two of the hulks could see me safely home without being pulled from their job. One of the dancing-girls who wasn't working that night ran in after last call was sounded.

"Hi, Jimmy," she said. "Hi, Ham." She was small and slender and short-cropped blonde and in her street clothes. I hadn't the foggiest idea of who she was.

"Hi, Eve," Jimmy said, saving me from potential embarrassment.

"Hi, Eve," I said, I hoped quickly enough neither of them noticed I needed Jimmy's prompt to get her name.

"I found out where the pretty one hangs out."

"Where?" Jimmy and I asked simultaneously.

"He likes the Red Prairie Oyster."

"You're kidding me," Jimmy said.

"No I'm not. A friend of mine is a waitress there. She told me he's in there two or three nights a week."

Jimmy laughed. "The Red Prairie Oyster. Oh my gawd, I would never have thought a tough guy would hang out there.

"What's a red prairie oyster from, an elk with hemorrhoids?" I asked.

"Huh?" "What?" they asked.

I looked at them blankly. I thought that at least Jimmy got the joke, that's why he was laughing, wasn't it? "A prairie oyster is a flop," I explained. "A cow flop, an elk flop, an antelope flop. Hell, I think even a moose turd can be called a prairie oyster."

Jimmy laughed again, said, "Ohmygawd," again. Then he grinned at me. "You don't know the Red Prairie Oyster?"

"Should I?" I'd never heard of the place.

Jimmy explained. "It's a wannabee place out on Industrial Highway. One of those pseudo-redneck joints. You know, the kind of bar where accountants can wear fake biker leathers and act just as badass as the banking management trainees in their dungarees, muscle shirts, and steam pressed sweat bands. I've been there a couple of times. Most of us have," he swept a hand around indicating the rest of the Side Car's staff. "It's good for a few laughs on a dull night." His eyes unfocused and he laughed so hard his breath came in gasps.

"Once when I was there some real bikers came in. I mean they were the kind you could smell before they even walked in the door. They came roaring up on their Harleys. When they walked in the place went stone silent. Somebody even pulled the plug on the jukebox, they were so scared. I was with a couple of the guys from here. We just grinned and sat back and waited to see what was going to happen. Well, the bikers bellied up to the bar and squeezed the Walter Mittys in their shiny black leather jackets away from it. Then one guy sort of tiptoed out. Someone else got up and tried to sneak out, but tripped on something and one of the bikers turned and looked at him. The poor wannabee looked like a deer caught in headlights, the way he froze in place. 'You,' the biker said, 'come over here and have a beer with me.' He grabbed a long neck off the bar and chugged it. The wannabee looked at him bug-eyed, then ran out. All of a sudden, it was stampede city. In like half a minute nobody was left in the place except the bikers and us. We laughed along with them. When they invited us to have a beer with them, we chugged and had a good old time."

Jimmy looked sort of misty at the memory. "So that's where Kallir hangs out. I never would have guessed."

Jimmy thought it was funny. I was perplexed. Why would a real tough guy hang out in a place like that? Then it came to me. He could go there and brag about what he did in real life. The Walter Mittys of the place would eat it all up. They'd think he was a fake, just like they were, only a better, more imaginative bullshitter was all. Somehow it made sense. A perverse sense, but sense none the less.

The hulks who saw me home seemed almost disappointed nobody was waiting for me. I wasn't.

CHAPTER THIRTY

Edward Bigler was an extremely dangerous man. He was probably also the kind of man who doesn't let grudges lie. He was settling his differences with other people by killing them. I tried to make him too busy to bother with me, but it hadn't worked. Even when he was in jail he could get people killed. Out of jail, he could get people in prison killed.

Somehow he managed to keep the DA's office from finding out about Kallir and company. No one in authority had any idea that he was connected with the dead man found on the street in my neighborhood. Kallir and Moose were free to continue going after me until I was dead. And they weren't averse to hurting, or maybe killing, other people to get to me. I had to put an end to that or I'd be in jeopardy from them for the rest of my life, and my life might prove to be a short one.

I figured the best way to get security from them was to do something to convince them to leave me alone. Something to show them I'm vicious enough it's in their best interests to leave me alone. Surviving five attempts like I had wasn't good enough-that only made them more determined to get me. There was only one way I knew that would positively, permanently convince Kallir and Moose to leave me alone. It might also be enough to convince Bigler that I was too dangerous for him to continue going after. Especially if he was tied up with his trial.

Of course I couldn't let anybody know what I had in mind. And I had to do it in such a manner that nobody would ever know I did it. Nobody but Bigler, Kallir, and Moose. First, I had to make a few preparations.

*

I vaguely recognized the young man who showed up at my place around brunch time. The face may or may not have been familiar, I wasn't at all sure about it, but he was the kind of hulk Clyde hires as bouncer-that's probably why he was familiar, I'd probably seen him at the Side Car. I took him out to breakfast. Mack must have passed the word, because he hadn't eaten yet.

Once we were properly fed, the hulk ate more than double what I did, I wanted to visit Clyde. We went in the hulk's car.

At the hospital, they were letting Clyde have two visitors at a time. He was feeling better. He was sitting up in bed when we got there and started off by asking if we were there to spring him out of the joint. Then he complained about having to do everything one handed and complained about the indignity of using a bedpan. After a while I could tell that Clyde was getting tired, even though he tried not to show it. I asked the hulk to leave us alone for a bit.

"I want to borrow your car, good buddy."

He cocked an eye at me and I laughed.

"No, I'm not going off on a wild goose chase," I said. "And I'm not trying to intercept someone catching a plane."

"Why?" Until I used his T-Bird to run off to the airport last week, I'd never borrowed his car. He had better reason to be suspicious than he realized.

I had my story ready. "There's somebody I want to impress. My Mustang doesn't give the right image."

He raised both eyebrows, more interested now than suspicious. "Anybody I know?"

"Yeah." I drew the word out. "You could say that."

"You've come to your senses regarding a certain someone?"

Good: He was buying my misdirection. Bad: I hated to deceive him. I didn't say anything, merely tried to look coy.

"You gonna tell Uncle Clyde about it, lad?"

"Maybe some day."

He grinned and shook his head. "No maybe some day about it, lad. Uncle Clyde's going to know."

"Don't bet on it." I looked smug, playing the game.

He tried to reach the bedside table to open the drawer, but the movement hurt something and he winced. "In the drawer," he said after a moment of silently dealing with the pain.

I opened it and got out his keyring. The car keys came off the ring easily and I left the rest of the ring.

"One more thing, Clyde. Tonight? I don't want a chaperon."

"I'll tell him to be discrete."

"No chaperon at all."

"It's dangerous out there, Ham."

"I know. Even if I didn't have to look at your ugly mug, I'd know it."

We went back and forth a little more, but finally he grudgingly gave in and agreed to call off his bodyguards for the night. But I think if he hadn't been tired and in pain, he wouldn't have agreed. As it was, I knew that later on he might still change his mind.

Clyde tried to continue to be the gracious host, but the effort was taxing. It was at least as difficult for me to be with him after my deception. We said our goodbyes.

Then I had nothing to do until the evening except get ready. Getting ready wouldn't take more than an hour, not even if I took a long, leisurely shower before going out. The hulk took me home and, after assuring himself that I didn't have any unwanted visitors waiting, and after I assured him that I'd call if I was going out or needed help, any kind of help at all, he took off for the Side Car.

Now I had to fritter the rest of the damn day away. I knew exactly what I was going to do tonight, so there was no more planning to do. My plans didn't need to be refined, and I'm not the kind of anal repressive who needs to plan for every contingency. I couldn't concentrate to write. I couldn't even concentrate to read. I tried watching the tube for awhile, but the made-for-TV sporting events couldn't hold my attention. I finally lost myself in computer games until dinner time.

I ate in, there's plenty of food in my larder. Then I took a lengthy shower. I dressed slowly, dragging out the time. I wore jeans that had seen better days, a muscle shirt, and a pair of clod-hoppers I normally only wear in bad weather. The last garment, I laid out on the bed to shuck into right before going out-a blue denim jacket that I hardly ever wear.

Then I went to one of my hiding places and got out the Security Six. I put .357 factory loads in five of the chambers and put the empty chamber under the hammer. Normally, I hate .357 factory loads, they have too much kick and shooting them hurts my hand. What I prefer is the much lighter powered Police Special .38s. But this was bear season. No way I was taking any chance on a bullet that doesn't have the greatest possible stopping power.

Next I got out my Marine issue K-Bar, the knife I told the supply sergeant I lost so many years ago. The K-bar isn't a pretty beast; it doesn't have the kind of balance you'd want in a throwing knife, and its clunky, seven inch blade is dark with bluing. That's okay, you don't use one to slice bread or carve a roast. It's designed to inflict ugly wounds on vital parts of the human anatomy. The only reason it exists is to maim, mutilate, and kill people. It's very utilitarian, and can scare the bejesus out of just about anyone it's pointed at. Way back when I carried that knife on the job, I wore its scabbard on a non-issue leather belt. I put it on one now and made sure the belt fit over my clothes properly, then put it and the pistol in its holster in a flight bag I use to carry my shooting things on those infrequent occasions when I go to the range.

I tore open a new deck of cards, drew out the ace of spades, and wrote, "Don't fuck with me," on it, then poked a hole through its center with a pencil. The ace and pencil went into a pocket of the jacket.

Then I surveyed my preparations and decided I was ready. Ready for anything but the cops if they stopped me when I was carrying either of the weapons outside the flight bag. Not only don't I have a carry permit for handguns, but the legal blade limit for knives in Philadelphia is three and a half inches.

I didn't like what I was about to do. It was dangerous, and I'd be violating more laws, more serious laws, than I already had. I reviewed my plans and knew they were pretty well foolproof. But what if something goes wrong? What if I run into a cop at the wrong time? What if Kallir or Moose is ready for me? What if one or the other of them has friends nearby who I don't see until too late? What if they're outside my place right now waiting for me to come out?

Ah, the hell with it. Just go. Go outside and hope nobody's waiting in the shadows. I put on the denim jacket, grabbed the flight bag, and left.

I didn't trip any anti-personnel mines on the steps or the sidewalk. No Mack trucks jumped the curb at me. No shots rang out from between the houses. They weren't here, I was being a worry-wart.

I timed myself just right to catch an east-bound trolley on Baltimore Avenue without having to expose myself waiting on the corner. I got off at the 33rd Street station and walked through the Drexel campus. I approached the Side Car Club from the rear entrance. Clyde's T-Bird was in its usual place. Nobody was taking a break and I didn't go inside looking to tell anyone I was there to take the car. Clyde might have checked with Martha, whichever dancing-girl she was, and found out I didn't have a date with her. I wasn't taking any chances on being stopped at this point.

I drove into Center City and kept an eye on the rearview mirror. I didn't notice anybody pull out anywhere and follow along. But I wouldn't notice anybody who really knew what he was doing anyway. To be on the safe side, I went down into Italian South Philadelphia, an area where unexpected little streets lurk among the regular streets, and rode around a few curlicues to throw off any followers I might not have noticed.

Finally satisfied I didn't have a tail, I wended my way to Penrose Avenue and went past the airport into Delaware County and onto Industrial Highway.

*

I found the Red Prairie Oyster a few minutes after 9:30. It was on a side street just off the highway, and its parking lot was on its far side. I pulled in and thought the '57 T-Bird had so much more class than the Miadas, BMWs, and Lexuses it had for neighbors.

There was a ten-foot wide pair of cow horns over the entrance. Saguaro and barrel cactus cutouts were on one side of the door and cutouts of a guitar and sombrero adorned the other. The building itself was pink stucco.

My first impression of the inside was I was glad it was night outside or I wouldn't be able to see a thing, that's how dark it was. My eyes adjusted quickly enough and I found my way to the bar. Except for the plush, naugahide stools at the bar, the fake Southwestern motif of the entrance was continued inside. Two stuffed Gila monsters were mounted behind the bar. An impossibly coiled rattlesnake guarded the cash register. More cutouts of cacti, guitars, and sombreros were plastered on the walls. Hats, holstered cap guns, and a pinata hung from the exposed-beam rafters. A life-sized, framed poster of a Harley dominated one wall. I knew Jimmy hadn't exaggerated in the least when he described the place.

The bartender wore pegged black trousers, white shirt, black dress vest, a red cummerbund, and a flat brimmed black riverboat gambler's hat. I ordered a bottle of beer and looked around at the other customers while he got it. I saw the same weekend-macho Jimmy had said was here. Two accountants in biker leathers and a bank management trainee in fringed buckskin were sitting in quiet consultation and nursing their pina coladas at the other end of the bar. The booths along two walls were high backed but I could see into all of them. Four of the booths were occupied by portfolio analysts discussing the day's market. The cowboy hats and western style shirts they wore weren't the uniforms of the accountants or banking trainee, so they must have been portfolio analysts. Kallir wasn't here.

When the bartender came with my beer I left a couple of dollars in a place where they looked like a tip and talked to him. Sure, he knew Kallir, came in two, three nights a week around ten, ten thirty. Except on those nights he came in later and told his tall tales about where he'd been and what he'd been doing to be so late. Privately, the bartender thought Kallir was a mutual fund salesman instead of the gangster he made out to be, but he'd never say such a thing to a customer's face. If I stuck around until, say, eleven thirty, the place would be hopping and I could get a real eyeful. He rolled his eyes at the amazement of it all. I think he had me pegged for a medical malpractice attorney.

I thanked the bartender for his information but, I told him, I had a hot party to go to and couldn't wait for Kallir to show up. It was his loss if he didn't make this party. I drank half my beer and left the two bucks in their obvious place. The bartender saluted me.

I moved the T-Bird to a nearby darkened street and took a moment to put my weapons on. I hung both belts, holster and scabbard, crosswise over my shoulders under the jacket. Hopefully, nobody would look at me close up and notice any peculiar bulges.

A clothing factory outlet facing the highway had its employees' entrance across the street from the Red Prairie Oyster. The light in the doorway was off so I stood in its shadows to wait.

A little after ten Kallir came rolling by my doorway like a sailor who doesn't have his land legs back yet. He was wearing a greaser-on-the-corner outfit that clashed with his blowdry. I just grabbed his collar, yanked him in and slammed him against the wall. He went crosseyed staring at the blade of the K-Bar pressed against the bottom of his nose.

"If you struggle you're going to look like Jack Nicholson did in *Chinatown*," I told him in an almost reasonable voice. "If you sneeze you're going to look worse than Jack Nicholson did." I increased the pressure enough to break the skin where the nose joins the upper lip. "As a matter of fact, if you say something I don't like, you're going to need a nose like Lee Marvin wore in *Cat Ballou*. Do you understand what I'm telling you?" I thought was an excellent idea to terrorize Kallir.

Sweat was popping out all over his face and his blow dried hair was starting to look as greased down as his clothes. He was beginning to tremble so badly I was afraid he'd hurt himself on the knife point. But he didn't. He was trembling everywhere but his face.

"I understand," he croaked. His jaw moved to talk, but his upper lip stayed still.

"Where's Moose."

His eyes flipped from the knife to me. "Why do you want Moose? Why should I know where he is?"

The blade had a keen edge. I slid the point along the base of his nose. Kallir had enough sense not to scream. A few drops of blood ran into his mouth and a few more runneled down the blade.

"That's your one chance to say something I don't like. Where's Moose?"

"I'm bleeding, you cut me." He went crosseyed again.

I increased the pressure. "If you don't tell me where Moose is right now I'm going to start cutting for real."

"He's at home," he said in a quick voice. "I think he's at home. He said he didn't have any money and didn't know any pimps who'd give him credit. He must be at home." An edge of panic entered his voice at the end.

"We're going there. My car's around the corner." I gave him another nip before taking the knife from his face and wiping the blade clean on his shirt. "Let's go."

"I'm bleeding, you cut me," he burbled. Honest, he burbled. It's not often you hear a tough guy burble.

"Press your hankie against it, it'll stop bleeding." As long as he was burbling I might as well talk down to him. He pulled something white out of his pocket and pressed it to his nose. The cut wasn't bad. Even without stitches it wouldn't leave much of a scar. I spun him around and slammed him over the hood to frisk. He had a 9mm in an ankle holster, I took it and stuck it in my hip pocket. Then I showed him my pistol.

"Mine's bigger than yours," I said.

He went bugeyed.

"You're not going to do anything stupid between here and my car. Are you, Kallir?"

"No." His voice squeaked and I wondered why I'd been afraid of him earlier.

I made him get in the passenger side and close the door before I got in. The .357 was in my left hand when I got behind the wheel. "I'm ambidextrous and can drive one handed," I said. My left hand rested in the crook of my right arm, the hand of which was on the wheel. The big muzzle of that magnum was pointing at him. "This car belongs to a good friend of mine. He thinks I borrowed it to impress a lady friend. If you bleed on his car, he's going to be very pissed off at me. If he gets pissed off at me, I will get very pissed off at you. Pissed off enough I'll probably have to shoot you. Got that?"

He clamped both hands to the handkerchief and nodded vigorously. As big as his eyes were looking at my gun, I didn't think I'd have to worry about him spilling any blood in Clyde's car. "What way?"

He mumbled some directions and I turned the ignition over, put it in gear, pulled away from the curb, and drove away from the Walter Mittys of the Red Prairie Oyster.

CHAPTER THIRTY-ONE

It turned out Moose lived in the shadow of I-95, just a few blocks from Bigler's drug lab. It was a rinky-dink area that I didn't think anybody could call a neighborhood. It was part houses, mostly boarded up, part wholesale commercial, part light manufacturing. There were only three streetlights on the block and one of them was out. Real estate people might claim it for either Olde City or Northern Liberties, but city maps would put a different name on it, and neither Olde City nor Northern Liberties would recognize it as being part of them.

Kallir pointed out a storefront we drove past and said Moose lived in a loft over it. I could see light seeping through curtains inside, so it looked like Kallir was right about Moose being home. No light shown from any of the other structures on the block. The street was so empty it looked abandoned. Still, I drove around the corner and halfway down the block before I eased next to the curb just past a dark alleyway between two buildings. I felt a touch of deja-vu and wondered if crackheads used the alley.

Kallir must have been getting his self-confidence back-now he was only using one hand to hold his hankie to his nose. "Now what?" he asked in something close to his normal tough-guy voice.

"Get out nice and easy," I said. I slipped out from behind the wheel without taking the magnum's muzzle away from him. When he came out I lifted my gun above the roof. "Make sure the door's locked," I said. "I wouldn't want anybody stealing my friend's car."

He gave me an annoyed look, but locked the door.

I nodded back down the street the way we'd come. "Lead on," I said.

Kallir gave an elaborate one-shouldered shrug and started sauntering like he didn't have a care in the world. Definitely getting his confidence back now that we were near Moose's place. He must have thought I was walking him to reinforcements.

Wrong. As soon as we were both on the sidewalk and his back was to me, I put the Security Six back in its holster and jumped him. It was no contest. He didn't expect me to do anything until we reached Moose's loft, and he didn't expect me to do anything with my bare hands. I threw the hold the Marine DIs taught me was called "the Killer" on him and had to hold myself back so I didn't accidentally kill him. Kallir struggled but he didn't do any of the things he should have in the brief instant he had to do them, so his struggling was useless. I held on for a few seconds after he went limp. Then I let go and hopped back in case he was that good an actor. He wasn't. Nobody can bounce off the pavement and fall back on it the way he did unless they're unconscious-or dead. I checked. He wasn't dead.

I got the first aid kit that Clyde carries in his trunk and shoved the roll of cloth adhesive tape from it into a hip pocket. Then I got the Mini-Maglite from the glove compartment and checked the alley to see if anybody was already there. I grimaced at the sound of rats scurrying away, but didn't find any suicidal people and didn't step on any crack vials.

I went back to Kallir, grabbed him by his ankles, and dragged him into the alleyway. The banging his head got on the sidewalk couldn't do his head any good, but hey, it would keep him out for a while longer, and that was a good idea. About twenty feet in from the street I stopped dragging him and trussed him like a stuffed goose. I folded his arms and wrapped the tape from his wrists to his elbows a few times, then wrapped some tape around his ankles and knees. I finished off by putting a few strips of tape across his mouth. Here's hoping he doesn't have any nasal congestion that could smother him. I rocked back on my heels and thought about it for a moment and decided one thing more needed to be done. I undid his trousers and pulled them down to his knees. Kallir wasn't going anywhere without help now, and probably nobody who came in here before I got back would give him any.

Now for Moose.

The loft's street entrance was in the blank wall next to the storefront's grungy display window. The substantial deadbolt lock it had was worthless. The lock was good, but the door frame suffered from dry rot. I gouged at the frame a couple of times with my K-Bar, then inserted the blade between the door and the jamb and gave it a twist. The keeper screws popped out with a dry rasp and the door swung open. No light showed in the entryway. I figured there must be a closed door at the head of the stairs. I quickly stepped inside and closed the door and stood to listen. A top forty radio station was blaring upstairs but I didn't hear any footsteps. I briefly flashed the flashlight to orient myself. The steps were just three feet inside the door. They went straight up to the second floor. I saw a heavy curtain hanging at the top of the stairs. Stepping carefully as close to the side of the stairs as possible to reduce the possibility of them creaking or making other noise, I climbed to the second floor. A hollow-core apartment door was behind the curtain. I listened with my ear against the door for a moment but all I could hear was the radio. Maybe Moose was asleep? I tied the doorknob, it was unlocked. I cracked the door open and peered through the slit to orient myself. I saw the front half of the room.

The landlord obviously expected his tenants to do their own fixing up. Or maybe Moose was squatting. The place wasn't a candidate for a spread in *House Beautiful*. The floors were bare wood that probably needed sanding and varnishing. It was hard to tell because more immediately it needed a good sweeping. Lighting was provided by two rows of industrial type fluorescent light fixtures hanging from the ceiling. Most of the tube brackets were bare and not much light filled the room.

There was a component stereo system piled on board-and-cinder-block shelves along the far wall. A record turntable sat on top of a CD player. Next to them I saw a receiver with more buttons and dials than I could imagine uses for, an equalizer with enough levers to control a studio taping, a Dolby black box, and a dual cassette deck. There were other parts I didn't recognize. A big pair of speakers bracketed the system and two more faced it from the opposite side of the room with a broken down couch between them. No records or CDs in sight, but a hell of a system.

A shiny king size brass bed hunched proudly with its head to the windows. Moose slumped in a recliner where he could get the benefit of all four speakers. He knew what was important, Moose did. A good stereo system, a bed big enough on which to do whatever he and his evening companion might want to do on it, and a good recliner for when he was alone. The rest of the furniture was unimportant. The end of the room I couldn't see must house the kitchen area and bathroom. That was probably where the TV and VCR were, if he had them. A few days worth of newspapers were scattered on the floor by the recliner but I didn't see any other reading matter-not even a skin mag.

I took a deep breath and held it to a count of five to steady myself, then opened the door wide and walked in.

"Moose," I said in a voice loud enough to crack over the volume of the radio.

He started out of the chair and spun as though to lunge at me. He froze when he saw the magnum pointed at him. His jaw hung slack and his blank face almost looked worried until he looked at my face and saw who it was. Then he grinned and relaxed a bit.

"Hi, Ham. I been looking for you. You know that?"

"That's why I'm here, Moose."

"And you brought a real gun this time."

"You hurt a friend of mine, Moose. You put him in the hospital."

He shrugged. "He wouldn't tell me where you were."

"He didn't know."

He shrugged again. "People get hurt all the time."

"You pissed me off, Moose. You made this personal in a way it wasn't before."

He yucked. The son of a bitch yucked at me. "What you gonna do? You're here with a gun. You gonna kill me for beating up your friend?"

Somehow it didn't surprise me that he didn't show any fear. I don't think he believed I could pull the trigger.

"You want to kill me." He grinned wider and started to advance. Maybe he thought he could get to me before I fired.

I held the magnum in both hands pointed at the middle of his face. He suddenly bellowed and charged. At the same instant I pulled the trigger. The thunder of the shot was deafening in the room and the fireball from the muzzle briefly blanched all color from his face.

Moose stopped. The impact of the heavy bullet didn't stagger him, he stopped on his own and stood erect. His eyes rolled up in their sockets as though trying to see where the bullet went when it crashed through his forehead. Slowly at first, then gathering momentum, he fell to the floor. Dead.

"Goddam you, Moose," I muttered, "even dead, you're trying to make life hard for me." He had fallen forward and landed on his stomach. I had to roll him over to finish this job. I put the magnum back in its holster and grabbed an arm to pull on. Nothing. I tried to use end leverage, rolling his feet around each other. He weighed too damn much. I knelt by his side and tried to lift that side. Moose's corpse was too big and too flat on the floor to budge. I kept trying to roll him over by brute force until my bad knee started talking to me.

Then I got smart and thought about the situation.

The solution was simple enough. I dismantled his stereo cabinet and used the planks and cinder blocks from it for levers and rolled him over that way. The shelves got reassembled and all the components replaced because I didn't want anyone guessing at what I had to do to get him on his back. The blood stain on the floor would tell whoever found him he was rolled over after he'd been shot.

Then I got to the serious part. "Sorry, Moose," I murmured. "I've only ever done this one time before, and that was a long time ago and a long way from here and I had to scare someone then, too. I'm not sure it worked then, but I sure hope it works now."

I worked fast with the K-Bar, trying not to let my mind pay attention to what my hands were doing. What my hands did was: cut open the front of Moose's trousers, grasped his genitals, cut them off completely and stuffed them in his mouth with the head of his penis poking out between his lips.

After I washed my hands I walked back to the mutilated corpse and knelt next to its head. The Ace of Spades and pencil came out of my jacket pocket and the pencil went through the middle of the card and then into the hole in Moose's skull. I positioned them to look like the card was nailed to his forehead by the pencil. The one other time I had done that I used a twelve penny nail instead of a pencil and drove it into the skull with the butt of my K-Bar. That time I had done it to show some nasty Al Qaidas who were mutilating American corpses and torturing prisoners to death that American Marines could be just as nasty as they were. The next day my battalion was moved out of that area, so I never found out what effect it had on the enemy.

Once I was finished with Kallir, and Moose's body was found, it wouldn't take the people who needed to know who had done this any time at all to figure it out. I hoped they'd take the message at face value and leave me alone.

My plan was to take Kallir someplace else and kill him there. Killing the two of them was the only way I'd been able to figure out of convincing them to stop trying to kill me. When I got back to the alley I decided against taking Kallir someplace else.

From the mouth of the alley I could hear a few thumps from a thrashing body. The thumps were accompanied by angry squeals from hungry rats. Shit. I turned on my flashlight and went in. The rats were at him. They ran away from me and the light, angry. I played the light on Kallir and almost threw up. He was alive, if that's what you want to call it. One eye was missing, chunks of his face were gone. His bare legs had been gnawed on. And there were more and more and more injuries. I used the K-bar to put him out of his misery.

Then I went back to Clyde's car, got in, and drove away, trying not to think about what I had done, what I had left behind.

CHAPTER THIRTY-TWO

Nobody saw me drop off Clyde's car. I found a cab on Market Street. Back home I thought about what I'd done, then did my damnest to not think about it. I went to a local video place and took out a bunch of tapes. On the way back I stopped in one of the bars along Baltimore Avenue and picked up a couple of six-packs. What I needed for proper anesthesia was a couple bottles of something much stronger, but the State Stores closed hours ago.

I stared at the movies flickering across my TV screen, don't ask what they were, I haven't the foggiest notion, and drank all of the beer. When it was gone I wanted more because I could still remember. The thing I remembered most was how Kallir looked when I went back to him. I managed to make it to the bathroom in time. Then I went to bed and pulled the sheet over my head so I couldn't see Kallir's image. The bastard got into bed with me and made me look at him. I rolled over to my other side. He changed sides of the bed. I screwed my eyes tightly closed and he crawled inside the lids.

It seemed to go on for hours, me trying new strategies for avoiding him, him finding new ways to get around my defenses.

Then, abruptly, it was early afternoon and I woke up. I didn't feel at all refreshed. My head protested. My stomach gave dire warnings about misuse. I stank from alcohol sweat and dream-fear. But Kallir wasn't there anymore.

I went into the bathroom, got into the shower, and stood under a stinging spray of cold water for a long time. Then I turned on the hot and scrubbed myself raw. I couldn't get rid of the feeling of filthiness. I wanted to vomit out the contents of my stomach; I wanted an enema. My stomach was empty; I didn't need the enema. I felt equally dirty, inside and out. A pot of coffee cleared my head enough for me to realize time was the only thing that was going to make me feel clean again after last night. I didn't look in the mirror while shaving and brushing my teeth-I was afraid I'd see Kallir standing behind me.

I knew food had to be the next step in my recovery. Soft food. I pulled on some clothes and went down the street because I didn't feel up to cooking myself. I got a tuna hoagie, mayo, no hot. I figured the tuna salad was the softest thing I could get. Some teenagers were making noise in the seating area, so I went a block farther with my hoagie and found a quiet corner of Clark Park to eat it in. A couple of times I thought I saw Kallir out of the corner of my eye, but when I looked it was someone else.

After a while I started feeling a bit human and made the terribly long trek home-all four blocks of it. I went slow, but still felt drained by the time I got back up to my second floor. I took some Alka-Seltzer and a couple of aspirin. The food sitting in my stomach kept it from rebelling at this assault. I sat at my computer and tried to play games, but had so little hand-eye coordination I kept hitting the wrong keys. When a tiny Kallir-figure ran across the screen chased by rats, I gave up. I sat in front of the television for a few hours. Kallir didn't have a role in any of the programs, didn't have an at-bat in that day's Phillies game.

Along about dinner time I dialed Bigler's attorney's number. His machine answered. I told it to check out Moose's place and look around for Kallir. I held onto the phone for several long seconds more without saying anything then added, "Bigler will understand."

I watched the 11:00 news. There was no mention of the murders.

*

Monday I visited Clyde. He was sitting up and looked stronger than before. He fixed me with a steely stare.

"I talked to Martha," he said.

I didn't say anything.

"You weren't with her Saturday night," he accused.

"I didn't say I would be."

"Lad, I feel betrayed. Who was she?"

I shook my head. "There was no she. You don't want to know about my Saturday night."

"Yes I do."

"Then let's put it this way. I don't want to tell you who I was with, what I did, or where I went. Who, what, where, when, and why. You know the when. The why is I had to. That's all I'm telling you."

After that there wasn't much point in me staying around, we weren't good company for each other. I didn't go back on Tuesday. They released him on Wednesday.

*

All week long I went out only to buy the paper. I watched the local news every night. It was Thursday before I could bring myself to do mundane things, like getting to work on the *Mother Jones* piece.

It was Friday before somebody finally found Kallir. The grisly manner of his death made a splash in the papers and on TV for the weekend. On Monday something else happened to take its place. During the time Kallir's death was being covered, the police didn't say anything about it beyond confirmation of a half-eaten corpse being found in an alley. No speculation on how it happened. There were no reports about Moose. Bigler must have sent someone to clean up the loft.

There were no more attempts on my life. Maybe I got my point across.

A week and a half after I killed Moose and Kallir my phone finally rang. I picked up the receiver and held it to my ear but didn't say anything. If it was someone who had business with me, they'd say something. If it was the call I was hoping for, I wanted to hear the voice first.

After a long pause I heard one word, "Truce?" It sounded like Bigler.

"Truce," I agreed.

There was a click on the other end and the line went dead.

I leaned far back and closed my eyes. It was over.

Except for one thing. I still had to write my report to Sindi DiWagne.

There was no way I could deliver it to her, of course. It didn't matter that my client was dead, I still had to write it.

I looked over the *Mother Jones* article and decided it was done. I wrote a cover letter and put it in an envelope, put proper postage on it, and took it out to a mailbox. Then I went back in to compose a report that would probably never be read by anyone but me.

*

It was a toughie. I started it slow and built up steam. By the time it was done it included everything I knew about who the characters were. Greg Hammond got a two paragraph bio. So did Llowlolski. Kallir and Company rated one paragraph each. Bigler rated three. Sindi started off with three pages, but when I read it over it was too confusing, so I cut it out completely. My feelings toward her were too ambivalent and it showed.

To the best of my ability, I wrote out all the double-dealing; Hammond vs Bigler, Sindi vs Hammond, Sindi vs me. I included a lot of speculation on motivations as well. Bigler's business problems and the further problems he ran into with his drug dealing. Sindi's involvement with the pension fund. Hammond's relationship with his wife and how that influenced him to get involved with Sindi and the plot to get the map. Why they wanted to use a stalking-horse-me-to throw off Bigler.

I left out all reference to my own culpability in the double-dealing-how I'd been so horny I let Sindi drag me around by my dick.

The provenance of the map as Sindi had given it went in as unconfirmed. I noodled a bit over the actual location of the buried treasure. It wasn't in Georgia. Atlantic coast Florida was probably out as well. As was the Gulf Coast of the US. No mariners mountains, you see. That left the Carolinas on up to the Delaware Bay as the likely geographical area. I even speculated that the location could have been anywhere in the Greater Antilles or in Mexico. Remember, I hadn't been able to read the legend on the map.

Damn, I wanted to find Sindi and present this report to her. And maybe have my way with that beautiful body of hers once more. She'd called it that once, having my way with her. But even if I could find her, I wasn't interested in necrophilia. I cursed myself as a fool for not making a copy of the map when it was in my hands. I could have had a lot more than five million dollars.

Damn.

Hammond's death went into the report, as did the prison riot deaths of Llowlolski and the chemist. Moose and Hondo went in as disappearances under mysterious circumstances. Kallir got marked down as being killed by person or persons unknown. I put down what was public knowledge of Bigler's upcoming trial, but not where the DA's office got the final piece of the puzzle they needed to bust him. I left out the commuter plane explosion that killed Sindi and fourteen innocent people.

After a little thought, I added in the attempts on my life. They were a part of what happened, even though Sindi was long gone by then and a case could be made that I was no longer doing "research" for this report.

When I was satisfied everything was in the report-everything I was willing to put into it, anyway-I printed it out and filed it away.

That night I went out and spent an hour or more in every one of the bars along the Baltimore Avenue strip. Then I went home and drank some more. My five million dollar share of the dead man's chest was gone. So was the most beautiful woman I'd ever laid serious hands on. Either of those was a good reason to get drunk. Together, they were cause for a long, long bender. At least Kallir was no longer haunting me.

But I didn't go on a bender, just the one night drunk. When I recovered from the hangover I took stock.

The *Good Housekeeping* check came through. I've got a payday coming from *Mother Jones*. *Sport* accepted my proposal for a where-are-they-now article about the 1960 Eagles team that won the NFL championship. Ditto *Score* for a similar piece on the '74 Flyers. *Atlantic City Magazine* wants me to do one on casino showgirl costumes. *PC Computing* said okay to a piece on setting up Word Perfect macros for manuscript formats.

And Sindi did pay me the retainer. The rent's paid, the utilities are up to date, the Mustang's gassed up, and I've got enough left over to keep me solvent for another month or two.

Tonight's a dancing-girl night at the Side Car Club. I think I'll head over there, bend my elbow, see if Clyde's willing to talk to me again, lay a few tips on the dancing-girls, indulge myself in a little harmless fantasy. Tomorrow looks a lot better than the last couple of months.

I think.

About the Author:

David Sherman began writing in 1983. His first novel was published in 1987, and he now has about three dozen books to his credit. Most of his writing has been military science fiction or fantasy, and most of what wasn't is either about US Marines in the Vietnam War, or other military SF. His books include the six book VN series *The Night Fighters*, the *DemonTech* books, the fourteen volume *Starfist* series he wrote with Dan Cragg, the three book *Starfist: Force Recon* series, again with Dan Cragg, and a *Star Wars* thingie, once more with Dan Cragg. He's written three other VN novels, a vampire novel, and this mystery novel. His books have been published in Czech, Polish, German, and Japanese in addition to America. He lives in South Florida. Please visit his website; novelier.com.

4916297R00114

Printed in Great Britain
by Amazon.co.uk, Ltd.,
Marston Gate.